THE LURE
Previously published as SWALLOW THE HOOK
S.W. Hubbard

D0963912

Chapter 1

The door of the Stop 'N' Buy wouldn't budge.

Yet the market was clearly open for business. Frank Bennett could see people inside partly obscured by the promotion signs, beer posters and garage sale flyers plastered on the windows and door. With another impatient push he felt the door yield slightly. When he finally got it open wide enough to squeeze his wiry body through, he found himself smack up against the well-padded posterior of Edith Marsden.

She brought up the rear of a line that stretched from the cash register, past the ice cream cooler, snaking around the chip-and-dip display, to end right inside the entrance. What the hell was this? There was never a line at the Stop'N'Buy—or anywhere else in Trout Run, for that matter.

Frank listened as Debbie Flint, the day shift clerk, attempted to run both the New York State lottery ticket machine and the cash register while cradling the phone receiver between her chin and shoulder.

"I don't know what happened—she's just not here. Of course I called. There was no answer. All I know is, I have to be out of here by four-thirty to pick up my kids. No, the sitter can't keep them any later—you'd better come in."

"What's going on?" Frank asked no one in particular.

"Mary Pat hasn't shown up for her shift," said a burly man wearing the trademark khaki pants and green shirt of a Stevenson's Lumberyard worker.

"Now Debbie's here all alone to deal with the afternoon crowd," Edith chimed in. Rush hour started early in the Adirondack mountain town of Trout Run, timed to the shifts of the lumber millworkers and the guards at the nearby prison boot camp, but it didn't amount to much. Waiting in line wasn't a familiar experience for the locals, even now in the fall foliage season, when tourists swelled the population.

"She's never been late before." Having hung up the phone, Debbie spoke to a customer at the head of the line. "In fact, she's always twenty minutes early. I'm kinda worried."

"She must be sick."

"She's never sick, but you know, she did buy some Tylenol yesterday—said she felt kind of achy," Debbie continued. "But she would've called if she needed to take a sick day. You think I should check the hospital?"

"I'll do it." Roger Einhorn, who volunteered on the Rescue Squad, stepped off the line and picked up the phone behind the counter to call the hospital, thirty miles away in Saranac Lake. Everyone in the store fell silent, listening to his end of the conversation, until it became clear that Mary Pat had not been admitted. Then the debate began again.

"Maybe you should investigate, Frank." Augie Enright, willing to wait any length of time to buy his weekly lottery ticket, elbowed Trout Run's police chief.

"I think people have the right to be late for work once in a while without bringing the police down on their heads," Frank answered with a smile.

"Yeah, Augie. If we called Frank every time you were late for work, he'd never have time to run the speed trap or anything," a voice called from somewhere in the store.

This brought laughter all around, except from Edith. But then she always walked around with a twist to her face like she'd just stepped in dog dirt. "I wouldn't be surprised if Mary Pat had an accident," she said. "It couldn't hurt for someone to look into it."

Frank took the "someone" as an arrow directed at him. Years as a detective on the Kansas City police force had taught him all there was to know about stakeouts and interrogating suspects, but had done nothing to prepare him for a job in which the primary qualification was the ability to endure unsolicited advice.

"She probably went shopping in Lake Placid and got stuck in traffic. You have to allow yourself more time to get anywhere, this time of the year," Frank reminded Edith. He meant to reassure her, but Edith's snort indicated she saw his answer as just another example of civil servants dodging their responsibilities.

Frank took this as his cue to leave. The line had barely moved in five minutes, and he was sensitive to any implication that he used the taxpayers' time to run his private errands. When his predecessor had retired two years ago, a faction in town had wanted to save money by turning Trout Run's slight law enforcement needs over to the state police. They'd lost the battle, but the war simmered on and Frank didn't want to supply any ammunition to the opposition.

"Well, I can't wait." He raised his hand in farewell to be certain everyone noticed he was leaving. "If Mary Pat doesn't show up by six, give me a call."

Was it his imagination, or did more than just Edith give him a cold stare as he left? Surely they didn't expect him to launch a manhunt for a grown woman who was half an hour late for work? In Kansas City he would have laughed at the suggestion. But this wasn't KC.

His spirits lifted on the drive from the Stop 'N' Buy to the center of Trout Run. The trip took less than ten minutes, except in September, when everyone, even the locals, slowed down for the view at the bend in the road where Whiteface filled the horizon. Color drenched the big mountain in autumn—stippled ruby and bronze highlighted by the lemon yellow of the birches. The mountain's smaller companions nestled beside it, so the wall of color seemed to stretch to infinity. For Frank, who had grown up on a farm surrounded by the flat, monochrome landscape of the prairie, the show never lost its appeal. Impossible to worry for long on a day like today.

All too soon he cruised past the score of buildings clustered around the Green that made up downtown Trout Run, and parked in front of the red clapboard Town Office. In the single large room devoted to the police department, Frank found Earl pacing.

"There you are!"

Frank made a show of consulting his watch, which read twenty minutes to five.

"I know, I know, but Howard Jenks said he could only wait around till five to show me the car he's got for sale." Earl had been without wheels ever since his previous car had fallen apart, literally, on the rutted dirt road leading to his favorite fishing hole.

"Howard Jenks! He's not trying to unload that old blue Plymouth with the brown fender, I hope?"

"Uh, that'd be it," Earl admitted. "He only wants $500 for it."

"That's about $450 more than it's worth. If you can wait till Saturday, I'll take you up to Plattsburgh and we can shop around the used car lots."

"I don't have the bucks to shop up there. My best shot is to buy direct from someone around here." At twenty-three, Earl was still young enough to live with his mother without embarrassment, since his modest salary as the police department's only civilian employee barely kept him in beer, gas and satellite TV.

"Just one problem with that—no one around here ever sells anything when it's still got some life left in it."

Earl shrugged his scrawny shoulders and ran his hand through his too long bangs, tics that surfaced whenever Frank criticized him. "I'll just go look at what Howard's got. I bet I can beat him down on the price some."

Frank lifted one eyebrow. Howard could make a trader in the Kasbah weep for mercy. Nevertheless, he tossed his assistant the keys to his own pick-up truck. "Don't be tearing over there like the devil's on your tail. I'll be here when you get back."

Earl grinned as he headed out the door. "Thanks, Frank!"

Normally, Frank set the phone to roll over to the state police by six on a weeknight, but since he couldn't leave until Earl got back, he let it go. No one called at six, and he relaxed. Mary Pat must've shown up at work after all. Then at six-fifteen, the phone rang.

"Hello, Frank, is that you?" Without waiting for affirmation the high-pitched voice continued. "This is Vivian Mays. Listen, we've got trouble over here on Harkness Road. I was walking my dog and I noticed a car pulled off the road into some bushes."

Frank's stomach tightened.

"When I stopped to see if they needed help, well, it turned out it was—"

"Mary Pat Sheehan," Frank finished.

"Yeah, how did you know?"

"Never mind. Have you called the Rescue Squad?"

"No. I, oh dear, I'm afraid it's too late for that. She's, uh–" Vivian stopped for a breath. "It's real bad, Frank. I came home to call, but I'll go back out and wait for you."

"I'll be right there." He slammed the phone down.

WITH THE SIREN BLARING on Trout Run's only patrol car, Frank headed out to Harkness Road. In a quarter of a mile he cut the siren; the road was empty and the urgent sound seemed hypocritical when only two hours before he'd discounted everyone's worry. Had the poor girl been bleeding to death while he stood around trading jokes in the Stop 'n' Buy? But even if he'd set off immediately to look for her, his search would never have taken him to Harkness Road. It was clear on the other side of town, nowhere near Mary Pat's home or job.

Still, he felt terrible. In Kansas City he had been able to put some distance between himself and the people he encountered in his work. The gang members selling drugs were not his neighbor's kids. The petty thieves he arrested didn't greet him at the supermarket. In Trout Run it was different. Answering a call on a domestic disturbance, he would find the young man who had cheerfully sold him some nails at the hardware store the day before, now turned nasty with drink and jealousy. He broke up a fight at the Mountainside Tavern, and the sheepish combatants waved to him the next afternoon as they ate lunch together in the park. Now he was on his way to pull poor Mary Pat Sheehan, who'd sold him snacks and gas almost every day for the past two years, from the wreckage of her crashed car.

He turned onto Harkness Road and pulled over when he spotted Vivian leaping up and down and waving her hands like a middle-aged pom-pom girl. Mary Pat's beige Ford Escort had been driven off the blacktop about fifteen feet into some tall meadow grass and scrubby bushes and trees. Approaching from the east, as Frank had, the car was almost totally concealed. Walking from the opposite direction, Viv had been able to see the rear end of the car jutting out of the trees, although cars driving down the road could easily have overlooked it.

"I opened the door and touched her," Vivian started in as soon as Frank got out of the patrol car. "I hope that was all right, but I thought I could help her. You see, she doesn't even look hurt. But she was...cold."

Frank peered in through the driver's side window and saw Mary Pat still strapped into her seat. With her head bowed and her hands lightly holding the steering wheel, she looked as if she were merely deep in thought.

Vivian began to sob softly. "Oh, this is terrible, terrible. What about poor Ann and Joe?"

"You did the right thing, Viv, " Frank put his arm around the distraught woman. "I'll take care of telling her parents. You just sit in the patrol car for a minute until I'm done here, then I'll run you home."

Frank opened the car door and automatically checked Mary Pat for a pulse, in case Vivian, in her agitation, had been mistaken. But the young woman was certainly dead, and had been for a while, which eased his guilt. In the fading light Frank couldn't see any obvious sign of injury–not even a bruise where her head must have hit the steering wheel.

He took a few steps back from the car and assessed its trajectory in leaving the road. Harkness Road ran straight and level at this point, without the slightest curve to challenge a driver. No rain in days. No skid marks on the pavement. Yet Mary Pat's car had left the road, flattening the grass for a good fifteen feet before coming to a stop against a birch tree. Only about four inches in diameter, it was really just a sapling–hardly obstacle enough to have caused a fatal impact to a driver wearing a seat belt.

"I can't believe she's dead—her car don't look beat up at all." Vivian had crept up behind Frank again and gave voice to his own thoughts.

"Yeah, that's the way it is sometimes with traffic accidents. Sometimes the car's barely dented and there's no survivors." But even as he said this to Viv, he felt unsatisfied with the explanation, and went around the car again looking for more damage.

"Maybe a deer ran in front of her, or another car came barreling down in the opposite direction and ran her off the road."

"Mmn." Let Viv believe what she wanted to believe. Frank suspected they wouldn't understand Mary Pat's death until the autopsy report was in, maybe not even then.

Viv grew weepy again. "Poor Mary Pat. She had everything to live for."

Frank nodded. Bit of an overstatement, there. The girl's life was awfully tame, even for Trout Run. Unmarried, pushing thirty, still living with her parents. She had a dead-end job as a clerk in a convenience store and, as his Aunt Aggie used to say, she was as plain as a post.

He stood back and took one last look at Mary Pat in the car. She was shaped sort of like a telephone pole, measuring about the same circumference at chest, waist and hips. Her broad face wasn't interesting enough to be ugly. Instead of the famed Irish peaches- and-cream complexion, Mary Pat was simply pale, with an over-generous distribution of freckles, colorless eyelashes and a mop of frizzy strawberry blond hair.

But Mary Pat had been unfailingly cheerful. She seemed to genuinely enjoy her work at the Stop 'N' Buy. Once she'd overheard him say that he didn't believe in gambling, and after that she had jokingly nagged him to buy raffle tickets for the Mother of Mercy Catholic Church in Verona so that her CCD students could have new catechisms. He'd often seen her eating dinner at Malone's Diner with her parents, laughing and chatting as if she couldn't have asked for two better companions.

Unaccountably, he felt his throat tighten. Ridiculous, really–he hadn't known her beyond those brief encounters. But somehow Mary Pat had always reminded him of his daughter, Caroline. Not that there was a physical resemblance—Caroline had her mother's delicate build, dark hair, and lively gestures. Maybe it was more that the Sheehans, as a family, called up the memory of what he'd once had, but had lost.

He and Estelle and Caroline had always been a team, unshakable in their loyalty. In her tumultuous teenage years Caroline had strayed, but never deserted them. Even when she had come east for college and stayed in New York after her marriage, the bond had not been broken. But Estelle's death had changed everything. The brain aneurysm that had felled her in a sudden cranial explosion had left him without a wife and Caroline without a mother, and somehow, both of them without each other. They were a tricycle missing one wheel; unbalanced, the other two wheels were useless, too.

Now it fell to him to tell the Sheehans that their team had also broken up. Mary Pat, their only child, was dead.

Chapter 2

Frank had seen hundreds of dead bodies in the morgue in the course of his career—bodies disfigured by violent death, bodies left to rot in a field or apartment—so the sight of Mary Pat's placid white face on the slab should not have been unduly upsetting. Her father had been quite brave, insisting on actually seeing the body, then gasping and making a quick sign of the cross when the sheet had been pulled back. Nevertheless, Frank had been feeling uncharacteristically glum in the two days since he'd accompanied Joe Sheehan to identify his daughter's body.

Morbid thoughts came to him at unlikely moments. The act of buzzing open the Starkist for his favorite tuna noodle casserole conjured up an image of Caroline crushed in that glorified tin can of a sports car her husband had bought her. Seeing the chairlift ferrying tourists up Whiteface to enjoy the view, he imagined Caroline tumbling down the steep steps of her vintage colonial and lying, mortally injured, until the boys found her body when they woke from their naps.

Finally he called her, but was at a loss for words once the initial surge of relief at hearing her cheerful voice passed. What could he say? "Are you still alive?" seemed ludicrous, yet that was all he wanted to know.

"Hi, how are you?"

"Fine. What's wrong?" Caroline answered.

"Nothing's wrong. Why should anything be wrong?"

"I'm just surprised to hear from you in the middle of the day. Shouldn't you be at work?"

"I just stopped by the house on the way back from a call. I thought this would be a good time to catch you." In the past few months it had seemed increasingly hard to find a time when Caroline could actually talk to him. If he called at dinnertime, his three-year-old twin grandsons, Ty and Jeremy, would be clamoring in the background and she would put them on for several minutes of unintelligible conversation. If he called in the evenings or on the weekend, he risked getting his son-in-law, Eric, and their conversation would flounder until Frank gave up and said good-bye.

"Oh, well you were right. I'm just here working on a project for a client. But it's nothing urgent," she added.

Ah, he'd forgotten about that. Now that the boys were in pre-school, Caroline had been doing freelance work which, so far as he could tell, involved her getting paid substantial sums of money for tapping away on her laptop and talking on her cell phone, dropping phrases like "strategic market penetration," and "enterprise-wide technology integration." The new job was another reason she never had time to talk, or visit, or invite him there.

"So how are you? How are the boys?" Frank forged ahead, determined to get her to talk for at least a few minutes.

"Oh, great! They love school. A zoologist is visiting today to talk to them about endangered amphibians."

"Whatever happened to gluing Cheerios to construction paper in the shape of the letter 'C?' I suppose they don't go in for that sort of thing anymore."

Caroline laughed. "Sure they do, Daddy. Except now they call it fine motor skills development. That way they can charge you a thousand dollars a month for it."

There, a flash of the old, teasing Caroline. Encouraged, he ventured on. "Say, it's really beautiful up here right now. Why don't you guys come up for the weekend? We could go canoeing."

"I'd love to, Daddy, but Eric's in California on business and he'll just be getting back Saturday morning. Oh, here comes the FedEx man—gotta run. Thanks for calling!"

Frank sat for a moment staring at the dead receiver in his hand. Then he hung up and headed for the office, feeling more blue than he had before he'd called.

Trotting up the stairs of the Town Office, Frank entered the inner office and pretended not to notice the Solitaire game vanishing from Earl's computer screen. He was looking for work to improve his mood, not worsen it. "Here you go, Earl. *The Mountain Herald*, hot off the presses." Earl's negotiations with Howard Jenks had not gone well and he was still in the market for a car.

Earl extended a slightly grimy hand to receive the weekly newspaper. "Garden Club Plans Perennial Border for Village Green," read the lead headline.

"Gee, nothing in here about Mary Pat? Well, it only happened two days ago," Earl continued. "Guess it missed the deadline."

"You oughta know Greg wouldn't put something like that on the front page," Frank said. With the motto, "The North Country's Good News Paper," the *Herald* was devoted to stories about Eagle Scouts, golden wedding anniversaries and High Peaks High School sports. A more accurate slogan might have been "All the News Everyone Already Knows." But Mary Pat's death wouldn't be official until a blurry family photo of her smiling face and the details of her sad end appeared in print. Maybe then customers at the Stop 'N' Buy would stop murmuring, "I keep expecting to see Mary Pat behind the counter. I can't believe she's gone."

Earl continued flipping through the paper. "I guess the obituary will be in next week. I'll tell you one thing, that'll be some funeral. Everyone knew Mary Pat and her parents."

"Everyone's related to them is more like it." Overhearing their conversation, Doris, the town secretary, popped her head in to offer her two cent's worth. "Joe has five brothers and sisters and I think Ann has even more. And them and their families all live around here."

"You're not related to them, are you, Earl?" Frank asked. He was forever sticking his foot in his mouth by making snide remarks about Trout Run natives, only to learn they were some distant cousins or in-laws of Earl's.

"Nah, they're all such serious Catholics. They don't go in for cross-breeding with us Presbyterians."

"Pity Joe and Ann only had the one child," Doris rambled on with her own train of thought. "They were married for years and Ann never could get pregnant. Then, after they'd given up hoping, wouldn't you know Mary Pat came along. Ann must've been pushing forty."

"Hey, look at this." Earl pointed to an ad in the *Herald* classifieds. He'd become as adept as Frank at diverting the flow of Doris's endless monologues. "'1989 Chevy pick-up. Four new tires. Runs good. $500 or B/O.' That sounds perfect. I'm going to call right now."

As Earl dialed, Frank casually leaned over his shoulder to scan the rest of the ads.

A large ad bordered in black dominated the always-short help-wanted column. Wanted: Experienced masons, carpenters and dry-wallers. Pay up to $20/hour. Call Sean at Nevins & Fine

"I can't believe they're still running this ad," Frank said after Earl left a message expressing his unquestioning desire to buy the truck. "They've already got every able-bodied man in the county working up at the Extrom house."

In the year since Rod Extrom had taken it in his head to build a mountain retreat at the crest of the Verona Range, the communications tycoon had become Trout Run's second biggest employer, next to Stevenson's lumberyard. Every contractor and craftsman from miles around had been put to work full-time building the huge stone and glass home, and any man who knew which end of a hammer to hold could pick up extra cash moonlighting there. Even Earl had done some framing and roofing. The work had continued from sun-up to sundown seven days a week all summer long.

"Everyone but you, Frank," Earl teased. "They could really use a good finish carpenter up there now."

Frank snorted. "I only build things for my own pleasure. I'd have to be on the bread line to work for a snot-nosed punk like that Sean character."

Frank's description of Sean Vinson was kinder than most. The project manager from the architecture firm that had designed the Extrom house took a lot of crude commentary at the Mountainside Tavern at the end of every workday. Still, regardless of their suspicions of Sean's sexual proclivities, no one walked off the job. Twenty dollars an hour wasn't easy to come by, and smoothed over a lot of moral outrage.

"Why don't you sign up for some wall-boarding, Earl? It'd give you some extra money for a car."

"Nah, I can't take all that dust." Earl ended the pressure to expand his employment by snatching up the ringing phone. "Some tourist just peeled out of the Trail's End parking lot right into Billy Feeney's truck," he reported. "No one's hurt, but they need to file a police report. I'll go."

No sooner had Earl left than the phone rang again. "Hi Frank, it's Dr. Hibbert." Frank rolled his eyes. The coroner was such a pompous ass always referring to himself as "Dr. Hibbert." The next time he called Hibbert he'd say, "Hello, Chuck, this is Police Chief Bennett."

"I have the results of the autopsy on the Sheehan girl. She died of septicemia."

"Septicemia? You mean an infection?" Why couldn't Hibbert just call a spade a spade instead of looking for ways to confuse the issue?

"Yes. Her death caused the crash, not the other way around. She probably lost consciousness and went off the road. Lucky she didn't kill someone else. That's why doctors say not to drive for at least a week, but these women nowadays just don't want to be tied down."

What was Hibbert on about? Not drive for a week after what?

"How long had she been home from the hospital?" the doctor continued before Frank could ask a question.

"Home from the hospital? She wasn't in the hospital at all that I know of."

"She had it at home?" Hibbert's voice registered his surprise. "She didn't look like one of those back-to-nature types."

"What the hell are you talking about?" Frank exploded.

"The baby."

"What baby?"

"Mary Pat Sheehan recently gave birth. From the looks of her, I'd say it was a good-sized baby. Part of the placenta wasn't delivered. It starts a massive infection when it's left in the uterus. Oftentimes a woman won't realize anything's wrong. She figures she supposed to be passing blood, she supposed to be weak and in some pain."

"Wait, wait. *What* did she die of?"

"She died of complications of childbirth."

"But she wasn't pregnant!"

Now it was Dr. Hibbert's turn to get testy. "I assure you Bennett, I've delivered enough babies to know what a woman looks like post-partum. Mary Pat Sheehan gave birth not more than a week ago."

"Her parents didn't say one word about this. And where's the baby?"

"You tell me. I have a feeling when you find out, I'll be doing another autopsy."

Chapter 3

*"*W*hy are you calling so late?"*
"*We have a problem. The coroner figured out why Mary Pat died."*

"I knew he would. You were unrealistic to expect otherwise. But you said no one knows you delivered the baby."

"They don't. I'm positive."

"Then relax—there's no problem."

A CASE LIKE THIS HAD been in the news recently, Frank remembered as he prepared to go see the Sheehans. A 14 year-old-girl living in a high-rise somewhere near Chicago had given birth in her family's apartment while her parents were at work. She had scrupulously cleaned up the mess, then threw all the telltale evidence—stained clothes and towels and the baby too—down the garbage chute. In the two or three days of notoriety that followed, the girl had faced the television cameras again and again with dead-eyed boredom, as if she couldn't understand what all the hoo-ha was about.

Could Mary Pat have done the same–just dispose of what didn't fit into her plans and move on? Frank heaved a sigh as he got into his truck and prepared to drive to the Sheehans'. Surely Mary Pat wasn't like that. First of all, she was twenty-eight. Not a worldly-wise twenty-eight, true, but not driven by the convoluted logic of a teenager. And then she was just so undeniably nice. Could someone like that suffocate her infant, or toss it in the trash? After twenty-five years of police work he ought to know the answer to that was yes, but still, in Mary Pat's case it seemed hard to believe. Of course, there was the religion. Would Mary Pat have committed one terrible sin to cover up another, one that by today's standards, even in Trout Run, people hardly blinked at?

Or it could be love. Maybe love for whatever man had gotten her into this mess had overwhelmed mother love, and Mary Pat had agreed to let the father get rid of the baby. He might even have tricked her–helped her deliver, then told her the baby was stillborn. That seemed more like it; Frank could imagine Mary Pat desperate to please the rare man who'd shown some interest in her.

He parked his truck in front of the Sheehan's house and sat for a moment, steeling himself for what lay ahead. The visit two days ago to break the news of Mary Pat's death had been bad, but this return trip to destroy her parents' illusions was even worse.

He gazed at the house, a tiny Cape Cod painted pale yellow with green trim, hardly bigger than a fancy suburban garden shed. How could the Sheehans have lived in such close quarters and not noticed the changes in their daughter?

His eyes traveled to the shrine in the front garden. An old claw-foot bathtub had been stood up and the drain end buried to create a makeshift grotto. Inside, a three-foot statue of the Virgin Mary wearing an iridescent blue robe, mournful despite the brilliant pink hue of her cheeks and lips. She stared at Frank reproachfully, oblivious to the ceramic bunnies and chipmunks cavorting at her feet.

"Don't look at me like that. You're part of the problem," Frank muttered out loud. Obviously Mary Pat would never have considered an abortion, even if she'd been able to find a doctor in these parts willing to perform one. And her parents' involvement in the church, and her own, would have made it hard for her to brazen it out as a single mother. As for homes for unwed mothers and quiet adoptions, common enough in his own youth, they had probably gone the way of other valuable services like home delivery of milk and doctors' house calls. Maybe hiding the pregnancy wasn't so crazy after all.

Noticing a movement of the lace curtains, Frank covered the distance between his car and the Sheehans' front door in a few long strides. Before his finger touched the bell, the door opened and Joe Sheehan ushered him in. The house was as impeccably neat as it had been on his previous visit, except that today sympathy cards covered every level surface.

"Sit down Frank," Joe waved him toward the afghan-draped sofa. The Sheehans faced Frank across the coffee table, each perched on the edge of matching gold-upholstered chairs. Grief had drained the usual animation from their faces and they stared at him, waiting. Silently Ann Sheehan reached out for her husband's hand. The thin gold band she wore on her left hand had sunk into her plump, freckled flesh over the course of forty years of marriage.

As Frank hesitated, trying to think how to start, Joe asked, "Is there some news on what caused Mary Pat's accident?"

"Well, yes, there is. The coroner completed the autopsy."

"Oh, thank the Lord," Ann said. "Now we can schedule the funeral. Father Ryan has planned a lovely Mass. The choir is going to sing…" A sob overtook her, and she trailed off into quiet weeping.

Frank took a deep breath. Already this was going badly and he hadn't even broken the news yet. "You see, when Dr. Hibbert examined Mary Pat's body he discovered she died of an infection. She apparently lost consciousness and that's what made her run off the road. The accident didn't kill her."

Joe looked at him quizzically. "An infection? What caused that?"

Frank focused his eyes somewhat to the left of Joe's shoulder. "She died of complications of childbirth. Apparently some of the placenta was left behind in the, uh, uterus."

The silence that greeted this statement was more terrible than any screaming or shouting. Mary Pat's parents could not have been more perplexed if Frank had suddenly started speaking Urdu.

"Dr. Hibbert estimates that she gave birth about a week ago." Frank hesitated. "I take it you weren't aware she was pregnant?"

Joe ran his hand over his face as if trying to brush away a cobweb he had stumbled into. "Mary Pat wasn't pregnant," he said, not agitated yet, just struggling to get things straight. "Hibbert must have confused her autopsy with someone else's."

Frank shook his head. "I'm sorry Joe, but there's no mistake. I know it's a terrible shock, but these things do happen."

Joe continued to look at him, expecting more explanation.

"Mary Pat was tall." Frank kept talking to fill up the silence. "If she didn't gain much weight, and the clothes the girls wear today are kinda shapeless–it's possible to conceal it."

Joe leaped up and turned his head from side to side as if he were searching for some escape route from the small living room. "You're talking pure craziness, man. My daughter was a good Catholic girl, and you're saying she got in trouble, and lied to us, and, and *had a baby*. Now how could she do that when she was right here with us every day? It's just plain crazy. It couldn't be," he said with finality, and sat back down.

Through all this, Ann had not spoken. Now her mouth began to move, but no words came forth. "Why? Why?" she finally gasped, then covering her mouth, she ran from the room.

Joe jumped up to follow his wife, then fell back and faced Frank, his fair, freckled face now etched with simple amazement. "But if she had a baby, where is it?"

Frank only raised his eyebrows.

Joe began cracking his knuckles, producing a sound so loud that Frank could not help but wince as each finger popped in turn. Joe finally spoke, his voice quavering as he choked out the words. "You think she killed the baby don't you? You think if you find where she had it, you'll find its little body, buried or in the trash."

Joe seemed to read agreement in Frank's silence. He leaned forward, his hands on the coffee table separating them. "I'm tellin' you Frank, that can't be. I *know* my girl."

Frank met Joe's defiant glare without blinking. Amazing how often he'd heard the phrase, 'I know my child,' when he presented irrefutable evidence to shocked parents. He himself had never been tempted to make that claim. He loved his daughter, was proud of her, enjoyed her company, usually. But know her, no he'd never say that.

He remembered when they'd brought Caroline home from the hospital. She'd cried and cried, her little face bright red and screwed up with rage, and he and Estelle had tried everything to calm her with no success. "I can hardly wait 'til she can talk," he remembered telling Estelle. "Then she can tell us what's wrong." But it seemed that every passing year had only taken Caroline further along a road that led away from him. He'd never understood her better than he had the day he'd first carried her into their house.

"We need to figure out when the baby was born and who might've helped her," Frank said to bring them back to neutral ground.

Joe's blue eyes met Frank's brown ones and the two men stared at each other for a moment. "I got to see to Ann now," Joe said.

"Maybe I could just look around Mary Pat's room for a minute?" Frank felt a twinge of guilt for pressing Joe in a weak moment, but sometimes that's what it took.

Joe hesitated, then raised his head. "Upstairs," he said as he left the room.

Frank climbed the short, steep staircase to the second floor. Below, he could hear Ann wailing, but he shut the sound out. Two doors opened on to a tiny landing; one led to a sewing room, the other to Mary Pat's room. Frank surveyed the cramped space. He could only stand up straight in the center, the dormers sloped so steeply. Pink and yellow flowered wallpaper covered the walls, interrupted only by a crucifix and a picture of Jesus in the Garden of Gethsemane. A nightstand, a chest of drawers and a small desk that must've dated from Mary Pat's grade school days completed the furnishings. One look at the impeccably clean pale yellow carpet told Frank Mary Pat couldn't have given birth here. Still, he went to the bed and pulled back the handmade quilt and white sheets until he could see the bare mattress—unstained.

The very sparseness of the place unnerved him—a calendar on the desk, an alarm clock on the nightstand. No make-up, no photos, no books. He opened the desk drawer: some note cards, stamps, pens. The nightstand drawer: pale blue rosary beads and a white prayer book. The closet: so shallow it barely fit the hangers with Mary Pat's meager wardrobe. The dresser drawers: underwear in the first, socks in the second, sweaters in the third. Could anyone's life really be this blank a book?

Frank tapped his foot —the room had to hold some clue, unless this baby was the second Immaculate Conception. He went back to the dresser. Feeling like a pervert, he slid his hand around underneath Mary Pat's big cotton panties and bras. Under the paper lining the drawer, his fingers touched a slightly raised area. Lifting the liner he found a plain white envelope.

Inside was a hand-written letter.

Dear Birth Mother:

We have been happily married for ten years and we want a child to make our family complete. We would be so happy if you would give us the privilege of becoming the parents of your baby.

We are both teachers, so children have been at the center of our lives for many years. If we are able to adopt your baby, Eileen plans stop teaching to be an at-home mom. We want to share all the things we love with the child we adopt—hiking, sports, music, travel and history. Most of all, we want to share all the love in our hearts.

We are not rich, but we own a home in nice neighborhood with lots of children. Your baby would have two sets of loving grandparents and lots of aunts, uncles and cousins.

We know this must be a terribly difficult decision for you. Sheltering Arms has told us that you want the adoption to be closed, and we respect that decision. We just want you to know that if you choose us to raise your child, you will never have to worry. We will love and cherish your child forever.

Brian and Eileen

Chapter 4

J oe emerged from the back hall as Frank came back into the house, after making a trip to his car for an evidence bag. "I found..." Frank cut himself off at the sign of Joe's finger raised to his lips.

"I got her lying down. Let's go outside."

Frank followed him through the doll-like kitchen out to the back porch. The lawn furniture sat shrouded under plastic, awaiting the return of spring, and Joe led the way through the fallen leaves, heading for a break in the shrubbery at the back of the yard. "I keep a path mowed down to the brook," he explained. "Ann says it's too buggy, but Mary Pat and I like to walk down there. Used to."

"The brook runs behind my house too," Frank said. "I have a bench there so I can sit and watch the water."

Joe smiled slightly, then nodded at the envelope that Frank had placed in a plastic sleeve. "What's that?"

Frank recited the contents of the brief letter. When he finished, Joe's eyes met his. "See, I *told* you she wouldn't kill her baby." He looked away and his bright blue eyes brimmed with tears that did not spill over. "She arranged this so we wouldn't be upset. She never wanted us to worry, even from the time she was a little girl."

Frank spotted a hawk circling, looking for a mouse or a toad in the tall meadow grass. He let his gaze rest there as Joe continued talking. "Once—she couldn't have been more than four years old—Mary Pat woke up feeling sick in the middle of the night. She ran down to the bathroom, but she didn't make it in time. She threw up in the hall. I heard a noise and d'you know how I found her? On her hands and knees, scrubbing the floor. And she said," now a sob choked his words, "she said, 'Don't worry Daddy. I got it all cleaned up.' "

They both walked for a while, lost in thought. Frank found Joe's story, meant to be touching, actually a bit chilling. He saw the four-year-old-Mary

Pat as terrified, not considerate. Maybe the passing of twenty-four years hadn't changed that at all.

Finally Joe spoke again, "So, I guess that settles it. The baby's adopted. No one needs to know about this."

"It's not quite that easy. I need to be certain of what happened to the baby. It would help to find the father."

Again the look of shock and amazement. Poor Joe, the punches just kept coming. First the death, then the pregnancy, the deceit, and now the realization that sex, too, had played a part in all this. "Was she seeing anyone?" Frank asked, although he suspected if there had been some obvious candidate Joe would have volunteered the name by now.

Joe's head wagged back and forth in an endless negative. "There was a fella, oh it's more than two years ago now, over in Verona. Worked in the garage. Ann never cared for him, thought Mary Pat could do better. Eventually they stopped seeing each other."

Eventually. Eventually after Ann nagged and complained and pointed out the poor guy's every flaw, Frank thought. Not good enough, as if there were an endless string of brain surgeons and corporate lawyers just waiting for their chance with Mary Pat. The girl's life was coming into sharper focus, and he could see the little twists and turns that had led to her sad end there in the crashed car.

Joe went on the offensive again. "Whoever the guy is, he's a bum. You don't need to talk to him. The baby's adopted. It's a closed adoption. You gotta honor that."

"All we have is this letter—that's not proof the adoption went through," Frank said.

"It's enough for me." Joe glared at Frank from under bushy brows that had faded from red to sandy gray.

Mary Pat had understood her parents all too well. Apparently propriety meant more to them than knowing if the only grandchild they'd ever have was safe in a good home. Frank felt his patience begin to crumble. "Doesn't it bother you she had the baby on her own? What kind of adoption agency would let her do that? These people could be responsible for Mary Pat's death."

Joe stopped and gazed off at the red and gold mountains outlined against the brilliant blue sky. Then he burst into tears. His shoulders heaved and tears poured down his face, although he hardly made a sound.

Frank rooted desperately through his coat pockets looking for some tissues. The best he could come up with were two undersized paper napkins from the carryout sandwich he'd eaten in the car yesterday. He offered them in mute solace, regretting that he'd pushed so hard.

Joe mopped ineffectually at his red, swollen face, "I'm sorry," he gasped. "This has all been too much."

"It's okay." Frank patted Joe awkwardly on the shoulder. Probably he'd judged the man too harshly.

Joe had a good twenty years on him, but they were both the fathers of only daughters. Caroline had once said that the best thing and the worst thing about being an only child were the same: you were the sole focus of your parents' attention. And now Joe had lost that focus. Even worse, the good memories of times they had shared, which might have been a comfort to him, must now be tainted by the realization that for the last nine months, they had been living a lie.

The sound of the rushing brook grew louder as they walked toward it in silence. Frank was reluctant to start in again, although he knew he had to.

Joe seemed to sense it coming because he let out all the stops. "Please, Frank, I'm begging you—leave this alone! Mary Pat's dead, nothing will bring her back." He turned and grabbed both Frank's hands in his. "You're a father—imagine how you'd feel if this was your daughter, your wife. This will kill Ann." His eyes welled up with tears again. "Please help me!"

You're a father—imagine how you'd feel. Joe couldn't have known that he had chosen exactly the wrong words to get what he wanted. Unintentionally, he'd echoed the words of another father, a father whom Frank had sympathized with a little too much, a father who'd turned out to be a killer. Frank had bungled that investigation in Kansas City, placing too much confidence in his instincts and not enough on proper procedure. It had cost him the job he loved, and he knew one thing: he might make other mistakes, but he'd never again overlook what had to be done in order to spare a man's feelings.

Frank pulled his hands back and shoved them in his pockets. He spoke without emotion. "When I get back to the office, I'll call the county social worker over in Elizabethtown and see what she knows about this Sheltering Arms agency. If the agency can prove to me that they did all they could to protect Mary Pat and that the baby has been legally placed for adoption, that'll be the end of it. If not, you better prepare Ann for a full investigation."

Joe stared at him for a moment, then turned away to watch the brook rush over stones worn smooth by centuries of contact with the water. "I better get back to the office," Frank said finally, but Joe didn't move, didn't even seem to hear. When Frank looked back from the top of the path Joe still stood there with his shoulders hunched against the breeze.

———————◈———————

ALL THE WAY BACK TO the office Frank kicked himself for the way he'd handled Joe Sheehan. He shouldn't have been so harsh—he could have jollied him along a little. After all, the man was still in shock. But he just couldn't accept that Joe was more concerned with what the neighbors would say about all this than he was about the fate of his grandchild. Personally, he'd never given a shit what any gossiping busybodies thought of him or his family. For that matter, he never cared much what his colleagues or even his bosses thought of him.

Now, he had to remind himself that utter disregard for other people's opinions was not necessarily a good thing. He tried to put himself in Joe's shoes. It was natural for a father to want everyone to remember his daughter for her good qualities, not for the one big mistake she'd made in life. If Estelle had done something foolish right before she died, wouldn't he want to keep it quiet?

Still, it all came back to the baby. He had to find out if the baby was safe, even if it meant hurting Joe and Ann Sheehan.

Frank parked his truck in front of the office and sat there for a minute rubbing his temples. Maybe he could dump the whole mess in Trudy Massinay's lap. He'd never had much use for the social workers he'd encountered in Kansas City–earnest young college girls with a yen to help the poor. But Trudy impressed him. She'd straightened out Ben and Laurie Hillier so that he didn't have to break up their fights every week, and if she could do that she could do just about anything.

As he got out of the truck, he could see Earl pacing back and forth in front of the office window, talking on the phone. He hurried in, thinking the state police might be on the line. Coming through the door he could hear Earl's end of the conversation.

"How many miles does it have on it? A hundred and eighty thousand!"

Good lord–no way would he let the kid take a car with that much mileage, even if they were giving it away.

"Well, I think I won't come to see it after all," Earl said, plopping down in his chair. "Thanks anyway.

"This sucks," he said to Frank. "I'll never find a car."

Unbidden, a vision of a car popped into Frank's mind. A car that was in good condition. A car without many miles. A car that had always been driven responsibly. "You know, it dawns on me I know a good car that's available," he said.

"You do? What car?"

"Mary Pat Sheehan's. It's still sitting over at Al's. I don't think Joe's going to want to keep it."

Earl looked at Frank as if he had just suggested grave robbing. "What am I supposed to say, 'Sorry for your loss, Mr. Sheehan. Can I take Mary Pat's car off your hands?'"

"I didn't mean you could get it right away. But mention it to Al. Then eventually Al will ask Joe what to do with the car, and he'll let him know that you're interested. I bet you'll have that car by next week."

Earl still looked squeamish. "But she died in it."

"It's not like there was blood." Frank was about to tell him the cause of death, but stopped himself. No point in telling Earl about Mary Pat's condition until he spoke to Trudy. If she could verify the adoption, then he could keep Joe's secret. "Depends on how bad you want a car, I guess."

Earl sighed, but a few moments later he stood up. "Maybe I'll go over to Al's and just look at it."

Any other day Frank might have objected to this squandering of government time, but with Earl out of the way he could call Trudy in peace, so he tossed him the keys to his truck and began dialing.

"Perfect timing, Frank!"

He smiled as Trudy's sultry voice came over the phone line. She sounded like a cross between Miss October and a late night jazz DJ. He'd been shocked the first time he met her in person: broad bottom in corduroy pants whose elastic waist rested right under her boobs. Frank supposed she must be about his age because the photos on her desk showed three kids in their late teens to early twenties. But she seemed so utterly maternal that she made him feel child-like.

"I have a few minutes to chat before the next problem arrives on my doorstep," Trudy continued.

"I think I am the next problem, Trudy. You did such a good job getting Ben Hillier going to AA, now I'm going to raise the bar for you. See if you can clear this mess up so easily." Frank proceeded to tell her the whole sorry tale of Mary Pat's pregnancy. He ended by reading her the letter.

She let out a low whistle when he finished, and Frank continued, "Joe wants to hush the whole thing up. He thinks this letter's proof enough that the baby's been adopted. But wouldn't an agency have given Mary Pat some counseling? Paid for her medical care? Why would she have the baby on her own if she had an adoption all arranged?"

"You're right. Something's strange here," Trudy agreed. "Let's start by checking out this Sheltering Arms agency. It doesn't ring a bell, but I have a list here somewhere of all the adoption agencies licensed in New York." Frank could hear rustling in the background and pictured Trudy before the towering pile of loose papers and frayed folders on the credenza behind her desk. Like a heron spotting a fish in the reeds, he knew she could pluck out the file she needed.

In an instant she was back. "Nope. Not licensed in New York. Our state's adoption laws are quite rigorous, some would say restrictive." Trudy explained, "It's perfectly legal to surrender your baby to an out-of-state couple, but you'd still need an agency licensed in New York to handle the details on this end. And of course, the baby has to have a birth certificate."

"So some agency other than Sheltering Arms would have to be involved?"

"For the adoption to conform to New York State law, yes. If I were you, I'd check the County Office of Vital Statistics here in Elizabethtown to see if the birth was registered. Then I'd track down this Sheltering Arms. I can give you a web site that has a nationwide listing of licensed adoption agencies."

"Thanks for your help, Trudy. And you'll keep this quiet, right?"

"You can trust me. But don't be surprised if the talk is already started."

Chapter 5

M alone's Diner was famous for large portions and leisurely service, a combination that made grabbing a quick bite virtually impossible. But Frank was encouraged by the number of empty seats at the counter. Sitting directly in Marge Malone's migratory path between kitchen and tables improved the odds of getting fed fast.

So hungry he could no longer concentrate on the expanding quagmire of Mary Pat Sheehan and her baby, Frank had decided to break for lunch but he was anxious to get back on the trail. The steps Trudy had advised him to take had only made it more obvious that something wasn't kosher with this adoption. Just three births had been registered in Essex County last week, all of them to married parents, all of them in the hospital. And Sheltering Arms had not been listed as a licensed agency anywhere in the U.S.

No sooner had Frank plopped himself on a stool at the counter than he regretted his choice. The window table behind him was occupied by two men he didn't recognize talking intently to a woman wearing a sacky dress, woolen tights and sandals: Beth Abercrombie. He shifted in his seat to catch a glimpse of her in the mirror that ran behind the counter.

Despite the outfit, Frank found Beth rather attractive, although there was no one in town he would have admitted it to. He barely admitted it to himself. Even after three years as a widower, Frank still thought of himself as married. Often he was quite shocked to find himself alone. Just the other day he had awakened and reached out for Estelle. Not finding her in bed, he had sleepily lay back in the covers, waiting for the smell of the coffee and pancakes she would fix him to coax him out of bed. But the smell never came; there was no cheerful clatter of pots and dishes, no singing with the radio. He had jolted wide awake with the terrible realization that Estelle was dead.

Now, almost against his will, Frank's eyes slipped above his menu and studied Beth Abercrombie in the mirror. Her thick honey-blond braid, coiled into a crown, balanced her strong-featured profile. A lifetime of outdoor pursuits had marked her fair skin with some fine lines around the eyes and mouth, which she declined to mask with make-up. When she gestured, her loose sleeves fell back to reveal strong arms covered with a light blond down. A potter and weaver, Beth owned a small craft shop catering to Canadians and downstaters. After twenty years in Trout Run, she knew everyone and everyone knew her. Still, she was decidedly "not from around here."

Over the clatter of dishes and the beat of country music on the radio, Frank strained to hear what Beth and the men were talking about. The better looking of the pair was about fifty, with dark wavy hair graying at the temples. He spoke in a low murmur that Frank couldn't make out. Beth seemed to be hanging on his every word, which Frank found unaccountably irritating.

"Of course, this kind of development would never be permitted by the Adirondack Park Authority today, but that operation has been there since right after World War II. It's grand-fathered." The other man, with a bushy beard and a rumpled blue suit, spoke in a loud, clear voice. Frank wasn't sure what that meant and his attention drifted back to the next step in the Sheehan case.

He knew he needed help from the State Police, but anticipated resistance from Lew Meyerson, the regional barracks commander. Lew would say there wasn't clear evidence of any crime. Lew would claim he couldn't spare the resources. Frank closed his menu without ever having read it and mentally ran through the responses he could make.

"He doesn't need to rape the land to put bread on his table." Bushy Beard's voice rose and Frank could see the flash of his waving hands in the mirror. "It's time the people of this town realize that he's exploiting them." Raping? Exploiting? What the hell were they talking about? Frank turned and stared blatantly at the window table, as did some other diners.

Beth's green eyes met his. She smiled, but he noticed her foot move under the table. The volume of the conversation at the window table dropped dramatically.

Marge chose that moment to lumber up. "Made up your mind, Frank?"

"Uh..., " he hesitated, still eavesdropping. "We'll see to that," he thought he heard the other man say.

"Frank!" she tapped her pencil on the waiting pad.

"How about liver and onions."

"That was yesterday's special."

"Oh. Well then, you better give me today's special."

Fifteen minutes later, a plate of stuffed cabbage challenged Frank to choose between starvation and indigestion. With some regret, he picked the latter.

———————◈———————

FRANK HAD HIT UPON a brilliant strategy for getting Lt. Meyerson to do what he wanted: he'd sent Earl to do the dirty work. Try as he might, Frank could never manage to request anything from Meyerson; the words always came out sounding like an order. Then Meyerson would get his back up, and Frank would respond in kind, and they'd be caught in a ridiculous deadlock from which neither would back down.

Earl, on the other hand, was genuinely terrified of the state police lieutenant. He couldn't say good-morning to the man without it sounding like a plea for mercy. So Frank had sent Earl into the lion's den with the letter from Brian and Eileen and told him to ask Meyerson to get the crime lab guys to dust it for prints. It was a long shot that a letter from some prospective adoptive parents would yield fingerprints that would match those in the system, but what else did he have to go on?

Earl had been gone for well over two hours. Frank was just about to call the state police headquarters to inquire when the kid stumbled through the office door and collapsed into his chair.

"How did it go?" Frank asked.

"He said there was no clear indication any crime had been committed. He said the likelihood of lifting usable prints from a paper that had been handled so much was very slim. He said the lab was all backed up with important cases." Earl paused for breath. "He said he'd have the results for us on Monday."

"Brilliant work, Earl! I'm proud of you."

"You owe me big time, Frank."

"Anything. Name it."

"You promised you'd help me study for the police academy entrance exam," Earl reminded him. He'd failed the test the first time he took it.

"Be glad to."

"And beer. Lots of beer."

Frank grinned. "All right—we'll study at the Mountainside."

Chapter 6

Number 12 Hawthorne Lane was in one of the new developments springing up on farmland all around Albany. Frank was on his way there, because, despite all of Meyerson's protests, the letter to Mary Pat had yielded a print that matched on ten of sixteen points to one Brian Finn, a man who had a felony assault conviction twenty-two years ago, but had not been in trouble since. Meyerson's report came with all sorts of caveats about the match not being close enough to hold up in court, but it was good enough to convince Frank to make the two-hour drive south.

He realized as he steered the patrol car through the twisting drives and cul-de-sacs that all the streets were named after authors: Melville Drive, Alcott Court, Whitman Place. Cute. The houses were cute too, each with their developer-issued tree and regulation five shrubs; most with an expensive swing set in the backyard. Twenty years of wear and tear would reveal the quality of the workmanship that went into them, but right now the neighborhood was bright with the hopefulness of young families just starting out.

He got disoriented driving around–God forbid someone should be out in their yard on a beautiful day so you could ask directions. Finally, he flagged down the UPS man, who pointed him toward Hawthorne Lane.

The woman who answered the door at number twelve looked to be in her early thirties. Everything about her radiated crispness: the short, styled hair, the rosy lipstick, the creased slacks, the sweater that looked as if that UPS man had just delivered it. Despite the fact that a uniformed cop stood on her doorstep, she faced Frank through the glass storm door with unquestioning friendliness. Her husband might be a convicted felon, but she showed no sign of animosity.

"Eileen Finn?"

"Yes."

"My name is Frank Bennett. I'm Chief of Police in a town upstate—Trout Run." He produced his ID, which she scanned briefly, without anxiety. "I wonder if you can help me with an inquiry I'm working on?"

"I'll be happy to try."

"I'm looking into a matter concerning the Sheltering Arms adoption agency. I believe you may have dealt with them?"

The smile on Eileen Finn's face disappeared. "My husband's not home right now. Maybe you should come back later." She edged backwards, her hand on the doorknob.

"I just have a few questions. Can I come in?" Obviously he'd hit on something, but he kept his tone bland.

"Do you have a search warrant?"

"I only want to talk to you. If you want me to shout my questions through the storm door, that's fine," Frank replied with a pointed glance at the neighbor's open windows.

She opened the door with a grudging shove and Frank followed her into a living room every bit as clean and crisp as Eileen herself. The curtains matched the chairs, a framed seascape hung squarely over the sofa, and the flawless pale carpeting made Frank feel that he should have kicked off his shoes before walking in. The impeccable appearance of Mrs. Finn and the house made him wonder if this lead was really going to pan out. New parents were usually haggard from sleep deprivation, their homes a riot of baby paraphernalia.

Eileen Finn sat huddled in a corner of the striped sofa watching him. He felt as welcome as a raccoon who'd gnawed his way into her attic.

He plunged in. "Do you know a young woman named Mary Pat Sheehan?"

She looked at him blankly. "No."

"I found a letter in her bedroom that was signed Brian and Eileen, and has Brian's fingerprint on it. What can you tell me about that?"

"I...we wrote a letter to prospective birth mothers, telling them that we wanted to adopt." She straightened up a little and tried to project more confidence. "There's nothing wrong with that."

"No, nothing at all," Frank agreed. "Except this particular birth mother is dead and we're trying to find the baby. Do you know what happened to it?"

Eileen Finn's makeup stood out as garish splotches on a face that was now drained of all its natural color. He'd pegged her age at about thirty, but now he saw lines that hadn't been noticeable when her cheerful façade was intact.

"The girl we wrote to—the birth mother—is dead?" she asked in a hoarse whisper.

Frank nodded. "No one knew she was pregnant and she had the baby without any medical help. A few days later, she died from complications of childbirth. We had no indication of what happened to the baby other than your letter. We want to know that the baby is all right. Is the baby here?"

Frank's question unleashed a torrent of sobs from Eileen. At that moment, Frank heard a door open and close in the back of the house and a man's voice cheerfully calling, "I'm home."

Frank scowled. What timing—he would have much preferred continuing to talk to Eileen alone, but there would be no way to separate a crying woman from her husband.

A burly man with close-cropped sandy hair appeared in the doorway. "Eileen! What's wrong? What's going on?"

Eileen nodded toward Frank. "He wants to know about Sheltering Arms. The birthmother we wrote to died after she had the baby. They found our letter because it had your fingerprint on it."

Brian dropped onto the sofa and put his elbows on his knees, propping his head up with his hands.

"The baby?" Frank asked again.

"We saw her ten days ago," Brian explained. "She was fine then. But we don't have her now. They took her back."

"They? Who's they?"

Brian groaned. "This mess just keeps getting worse and worse. This is what happens when you try to pull an end-run around the rules." Eileen had drawn away from him; they were each alone in their misery.

Frank felt sorry for them, but he wanted the whole story. "Why don't you start at the beginning and tell me everything."

Brian stood up and began to pace. "Eileen and I tried to have a baby for ten years. We finally decided to adopt. Thought it would be no big deal. We're good people, have a nice home. So we go to the adoption agency..."

"Sheltering Arms?" Frank interrupted.

"Oh no, this was a *real* agency. That's when we found out we weren't eligible to adopt." Brian sighed. "If you traced me through a fingerprint, I guess you know I have a record for assault. In high school I had this girlfriend–we were obsessed with each other. After graduation, we ran away and got married. It was two years of pure insanity. We drank and took drugs and lived like bums. One day we got in a fight over another man we were crashing with. I tried to punch him and she got between us and I knocked her out cold. I got arrested and my family couldn't afford the kind of lawyer that can get you out of situations like that, so I pleaded guilty to get probation. So I now have a record for spousal abuse, and the law in New York says you can't adopt if you were ever convicted of abusing your wife or a child. That one mistake I made as a kid keeps us from having a family."

Eileen mopped her face with the sleeve of her yellow sweater. "It's so unfair. Brian is the kindest, gentlest man. He'd make a great father. That's why we decided to follow an, uh, alternative route."

Alternative route? It seemed to him they had out-and-out deceived Mary Pat to get her baby.

"Back up a minute. How did you get from the agency who told you didn't qualify to Sheltering Arms?"

"We started to do some research on the Internet," Brian explained. "We found out that if we located our own birth mother, one who said she wanted us to raise her baby, we might be able to move ahead with an adoption, maybe in a state where the rules aren't as strict. We didn't have the slightest idea how to go about finding a birth mother. But one of these adoption web sites had a chat room where you could ask questions, share your frustrations, that sort of thing. So we posted a few times, and the next thing you know, we got this email from Sheltering Arms."

"They contacted you?"

"Yeah. I guess that should've been our first clue that something wasn't right. But it sounded so perfect. They said they had a birth mother who wouldn't care about my past—just wanted loving parents for her child. All we had to do was write a letter that described ourselves and how we'd raise the child. If she liked us, she'd be willing to say in the paperwork that she wanted us to have the baby, and they would arrange everything else."

"So Mary Pat agreed that you should adopt her baby—how long ago was that?"

"August—she was pretty far along in her pregnancy. We were thrilled that it was going so fast," Eileen explained. "We paid Sheltering Arms $10,000 to pay for the mother's medical expenses."

Frank scowled. Mary Pat's medical expenses had amounted to the buck ninety-eight she'd spent on Tylenol the day before she died.

Brian took over the story. "Two weeks ago, we got a call that the baby had been born on September 17th. We met a woman named Betty in a park outside of Glens Falls, about fifty miles north of here. She brought Sarah—that's what we were going to name her—so we could see that she was healthy."

Eileen spoke in a dreamy, faraway voice. "She was beautiful, perfect. With big dark eyes and a headful of black hair and the longest, most delicate little fingers." She wiped her eyes with a shredded tissue. "Betty let us spend all afternoon with Sarah. We fed her and changed her. We walked her in her stroller and people smiled at us and asked how old she was. One lady told me how good I looked—" Eileen choked, her face crumpled and she started crying with the wholehearted abandon of a small child.

Brian put his arm around her and pulled her close. "At the end of the day Betty told us she had to take the baby back until all the paperwork was completed, but then she would be all ours." He snorted. "That night when I got home, I checked my email. There was a message from Sheltering Arms saying that the mother had experienced unusual medical expenses and we'd have to pay another $50,000 if we wanted Sarah. When I replied that we just didn't have that kind of money, they said they were going to have to place her with someone else."

"We believed them," Eileen said. "I mean, things can go wrong. We knew we were taking a risk when we sent our money to Sheltering Arms–that there were no guarantees—but what other choice did we have? They told us that for another $10,000, we could try for another baby—one with no problems. We were actually considering it."

"*You* were considering it," Brian corrected. "I thought they were tempting us with that baby. They tried to get us hooked, then upped the amount we had to pay to get her."

"You were right, Brian," Eileen said as she gnawed on her thumbnail. "The birth mother never received any medical help at all. That poor girl died because she had the baby outside of a hospital—" She buried her head in her husband's shoulder.

Frank stood and began to pace around the living room. There was still no hard evidence that the baby the Finns had been shown was Mary Pat's baby, but the timing sure seemed right. "So, who has that baby now?"

Brian scowled. "Someone who didn't flinch at coughing up a lot more money than we have, apparently."

"We ought to be able to trace Sheltering Arms through the money," Frank said. "How did you pay them the first ten thousand?"

"By wire transfer to a Bank in the Cayman Islands. All our dealings with them were electronic. We never met or spoke to anyone."

"Except this Betty," Frank said. "Can you describe her?"

Brian shrugged. "She was pretty average. Older than us—maybe mid-fifties. Brown hair, eyes, I don't know, brown, maybe gray. Medium height, not heavy. Frankly, we were so excited about the baby, we hardly looked at Betty."

"What about the letter you wrote? How did you get that to Mary Pat?"

"They said the letter should be hand-written—more personal—and that we should include a photo. We mailed it to a PO Box in New York City."

Frank rose with a sigh. Hard to believe people who seemed as reasonable as the Finns could be so gullible. "Well, get me that address, the email address, the wire transfer address. We'll get to work tracking them down."

Brian sighed. "You can have them, but somehow I doubt it'll do you any good. I think Sheltering Arms is gone. Our money is gone."

Eileen pulled her tear-streaked face away from her husband's shoulder. "Who are these people? What are they going to do with Sarah?"

"They're going to use her to lure another couple." Frank answered. "See how much money they can get from them."

"But this is so unfair to Sarah," Eileen pleaded. "She's just a baby. She needs a mom and dad."

Frank knew the Finns were suffering, but he couldn't help feeling they were partly responsible for this mess. Now that the game they'd been playing had turned against them, they were worried about Sarah. But when they'd thought they would win, they hadn't minded gambling on that baby.

He looked at the couple: Eileen trembling, Brian morose. "I suppose she'll get parents eventually," he told them. "When her usefulness runs out."

Chapter 7

"I don't understand—why aren't the Finns getting this baby? They really were good with her."

"I have someone else who's willing to pay more. I gave the Finns an opportunity to match the offer. They couldn't do it."

"I don't like it. It's not right."

"If you don't like the way I do business maybe you should go to work for a real adoption agency. I wonder what that pays?"

"Don't threaten me. You need me."

"And you need me."

FRANK HAD PLANNED ON driving down to the Finns' and back the same day, but after he left their house, a terrible weariness came over him. He spent two hours in a dark little roadside tavern nursing a beer and thinking.

How had Mary Pat connected with Sheltering Arms? The Sheehans didn't have a computer. He supposed Mary Pat could have used one at the library in Lake Placid or at the county college. If she had, would he be able to trace it? Would they be able to track down the agency again on the Web? He didn't relish the prospect of hours in front of a computer screen, using search engines to come up with seventy-nine thousand possible sites to check out. Earl could help with that—his patience was limitless.

He thought about Mary Pat's baby, who had been a faceless infant but now was a little girl named Sarah. He found it perversely reassuring to know she was such a valuable commodity; her monetary worth meant whoever had her would want to keep her safe. But Sheltering Arms had allowed Mary Pat to deliver without medical attention, so presumably the baby hadn't been examined by a doctor. Anything could go wrong—he remembered Caroline needing special treatments for jaundice in the days after she was born.

Would these con artists even recognize a problem if Sarah wasn't healthy? They might know their way around the Internet and offshore banking, but would they realize if she wasn't eating right? And how long could Sarah be shunted around to different caregivers before that treatment took its toll?

By the time he came out of the tavern, the sun had set, his head was pounding and the Motel 6 across the highway looked irresistibly inviting. Despite the lumpy mattress and musty-smelling sheets, he slept soundly. He leapt out of bed the next morning, shocked to see "7:30" blinking in red on the bedside clock. Heading north at top speed, he exited the Northway by nine-thirty.

The patrol car crested the hill and the long sweep of Route 73 leading into Keene Valley, just west of Trout Run, unrolled before him. Pockets of mist still swirled in the low areas as the sun began its climb. The car picked up speed as it coasted down, and Frank's mind glided along, unshackled as yet by the problems of the day. Luckily, his unconscious reflexes were still engaged. When a man shot out of the parking area near the Giant trailhead and stood in the middle of the road waving his arms, Frank slammed on the brakes and the patrol car skidded to a stop, close enough to spray the man with gravel.

Frank jumped out of the car ready to yell.

"Oh man! Thank God you came along!" He was a stocky man in his late thirties, and his words came in bursts between gulps of breath. "There's a guy up there on the trail. Oh man, I think he's dead."

Frank put a steadying hand on the hiker's shaking shoulders. "OK, slow down. What's your name? Where is this man?"

"Only about a quarter of a mile up the trail. My name's Milton Miyashiro. I just came up here from New Jersey for a couple of days of hiking. I camped on Giant last night, and I was on my way down when I found this guy lying face down on the trail. I thought about giving him CPR. But, I don't know, there's blood, I think it's too late."

Frank radioed for an ambulance and the state police and told Milton to come with him back up the trail.

The lower part of the trail was neither steep nor rocky and Frank made good time even though he wasn't dressed for hiking.

"I think we're getting close," Milton said. A moment later they turned a bend in the trail. Sprawled across the trail lay the body of a man.

"You OK?" Frank asked Milton, whose face looked gray behind a two-day stubble of beard. He didn't wait for a reply before dropping to his knees to examine the man on the trail, who lay on his side with his left arm pinned beneath him. Milton kept up a running commentary that Frank heard with half an ear.

A quick exam told him the ambulance would be making a trip to the morgue, not the emergency room. The body was dry and still warm—certainly it hadn't lain there all night. A bloodstain radiated out from the center of the man's chest, darkening his blue anorak, and blood had soaked into the hard-packed earth of the trail. "You turned him like this?" Frank asked.

"Yeah. I'm sorry if I shouldn't have. But he was face down, and I thought he had fallen, or had a heart attack or something. I thought maybe I could help."

"It's all right." Crouching, Frank looked at the back. He grunted at what he saw: a small, perfect round hole through the back of the jacket.

"What is it?" Milton asked. "How did he die?"

"He was shot."

"Like, with a gun? But there's no hunting allowed here."

Frank didn't answer. This was no hunting accident. The entrance wound was so tiny it had to come from a small caliber handgun at very close range. He felt his heart rate ratchet up a bit, the way it always had when he had been called to the scene of a murder in Kansas City. But this wouldn't be his case. The death had occurred on a trail in the Adirondack Park, so the state police would investigate.

Still, he couldn't stifle his instincts. He studied the dead man: expensive but well-worn hiking boots, fancy sports watch, Gortex anorak, a fanny pack. Definitely a tourist, yet the face, slack and expressionless in death, seemed familiar. The baseball cap had slipped back, revealing dark wavy hair streaked with silver. Then it came to him—this was the man who had been talking to Beth Abercrombie at Malone's.

LIEUTENANT LEW MEYERSON barked out orders like the Marine sergeant he once had been. The woods crawled with crime scene investigators. Dr. Hibbert had arrived to confirm that the body was indeed dead. Uniformed troopers directed traffic and sent away prospective hikers. Frank sat seething on the sidelines with Milton Miyashiro.

Instead of thanking him for securing the crime scene and keeping the witness close by, Meyerson had reamed him out for approaching the body at all. He wouldn't let Frank return to his office until he'd debriefed him, but he was taking his sweet time about it. Frank knew he was being reprimanded and it really ticked him off.

Finally, Meyerson approached the patrol car, where Frank leaned with his arms folded across his chest. The lieutenant signaled Milton over, too.

"All right. What time was it when you discovered the body?" Meyerson demanded.

Milton looked at Frank and shrugged. "Uh, I don't know. Did you look at your watch?"

"It was nine-forty when you flagged me down. Had you been standing there long?"

"No, I tried to stop one other truck, but he passed me by. Then you came along."

"O.K. So it took you how long to get down the trail?"

"Less than ten minutes."

"Then you came upon the body at approximately nine-thirty," Meyerson clarified. "Did you pass anyone on the trail?"

"No one. I was the only ones camping at the lean-to. And no one else came up the trail as I was coming down."

"Did you hear anything? Shouts? Screaming? The shot?" Meyerson asked.

Milton looked perplexed.

"It would have just sounded like a loud pop," Frank explained, despite Meyerson's glare.

"If I heard it, it sure didn't make an impression."

"And you found the body in what position?" Meyerson asked.

"Face down, in the middle of the trail. I rolled him partway over because I thought he might've hit his head or had a heart attack or something. But when I saw all the blood on his chest, and he had no pulse, I just left him alone." Milton looked at Meyerson for reassurance, but the lieutenant only grimaced.

"When you got down here to the parking area, did you see a car other than your own and that old green Volvo?"

"No." Then Milton caught on. "Oh, is that his car? It wasn't here when I hiked in yesterday."

"The victim is one Nathan Golding, resident of Brooklyn, New York according to his license," Meyerson said. "And that car is registered to him."

"*The* Nathan Golding?" Milton asked.

"You know him?"

"Know of him. He's the head of Green Tomorrow, the environmental group. The one that blows stuff up."

Frank's eyes met Meyerson's and he knew they were thinking the same thing. What was Golding up to in the Adirondack Park? He also knew he could probably provide Meyerson with a quick answer by telling him about the conversation he'd overheard in Malone's. But why should he? If Meyerson knew so damn much about running a murder investigation, let him work it out for himself.

A tiny muscle near Frank's left eye began to twitch. He no longer heard what Milton was saying to Meyerson. What would he do with the information if he didn't pass it on to Lew? Investigate himself?

Well, why not just look into it? He didn't like the idea of bringing the State Police down on Beth's head. Besides, if she knew anything, she'd be more likely to tell him than some ass-kicking trooper.

Christ, what was he thinking? He couldn't withhold information from the officer in charge of the case. Where was Meyerson?

The lieutenant was handing the hiker his card and telling him to call if he remembered anything else. He glanced up and noticed Frank watching. "You're free to go, Bennett."

The muscle near Frank's eye pounded.

"Thanks, Lew. Don't work too hard."

——————◆——————

AS SOON AS FRANK STEPPED through the door to his office, Earl and Doris were on him like two puppies on an old shoe. "Who got shot on Giant?" "How did it happen?" "Was it poachers?" "Did you arrest anyone?"

"Jesus H. Christ! Why don't you two consider doing a little work for a change? You obviously spent the whole morning listening to the radio."

His words had the effect of a rolled newspaper raised to strike. Doris and Earl slunk off while Frank sank into his chair and massaged his throbbing temples. He glanced at the clock. Ten after one and all he'd had to eat all day was a lousy donut and coffee in Albany—no wonder his head hurt. Too bad he'd snapped at Earl like that. He could hardly ask him to go to The Store for a sandwich now.

As he was about to get up and go himself, Doris's mousy brown bouffant appeared around the edge of the door. "Joe Sheehan is here," she whispered. Doris always spoke softly in the presence of tragedy, to keep it from turning its attentions to her. "Should I send him in?"

Frank nodded and sat back down as Joe entered, shutting the door behind him. "Well, what did you find out?" Joe asked.

When the fingerprint match had come through, Frank had told Joe he'd be going to Albany to see the Finns. But with all that had happened since he left Trout Run yesterday, he hardly had given a thought to what he would tell Mary Pat's parents about the visit.

Frank began systematically straightening a paperclip, keeping his eyes fixed on his task. "Well, the Finns are the people who wrote that letter I found in Mary Pat's room. Unfortunately, they don't have the baby." Frank explained the entire Sheltering Arms story, ending with the money the Finns had paid for the baby they never got.

Instantly, Joe's hackles went up. "Now wait a minute! First you accused my girl of killing her baby, now you're saying she sold it for money! Mary Pat didn't have but three hundred dollars to her name when she died. I'll show you her bank statement."

"I didn't say Mary Pat sold her baby, I said Sheltering Arms did. Now the Finns found out about this so-called agency through the Internet. Did Mary Pat have a friend with a computer? Did she go to the Lake Placid library a lot?"

Joe shook his head. "Nah, Mary Pat didn't have no interest in computers. She had trouble just typing a letter on the one in the church office."

"Does that computer have Internet access?" Frank asked.

Joe shrugged, then shifted his body in his chair to pull a large blue handkerchief from his pocket. He dabbed at his eyes. "This is just getting worse and worse. I thought you'd come back and tell me that this nice couple adopted the baby fair and square. And then I could tell Ann that everything was settled."

"Well, I'm sorry I couldn't oblige you," Frank said, unable to keep the sarcasm out of his voice. He'd just told the man his granddaughter was being sold like a steer at a cattle auction, and all he cared about was being able to tell his wife their messy problem was cleared up.

But the remark apparently sailed over Joe's head. "That's all right," he said. "What's next?"

"The Finns said Sheltering Arms told them the baby had been born on September 17th. If we knew where Mary Pat was that day, we might discover someone who helped her. And that person might know how Mary Pat hooked up with Sheltering Arms."

"The 17th—what day of the week was that?"

"Wednesday."

Joe rattled off the litany of Mary Pat's well regulated life—shopping on Monday, her day off, volunteering at the church on Tuesdays, at the clothing bank on Fridays, helping her mother with housework and her father with yard work—punctuated with the mantra, "same as always."

"And did she come straight home after work every night? Were you awake when she got home?"

"Of course she came straight home—she knew her mother could never sleep until she was in," Joe explained, then added, "except for Wednesday, now that you mention it."

"What happened then?" Frank prompted.

"She spent the night at Debbie's," Joe said, his mouth pursed in disapproval.

"Debbie...?"

"Flint, who she worked with at the store. You know she's got those two little kids and her husband run off and left her, so whenever her regular babysitter would stand her up or she wanted to go gallivanting with some man, she'd want Mary Pat to come over after her shift at the store and watch the kids, and Mary Pat would never say no."

"I take it you disapproved." Frank wondered what poor Debbie, who had always struck him as a decent, hard-working woman, would think of this take on her social life.

"Well, Mary Pat's just too good-natured. We thought Debbie took advantage, is all."

"And Mary Pat would spend the night when she babysat?" Frank asked.

"Yeah, Debbie would stay out 'til all hours and then Mary Pat would be too sleepy to drive home so she just slept over on the sofa, and came home early in the morning."

"And that's what happened Wednesday the seventeenth? What time did she get home on Thursday morning?

"Well she didn't come home that morning. She called around seven and said Debbie was taking her and the kids to that new pancake restaurant that opened on the way into Lake Placid, and that she thought she might just do a little shopping over there afterwards. See, I had to take Ann to Plattsburgh for a doctor's appointment later that morning."

"So you didn't see Mary Pat from the time she left for work at 2:30 on Wednesday, till she got home from work at 11:30 on Thursday night," Frank clarified.

"Yeah, that's right, " Joe agreed. "So you think she had the baby while she was over at Debbie's? I knew that girl was no good. Why would she let Mary Pat do such a thing and not call a doctor?"

"Hold on, we don't know that Mary Pat had the baby there—she could have been anywhere that night. We'll have to talk to Debbie." Frank thought back to the afternoon in the Stop 'N' Buy when Mary Pat hadn't shown up for work. If Debbie had known about the birth she would have suspected the reason for Mary Pat's absence, but she had seemed truly puzzled. He didn't think she was that good an actress.

Joe looked at Frank in confusion. "You think Mary Pat lied? That she just told us she was at Debbie's and she wasn't really?" This seemed to shock Joe almost as much as the pregnancy.

"Did this babysitting thing come up suddenly?" Frank asked.

"Yeah, as a matter of fact, it did. She just told us about it an hour or so before she left for work. That's what got Ann so riled up. She said Debbie just had Mary Pat at her beck and call. But Mary Pat would never hear a bad word spoken about anyone. She said Debbie had a rough life and deserved a little fun and she didn't mind helping her out."

"Maybe she felt some contractions and figured the baby was coming, so she better make a plan. Although how she managed to get through her shift at work if she was in labor–" Frank shook his head. "Do you know who she would have been visiting on Harkness Road?"

Joe shrugged. "I don't know. I can't really think of anyone she knew over there."

Frank hit the intercom button and told Doris to bring in the property tax record book. She responded with unusual alacrity, then dragged her feet on the way back out, hoping to gather a tidbit of information. Frank remained silent until she was back at her desk.

"Here Joe—look over the list of property owners and see if that jogs your memory."

After studying the book, Joe shook his head. "I recognize most of the names. Mary Pat probably knew most of them by sight too. But I don't think any of them were special friends. She never mentioned visiting them."

Frank sprang up, startling Joe. "I'm going to have to talk to Debbie Flint about Wednesday. And I'll have to go out to Harkness Road and talk to everyone there. I don't think this can stay secret much longer, Joe. You better do what you can to prepare Ann." His voice sounded harsh even to his own ears, but he didn't care.

Joe nodded silently and slowly headed toward the door. With his hand on the doorknob, he turned back to face Frank. "I lost everything here, Frank. My daughter. My granddaughter. The life we used to live. Ann is all I got left. Don't blame me for wanting to keep her safe."

Frank stared at the door that had closed behind Joe. He didn't think he could have felt any worse than he had when the man had opened it, but he did.

Chapter 8

It would be impossible to talk to Debbie while she was working at the Stop 'N Buy, so Frank decided to head over to Harkness Road first, then swing by and talk to Debbie after her shift.

He stepped into the outer office where Doris sat chatting animatedly on the phone while making occasional stabs at her keyboard. He might have known she wouldn't be fazed by his sharp words. Earl was another matter. He sat at the desk shared by the tax collector and the building inspector when they were in, typing with unusual speed. Frank could tell by the uncharacteristic straightness of his assistant's back and the elaborate attention he paid to the computer screen that Earl was truly pissed.

"Earl, I have some interviewing to do out on Harkness Road and I'm going to need your help," Frank announced loudly. Earl made a great show of finishing his typing and shutting down the computer before he looked at Frank. He maintained a dignified silence all the way out to the patrol car.

"Hey, I'm going to pick up a sandwich at the Store before we take off? You want a donut? A Kit-Kat?"

"No thank you," Earl answered.

Frank pressed his lips together; he didn't like having his peace offerings declined. He bought the candy bar anyway and left it on the console between their seats in the car. Steering with one hand, eating with the other, he filled Earl in on the Sheehan case as well as the shooting on the Giant trail.

"Right here!" Earl warned, as the car threatened to shoot past the faded sign that marked the beginning of Harkness Road.

Frank succeeded in making the turn, but not without sending up a spray of gravel from under the patrol car's rear wheels. "I told you I needed your help."

Earl grinned and reached for the Kit-Kat.

The houses on Harkness Road, though modest, all sat on large acreages. They had big, wild yards that ran into thick woods at the back of the properties. Frank drove past the first two houses. He'd found Mary Pat's car beyond these two, heading back out to the main road, so she couldn't have been visiting them. The next house after the spot where Mary Pat's car crashed belonged to Vivian Mays, who'd found the body. As he'd already spoken to Viv at length, Frank kept going. They stopped at the fourth house despite the fact that Earl said the couple who lived there both worked in Plattsburgh and wouldn't be home. He was right, and they continued on.

Frank followed a bend in the road around a tall stand of white pines and the next stretch of Harkness Road lay before them. Two green-painted Adirondack chairs sat in the middle of a meadow-sized front lawn belonging to a small, log-cabin-style house. A man sat in one of them, enjoying the pleasant, if limited, view of the meadow-sized lawn across the street.

"Ah, this looks promising," Frank said as they pulled into the driveway.

"I don't know," Earl cautioned. "That's Mr. Nyquist—he's about a hundred."

Frank suspected that Earl regarded everyone over sixty as "about a hundred," but as he crossed the lawn he saw that Mr. Nyquist was indeed quite elderly. Still the old fellow seemed alert enough, straightening up in his chair and waving cheerily at the prospect of company.

"Why, Earl Davis, is that you?" Mr. Nyquist shouted. "I bet you growed another foot since the last time I seen you. How's your sweet grandma?"

"She's just fine, Mr. Nyquist, how are you?"

"Can't complain, can't complain. And if I did, ain't nobody to listen," he grinned, revealing a broad expanse of pink gums interrupted sporadically by some stumpy brown teeth. "And this must be the new police chief, who replaced Herv," he continued, turning his attention to Frank. "I been hearing some good things about you. You must be here about a year now, huh?"

"Going on two," Frank answered, reaching out to shake Nyquist's hand. He found the old man's grasp surprisingly strong.

"Well, you can't be here to arrest me. I don't move fast enough these days to get into any trouble," he said, slapping his bony knee. "So what can I do for you?"

"It's about Mary Pat Sheehan," Frank began.

"Don't think I know her, although the name kinda rings a bell."

"The girl who was found dead in her car out here last week," Earl explained.

"Oh, oh, her. Yup, that was quite a bit of commotion." Mr. Nyquist's eyes glittered with remembered excitement. "Pity—can't imagine what caused her to crash. It's not like she didn't know the road."

Frank and Earl exchanged glances. "You saw her out here a lot?" Frank asked.

"Sure, recently that is. She drove a beige Escort."

"Who did she come out here to see?"

"Couldn't tell you that. I'd just see her drive by; then about an hour later, sometimes less, she'd drive back."

"So whoever it was, they must live beyond your house," Frank clarified.

"Yessiree."

"And when did you first notice her car out here?"

"It was in May. That's when I start sitting out, when things warm up. In the winter I sit by the window in the house, but I can't really see the road too good from there."

"So she might have come before that?"

Mr. Nyquist nodded.

"What about last fall—did you notice her then?"

"Oh, no definitely not then."

"Thanks, Mr. Nyquist, you've been very helpful," Frank said.

"I have? How?" But despite the old man's prying, Frank managed to extricate himself and Earl without revealing any of the details of Mary Pat's situation.

"Now we're getting somewhere, " Frank said as they got back into the car. "We can concentrate all our efforts on the houses down at this end of the road."

Unfortunately, no one was home at the first two. At the third, the door was finally answered, after a long period of ringing and knocking, by a middle-aged woman named Donna Milford. "I'm sorry," she said breathlessly. "I was clear back in my workroom, and with the sewing machine running I can't hear the bell." A few minutes' conversation put Mrs. Milford out of the picture. She knew Mary Pat only from visits to the Stop 'N' Buy, and although she was home all day, she worked at the back of the house, making curtains and slip covers, and never noticed what traffic passed in the front.

"What about the folks in the two houses between yours and Mr. Nyquist—are they usually home during the day?" Frank asked.

"Well, Judy Penniman works all day and their son's at school. Her husband Doug's a trucker. Sometimes he's home during the day, but then he's usually sleeping. And the Stilers, they're retired, so they're in and out most days, I guess."

Frank didn't know what to make of this information. Would the trucker husband be brazen enough to have his girlfriend Mary Pat meet him at his own home in broad daylight? Or maybe Mary Pat was friends with the wife, who let her use their empty home to meet her lover. Or could the retired couple be helping her in her predicament? He'd have to come back again in the evening to check out the remaining houses.

Leaving the Milfords', they saw a car pull into the Stilers' driveway. "Looks like we're in luck. They're back home," Frank said. "Isn't she the woman who's so involved in organizing the concerts on the town green in the summer?"

"Yeah," Earl agreed. "Her husband's got something wrong with him. He walks real stiff and he doesn't say much."

Frank pulled into the driveway behind the Stilers and got out of his car with a cheerful wave. Mrs. Stiler acknowledged him, but went to the passenger side of her car and opened it. As Frank approached, he could see her moving first one and then the other of her husband's legs out of the car. He stepped forward to help her but she waved him off. With one practiced move, she swung her husband from the car. They both staggered slightly, then regained their balance.

"There now." Mrs. Stiler turned toward them with a smile and extended her hand. "I know who you are and I imagine you know who I am, but I don't think we've ever officially met. Constance Stiler," she shook Frank's hand firmly, then Earl's. "And this is my husband, George." Frank offered his hand to the man but he didn't respond. "George has advanced Parkinson's disease. He finds it difficult to shake hands, and to converse, but he enjoys having company. Come on in."

They followed the Stilers through their back door into a large and cheerful kitchen. Patiently, Constance helped her husband ease into a chair that looked out over the yard behind the house. Frank studied her movements. He imagined she must be in her mid-sixties, but she moved like a much younger person. Tall and lean, she looked like she had always been athletic and still kept up with her exercise. Dressed in khakis and a sweater, she nevertheless projected a rather elegant image. Her most striking feature was her hair: thick and wavy, it had turned a pure, gleaming silver over time.

Motioning them into more comfortable chairs, she pulled a straight-backed chair away from the table and perched on the edge. "What can I do for you?"

"We're here about Mary Pat Sheehan," Frank began.

Immediately Constance began shaking her head. "A terrible tragedy. The poor girl. Do you know what caused the accident?"

"We're looking into it. Right now I'm trying to figure out who she was visiting on Harkness Road."

"Why would that matter?"

Frank sidestepped the question. "Mr. Nyquist said he noticed her driving out to this end of the road many times over the summer."

Constance smiled. "Mr. Nyquist is nothing if not observant."

"Was she visiting you?"

"I think she may have been here once early in the summer to pick up some posters for the concert series. She offered to put them up at the Stop 'N Buy and her church."

"And that's it? She didn't stop by on a regular basis?"

Constance arched her eyebrows. "I don't know what you're getting at, Chief Bennett. I only knew the girl in passing. What does who she was visiting have to do with her car accident?"

Frank hesitated, his eyes scanning the small details of the Stilers' home: the canvas PBS tote bag hanging on a hook, the wall calendar with a famous painting that he recognized but couldn't name; the Julia Child cook books on the shelf. No, he didn't imagine that Mary Pat and Constance had been fast friends. Still, something held him back from telling her what he was after.

"We're trying to determine who she was with immediately before the accident. Did you ever notice her across the street at the Pennimans'?"

Constance regarded him with her steady, intelligent gaze, letting him know that she understood this was only a partial truth. "Well, she certainly wasn't here. And since I don't watch out my front window like Mr. Nyquist,

I really couldn't say about the Pennimans." Somewhere across the kitchen a timer let out a tinny, persistent beep. "Is that all you needed? It's time for George's medication."

"That's all. We won't keep you."

Back in the car, Frank continued down the road, even though there were no more houses to visit. Harkness Road ended in what would be called a cul-de-sac in the suburbs, but in the country the wide, gravelly area surrounded by dense woods was simply known as "the turn-around." On one side, a slightly overgrown path extended into the woods. Earl pointed to it an explained, "That's the old logging trail, where kids ride their ATVs and dirt bikes."

On the other side, a narrow but hard-packed dirt road led out of the turn-around. A crudely lettered sign nailed to a birch tree read, "Privit Prop Kep Out."

"Where's that go?" Frank asked.

"To the Veeches. I've never been back there." The look on Earl's face showed he wanted to keep it that way.

"What's the big deal? Who're the Veeches?" Frank asked as he carefully steered the patrol car up the rutted dirt road.

"They're this weird big family. They all live back here and they never bother with anyone in town. They're dirty and none of 'em work, and there's something wrong with all the kids."

"Wrong in what way?"

"I don't know," Earl said as he peered out the window at the dense woods. He seemed to expect sniper fire at any moment. "Slow, I guess. One of them was in school with me for a while. He was about fifteen and still in the sixth grade, then he just stopped coming. Everyone made fun of him." Earl paused, thinking back on the bad old days when he'd been in school. Frank suspected Earl had endured a fair amount of teasing himself.

"There was a joke they all told about the Veech girls," Earl continued. "What's the Veeches' definition of a virgin?"

"What?" Frank prompted.

"A girl who can run faster than her brothers."

"Earl, that's terrible," Frank said, but snickered anyway. "So what do they do back here, farm?" He winced as his well-maintained patrol car bottomed out on the increasingly steep road, wondering how much further they had to go before they'd come to a house.

"Nah, they just collect welfare. Sometimes you see one of them in the supermarket in Verona. They always pay with food stamps." Earl's voice vibrated with contempt.

Plenty of families lived on the brink of poverty in these small mountain towns, but Frank had noticed that even the poorest workers seemed to be staunch Republicans, fiercely opposed to government handouts of any kind. The Veeches might run counter to the local character, but they must be law-abiding because he'd never had a complaint about them, and their names had never been suggested as suspects in the few petty thefts or vandalisms that constituted his usual workload.

Just as he began to despair of ever getting off this lousy road, the light brightened, the trees thinned out, and the first of several ramshackle houses came into view. Frank pulled up in front of it and turned off the car, then hesitated. Surely this house wasn't inhabited. The front door opened about three feet above ground level, with no porch, stoop or step leading up to it. Several windows were broken, patched with cardboard, and the remaining glass ones were shrouded by tattered sheets serving as curtains. The central part of the house had been built of wood, and several haphazard additions flowed from it, including one wing consisting of a small Airstream trailer that had apparently been backed right into the side wall, then attached with some roughly nailed-up boards.

In a passing fit of enthusiasm, someone had once started painting the place bright blue, but had laid down his brush in mid-stroke, as if called to the phone, and had never picked it up again. The garish color covering half the house made the rest of it look even more dismal.

"No one could possibly live here," Frank said. "We better drive up to the next house." He started up the car again and hadn't gone more than a few feet forward when Earl cringed away from the passenger side door, shouting, "Look out!"

A huge, brindle-coated dog had sprung out of the trees and lunged against Earl's side of the car. Frank stopped with a jolt as the big brute leaped again, putting paws the size of saucers against the window and baying ferociously. Two more dogs ran down the road from the direction of the other houses, surrounding the patrol car. Although smaller, they were no less fierce. Frank could hear their claws scratching his car, as one and then the other showed his head above the car hood.

Frank let out a few whoops of the police siren and the dogs backed away momentarily, but despite all the racket, no one emerged from any of the houses. He turned on the bullhorn. "Hello, Mr. Veech? Could you call off your dogs please?"

Still no sign of life. "We just want to ask you a question about the accident Mary Pat Sheehan had out here last week. Could you help us out?" No response.

"Now what?" Earl asked, as the dogs closed in again. The big one slobbered all over the window, looking for a way to tear Earl's throat out.

"I think we beat a tactical retreat." Frank put the car in gear, not caring if the dogs got out of the way. "We'll wait and see what the Pennimans have to tell us before we come up here again."

"Next time, we better bring the state police animal control officer with us," Earl said.

"That's an option. But it could be the dogs were guarding the place because no one is home today."

But as they passed the first house, they saw the ragged curtain in the upstairs window fall back into place.

Chapter 9

"What's today's date?" Frank demanded out of the blue as they drove back toward town.

"October first."

"Shit! Caroline's birthday is just four days away and I haven't bought her present yet."

"So she'll get it a day or so late—what's the big deal? She's not a little kid."

Earl was right of course, but Caroline had always regarded her birthday as a national holiday, and since she was an only child he and Estelle had indulged her in this, even after she was grown. She looked forward to his present and would be disappointed if it weren't there on the right day. He didn't want to let her down, especially with the coolness between them now.

"If I buy something today and send it express she'll have it by the fifth," Frank said.

"What're you going to get her?"

That was the problem. Now that Caroline was married to Mr. Wall Street, there wasn't a thing Frank could get her that Eric couldn't provide a better version of. There was nothing she truly needed, and Frank didn't understand her wants anymore.

Then, as if the hand of God were guiding him, Frank rounded the next bend in the road and a sign came into view. "Adirondack Artisans—Pottery, Weaving, Jewelry"—Beth Abercrombie's shop.

The last time Caroline had visited she'd seen that sign, but when they stopped, the store had been closed and Caroline had stood with her nose pressed against the glass, oohing and ahing at what she could see through the window. Some arty little knick-knack from Beth's shop would be right up Caroline's alley, and it had the advantage of being something that Eric couldn't deliver. Best of all, the pretext of shopping would give him a chance to ask Beth about Nathan Golding.

"I just got a shopping brainstorm, Earl. I'll drop you at the office. See what you can turn up searching the Internet for Sheltering Arms–I'll be back in half an hour." Frank soon dropped Earl off in the town office parking lot, then doubled back to Beth's shop.

The Adirondack Artisans sign stood on the main road between Trout Run and Verona, but the shop itself was down the little unmarked country road just beyond the sign. In less than a quarter of a mile, Frank spotted the shop, nestled in a clearing surrounded by white pine and birch. Its cedar shake siding, stained a deep green, allowed the little building to blend into the woods, as if it had sprung up there naturally.

Beth must have had the place built to suit her needs. The front door, flanked by two large plate glass windows, opened directly into the shop, while a side door led into her living quarters behind and above the store. The little graveled parking area was empty.

Frank followed a flagstone walk past some chrysanthemums blooming bravely despite the chill, and hesitated before the door. Maybe this hadn't been such a good idea after all. Clearly, he would be the only customer. What if there was nothing he thought Caroline would like? He'd have to buy something—he couldn't very well say "just looking" and saunter out like you could in a big department store. But maybe the shop wasn't even open today. He reached for the doorknob, half hoping it wouldn't turn, but it opened and the breeze immediately set some wind chimes into a melody announcing his entrance.

A wonderful scent of pine impressed him before his eyes registered anything. Not the cloying, suffocating smell of those pine air fresheners or green scented candles—just the terrific smell of a fresh Christmas tree the day you first bring it into the house. But there was no tree, and no Beth either.

Frank prowled around the deserted showroom, taking everything in. Three tiers of shelves ran around the perimeter of the room. The carpenter in him immediately noticed the fine craftsmanship of the shelves—the finely mitered corners, the beveled trim, the satiny finish. Then he thought to look at the pottery displayed upon them: bowls, plates and vases, no two items exactly the same, although all clearly made by the same hand. A rack in front of the window held multicolored woven wool shawls, and another displayed cotton area rugs. In a case by the cash register, silver jewelry sat on black velvet pads. The overall effect was quite pleasant and restful, not at all like shopping in the mall. Still, Frank wondered how Beth could make a living with such a small inventory.

He reached out and picked up a large green vase that caught his eye. Turning it over, he held it at arm's length to make out the tiny writing on the discreet price tag. Twelve dollars? No, one hundred and twenty! Good grief, she couldn't sell many of those around–

"Why hello, Frank. What brings you here?"

The sound of Beth's low, mellow voice surprised him so much that he nearly dropped the vase, which would have been a real catastrophe.

"I'm sorry. I didn't mean to startle you. I heard the bells chime but I had a pot on the wheel and couldn't come right out." Beth smiled. She radiated a placid stillness, as if the atmosphere of the shop emanated directly from her.

Her calmness inspired an equal level of nervousness in Frank. He felt like she'd caught him shoplifting and for a moment his tongue stayed glued to the roof of his mouth as surely as if he'd just taken a big bite of peanut butter sandwich.

"Hi, Beth," he finally managed to stammer. "I, uh, I'm looking for a birthday gift for my daughter. Thought she might like something from your store."

"Aren't you a sweet dad! Is she a college girl? She might like some earrings, or a shawl."

"Oh, no," Frank answered. "She's out of school. She's going to be twenty-six."

"Twenty-six!" Beth put her hand on his forearm. "You can't have a daughter who's twenty-six! You must've been twelve when she was born."

Frank felt a silly rush of pleasure at her joke. Did she really think he only looked thirty-eight? That was about how old she was, he guessed. "No, I was twenty-one when Caroline was born," he admitted. "But sometimes I felt like I was twelve."

"Yes, having children knocks the know-it-all right out of you, doesn't it?" Her green eyes, flecked with gold like a cat's, looked directly into his. Frank's mind went blank as he felt his heart quicken and his throat go dry. Good lord, he hadn't had this reaction to a woman since Bettina Albert had paralyzed him with her presence in eighth grade French.

"Do you have children?" he finally managed to choke out, keeping up his end of the conversation. He'd picked up from someone that Beth was divorced, but he hadn't noticed any sign of children.

"Yes, two boys. Gregory's at the University of Oregon and Theo's a junior at Oberlin."

"Now it's my turn to be surprised. I would've expected grade school kids." Perhaps she was a little closer to his age than he thought.

"No, they're out of the nest." A wistful look crossed her face as she gazed out the window. "I miss them, but I never expected they would stay around Trout Run." Beth brought her attention back to him with a little shake. "Enough about that—let's find a gift for your daughter. You were interested in that vase?"

Frank coughed. "Actually, I'm thinking a bowl might be better—more practical." He gestured toward a medium-sized bowl glazed the same rich green color as the vase, but with less detail-work. Hopefully this one was a bit cheaper; he didn't have the nerve to turn it over and look.

"You have a good eye."

Again, that ridiculous flutter of satisfaction. As she reached out for the bowl he noticed that her hands were stained with the clay she had been working. Somehow, that made them more attractive.

"She can use this to serve food, or it would look nice with a seasonal arrangement. Some gourds, or pine cones and berries," Beth said as she held the bowl up for his inspection.

Frank nodded in agreement, although what he knew about seasonal arrangements wouldn't fill a matchbook. "I'll take it. Could you pack it up? I have to ship it to Chappaqua."

"I can take care of all that for you. The UPS man stops here every day."

They moved to the cash register and Frank handed over his credit card. As he filled out the shipping form he said, "I guess you heard about the shooting over on Giant this morning?"

"Shooting? Who would be hunting over there?"

His heart sank as he realized he was going to be breaking the news of Golding's death to her. He'd just assumed that news this big would have reached her by now, but of course no one from town shopped here, and if she'd been working all morning without the radio on she wouldn't have heard. "It wasn't an accident. And I'm afraid the victim was someone you know."

Beth looked up from wrapping the bowl.

"Nathan Golding."

She took a step back and plopped onto a stool behind the counter. "Is he badly hurt?"

Frank's hesitation answered her question.

"He's dead? But I just saw him the other day!"

"I'm sorry, Beth. Was he a good friend?"

"Well, not exactly. I mean, he used to be, but I hadn't seen him for years until he showed up on Thursday here at the shop." Frank's curiosity must have been apparent, because she kept explaining. "I met him when I was in college at Cornell. He was a grad student there when I was a freshman and sophomore."

Beth stopped talking and her eyes got that same faraway look they'd had when she was talking about her sons. Frank waited.

"Nathan was so, so...vibrant. People just flocked to him." Beth smiled at Frank. "You remember what college was like in the early seventies. We were all so idealistic, so passionate. And Nathan was at the center of it all. Leading every protest, organizing marches, circulating petitions—all for the environment."

Frank forced his lips up a little in response. That might've been what college had been like for Beth and Golding, but he had worked his way through UMKC at night when he was already married, a father and a cop. It'd taken eight years and there certainly hadn't been any time for waving banners and marching on the dean's office. He imagined Beth as an eighteen-year-old hippie-chick—he probably wouldn't have given her a second glance in those days.

Beth didn't seem to notice that Frank wasn't agreeing. She continued down memory lane. "When I was nineteen I would've walked across hot coals for Nathan Golding. But then he dropped out of grad school, I finished college, got married, and came here. Of course I knew what became of him—I followed all the news about Green Tomorrow. I even sent the organization a few donations. He said that's how he tracked me down."

"Why did he suddenly want to track you down after all these years?" Frank asked.

Beth began fussing with the packaging of the bowl again. "He was in the area, uh, conducting some research. He said he always likes to look up local supporters when he's working in the field. It was wonderful to see him. Even with the gray hair and a few wrinkles he was just the same. Still so intense, so committed. I just can't believe he's dead."

"What kind of research?" Frank persisted.

Beth looked up from her wrapping and her eyes locked with Frank's. "Are you investigating his death? Is that why you came in today?"

Frank felt a wave of heat rise through his body. He wondered if he was blushing noticeably. "No, it's the State Police's case. I came in to buy a gift. But I saw you talking to Golding at Malone's, and now he's turned up dead. I can't help but wonder—" Frank broke off. Why did he feel the need to explain to her?

"The State Police are going to need to know why Golding was here," he continued. "If you can help them, you should come forward."

A furrow of worry appeared above Beth's eyes. "Nathan's been active in protesting the commercialization of wilderness areas. New ski resorts in the Sierras. Golf courses in the desert. He was here looking into Raging Rapids."

"Raging Rapids? That's just a dinky little tourist attraction." Frank had taken his grandsons there last summer to walk across the catwalks that crossed Stony Brook as it plunged into a deep gorge. "Why would Golding care about that?"

Beth shrugged. "Nathan was involved in far more controversial things, and he certainly had enemies. That must be why he was killed—I doubt it has anything to do with Raging Rapids."

The sound of gravel crunching outside made them both look up. The UPS truck was pulling into the parking area. Beth put the last piece of tape on the box containing Caroline's gift.

"Just in time," she said. "Let me know how your daughter likes the bowl."

"I will." In a rush he added, "Maybe we could have lunch sometime."

"I'd like that."

Then, before she could say anything else, he left as fast as a mouse that has nabbed a piece of kibble straight from the cat's bowl.

Chapter 10

Debbie Flint lived in a trailer parked on a long, narrow lot that fronted the main road out of Trout Run. Now that it was past five, Frank was sure Debbie would be home from her shift at the Stop 'n' Buy.

The trailer, which looked to be about fifteen or twenty years old, had been set up with the least amount of effort, barely a car's length back from the road. There was no driveway, only hard packed earth where Debbie's ancient Crown Victoria was parked. A tangle of trikes and trucks and dolls lay in the weedy grass, and out back a row of tiny shirts and pants flapped on the clothesline. Frank climbed up the unstable pile of concrete blocks that passed for a front stoop. Knocking on the door was like rapping on tin foil.

But Debbie's trailer was clean and cheerful inside. Dinner was cooking in the galley kitchen, and the children were working on a jigsaw puzzle on the living room floor. A flowered curtain separated the main room from the bedroom. If Mary Pat had given birth here, she had certainly had very little privacy.

"Hi Debbie, I need to talk to you about Mary Pat Sheehan for a minute," Frank said as the young woman let him in. "Was Mary Pat over here on the evening of September 17th? That's the Wednesday the week before she died."

"Here at my house? Of course not—why would she be?"

"Her parents said she babysat for you that night and slept over. That she babysat for you all the time. Is that true?"

"Babysat? For me? The only person who watches my kids is Sue Estes, while I'm at work."

"So Mary Pat never babysat for you?" Frank confirmed.

"Well, I take that back. Once, about a year ago, I had a court date in Elizabethtown about my support payments, and Sue got sick and I was upset about it at work and Mary Pat volunteered to watch them and so she did stay with them for a couple of hours that one time." Debbie gulped a breath. "Now, what's this all *about*?"

"Mary Pat's death was not quite what it seemed," he began, and then listened to the now familiar chorus of disbelief as he told about the concealed pregnancy, the birth, and the sale of the baby through Sheltering Arms. "So," Frank concluded, "it would appear that Mary Pat was using you for a cover when she would meet her boyfriend. And, I'm pretty sure she gave birth that night when she told her folks she was babysitting for you. Now I have to figure out where she really went, and who she was with, and who put her in touch with Sheltering Arms. Any ideas?"

Debbie shook her head, her dirty-blond hair swinging back and forth with the vehemence of her denial. "Wow, and I thought *my* life was screwed up!"

"Can you remember if there was anyone she talked about a lot? A man she went out of her way to talk to, or flirted with–"

"Flirted!" Debbie interrupted. "Mary Pat didn't even know how to flirt. She was just the same nice Mary Pat to everyone, young, old, ugly, handsome. It didn't matter to her."

"Well, she treated *someone* different, and the Stop'N'Buy's gotta be the link," Frank said. "Where else would she meet anyone? She spent all her free time with her parents or at church."

"Mommee?? I'm hungry!" a little voice piped from the sofa.

"I'm coming sweetie." Debbie opened the door for Frank. "I guess the guy must've been someone who came in later in her shift, when she was alone. Maybe Anita would know something. She comes in three nights a week to clean."

"Anita who?"

"Anita Veech."

————— ❧ —————

ON THE SHORT RIDE INTO town, Frank thought about Mary Pat's lover.

Was the guy grief-stricken now or relieved? Had he known how sick Mary Pat was in the days before she died? Had he urged her to see a doctor, or had they both been so anxious to keep the pregnancy quiet that he'd done just the opposite–prevented her from getting the help that could've saved her?

Or could he have just been a one-night stand, someone passing through that Mary Pat had gone with out of sheer loneliness?

Such a waste. Such a terrible, terrible waste, and nothing Frank did could change that. He'd spent the whole day getting bad news and giving bad news. He hadn't accomplished jack shit. Now he felt an overwhelming need to fix something. To just use his hands and head to make one thing, one stupid little thing, come out right. And then he got an idea.

Driving back to the office, he switched the patrol car for his own pick-up, checking to see that his toolbox was in there. Then he headed out to the Iron Eagle Inn.

Edwin and Lucy Bates owned Trout Run's one entry in the charming country bed and breakfast category. They'd escaped the high-pressured life in Manhattan, and now spent their days catering to the whims of the type of people they used to be.

The Inn was one perpetual repair project, as Frank had discovered when Caroline had booked him into the Iron Eagle for a restorative fishing trip after Estelle's death. During his stay he'd walked in on a contractor giving Edwin some hare-brained advice on porch repair. Unable to stand by quietly as a catastrophe unfolded, he'd replaced the rotting floorboards himself, and an unlikely friendship was born.

Edwin and Frank had nothing in common. Edwin, a former English professor who hadn't made tenure, was particular about everything: the books he read, the clothes he wore, the food he ate. Frank was an omnivore: he read everything he got his hands on, ate anything that was put in front of him, often with disastrous consequences, and wore whatever was given to him for Christmas and his birthday.

But one thing they shared–Edwin understood what it meant to lose a job you loved, and he had persuaded Frank to reject the new career in corporate security he'd been considering in favor of taking over the police chief's job in Trout Run. It was the best advice Frank had ever received and he repaid Edwin by continuing to repair things at the Inn.

Frank glanced at the dashboard clock. Almost seven—he could get some satisfaction from fixing Edwin's latest plumbing problem, and get a free meal in the bargain. He hoped it wasn't anything too weird. The last time he'd eaten there, Edwin had fed him ratatat-something, full of eggplant and tomatoes and suspicious little flecks. It had tasted all right on the way down, but had roiled his digestive tract for hours afterward.

Frank marched into the kitchen without knocking, encouraged by the comforting smell of garlic and roasting meat. Jen Verhoeff, who helped Edwin with the cooking, was flying around, muttering under her breath, "Seven minutes to cook a whole pot of green beans, my ass! Fine if you're feeding beavers, but people like to be able to chew their vegetables."

"How's it going?" Frank asked, sitting down at the long oak table, well away from the big six-burner stove.

Jen let out a little shriek. "Geez! You scared me. Where did you come from, Frank?"

"Sorry. I came to scrounge a meal."

"Well, get in there. You missed the appetizer, but I'll set you a place for the main course."

Frank tugged at the khaki shirt of his uniform. "I'm not dressed for company. I thought I'd fix the toilet in the Blue Room, then just eat leftovers out here."

"I guess that's all right, if you can finish before the guests are done with dinner. Go up the back stairs."

Frank carried his toolbox up the narrow steps and crossed the hall to the Blue Room. He tapped on the door, and when no one answered, walked in. None of the Inn's locks worked–it catered to trusting souls.

The guest's suitcase lay open on the floor. Instinctively, he checked out the contents as he stepped over it to get to the bathroom. He could hear the toilet gurgling away.

"I can't believe people pay Edwin $125 a night to stay in a room with a little sign taped to the toilet telling you how to jiggle the handle to get it to flush," he said to himself as he set to work installing a new ball and plunger. In just a few minutes, the toilet responded to his test with a gratifying whoosh. He pulled the sign off, but stopped short of throwing it away. Might as well save it for when the next one broke.

Frank came down the back stairs just as Edwin entered the kitchen from the dining room. "Frank, what a nice surprise. What brings you here?"

"Fixed your toilet." Frank took the half empty serving platter from Edwin's hands. "I'll take my payment in roast beef."

"Lamb," Edwin corrected. "And don't wrinkle your nose like it's fried goat eyeballs. I'm just going to serve the guests dessert, then Lucy and I will come back and have coffee with you."

Frank watched as an impressive-looking chocolate cake rode out to the dining room on a serving cart. He hoped there would be enough left over. But his fears were groundless. Before long, Edwin and Lucy both were back in the kitchen, bearing nearly half the cake. "So many people on diets these days," Edwin complained. "It's hardly worth baking. I should just serve fresh fruit."

"Don't be rash, Edwin. You can always count on me," Frank said, slicing himself a large piece.

"Ah, if only everyone had your metabolism, Frank," Lucy said as she served herself a piece of cake so thin it dissolved into a pile of crumbs on her plate. Lucy complained constantly that Edwin's cooking would soon push her from a size six to a size eight, a lament that didn't earn her much sympathy from the other women she knew.

Edwin poured coffee all around, as Jen loaded the dinner plates into the dishwasher. "Well, the talk at dinner was all about the shooting on Giant. I hope they're all talked out, otherwise I don't know what we'll do at breakfast tomorrow."

"Meredith Golding, Nathan's widow, is staying here," Lucy explained. "She arrived this afternoon, but she had to go right out to the morgue to identify the body. She hasn't come back yet—I guess the police are still talking to her."

Frank raised his eyebrows. "She had time to find a cozy little B&B when her husband's just been murdered?"

"Oh, we know them. She and Nathan have stayed here before—they both like hiking in the High Peaks."

Frank set down his fork with a bite of cake uneaten. "Nathan Golding was here last night?"

"No, no—he wasn't staying with us. Apparently he's been up here on business. I heard in town he was staying at the Mountain Vista Motel. It's cheaper over there, and Nathan's pretty thrifty. Why are you so interested? Will you be part of the investigation?"

"No, this belongs to the state police. I've got my own problems."

"You sure do. Tell us all about this scandalous secret life that poor Mary Pat Sheehan was living," Edwin said, settling into his chair as if it were a theater seat.

Hot coffee sprayed from Frank's mouth. "How the hell do you know about that? Did Earl tell you? Wait'll I get ahold of him..."

"Earl? No, we haven't seen him for days. We heard it from Jen," Edwin explained. "Her nephew's engaged to Dr. Hibbert's secretary. She transcribed the autopsy notes."

"Man, you can't keep a secret in this town for more than a few hours," Frank said.

"Mary Pat seems to have kept a pretty big secret for nine whole months," Lucy pointed out.

"It beats me how she managed it," Jen said from her spot at the big, old cast iron sink. "Whenever I was pregnant, Bill used to swear I'd grown a couple of inches every time he looked at me."

"Maybe that's how she did it," Edwin said. "No one ever really *looked* at Mary Pat, did they? She was just part of the background."

They all sat for a moment until Lucy broke the unnatural quiet. "So what do you have to do with this, anyway, Frank? After all, even if Mary Pat did something to the baby, she's dead now too. There's no one to arrest."

Frank hesitated. Part of him still wanted to protect Mary Pat and her family from the wagging tongues in town. But Debbie Flint already knew about the baby-selling scheme and tomorrow he'd have to tell Anita Veech. So told them about the letter and the Finns. "So now I'm trying to figure out who helped Mary Pat with the baby and who put her in touch with this Sheltering Arms," Frank concluded.

Jen's mouth had dropped open halfway through the story and now she wagged her head as she spoke, "I just can't believe she'd sell her own baby. I mean, when you've given birth and you see that little face looking up at you for the first time, you just melt." Jen paused in her relentless scrubbing of the counters, her eyes lost in wistful memories. "You're in love."

"Maybe the experience is a little different when you're giving birth on a dirty bathroom floor, with the jerk who knocked you up as your midwife," Lucy said. Edwin, Frank and Jen all turned to her, surprised by the harshness in her voice.

"It's not like that," Jen objected. "When you're a mother–"

"Oh, right. *I* wouldn't know. I haven't been there. I'm not a member of the club." Lucy began picking up the dessert plates, not bothering to remove the forks, so they teetered in an unsteady tower in her shaking left hand.

Jen's eyes opened wide in amazement. "Lucy, I didn't mean..."

"It's nearly nine, Jen," Lucy cut her off. "I'll finish up here—I know you like to get home before your kids are in bed."

Jen looked at Edwin for support, but he simply shook his head very slightly. "I'll see you tomorrow, Jen. Thanks for your help."

Frank rose as well. "I'd better be going too."

"No, no Frank. Go on out to the parlor. We'll have a glass of port," Edwin instructed. Frank edged nervously toward the dining room door, watching as Edwin put his hand on Lucy's shoulder as she stood at the sink. He murmured something, his head bent close to hers.

She nodded and straightened her back. "I'll just get the dishwasher going," she said with studied brightness. "I'll join you in a minute."

In the parlor, Frank sank into the worn leather chair next to the crackling fire. Suppressing the urge to blurt, "what was *that* all about?" he accepted, guiltily, the rosy–gold glass of port that Edwin offered. It reminded him of the homemade elderberry wine his grandmother used to give him for a sore throat.

Edwin rolled his port glass between his palms, warming it, before he spoke. "Lucy and I tried for eight years to have a baby. Drugs, surgery, inseminations, in vitro—we did it all, in every fertility clinic in Manhattan. It was like a merry-go-round you couldn't get off. Every time we'd make up our minds to stop trying, some 50-year-old we knew would get pregnant with a new treatment or a new doctor, so we'd start all over again. The doctors kept feeding our hopes– it was like they wouldn't give us permission to quit. The constant disappointment was eating away at Lucy.

"If I'd won tenure at NYU, we'd probably still be at it. Buying the inn was the best thing we could have done. We're hundreds of miles away from the nearest fertility clinic, so the temptation is removed. We've made up our minds that we can have a happy life without children," Edwin said.

Frank nodded, but he must have looked doubtful, because Edwin continued on the defensive.

"I guess you wonder why we don't adopt?"

Frank held up his hand to stave off the confession. "I don't wonder anything."

But Edwin seemed determined to confide. "We've discussed it, and Lucy would probably pursue it if I showed a little more interest. But I have reservations about adoption."

Frank twisted in his seat to see if any of the other guests were headed for the parlor to rescue him. He didn't want to know all this personal stuff, but the hall was empty and Edwin clearly expected him to show some interest.

"Oh?" he managed.

"We went to this adoption support group once, and someone there said, 'I know I could love an adopted child, I'm just not sure I could love *any* adopted child.' That's how I feel. I'm not sure I could love whatever baby we happened to get. I can't take the chance that I wouldn't love it—that would be too terrible, for both of us." Edwin looked down at his hands. "I guess you think that's horrible."

"No, I don't. I—"

As if on cue, Lucy entered the room and spared him from having to offer more comfort. She perched on the wide arm of Frank's chair. "I'm sorry I'm such a grouch."

Roughly, Frank patted her knee, "Everyone's entitled to be grouchy sometime. Hell, I'm always a bear—ask Earl."

Lucy was about to answer when a movement at the door caught her eye. She leaped up. "Meredith! Oh, Meredith, how are you? What did they say? Edwin, pour her a drink," she ordered as she hugged the slender, auburn-haired woman and ushered her into the room.

Frank observed, fascinated. Police work didn't throw women like Meredith Golding in his path much, but he'd seen plenty of her type in the four years Caroline had been at Princeton: women born knowing what fork to use, what dress to wear, what gift to bring. He wouldn't have pegged Meredith as the wife of an environmental activist in a million years.

"Thank you, Edwin." The glass of cognac she accepted trembled slightly in her smooth, well manicured hand. She looked at Frank. "Are you here to talk to me? I just spent four hours with the state police."

"No, no," he and Lucy answered simultaneously. "Frank Bennett is the chief of police here in Trout Run, and a good friend of ours," Lucy continued.

"I was on the scene at Giant for a while this morning, Mrs. Golding. I'm sorry for your loss."

Meredith accepted his condolences with a nod and sank into the other chair by the fire. "Maybe you can tell me if it's usual for the state police to be so harsh to a victim's family. They asked me a million questions about Nathan's schedule and his plans and then they got annoyed when I told them I simply do not keep tabs on my husband twenty-four hours a day."

Frank tried to look sympathetic. "I'm sure they're just trying to determine the chain of events."

"I told them they should be talking to Barry Sutter, Green Tomorrow's lawyer, about Nathan's schedule. But they can't seem to track him down. I can't imagine why—he was supposed to meet Nathan up here this afternoon." Meredith turned toward Lucy, "I went to visit my sister in Saratoga for a few days. I hadn't seen Nathan since I left on Friday. Then right before lunch, the police called me on my cell phone—" Meredith's anger dissolved into soft weeping.

Lucy came and knelt beside Meredith's chair, taking her hand, "I can't even imagine what you must be going through. But I'm sure the state police will find whoever did this."

They all fell silent as Meredith searched out a tissue in her purse.

"I bet you haven't eaten all day," Lucy said finally. "Edwin can fix you a little plate."

Meredith raised her hand in half-hearted protest but Edwin was already on his feet. "Good idea," he said

Frank rose too. "I'll be leaving now. Goodnight Lucy, Mrs. Golding."

Following Edwin to the kitchen, Frank perched on a stool and watched Edwin fixing a plate of cheese, fruit and pasta salad. "Well, she's certainly not what I expected."

"Tell me about it. Old money WASP meets left-wing Jew–she and Nathan were definitely the odd couple. But they seemed devoted to each other."

"Kids?"

Edwin shook his head. "He was married before. I think he had kids, but none with Meredith."

"Lucy seems very concerned about her. Are they good friends?"

Edwin shrugged. "You know Luce—always ready with the shoulder to cry on. Meredith and Nathan have been up here maybe three times. But she and Lucy seemed to hit it off. Meredith used to be in corporate PR. The two of them would reminisce about the days when they wore suits and high-heels to work. Lucy gets a little lonely in Trout Run sometimes." Edwin handed Frank a Tupperware container and a fork. "Here, finish this pasta—there's not enough to save. I've got to bring this to Meredith."

Frank obliged, although Edwin's salads tended to be full of landmines like black olives and artichokes. As he ate alone in the kitchen, he wondered why Golding had only recently looked up Beth Abercrombie if he'd been to Trout Run several times.

A piercing shriek echoed back to him. He followed the sound out to the front hall, where Meredith Golding stood staring at the bushy-bearded man who'd been with Nathan and Beth at Malone's.

"Barry, where have you been? How could you have let this happen?" Meredith faced him like an angry cat, claws extended, back arched.

"I was supposed to meet Nathan at 2:00, but he never showed. I've been looking for him ever since." He patted his pockets apologetically. "I seem to have misplaced my cell phone. Where is he? What's wrong?"

"Nathan is—" But Meredith couldn't bring herself to say the words.

Edwin and Lucy also seemed paralyzed by the situation, so Frank stepped forward. "Mr. Sutter, I'm afraid Nathan Golding was murdered this morning on the trail to Giant. The state police need to speak to you. I can take you there now."

Sutter staggered backward a few steps. "No..." he said weakly. "Meredith?" he turned to her, looking for support.

Meredith's anger had passed. "You'd better go and talk to the police now, Barry. Come back here when you're done." Her eyes locked with his. "I'll be waiting up for you."

Chapter 11

"*What are you calling about? Do you have a new prospect?*"

"*No, we have a little problem. Kimba and Chip Braithwaite don't want the baby.*"

"*What do you mean, we have a problem? I told you to leave her with the Finns.*"

"*I don't remember you protesting too loudly when your heard what the Braithwaites were willing to pay.*"

"*So why did they change their minds? Did Kimba get pregnant?*"

"*They didn't like the looks of her. She's not enough like them—no blond hair and blue eyes.*"

"*That beautiful, perfect baby isn't good enough for them? God, we should have known people named "Kimba" and "Chip" would be nothing but trouble. So give the baby back to the Finns. She'll be better off with them anyway.*"

"*We can't, now. They know this is an illegal adoption. And Bennett knows about them.*"

"*We can get around that. They were crazy about the baby.*"

"*Let me think about it. In the meantime, come and get this kid. I'll meet you halfway.*"

FRANK ENTERED HIS OFFICE the next morning with Doris hot on his heels.

"Frank, Frank—I need to know what to do about this."

Frank raised his shoulders towards his ears, an involuntary protective re-action to the sound of Doris's piercing voice. The town secretary waved a piece of typewritten paper in one hand, but he was momentarily distracted by the sight of her hair. It had changed color overnight, from the familiar dingy brown to an extraordinary shade of red, bordering on magenta. She looked like Lucille Ball viewed on a TV with faulty color control.

"What—?" 'What happened to your hair?' Frank had been about to say, but he caught himself and finished the sentence, "do you have there?" He extended his hand and took the paper Doris clutched.

"It's a letter from Katie Conover requesting a permit to stage a demonstration."

"A permit?" Frank's brow furrowed as he began to read. "What kind of permit? What kind of *demonstration*?"

Doris's shrill commentary made it difficult for Frank to follow what he was reading, but the gist of it seemed to be that the writer wanted to hold a demonstration on Stony Brook Road next Wednesday. It was signed Katherine C. Petrucci, Chair, Concerned Citizens of the High Peaks.

"Who's Katherine Petrucci?" he asked. I thought you said Katie Conover wrote the letter?"

"Petrucci is her married name," Doris sniffed. "Except a lot of folks don't believe she really is married to that fella. She met him in New York City and he followed her up here, you know. She still went by Katie Conover, even though her mom kept insisting they were married. Now that they have kids, suddenly she's Katie Petrucci."

"Women don't have to take their husband's name when they get married, Doris."

"Well, I'm not the only one who thinks Katie Conover Petrucci whatever has gotten just a little too big for her britches ever since she won that full scholarship to NYU. Naturally her parents didn't want her going to college in Greenwich Village with all them drug addicts and subway murderers and such, but they had five kids and it was totally free, so what could they do?"

Doris shifted in her seat, crossing one skinny leg over the other as she warmed to her story. "Anyway, she just turned weirder and weirder. First she wouldn't eat meat, and then she announced she was going off to South America to help the Indians or peasants or whatever they have down there."

"Okay, okay, I get the picture. What's it got to do with this protest she's planning?"

Doris straightened the lapels of her polyester pantsuit. "I'm just trying to give you a sense for what kind of person she is. So, after she finished college she moved back here with this fellow Mark and they both started teaching at the North Woods Academy."

Doris said this with the same tone she might have used to announce they'd gone to work for the Church of Scientology. The North Woods Academy was a boarding school catering to rich kids who couldn't get into—or had been kicked out of—more prestigious institutions.

"And then she had kids and breast-fed them till they were two years old! Why I remember one Fourth of July, Katie's little one—mind you he could talk and had a full set of teeth—walks over to her, pulls up her shirt and starts suckin' on her tit—pardon my French—right there at the parade with the fire trucks and the Verona Drum and Bugle Corps going right by."

Frank laughed out loud, which encouraged Doris to continue. "Anyhow, now that she has kids she doesn't teach at the Academy anymore. She organized a little co-op nursery school three mornings a week over at the Presbyterian Church. So that's probably how she got the other girls to go along with her on this protest."

"But what are they protesting *about*?"

"It says right there in the letter," Doris came around behind his desk and pointed to a sentence in the middle of the letter that read, "We wish to alert the public, especially people with young children, to the unsafe conditions tolerated at the Raging Rapids attraction and the irreparable harm it causes to the environment."

"Raging Rapids?" Frank snatched up the letter and read it word-for-word, but there was no mention of Green Tomorrow or Nathan Golding. He sat thinking for a minute until Doris started in again.

"Well, what should I do?"

"Go ahead and give Katie her permit." He didn't understand what was behind this sudden interest in Raging Rapids, but he had a feeling the demonstration might shed a little light on the matter. And he suspected Meyerson would agree.

"Really? Abe Fenstock won't like that one little bit," Doris warned.

"I know, I'll go see him today and warn him."

The morning's excitement over, Frank turned his attention to the stack of papers in his in-box. Doris continued to sit silently in the chair opposite his desk. Frank looked up. "Well?"

"What should I do about the permit?"

"Didn't I just say to give it to her?"

"Give her what?"

"The permit!" Frank felt like he was in the middle of a "who's on first?" routine.

"But we don't have any demonstration permits. The last time someone wanted to demonstrate was over replacing the old covered bridge. Clyde Stevenson made Herv reject the request. Said we couldn't afford the police overtime."

"Well, I think Earl and I can work this into our busy schedule, so just call Katie and tell her it's okay."

"The Ordinance says..."

"Okay, okay, okay!" Frank could see that further argument would be useless. "How about this—go over across the hall and get a Building Permit. Cross off "building" and write in "demonstration," then fill in the date and send it off."

Doris jumped up immediately. A few minutes later, she was back showing Frank her handiwork.

"That was a really good idea, Frank."

He sighed. "That's why they pay me the big bucks.

FIFTY CARS AND TWO big tour buses already filled the Raging Rapids parking lot when they arrived. As they walked toward the entrance in the long, low frame building they could hear the sound of Stony Brook rushing along.

"I don't think I've been here since the fourth grade," Earl said.

"I brought my grandkids here last summer, just to see what it was," Frank answered. "I bet a lot of people who live in Trout Run have never been here at all."

"Yeah, why pay five dollars just to see a waterfall when you can hike up Giant and see a really cool one for free?"

"You have to be in good shape to hike Giant," Frank reminded him. "This is for old geezers and little kids. And..." Frank nodded toward a couple passing them on their way out, young, but seriously overweight.

As they approached the entrance, they could see a hint of what lay beyond the gate—Stony Brook rushing fiercely over huge, jagged boulders, then twisting and descending out of sight. A system of metal catwalks and open-riser stairways allowed visitors to follow the path of the brook without any rugged hiking. Eventually they would reach the dramatic falls, which dropped about seventy-five feet over a sheer rock wall into a deep pool surrounded by dense forest.

Frank and Earl entered the building just as a mob of elderly tourists was leaving through the separate exit.

"Bye, now," April Fenstock, Abe's daughter-in-law, called from behind the ticket desk. "Be sure to tell your friends about us!"

"Oh we will," a blue-haired lady in tennis shoes said. "We really enjoyed it."

"Hi Frank, Earl! Come to do a little sight-seeing?" April spoke with her customary good cheer, but Frank noticed a wariness about her eyes. She seemed to know that this visit could only be bad news.

"Earl wanted to get a stuffed moose in the gift shop." Frank kept his tone light too. "Is Abe around?"

"He's in his office—go down that way and turn left before the snack bar."

The smell of fresh coffee guided them, tempting Frank, but he turned as April had directed and knocked on a door marked, "Office—Private."

"One more door down for the bathrooms," a voice bellowed from within.

Frank turned the knob and opened the door part way. "Sorry to disturb you, Abe. It's Frank Bennett."

Abe looked up from some papers he had been reading. Immediately, frown lines furrowed his brow. "Hi. Come in." He rose and shut the door behind them. "What's wrong?"

"Oh, nothing serious. I just wanted to warn you about a little"—Frank paused to select the right word—"disturbance headed your way."

"Disturbance? Whaddya mean, disturbance?" Abe remained standing. He was a good deal shorter than Frank, but with a neck that was twice as thick, and powerful, hairy arms.

"Katie Petrucci is planning on staging a demonstration against what she calls unsafe conditions and environmental problems here at Raging Rapids," Frank told him.

"Unsafe? We've never had a serious injury here." Abe threw back his shoulders and his dark brows met in a line above questioning eyes. "And what kind of environmental problems?"

Frank held his hand up. "I didn't say there was any merit to her claims. I'm just telling you she's planning on staging a demonstration out on the shoulder of the road. She asked for a permit and I didn't have any grounds for turning her down."

"Didn't have any grounds? How about that she's destroying my business at the height of the tourist season?" Abe paced furiously around the small, cluttered office. "Who did you say is behind this?"

"Katie Conover," Earl said.

"Bill's daughter?" Not waiting for confirmation, he snatched up the phone and began dialing. He paused in mid-number. "Wait a minute. Katie..." He turned to Earl for guidance. "Is that the nutty one?"

Earl nodded.

"Oh, Christ!" He slammed the phone back down. "That girl's always been a headache. Why's she got this bug up her ass about my place?"

Briefly, Frank explained the connection to Green Tomorrow and Nathan Golding.

"You mean to tell me," Abe's voice rose in a steady crescendo, "some lunatic who's not even from around here is agitating for my business to be closed?" The question ended in a shout just as the office door was flung open.

"Dad, what's going on? Who wants to close the business?" Roy Fenstock looked remarkably like his father, except that the older man projected an air of kind-hearted grumpiness, while the younger just came across as mean. He glared at Frank. "What's this all about?"

Frank began the explanation all over again, playing down the significance of the demonstration as much as possible. "It won't amount to anything, Roy. Just a few girls with signs. I'll keep them on the shoulder—won't let them block the drive. It just seemed better to let them go ahead until they run out of steam."

"Better for you, maybe," Roy answered. "You're just trying to take the easy way out. When Herv was police chief, we never had crap like this going on."

Now Frank had his back up too, and he struggled to keep his voice from climbing to Roy's level. "If we try to prevent it it'll make them more determined. Just ignore them. If you make them feel like they're totally unimportant, they'll give up."

"Ignore them!" Roy pounded the wall with a ham-hock fist. "Like hell I'll let these lesbian, hippie freaks push me around!"

"That's enough!" Abe yelled. "Frank, you and Earl will be here during this whole thing on Wednesday, won't you?" he asked as he herded them toward the door.

"Absolutely, Abe. We won't let them disrupt your business."

"Fine." As the door shut behind them, father and son resumed their shouting.

"That didn't go too good," Earl commented on the way back to the car.

Frank only scowled. So much for teaching Earl how to deal with irate citizens.

⎯⎯⎯⎯⎯◉⎯⎯⎯⎯⎯

"WHAT IS THE MOST DANGEROUS part of a domestic disturbance call?" Frank asked.

"When approaching the scene," Earl answered.

"Very good!" Frank and Earl sat in the dining room of the Trail's End waiting for a waitress to take notice of them. Earl had wanted to combine lunch with another police academy study session, but he objected to being quizzed in front of all the prying eyes at Malone's, so the Trail's End had been their compromise, although neither was fond of the food.

"Have you ever tried quinoa and pinto bean stew?" Earl asked.

"Don't even look at that side of the menu. Get a hamburger."

"They don't have French fries here. You have to take it with *salad*."

"A little lettuce would do you good." Frank craned his neck. "Where is everybody?" Then he grinned as he saw a flustered waitress scurrying toward them, tying on her apron as she went. 'Well look at this! Melanie Powers, when did you start working here?"

"Hi, Chief Bennett. Hi, Earl," Melanie skidded breathlessly to a stop in front of their table, her ample bosom heaving. "Sorry I kept you waiting. This is my first time working alone."

A pair of skin-tight black pants and a stretchy top with a deeply plunging u-neck displayed all Melanie's assets. She teetered on heels that would cripple her if she stayed in this line of work. The waitress apron was a coquettish accessory. She leaned over the table to put down their napkins. "Are you ready to order?"

Earl's eyes widened. Try as he might, Frank was not able to keep his eyes focused attentively on Melanie's face, and to give his willpower a rest, he buried his nose in the menu. "I'll have the grilled trout."

Melanie smiled at Earl, and stood beside him to read the title of his book. "What's that for?"

Her question inspired a palsied flinch of his hand that sent the saltshaker skidding across the table. "I, uh, I'm studying for the police academy entrance exam."

"Cool!"

"But I, I don't want everybody to know about it," Earl stammered.

"Don't worry. I can keep a secret."

Frank smiled. Melanie was an irrepressible chatterbox. Of course, she *had* managed to keep an important secret that had slowed him down during his investigation of Janelle Harvey's disappearance a few months ago. But he had a feeling Earl's plans would be public knowledge before long.

Melanie bounced on her high heels. "So, what did you want to order?"

"Oh, I'll have a hamburger," Earl choked out.

"All right, the show's over," Frank said as Melanie's round bottom disappeared into the kitchen. "When should a person be advised of their Constitutional Rights?"

"After they're taken into custody but before they're questioned."

Frank continued the quiz until their food arrived. "You know this stuff backward and forward Earl. You oughta ace the exam this time."

Earl smiled and ran his fingers through his hair. Frank's praise made him almost as nervous as his reprimands.

A few minutes into the meal, Melanie reappeared at their table. "How is everything?"

"Very good. Our compliments to the chef."

Melanie continued to stand there, watching them eat. Frank smiled at her attentiveness. "Could I have some more water?"

Melanie left and came back with the water pitcher. She refilled their glasses and again stood and watched them eat.

This was getting unnerving. Frank stared back at her.

"Have you figured out what happened to Mary Pat Sheehan's baby yet?"

"No." Frank reapplied himself to his dinner. He hated being pumped about open cases. But Melanie didn't consider herself dismissed.

"Listen," she blurted. "This might be nothing, but after what happened with Janelle, I feel like I better tell you, just in case."

Frank stopped eating. "Tell me what?"

"Last spring, this, uh, friend of mine had a problem, and she wanted my advice. She showed me an ad in *Mountain Herald* that she was thinking about answering. It said something like, 'loving couple wants to adopt healthy white infant,' and then it gave an email address to respond to, and said everything would be kept confidential."

Melanie had Frank's full attention, and not for the usual reason. "And did she respond?"

"Well, no. It turned out that, uhm, she had a miscarriage, so then she didn't need to contact them anymore. But since I heard what happened to Mary Pat, I kept thinking, what if Mary Pat answered the ad, and then everything turned out so bad." Melanie's full lips began to tremble and her blue eyes teared up, threatening disaster for her extravagant eye make-up.

"And when did you say this ad ran in the paper?"

"It was sometime in May, I think. But listen, you can't, like, talk to my friend about this, because she'd kill me if she knew I told you."

"Miss, miss." Two elderly ladies waved their menus at Melanie.

"Okay. I gotta go."

Frank stared at his plate without seeing the trout, rice and string beans arranged there. If an ad had appeared in the *Mountain Herald*, then Mary Pat might not be the only local girl that Sheltering Arms had victimized. Were other babies from the area up for sale right now?

"You want me to stop by the *Herald* first thing tomorrow and get that ad?" Earl offered.

Frank speared a forkful of fish. "I'll do it."

"Are you going to try to find out who Melanie's friend is?"

Frank opened his mouth to say, "There is no friend, Earl." But he changed his mind, and merely shook his head. If Melanie's story had convinced Earl, there really was no reason to blow her cover.

Chapter 12

The *Mountain Herald* only survived because Greg Faraday was reporter, editor, ad salesman, designer and secretary rolled into one. A monument to efficiency, he located the ad in question within minutes. Frank studied the small ad in the classified section.

Are you pregnant?

Loving couple seeks to adopt healthy white infant. We will provide your child with every advantage. Financial assistance available for expenses during your pregnancy. All inquiries strictly confidential. Email: jgp487@webnet.com

"So who placed that?" Frank asked.

"I don't know. They just send in the ad copy and a money order to pay for it to run twice, and it's always for a little more than the cost."

"Always? You mean you've had more than this one ad?"

"Yeah, one a few months before this. But don't go telling me it's illegal, because I checked that out before I ran the first one."

"That's not why I'm here," Frank reassured him. "But what do you mean, you checked it out?"

"With my chapter of the American Association of Newspaper Publishers. If you have a question about the ethics of accepting a certain ad, you can call them for advice. And they said couples who want to arrange an independent adoption run these kinds of ads all the time in papers like the *Herald*."

"Small weeklies? Why?"

"It's not so much that we're small, it's that we serve a rural population. A rural, *white* population. See, they don't want babies from minority mothers. And they think babies from the country are going to be healthier than babies from the Bronx. 'Cause everyone knows teenagers in trouble up here eat their veggies and drink their milk."

"Okay, I get it. Do you think these ads are sent by the same person?"

"I don't know. The first one had a different email address to respond to. But they both came in the same way. Envelope with no return address, no cover letter, money order to pay, no names anywhere."

"And have you had any more of these since this one ran in May?"

Greg shook his head. "I'm sorry, Frank. I should have called you when I heard what happened with Mary Pat Sheehan. But the ad was so long ago, I never made the connection."

"That's all right—it could be nothing. But Greg, do me a favor—don't mention this to anyone until I track this down, okay?"

"This is great!" Earl said when Frank returned to the office with the ad. "All you have to do is call up the Internet provider and find out who owns that account."

"Not that easy, I'm afraid. We'd need a subpoena, and we don't have enough evidence to prove that Sheltering Arms placed this ad. It could've really been placed by a couple, just like it says."

Earl wrinkled his brow. "Well, could we send an email to that address—you know, write it like it's from a pregnant girl?"

"Yeah, we'll try. But we'll have to send it from an email address they wouldn't recognize. Edwin and Lucy have a personal account separate from the one they use for Iron Eagle business, so I thought you could go over there and send it." Frank began to write. " 'I am three months pregnant, but nobody knows. I can't keep this baby, but I don't want to get an abortion. Please tell me about yourself and how you can help. Molly.' What do you think?"

"It's good except for the name. No one's named Molly anymore."

"My age is showing–you pick it."

"Uh, how about Brandy?"

"Brandy it is."

Minutes after Earl left to send the email, Doris's voice screeched over the intercom, "Lt. Meyerson's here to see you, Frank."

"What can I do for you, Lew?" Frank kept his eyes focused on some papers on his desk.

"Probably nothing," Meyerson said, taking a seat but maintaining his usual ramrod posture. "The Feds have taken over the Golding murder investigation. They've put me in charge of following up dead ends."

Now Meyerson had Frank's full attention. "The FBI has taken over? Why?"

"Seems like some of Golding's followers got a little carried away last year in Colorado. Blew up some earth-moving equipment being used to build a deluxe hunting lodge. Now Green Tomorrow's on the FBI's radar screen as domestic terrorists. They seem to think Golding's murder could signal the beginning of something big."

"Left wing extremists versus right wing extremists?"

"Exactly. War of the crackpots."

"So they think someone from this hunting lodge place killed him?" Earl asked.

Meyerson flipped his hand dismissively. "No. Green Tomorrow's gone on to bigger pastures. Now they're involved in trying to stop old growth logging out in Oregon. They've deployed a bunch of hippie chicks to sit up in trees.

"The logging company claims it'll go bankrupt if they can't cut these trees, the loggers are all up in arms over their jobs, and the locals are about equally divided and going after each other every day. The FBI figures Green Tomorrow's opponents in Oregon sent someone to kill Golding here to deflect suspicion from them."

"Doesn't seem to have worked," Frank observed. "The FBI must have some evidence to back that theory up."

"They probably do, but they're not sharing it with me," Meyerson complained. "Just to make sure they've got their asses covered, they've got me checking out Mrs. Golding and the sidekick, Barry Sutter."

"And do they have alibis?" Frank asked.

"Ironclad. Sutter was still on the Thruway at the time of the murder, on his way up here to meet Golding. Several employees at the Malden rest area remember him—apparently he got into a rather loud debate about the environmental implications of fast-food packaging. And Mrs. Golding was with her sister in Saratoga Springs."

"The sister could be lying to cover for her," Earl pointed out.

Meyerson twisted in his seat and stared at Earl for a full five seconds before replying. "Three neighbors saw Mrs. Golding out walking the sister's dog at 6:30 A.M. It takes two hours to get from Saratoga to here. Golding was killed before 8:30."

Frank spoke up before Earl could dig himself in any deeper. "So what did you need my help with?"

"Apparently Golding was seen talking to a woman from Trout Run the day before he was killed. A," Meyerson paused to consult his notes, "Beth

Abercrombie. She's not at that craft shop she runs. Any idea where I could find her?"

Frank rolled back his desk chair and began rooting around in a file drawer to buy a little time. He'd been meaning to call Meyerson to tell him what he'd learned from Beth, but the lieutenant's arrival in his office had caught him off-guard. "Actually," he began, "I happened to run into her yesterday afternoon. She hadn't heard about the murder yet, and when I told her the news she was shocked. Seems she knew Golding from her college days." He glanced up to see if Lew was ready to start blustering, but he looked only vaguely interested.

"I wonder why Mrs. Golding was walking her sister's dog so early in the morning?" Earl said.

This time both Frank and Meyerson stared him into silence. Frank resumed his story. "Beth said Golding looked her up recently. The day she was seen with him in Malone's, they were discussing his plans to try to shut down Raging Rapids."

"Raging Rapids? Why would he care about that?" Meyerson asked.

"That's what I wondered."

Frank and Meyerson locked eyes for a moment, then Meyerson shrugged. "It's probably nothing. According to the Feds, Green Tomorrow and a lot of these other environmental groups are just a bunch of loosely organized cells. The way they work is, the leaders go around rabble-rousing and getting the locals worked up about something, then they step back and let the locals take over the protests. That way, the left hand never knows what the right hand is doing and they can't rat each other out. For instance, Golding claimed he knew nothing about the bombing in Colorado. Said he couldn't help what his followers do."

"Yeah, but why has Green Tomorrow chosen Raging Rapids as the next project?" Frank asked. "It's small potatoes."

"The hunting lodge was no big deal either," Meyerson said, "until the bombs went off. I think his strategy is –was—to sow his seeds far and wide and see what sprouts."

"What's sprouting here on Wednesday is a demonstration in front of Raging Rapids lead by Katherine Petrucci. She runs the nursery school at the Presbyterian Church. I don't know if Beth will be involved in it or not."

Meyerson sighed. "I'm sure it's another dead-end, but I better go talk to her."

"It couldn't hurt," Frank agreed.

"I'll let you know what I find out."

"Thanks, Lew." Frank smiled as he watched Meyerson trudge across the Green toward the church. He liked Lew a lot better when he was the FBI's gofer than when he was running his own show.

————————⬤————————

"THERE'S A MRS. FINN for you on line one," Doris announced.

Frank pressed the blinking button eagerly. Maybe Sheltering Arms had contacted the Finns again.

"Hi, Mrs. Finn—what can I do for you?"

"I, I'm sorry to bother you—"

Her tentative tone didn't sound promising. "No bother. Do you have some new information for me?"

"No...I was hoping *you* might have some news. Have you discovered anything more about Sheltering Arms?"

"No, ma'am. I'm afraid your husband was right. They were very good at covering their tracks. We'll keep trying to recover your money for you, but it doesn't look promising."

"Oh, the money. I don't care about... I mean, I do care, but that's not why I called. I wondered if you had any news about Sarah?"

"No, we haven't been able to locate the baby."

"Oh." Her voice sounded tiny and crushed. There was a long pause, then she began to speak in a rush. "I'm sick about this, sick. I just want to know that Sarah is OK. I've accepted that she'll never be ours, but I have to know that she's with a good family and not some, some..."

Horse traders. Frank supplied the word in his mind, but spoke gently to Mrs. Finn. "I know it's upsetting ma'am. I'll be sure to let you know when I have some news."

"Okay. Thank you."

She hung up, just as Earl came in looking forlorn. "After I sent the email, Edwin made me a snack, and then we checked just to see if they had answered yet. But the message bounced. It came back 'not a known address.'"

Frank didn't bother to look up from what he was doing. "That doesn't surprise me. They're covering their tracks. Close one account, open another."

"What did you make me go over there for if you knew it wasn't going to work?" Earl sulked.

"Never take anything for granted, Earl. Do you want to work on the next lead, or do I have to promise you it's going to pan out?"

Earl sighed. "What?"

"Do a search—see if you can find any references to Sheltering Arms on the Internet."

"Any luck?" Frank asked, after Earl had been working quietly for half an hour.

"Not yet. The top hit for "Sheltering Arms" is the website for some romance writer named Aneliese Dupree. Then you get a lot of hits for animal shelters, battered women's shelters, injured wildlife shelters. Now I'm going to search on 'independent adoption'—see what that turns up."

"That's why you're better at this than me, Earl. I would've given up already."

Earl smiled, pushed his lank hair out of his eyes and reapplied himself to the search. Frank watched him for a moment. Paying the kid a compliment worked wonders on his productivity—he ought to do it more often.

They worked in companionable silence for more than an hour. Finally, Earl glanced up. "What are *you* doing?"

"I've been making a list of papers in a hundred-mile radius of here. When you're done with what you're doing there, call them all and see if an ad like the one in the *Herald* has run recently."

The 'why?' was written on Earl's face although he didn't speak it.

"After what happened to Mary Pat, they're not going to try to recruit again in Trout Run," Frank explained. But I figure the Adirondacks are too a good territory for them to give up. A rural, white population, not far from their buyers—couples with money in Albany, Westchester, New York City. It beats getting the babies from West Virginia, or Arkansas."

"I may as well start now. All I've found so far are lots of chat rooms and newsgroups and discussion lists about independent adoption. It'll take forever to visit them all."

"All right. Save the notes on what you found. It might still come in handy."

Chapter 13

"What do you have in the pipeline?"

"Nothing. You said to stop running the ads for a while."

"I know, but I was hoping—"

"What?"

"Those damn Braithwaites are making trouble again. I told them it would be months before we could find them another baby, but they're not willing to wait. Chip says he paid his money and we didn't hold up our end of the bargain when we offered them Mary Pat's baby. As he put it, 'clearly not what we specified.'"

"Specified! Does he think he's ordering a new BMW? Tell him to get lost."

"Believe me, I'd like to. But he's threatening to expose us if we don't produce a nice WASP baby for him right away."

"How can he expose us without getting in trouble himself? No one would believe he didn't know what he was doing was illegal."

"He knows politicians. He knows high-priced lawyers. He'll act like a pathetic victim and get out of it with a slap on the wrist and we'll be screwed. We have to give him what he paid for."

"Can't you just give him back the money?"

"The money? The money is long gone."

FRANK HAD LEFT A MESSAGE on the Pennimans' answering machine saying he wanted to schedule a time to come out to Harkness Road and talk to them both. Judy Penniman, sounding none too friendly, had called back to say he could come at seven. He'd learned from the owner of the Stop'N'Buy, that Anita Veech would be working tonight, so he figured he'd swing by and see her after he finished with the Pennimans. By the end of the night, he ought to know what Mary Pat was doing on Harkness Road.

When he pulled into the Pennimans' driveway he noticed the cab of Doug's eighteen-wheeler parked beside the garage. He could tell from the size of it that it had a sleeping berth behind the driver's seat. Doug must make long-distance hauls. Maybe that explained why the yard looked so overgrown and the paint on the front door was peeling. With Doug away, most of the work around the house must fall on Judy's shoulders.

He rang the doorbell and immediately heard heavy footsteps pounding and a male voice yelling, "I'll get it! I'll get it!" A female voice replied in a softer tone, and when the door opened, it was Judy Penniman who greeted him. A good-looking, broad-shouldered boy stood behind her. Frank didn't recall ever seeing him hanging around town with the other local kids.

"Come on in," she said. "Doug's in here." She led the way to the dark-paneled living room, where Doug Penniman was stretched out in a plaid recliner before a blaring TV. A rack full of guns stood in the corner. He sat up and pressed the mute button on his remote, but let the baseball game continue to flicker across the screen. The boy had followed them in, and was pacing around the room, running his fingers through his wiry dark hair.

"Do you like baseball?" he asked, before his father could even say hello. "Do you like the Red Sox? I love the Red Sox, but they never win the World Series. It's the curse of the Bambino. Do you know what that is?"

"Yes, I—"

The boy steamrolled over Frank's attempt to answer. "Back in 1920 the Sox got rid of Babe Ruth and—"

"All right, Bill. Chief Bennett didn't come out here to talk about baseball," Doug said.

Bill kept talking, as his pacing became more agitated. "They should never have gotten rid of the Babe. Once the Babe went to the Yankees..."

"Bill!" Doug raised his voice. The muscles in his powerful arms flexed as he made to get up from his chair. "That's enough."

Frank watched as Judy shot her husband a dirty look. "Billy, you need to go to your room now and finish your handwriting assignment." She spoke to Bill in a low, patient voice, like a horse trainer soothing a high-strung thoroughbred. "If you don't go, I'll have to take away your baseball cards for the evening. I'll count to three. One. Two."

"No, no! No three!" Bill shouted and he ran out of the room.

Frank's amazement at seeing a kid who looked to be high-school age act like this must have been written on his face.

"Sorry about that." Doug clenched and released his big hands. "Bill's got Asperger's Syndrome. He—"

"You don't have to apologize for him," Judy snapped. "He's doing great, and he'd be even better if you—"

Frank, who had taken a seat between the two parents, extended a hand toward each. "Look, don't worry about it." He smiled at Judy and used a de-escalation ploy he'd learned as a beat cop. "Could I trouble you for a glass of water? I don't know why I'm so thirsty today."

Judy stamped off toward the kitchen and Doug sat in his recliner massaging his temples. Each finger had a tuft of thick, black hair, but no wedding ring, Frank noticed. As the tension dissipated, he seemed to remember he wasn't alone. "So what was it you wanted to talk to us about?"

"Mary Pat Sheehan."

"I just heard about her dying when I got home yesterday. That's a shame."

"You were away all week?" Frank inquired.

"Yeah, New York to California, to Texas and back again."

"Did you know Mary Pat well?"

"The Stop'N'Buy sells diesel, so I fill up there a lot. You know how friendly Mary Pat is. Was."

"Did she ever visit you here at home?"

"Visit us?" Judy asked as she came back. "Why would she visit us?" She handed Frank the water, sloshing some out of the hazy, jam-jar glass.

"I'm trying to determine who she was with right before she died. You may have heard that she didn't die because of the crash."

"We heard," Judy said.

"What do you mean?" Doug asked simultaneously.

"She was pregnant and she died of complications from the birth." Bitterness, not the force of gravity, had tugged Judy's features toward the floor. "I *told* you. You never listen." Then she turned her irritation on Frank. "I don't see what it's got to do with you anyway. Her parents don't want you stirring things up. You oughta respect that."

Frank didn't appreciate hearing what he ought or ought not to do from Judy Penniman. "I'm trying to find out what happened to her baby," he said, and then focused on Doug. "Any idea what brought her out here that day?"

"She must've been dropping something off, doing someone a favor. Once Bill left his baseball cards in the Stop'N'Buy and she brought them back here. She was that kind of a person—she'd go out of her way for you."

Frank would have accepted that explanation if it hadn't been for Mr. Nyquist. "Your neighbor, Nyquist, says he saw Mary Pat out here on a regular basis."

Judy snorted. "That senile old fool. He talks just to hear himself."

"He's lonely, Judy. It wouldn't kill you to stop and chat with him sometimes," Doug said.

"Oh, and when am I supposed to fit that in? Between working full-time, taking care of Billy, trying to keep this house from falling down around our ears..."

Frank could tell they were heading down a road the Pennimans had traveled many times before. "So, Judy," he interrupted before she worked up a full head of steam, "you're not around much during the day, are you? Would you have noticed if Mary Pat was out here?"

Judy shook her head. "I'm gone from six AM to six PM, Monday through Friday, and most of the day Saturday too. I'm an LPN and I work with the homebound—bathing them, changing the sheets, checking their vitals. "

"And what about you, Doug?" Frank made direct eye contact with him, but Doug dodged his gaze. "When you're not driving, are you home during the day?"

"Dead to the world," Judy answered for him. "And you better believe when he *is* awake, he's not spending any time here, between bowling, softball, hunting."

"And working construction whenever I can," Doug defended himself. "You seem to forget that."

Frank stood up; he'd had about all he could take of the Bickersons here. Judy was sure no Cupid, so it didn't seem likely she'd have loaned their house for Mary Pat's trysts. Billy had the physique of a grown man, but he couldn't picture Mary Pat seducing someone who had a disability. There certainly was no doubt the Pennimans were unhappily married, which made Doug a reasonable candidate to be Mary Pat's lover. He was a good-looking man and probably only in his mid-thirties, although the circumstances of his life made him seem older. Of course, he wasn't going to admit to that in front of his wife. But with the schedule Judy kept, it shouldn't be too difficult to catch Doug alone tomorrow.

"Thanks for your time," Frank said. "I can let myself out." As he closed the door, he could hear their voices raised again. He headed out to the Stop'N'Buy, hoping that when his time came, he'd die in the saddle and never have to face being cared for by the likes of Judy Penniman.

———◦———

IN TWO YEARS OF LIVING in Trout Run, Frank had never once met Anita Veech. He could be confident in this because Anita wasn't a woman anyone would be likely to forget.

He couldn't accurately estimate her weight—the difference between 350 pounds and 450 or 500 was largely academic. She wore black knit pants, pilled from the constant friction of her massive thighs. Her arms appeared disproportionately short, flipper-like, because the size of her gut prevented her fingertips from extending past her waist. With eyes, nose and mouth subsumed by fat, her face seemed almost featureless. Wheezing with every step, Anita came toward him.

Frank extended his hand. "Hello, Anita, I'm Frank Bennett. I don't believe we've ever met."

Her mouth stretched open in what passed for a smile. Two teeth were missing and the others were crooked and brown. "That's because I like to steer clear of the law."

"A good policy. Say, I just wanted to talk to you for a minute about Mary Pat Sheehan. I guess you heard by now the reason she died?"

"Coulda knocked me over with a feather—and that wouldn't be easy!" Anita slapped her thigh, setting waves of fat in motion.

"So you didn't know she was pregnant? She never confided in you?"

"Nope. I did notice she was gaining a little, but I'm not one for mentioning other people's weight."

"Was she in the habit of coming out to visit you at home?"

"Visit me!" Anita's snorting laugh added to the overall impression of a malevolent pig. "Pap told me you all was out to our property the other day. Set the dogs on ya, didn't he? No, Pap's not one much for company, see?"

If that was the way Pap welcomed all guests, Frank supposed it wasn't Anita Mary Pat was visiting on Harkness Road. Doug Penniman was starting to look more and more likely. Still, there must be some people for whom the dogs were called off. He let the matter of the visits drop for the moment and changed tacks.

"It would be helpful if we could figure out who the baby's father was. It might've been someone Mary Pat met here at the store. Was there anyone she was unusually friendly with?"

Anita cocked her head and pushed aside a strand of greasy dark hair. "Well, there might've been..."

Frank stood waiting, but Anita said no more. He had the distinct impression the ball was back in his court.

"The man wouldn't be in any trouble," Frank assured her. "I'd just like to talk to him. It could help us locate the baby."

Anita's eyes scanned the store, focusing on everything but Frank. "Well, see, I feel like I'd be breaking my word, in a way."

Frank couldn't keep the eagerness out of his voice. "I know Mary Pat wanted to keep the relationship secret, Anita. But her death changes everything. This adoption she tried to set up wasn't legal. With the father's consent, we could get the baby placed in a good home."

Anita waved her hand. "The father, he don't want nothin' to do with the baby, that much I can tell you."

"What do you mean? I thought you said you didn't know she was pregnant?"

Anita shifted her weight from one leg to the other. She looked down at her feet oozing out the sides of unlaced sneakers. "I didn't. But I got the feeling the guy who was doing her was married."

"Anita," Frank barked, "do you know who Mary Pat was seeing or don't you?"

Anita looked him square in the face, her tiny eyes reduced to slits. "Seems to me you're asking me a big favor. When someone does you a favor, seems to me you should do them one in return, don't it?"

Frank pursed his lips. "And what might that be?"

"My brother Ralph ran into a little trouble over by Placid. Something about drunk and disorderly–they're always pickin' on him over there."

"I'll see what I can do. Now, what about Mary Pat? Who's the guy?"

Anita pulled a stool out from behind the counter and propped herself on it. "Don't get me wrong. I didn't say I knew exactly who he was. Just from things she said, I got my suspicions."

Frank took a deep breath. "OK, then, share your suspicions please."

"Like I said, I think he's married."

Doug Penniman? But Frank didn't want to put ideas in Anita's head. Better to see how much she really knew. "Why?"

"One night, we was talking and she said to me, do I believe two people could be destined for each other, could be, what'd she call it? Soul mates." Anita cackled. "I told her all men just lookin' for one thing—a little pussy. They take it where they find it." Anita leered at him. "She didn't like that too much. She said sometimes two people are meant for each other, but circumstances keep them apart."

Circumstances like being married to a shrew and having a handicapped son? Frank waited, but Anita said nothing more.

"That's it?"

"Here comes the boss. I'm supposed to be cleaning," Anita said, heaving herself off the stool and shuffling toward her mop. She looked back at him over her shoulder. "You see about my brother. Maybe something else will come to me."

Chapter 14

"The police chief, Frank Bennett, has been out to Harkness Road talking to everyone, trying to find out who Mary Pat was with before she died."

"All you need to do is be quiet. He'll give up eventually."

"Yes, but one of the neighbors told him that he saw her drive past his house a lot. So now Bennett knows she had to be visiting someone at the end of the road. Maybe I should—"

"Don't try to be clever. Just keep your mouth shut. And find me another pregnant girl."

THE MORNING OF THE great Raging Rapids protest dawned clear and bright. The ground was still warmer than the chill dawn air, so a light mist swirled through the low-lying areas of Frank's property. With a full coffee cup to keep him warm, he looked out at the peaceful scene from his screen porch: the brilliant reds and yellows of the trees softened by the ghostly mist; a few barn swallows swooping and diving over the meadow; a blue heron standing so still in the brook that he merged with the gray rocks around him. Frank could happily have sat there all day, but no, he had to go attend to this hare-brained protest, a protest that he probably could have squelched without much effort at all.

Why hadn't he, just like Herv would have done? No danger of the ACLU coming after him in Trout Run, that was for sure. He'd convinced himself the protest should go forward as a way to shed some light on Nathan Golding's murder. But Golding's murder was not his concern—Lew had certainly made that clear.

When he'd first come to Trout Run after being forced out of his job in Kansas City, he hadn't felt up to any challenges. But solving the Janelle Harvey case—his first, and only, big investigation in Trout Run —had restored his confidence. Maybe the satisfaction he'd gotten from unraveling that mess had given him a taste for bigger prey than speeders and Saturday night brawlers. Had he made it easy for Katherine Petrucci to stage her protest because he wanted to get a piece of the Golding investigation action? Just to provoke a little excitement?

Well, the strategy had most likely backfired. The more he thought about it, the more the Fed's theory of the case made sense. After all, shutting down a logging operation put a lot more money and jobs at risk than shutting down Raging Rapids, and it provided a lot more motivation to kill. Meyerson's report on Katherine Petrucci dismissed her as "a hysterical housewife with too much time on her hands."

Worst of all, poor Abe Fenstock was just fit to be tied. Most people in town, Frank felt sure, supported Abe. If anything happened today to ruin Abe's business, Frank would take as much blame as Katherine and her followers.

He shrugged off his worry. Really, how rowdy could the thing get? A few hippies, a few moms, a few signs—the whole charade would fizzle out by noon.

He drained his coffee and headed out to Raging Rapids.

When Frank arrived, Earl was already there. He'd taken the patrol car home last night, while Frank had loaded up the back of his own pick-up with orange cones and slow signs from the road department. Together they blocked off an area for the protesters to march, and prepared to direct traffic around them.

"Put this other slow sign up ahead where the road bends, Earl," Frank directed. "I don't want any cars tearing around that curve."

Abe had apparently seen them at work and came trotting across the parking lot, an anxious frown creasing his face. "I've got five tour busses scheduled between ten and twelve. Are you sure they'll be able to get through?"

"Absolutely. We'll keep the marchers over here." Frank indicated a twenty-yard strip of shoulder to the right of the driveway.

"There's only you and Earl. Maybe I should send my son out to help," Abe said.

That was an offer to put out the fire with gasoline. "No, we'll be just fine," Frank assured him. "You attend to your customers, just like any other day."

Reluctantly, Abe left them, glancing back over his should several times as he returned to the main building. No sooner had he gone inside than a dusty old station wagon pulled up. All the doors opened at once and six young women spilled out.

Frank studied Katie Conover Petrucci as she approached: thick wavy hair pulled into a haphazard pony tail, saggy green khaki pants and a shapeless sweater, clunky hiking boots, and not a lick of make-up. He'd never seen such a pretty woman so hell-bent on hiding her light under a bushel.

Katie extended a slender hand and fixed her steady gaze on him. "I'm Katherine Petrucci," she said without letting a smile touch her delicate lips.

Frank shook her hand, amiable but authoritative. "I'd like your group to stay right in this area on the shoulder. Remember, Raging Rapids is private property and you are not permitted to trespass or block the drive. Follow those guidelines and we won't have any problems, all right?'

Katie nodded. "If you say so." She turned to her cohorts, all of whom Frank recognized as young mothers from Trout Run. "Let's unpack the signs."

The others dutifully followed her to the back of the station wagon, but Frank thought Cassie McDonald and Deedee Peele looked a little sheepish. They pulled out signs mounted on wooden poles.

Another van pulled up and five more women got out. Beth Abercrombie was in this group. Frank and Earl exchanged a nervous glance. Hopefully, this was it—the letter had said approximately 15 protesters, but Frank hadn't believed Katie could round up that many.

Soon, Katie had her followers lined up and they took their positions in the area Frank had laid out for them. Each carried a sign: close raging rapids, birds & fish not $$$, dangerous conditions ahead. Beth carried a stack of large, white placards each with a loop of yarn at the top, which she set on the ground near the driveway. She smiled at Frank and he nodded back.

Quietly, they marched up and down. When the occasional car drove by on Stony Brook Road, they turned to face the road and waved their signs. Often, the drivers waved back or tooted their horns. So far, so good. He watched Beth as she carried her sign, the slanting sunlight reflecting off her golden hair. What had possessed her to join this goofy troupe? Still, she looked kinda cute, especially in that orangeish sweater.

"What do you think those other signs are for?" Earl asked as they stood watching the totally uneventful event.

"Beats me."

When Raging Rapids opened at ten, the first customers of the day pulled in and Frank braced himself for possible trouble. But the women continued to march up and down in their designated spot waving their signs toward the drivers, who seemed perplexed by the protesters, if they noticed them at all.

Frank grew tired of all the standing and perched on the guardrail. He checked his watch—one more hour to go. The worst part of this protest was the tedium. He considered sending Earl inside for coffee from the snack bar. Better not—he couldn't very well pee in the weeds in front of all these women. He yawned and listened to the distant knocking of a woodpecker. It sure was shaping up to be a nice day.

"I see the first bus!"

The shout startled Frank onto his feet. Suddenly all the protesters had thrown down their signs.

"Link arms!" Katie shouted.

Frank watched in astonishment as all of the women ran to the driveway. Some picked up placards from the stack and hung them around their necks. Then they rearranged themselves, and linked arms to form a human chain. The two on the ends each grabbed a gatepost. The six in the middle formed a word with two-foot letters on their chests: unsafe.

The tour bus, first in a convoy of five behemoths, pulled up to the driveway and honked its horn. The women refused to move and began to chant: "Raging Rapids kills fish and birds! Raging Rapids is unsafe for children and seniors! For a green tomorrow, close Raging Rapids today!"

Frank ran over to them. "All right, Katie—that's enough. We agreed you wouldn't block the driveway."

"I don't recall agreeing with *you* on anything."

"Ladies, break it up. Let's move along back to the shoulder, please," Frank demanded.

But they all clung to each other fiercely and refused to move. Frank felt as helpless as he had when his grandsons had refused to get out of the spaceship ride at the mall until he put in two more quarters.

He put his hand on Cassie McDonald's elbow and tugged slightly. "Come on, now, Cassie. Let go of that gatepost."

"He's hurting her!" Katie shrieked. "Stand firm, Cassie."

Cassie looked from Frank to Katie, wide-eyed. Clearly, she was more intimidated by Katie, because she didn't let go of the gatepost.

Next he tried his luck with Beth. "Be reasonable, Beth," he said in a soft voice, looking her straight in the eyes. "You guys can't block the drive like this. Get the others to let go."

Her face, flushed by the excitement and the cool breeze, was inches from his own. If he hadn't been so thoroughly annoyed he would have been tempted to kiss her. She looked away from him. "I can't, Frank. This protest is important. It's something we've got to do."

By this time, Abe had shown up. "Arrest them!" he demanded.

But that was easier said than done. With just him and Earl, one set of handcuffs, one patrol car, what could he do? These were girls from Trout Run—he couldn't very well start whacking their arms with his nightstick. They had him between a rock and a hard place.

"I'll have to call the state police for back-up," Frank said.

"That'll take too long. These busses aren't going to wait forever," Abe shouted at Frank. Then he banged on the door of the bus. "Tell everyone to get off," he told the tour director. "They can walk into the complex on this little path through the trees."

A broad-beamed lady with a clipboard and a hairdo like a curlicued football helmet stepped down on the bus steps and peered out. One look at the chanting protesters and the overgrown path Abe wanted her elderly group to use sent her scurrying back on board. A few moments later, the busses lumbered off.

"Come back!" Abe shouted. "You can come back this afternoon." But his voice was drowned out by the diesel roar.

Abe turned on Frank, apoplectic with rage. "Nearly three hundred people at seven dollars a head—I just lost two thousand dollars! I knew you couldn't control this. And you—," He spun around and turned on Katie, but Frank held him back.

The need to call the state police was now past. The protesters had broken their line and were jumping up and down, cheering and giving one another high fives.

"We did it! We did it! Way to go, Green Tomorrow!" Katie screamed. The protesters began retrieving their signs and chatting excitedly. Katie stepped back, standing on the edge of the road and clapping her hands to get their attention. "Our next meeting will be—"

Just then, a big extended-cab pickup appeared from around the bend. Instead of slowing, as the sign warned, it picked up speed and headed straight for Katie. Frank, still trying to calm Abe, could only scream a warning.

Chapter 15

Ten seconds of chaos seemed to elapse over an hour.

Earl lunged forward, grabbed Katie by the sleeve, and tumbled with her onto the shoulder. The truck careened past, just inches from their sprawled legs. The other protesters ran screaming in every direction, blocking Frank as he tried to reach Katie and Earl. Earl sat up, rubbing his head, then pulled Katie to her feet. He waved Frank off. "We're all right."

Frank leaped into the patrol car and took off after the truck. It was already well ahead of him, out of sight. But the road followed Stony Brook here for several miles, so there was no place to turn off to the right. And to the left rose the Verona Range, with only a few parking areas at the trailheads. With sirens blaring and lights flashing, he pushed the car up to sixty, but as he tore around a blind curve he knew it wasn't safe to him or anyone who might be coming in the opposite direction to be taking the road at that speed. He slowed a bit, and continued toward Lake Placid, without seeing any sign of the truck. When he reached the intersection of Route 73, he had to accept that whoever had tried to run down Katie Petrucci had gotten away.

THE FIFTEEN PEOPLE present at the protest came up with almost as many different impressions of the color, make, model and license plate of the truck. Finally, relying most heavily on his own, Earl's and Beth's recollections, Frank put a search through to Motor Vehicles to see what would turn up. If the truck was local, he was sure he'd recognize it when he saw it again.

The stunt struck him as the kind of thing Roy Fenstock would pull, but Roy must have been working inside Raging Rapids at the time, since his father had wanted to send him out to help manage the protest. Had Abe said that as a cover for Roy, knowing that Frank would never take him up on the offer? Surely Abe wouldn't go along with a scheme that might have gotten someone killed. Or had Roy lined up some yahoo friend of his to do the dirty work?

But maybe it was more serious than that. Maybe whoever had killed Nathan Golding was determined not to stop until he had destroyed the entire Green Tomorrow organization and scared off all its supporters. In that case, Beth Abercrombie and all those girls who had been swept up in Katie's fervor could be in for a lot more trouble than they ever bargained for.

The problem was convincing them that he wanted to protect them, not shut them up. Especially since he wouldn't mind if shutting them up was a by-product of protecting them.

He stood up and stared out the window, watching the wind drive little tornados of leaves across the green. Tomorrow might be a good day to try to have lunch with Beth. Maybe he could get her to tell him why she and Katie and Green Tomorrow were so determined to close down Raging Rapids. And then what? Convince her to give it up?

A cold front had moved in since this morning, replacing the blue skies with dark, lowering clouds. A few storms like the one that was brewing would bring all the leaves down and mark the end of the best season of the year.

He shifted his gaze to the parking lot, where Mary Pat's Escort sat in a reserved space. True to Frank's prediction, Joe had offered Mary Pat's car to Earl at a very reasonable price. He wondered how well the little car would do this winter, when Earl had to make the drive in from the outskirts of Trout Run.

He pivoted. "Earl, is your car unlocked?"

"Yeah, why?"

"I want to look inside."

"At what?" Earl trotted after Frank out to the parking lot.

"I never searched Mary Pat's car. It just struck me that if Mary Pat wanted to hide something from her parents, especially her mother, her car would be the best place. Ann doesn't drive anymore, so she'd never be in it without her daughter. But, maybe it's too late now."

"It was still at Al's Sunoco when I picked it up, but it's clean as a whistle inside."

Frank opened the glove compartment: map, owner's manual, registration and insurance. Under the seats: nothing. He popped the trunk: a spare tire and one of those roadside assistance kits. He opened the case, pulled out the jumper cables and flares, and there it was: a square white envelope.

Inside was a card with the standard-issue Hallmark drivel. On the cover, a wildflower in a beam of sunlight; inside, the printed inscription "special people like you set the world alight." It was signed with a very ornate scribble.

"What does that look like to you?"

Earl studied the handwriting. "I'm not sure. That first letter could be an L or maybe an S. Then it looks like there's a Y or a P—something with a lower loop—there in the middle."

How galling to have the lover's name right here in his hand and not be able to read it. "Could it say 'Doug'?" Frank asked.

"Nah—it looks longer than that. There's letters after the G."

"Douglas. Or maybe it's a pet-name."

Earl squinted at the card. "Really, it doesn't look like a guy's handwriting at all. It's too... too fancy, or something."

Earl had a point. It was unusual-looking script–cramped, yet with flourishes. "But it has to be from a man," Frank said. "Why else would she have it hidden in this road kit?"

Earl shrugged. "Have it dusted for prints. Maybe you'll get lucky again."

Frank scowled. He didn't relish another battle with Meyerson over resources.

He looked back at the open box in the trunk. There was still a little first aid kit in there, and he opened it. The usual stuff—he dug through the Band-Aids and cold pack just to be thorough. And then he saw it: an orange prescription bottle half-full of big white pills.

"Look at this, Earl. Bactrim–that's an antibiotic, I'm pretty sure. Filled at a pharmacy in Lake Placid on September 19th, two days after the birth. She *did* go to a doctor. She knew she was seriously sick."

"But wouldn't a doctor have made her go to the hospital?" Earl asked.

Frank nodded. "He would if he knew what he was up against. Hibbert says any doctor would know a retained placenta can be life-threatening."

"So maybe this guy didn't know what was really wrong with Mary Pat, because she didn't tell him about the birth."

Frank studied the pill bottle. The prescription label referenced Dr. Stephen Galloway, Cascade Clinic. "Either that or whoever gave her these pills also wanted to keep the birth secret, and intentionally kept her away from the hospital. If they really knew how sick she was, that's depraved indifference, and it's a felony."

Frank put the bottle in his pocket. "I'm going over to the Cascade Clinic to talk to this Dr. Galloway."

Chapter 16

The Cascade Clinic was a good twenty-five minutes away, on the far side of Verona, but it was the only doctor's office between Trout Run and Lake Placid. The parking lot surrounding the small, cedar-shake building was full, and Frank walked into a waiting room packed with crying babies, sniffling toddlers and sighing adults. He didn't want to think about all the germs he was breathing in.

"Sign the log, fill out the yellow form and have your insurance card ready when you're called," the woman behind the check-in counter said without glancing up.

"I'm Chief Bennett of the Trout Run police. I need to speak to Dr. Galloway when he's done with his current patient."

The woman looked even more exasperated. "We're terribly busy—can't it wait?"

"No."

"All right—go into his office."

Galloway's office was a cubbyhole barely big enough for a desk and a bookcase. Frank just had time to check out the diploma on the wall—Georgetown University Medical School—when Galloway entered.

"Yes, what is it?" he demanded, without introduction.

Frank sized him up: early thirties, short and a little pudgy, with shaggy dark hair and a complexion that hadn't fully recovered from adolescent acne. The brown eyes that met his were intelligent, but wary.

"Frank Bennett, Trout Run police. I'm here about a patient of yours—Mary Pat Sheehan."

Galloway shrugged. "I see scores of patients everyday. You'll have to give me a little more clue than that."

"Well, this one's dead." That caught the doctor's attention. Frank pulled out the prescription medicine bottle. "She died of septicemia after giving birth. You wrote her this prescription. What kind of medication is that?"

Galloway snatched the bottle. "Sheehan? Sheehan? September 19th? The only post-partum patient I've seen in September was Fogelson. She was in yesterday for her follow-up appointment and she's okay." A fine sheen of sweat appeared on his brow. He punched the intercom button on his phone. "Stacey, get me the chart on Mary Pat Sheehan. Right away."

Galloway turned back to Frank. "Did you check with the hospital to see who delivered this baby? I don't deliver babies—I just help out with pre-natal and post-partum care if they can't make it to Saranac Lake to see an obstetrician regularly."

"I already know she didn't have the baby in the hospital. She kept the pregnancy a secret from her family and friends. I want to know if you treated her for this infection after the baby was born." Frank shook the pill bottle. "What is this?"

"Bactrim is a broad-spectrum antibiotic."

"So, that's what you'd give for a post-partum infection, isn't it?"

"It depends on what was causing it." The doctor turned and stuck his head into the hall. "Stacey," he pleaded, "where's that chart?"

"I'm looking. I can't find any Mary Pat Sheehan. The only woman "sh" is Mary Sherman."

"You see—we don't have a chart on her. Besides, if a teenager had presented with a post-partum infection recently, I would remember that." Galloway clicked his pen and eyed the door.

"She wasn't a teenager, she was twenty-eight. And what if she just came in telling you she was feverish and achy, never mentioning the pregnancy. Would you give her that antibiotic?"

Galloway puffed out his chest and tried to look stern. "I don't pass out antibiotics indiscriminately. Symptoms like that would usually indicate a viral infection, not bacterial."

"So how do you explain these pills?"

Galloway threw up his hands. "I don't know. What's the big deal? It's only an antibiotic, not morphine or oxycontin."

"I'll tell you what's the big deal." Frank dropped his voice and took a step toward Galloway. "Someone knew this girl was seriously ill and instead of taking her to the hospital, they wrote her a prescription for an antibiotic to try to patch her up. She died. And I want to know who that person was, all right?"

Galloway squinted his left eye. "Someone could have stolen a sheet off my prescription pad."

Frank looked at the doctor's white lab coat. "Take it right out of your pocket, there?"

"Oh, please!" Galloway looked at his watch. "You see how over-worked I am. Maybe I took it out to write a prescription, got distracted, and left it in an examining room. Anything's possible."

Galloway's frazzled irritation was fairly convincing. At any rate, it would be easy enough to check. The pharmacy would still have the original prescription slip on file, and the handwriting could be compared to a legitimate prescription Galloway had written. "What about the nurses?" Frank asked.

Galloway flexed his fingers. Frank noticed he wore no rings. "Elaine's incompetent, but trustworthy. Connie's only here three mornings a week, unfortunately. She's the only one I can count on to do things right."

Galloway didn't seem very happy in his work here at the clinic. "You're not from around here, are you doc?"

"I'm from New Jersey. I agreed to practice in an underserved area for three years to pay for medical school. I have one more year to go."

That explained the attitude; you couldn't expect an indentured servant to act like Marcus Welby. "Are you married?"

Galloway frowned. "Engaged. Leah's in graduate school at UCLA. We try to fly back and forth as often as we can, but it's tough."

So, Galloway was broke and lonely. He had been in the area long enough to have known Mary Pat. Under normal circumstances, the young doctor wouldn't have looked twice at a woman who clerked in a convenience store. But he had the grad student fiancée for long-distance, intellectual chats. Mary Pat could have supplied what was missing close to home.

Frank regarded Galloway with more interest. "You said you don't deliver babies, but you must know how to, right? Doesn't everyone learn that in medical school?"

"Everyone does a rotation in obstetrics, and I've been in the ER when women have delivered. What are you getting at?"

Frank ignored the question and pressed on. "Do you shop at the Stop'N'Buy on Route 12?"

Galloway edged toward the door. "I've bought gas there occasionally, a quart of milk. Why?"

"Mary Pat Sheehan worked there nights. But maybe you know that."

Galloway blinked his eyes rapidly. "Why would I know? I never noticed who waited on me."

"She was kind of a lonely young woman. You're up here all by yourself. One thing leads to another. Next thing you know, she's pregnant with a baby she doesn't want, and you're delivering it. Only you didn't do such a good job."

Galloway's mouth fell open. "That's insane!" The words came out broken and squeaky. "You have no evidence of that."

Frank shrugged. "Give me time. Maybe I'll find some."

Chapter 17

The next morning, Frank sat at his desk studying several photocopies. He'd gone to the pharmacy in Lake Placid and got copies of the original prescription for Mary Pat's Bactrim. After some haggling, he'd convinced the pharmacist to find some other prescriptions written by Dr. Galloway and copy them with the patients' names blocked out just so he could compare the handwriting. The results were intriguing.

In each instance, the name of the prescribed drug had been printed in block letters, some neater than others. And in each case, the prescription had been signed with an illegible cramped signature. It was hard to tell if the signature on all the prescriptions was exactly the same—he was no handwriting expert—but Mary Pat's prescription wasn't an obvious fake. But what really interested him was comparing the doctor's signature with the name signed on the card he'd found in Mary Pat's car. Of course, the card had only a first name, whereas the prescriptions had what appeared to be Galloway's first initial, "S", and his last name. Was the first letter on the card an "S" and was the letter that dipped down in the middle the "p" in Stephen? It seemed plausible, more plausible than "Doug."

Doris buzzed him. "It's your daughter on line one."

"Hi sweetheart! Happy Birthday!" Frank said. "You're calling me before I got a chance to call you."

"I wanted to thank you for the bowl. I love it! Is it from that little shop that was closed the last time I visited?"

"Yeah, I remembered you seemed to like the stuff there."

"You are so sweet. It's just beautiful—so original, so different. Did you pick it out yourself?"

"Well, the owner helped me a little." He didn't want to go there. "I'm very glad you like it. What else are you doing to celebrate your birthday?"

"The boys built a castle with Legos for me—isn't that cute? Eric is closing a big deal in South Carolina, so we'll do something when he gets back."

"Can't let a birthday get in the way of a big deal." The moment the words were out of his mouth he wished he could have reeled them back in. The conversation had been going so well–the last thing he needed was to sound sarcastic about his sainted son-in-law.

Caroline reacted with a predictable, "*Dad*-ee."

"I just meant, I hate to see you all alone on your birthday. If I knew, I would have come down and taken you out."

"Oh, it doesn't matter—I'm a big girl. Or so I'm told."

Was that a quaver he heard in her voice? "Honey, are you okay? Tell me what's wrong."

"Don't be silly. Nothing's wrong."

"Caroline, that's not true. I know something's bothering you. Let me help."

"I don't need you to– Oh, Jeremy, no! What a mess. I've gotta run, Daddy. Thanks again for the gift."

And the phone went dead.

In the silence of the office, he mulled over what Caroline had said, and not said. He struggled to remember when this coolness toward him had started. She'd been fine in the spring, hadn't she? But maybe he'd been so preoccupied with the Janelle Harvey case that he hadn't noticed the change coming over her.

Could it be some trouble with Eric? No, that was just his natural mistrust of every man who'd ever shown an interest in his daughter, from the kid who tried to kiss her in the sandbox on up to her husband. The last time he'd seen Caroline and Eric together they'd been embarrassingly affectionate.

Maybe she was sick? A shudder of fear passed through him. Caroline was young and healthy–he wouldn't even consider that. But when he rejected the obvious, he was left with the nagging worry that he and Caroline were drifting apart because she had no need for him in her life.

The conversation with Caroline, as unsatisfactory as it had been, at least gave him a pretext to call on Beth. After all, she *had* asked to know how his daughter liked the bowl. And suddenly, the office seemed unbearably small and stuffy.

Frank quickly drove the two miles to Beth's shop. Relieved to see no other cars parked in front, he entered and followed a humming sound directly to the curtained doorway in the back of the showroom. Pushing the fabric aside, he stood and watched as a pear-shaped vase took form on the potter's wheel under Beth's nimble fingers. It grew magically from a lump to a graceful column, with only the slightest coaxing from its creator. She smiled slightly, but her eyes never left the wheel, so he perched on a stool and waited for her to finish.

In a minute or two, the wheel slowed and stopped and Beth looked up. "Sorry, once I start, it's not easy to stop."

Frank smiled. "You could say that about a lot of things."

Beth relaxed. "I thought you might still be mad at me."

"And that worried you?"

He watched with amusement as she blushed and fiddled with something on her wheel. He was getting better at this flirting business.

"I wanted you to know my daughter really likes her bowl. I thought I'd take you out to lunch to celebrate our success."

"What a good idea!"

Ten minutes later they were settled in a booth at the Trail's End. Frank wasn't thrilled to be perusing their menu again so soon, but food wasn't really the point of this lunch.

"You should order something vegetarian, Frank," Beth teased.

"Real men don't eat quinoa. I'll have the chicken," he told the young man taking their order.

Beth settled back in the booth and smiled at him. "You're very "not-from-around-here." Tell me how you happened to move to Trout Run."

So he told her about the spectacular mess of his last case in Kansas City, about Estelle's sudden death and the loss of his job. And she told him about the slow but steady growth of her business, and the slow but steady decline of her marriage. He barely noticed when his food arrived, and unconsciously ate the artichokes he'd intended to scrape off. Without much arm-twisting, Beth agreed to coffee and a shared piece of pecan pie, which led, somehow, to more talk about books, and hiking, and music. Eventually, Frank noticed their waiter pacing anxiously near the cash register–they were the only two left from the lunch crowd.

"Oh, my! It's three o'clock," Beth said. "I've got to get back to the store."

In all this time he'd never managed to bring up Green Tomorrow. Now, all he had left was the brief ride back to Beth's place. As he paid the check, he thought of casual ways to steer the conversation in that direction.

"So," he said, guiding Beth through the door with his hand on her back, "how's Katie holding up after her near-miss the other day?"

"I think it's made her more determined than ever."

"Why is that, Beth? After all, Raging Rapids has been there her whole life. Why did it take Nathan Golding coming to town to get Katie all up in arms." He didn't add, "and you" but the implication hung there.

Instantly, he felt Beth pull away.

"Sometimes it takes someone with a fresh perspective to open your eyes to a problem," she said.

"True. But sometimes a person with his own agenda can get others to do his bidding."

Beth stepped quickly toward his truck and pulled on the passenger door.

Frank came up beside her with the key in his hand but made no move to unlock it. "Are you planning on staying involved with Green Tomorrow?"

"Is that why you asked me out to lunch? To see if you could recruit an informant?"

"Don't be ridiculous. I'm worried about you."

"I don't need a watchdog, Frank. I've been taking care of myself for a long time. I know what I'm doing."

"There's something bigger going on here, Beth, something you and Katie aren't being told."

"Like what?"

"I'm not sure. Aren't you curious why Golding targeted a little operation like Raging Rapids as his next project, when he's involved in much bigger things out West?"

"Nathan grew up in New York. The Adirondacks are the last great wilderness area in the East. He is—was—committed to preserving them for future generations. I feel an obligation to continue his work."

"An obligation? You hadn't seen the guy in twenty-five years."

Beth tossed her long hair over her shoulder. "Don't be cynical, Frank. It's not at all attractive."

Frank unlocked the truck door and yanked it open without bothering to help Beth into the cab. They drove in tense silence all the way to the sign that marked Beth's road. As he made the turn, Frank glanced over at her. She looked as miserable as he felt. He reached out and took her hand. She looked surprised but didn't pull away. Steering with one hand into her parking lot, he stopped the truck and turned to face her.

"Look, Beth, I admire you for having strong convictions. Just be aware that not everyone's motivations are as pure as yours. Someone murdered Nathan Golding, and Katie came damn close to being killed, too. If anything happens that doesn't seem right, don't be afraid to ask me for help."

She brushed her fingertips against his cheek. "I know you're a good man, Frank. I'm sorry we have to be on opposites sides of this thing."

Not as sorry as me, he thought as he watched her slip out of the truck.

He didn't back out immediately, but sat staring at Beth's shop without seeing it. Why was this so goddam hard? How had his lunch gone from fun and comfortable to angry and defensive?

And where could he go for advice? He'd always turned to Estelle when there was some personal conflict at work or a rift with a friend. Even now, when he found himself in some sticky situation he'd try to imagine what Estelle would do. But he felt like a philanderer even thinking about Estelle and Beth at the same time.

Oddly enough, he thought Estelle would like Beth—her artistic bent, her independence. Maybe the idea that Estelle would approve was part of the attraction. How weird was that, picking a girlfriend that you thought your dead wife would like? A shrink would have a field day.

Frank sighed and put the truck into gear. He was too old for this game.

Chapter 18

"*Any luck?*"

"*No. I've been going back through my old contacts, but so far all of them have changed their minds about giving up their babies.*"

"*I'm doing a little better. I have another couple for Mary Pat's baby.*"

"*Great! Then we can use that money to pay off the Braithwaites.*"

"*It won't be enough. They're only paying $20,000.*"

"*Twenty thousand! That's less than the Finns would've paid.*"

"*Don't remind me. But I don't have time to shop around for a better prospect. We've got to get that baby placed. It's making me nervous leaving her where she is.*"

"*You can say that again. When should I bring her?*"

"*They want to see her tomorrow. Then it will take them a few days to come up with the cash.*"

"*Good. I need the money.*"

"*You don't get any of this money if you don't find another baby for the Braithwaites. Get busy.*"

"WHERE HAVE YOU BEEN?" Earl looked about ready to burst when Frank got back to the office. "I worked my way through the whole list of newspapers you left for me. Boy, they've been running that ad all over the place—Saranac Lake, AuSable Forks, Willsboro, Schroon Lake."

"Always the exact same ad?"

"The words are the same, but there's three different email addresses they use. The one we tried this morning, and two others."

"Are the ads still running now?"

Earl shook his head. "The most recent one was August fifteenth."

Frank flopped down in his chair. Less than a month ago. That meant Sheltering Arms could still be actively recruiting. How could he flush them out?

"All right, Earl, let's brainstorm here." This was a code word that meant that Frank would think aloud and Earl would not interrupt with any remarks about how unworkable the ideas were.

"Say we send our message from 'Brandy' to those other two email addresses in the ads, and one of them actually goes through. Then what? Eventually, they're going to want to set up a face-to-face meeting. Who are we going to send? We can't involve a teenage girl in a police sting operation."

"A woman cop?" Earl knew his role as straight man: throw out the obvious solutions for Frank to shoot down.

"The only female trooper under Meyerson's command is Pauline Phelps." Frank and Earl both snickered. Pauline was a terrific cop and a hell of a nice person, but she was built like a Giants linebacker. Passing her off as a girl in trouble would never fly.

"Maybe Lt. Meyerson could find us someone from another barracks," Earl suggested.

Frank scowled. "That would be ideal, except that he's under tremendous pressure right now with this Nathan Golding investigation. He won't want to bother with trying to set that up, especially since we're still not sure those ads are placed by Sheltering Arms."

Frank stood up and began to pace. "How about this? What if we come at it from the buyer side? Go to some of those independent adoption chat rooms that the Finns mentioned and those bulletin boards you found and post messages saying we're a couple looking to adopt a healthy white infant. We'll drop hints that we've got money and we're willing to pay to make it happen fast. Then we'll see if Sheltering Arms contacts us."

"But we'll still need someone for the sting."

"That's the beauty of it. We can use any middle aged male cop to pose as the prospective adoptive father."

"What if they don't contact us?" Earl asked.

"We'll cross that bridge when we come to it." Frank sat down in front of his computer. Long periods of thinking were interspersed with short, rapid burst of typing. He hit the print command and handed the sheet to earl.

"Here. Post these messages. I'm going to do the afternoon patrol."

FRANK CRUISED PAST the high school in time for the end of the football game, idling by the rear parking lot to discourage lead-footed departures by both players and fans. Then he swung by the lumberyard to give the owner, Clyde Stevenson, an opportunity to see his tax dollars at work. Crossing over Stony Brook on the new bridge, he drove along Route 12 with no particular destination in mind. Homes and businesses were mixed together here: a small engine shop that repaired chain saws and ATVs, an old Victorian homestead, a new vinyl-sided ranch house. And on the right, the Rock Slide, a store that sold hiking, camping and rock-climbing equipment. From the Adirondack chairs on the wrap-around porch, customers could admire the view of the Verona Range while snacking on trail mix and Snapple from the juice bar.

The store had reported a break-in last month, in which some expensive climbing equipment had been stolen. Frank had spent several hours with the owner, showing him ways to improve security. Deciding to check if the fellow had followed his suggestions, Frank pulled in and parked near the back door of the store, where the burglars had jimmied a flimsy lock.

Frank was pleased to see that the owner had installed a new metal door with a heavy deadbolt. He continued around the perimeter of the building, noting with satisfaction the new floodlights and the shrubbery that had been trimmed back from the windows. He turned the corner of the building and came along the side of the porch. There, sitting on two adjacent chairs, were Stephen Galloway and a young blonde woman. Their backs were to him and he could only see their faces in profile as they leaned toward each other past the high-backed chairs. He couldn't make out their words, but they seemed to be discussing something intently. Perhaps this was the California girlfriend, come east for a visit. Either that, or Galloway was on the prowl for a new local amusement.

Frank watched them for a while, not sure why he was so interested. Then the young woman stood up, and he could see she was much younger than Galloway. She stepped down off the porch and headed for a pick-up with New York plates, turning when she got there to offer the doctor a half-hearted wave. Then, she heaved herself with some difficulty into the driver's seat. She was hugely pregnant.

FRANK DECIDED TO FIND out what the pregnant girl's story was before he confronted Galloway. He took down the license plate number of her truck, and traced it when he returned to the office. The vehicle was registered to a John Sarens in the town of Willsboro. He tried several times to call the Sarens's home, but each time the phone rang endlessly.

Finally, he gave up. It was dark and he was hungry. Earl was long gone. He'd drive up to Willsboro first thing in the morning, and catch the family at home since it was Sunday. To make sure he was on the road early, he decided to leave his truck at the office and drive the patrol car home.

Circling the deserted green, he headed toward his snug little house on the bank of Stony Brook. A half-mile away from the center of town, a pick-up truck pulled out in front of him. One of its taillights was burned out. Frank didn't like to write a ticket for this offense—it was possible the driver didn't even know it had happened. He figured he'd do the guy a favor and pull him over to let him know—it would save the driver the trouble of being ticketed by a less magnanimous state trooper somewhere else.

He put his lights on and gave the guy a minute to notice. The truck made no effort to pull over, but the road was narrow here. Frank gave him a while longer. The road widened, but still the truck didn't stop. Frank let out one whoop of the siren, the "yes, I really do mean you" warning.

Instead of slowing, the truck sped up. Now, what the hell was this about? Frank accelerated, and the truck shot further ahead.

Frank threw on the sirens—this guy *would* pull over, or he'd know the reason why. He probably had an open beer in the truck, or a few joints—Frank watched to see if anything flew out the window. It was hard to tell in the dark, but the fellow seemed to be hunched over the wheel, intent on his driving. They had been climbing a hill, and as the two vehicles crested it, the truck shot ahead on the long, straight descent, getting up to eighty.

What in God's name did this guy think he was doing? He must really have something to hide to drive at that speed on these dark mountain roads. Frank radioed the state police for assistance, and kept up the pursuit, although he refused to risk going that fast here. The truck's taillights disappeared from view around a bend at the base of the hill. As Frank reached the bottom he heard it, even over the siren: a sickeningly loud thump, the crunching of metal, the shattering of glass.

He came around the turn and found the truck flattened against a large outcropping of rock that jutted out almost to the edge of the road. The hood was compressed all the way into the passenger compartment. The driver, who- ever he was, was clearly dead.

Chapter 19

The cleanup of the accident, the removal of the body, and the notification of the family took almost until midnight. When Frank finally fell into bed, his body yearned for sleep, but his mind raced. The driver of the truck had been one Dean Jacobson, nineteen years old, who lived with his grandfather in Verona and worked sporadically as a gas station attendant, chairlift operator, and golf course maintenance man. What could have made the young man run like that when Frank tried to pull him over? He had no criminal record, but his grandfather, although distraught, had seemed oddly unsurprised by the news of his grandson's death.

"He's been acting funny lately—just hasn't been himself," the older man had said when Frank broke the news. But he couldn't or wouldn't speculate on what the problem might be. He just kept shaking his head and sighing.

Frank wouldn't know anything to relieve his guilt until the state police picked apart what was left of the truck, and the coroner delivered the autopsy report. Finally, he sank into an uneasy sleep.

Soon after the sun awakened him, Frank headed out to the Sarens's home in Willsboro. The woman who answered the door looked a lot like the house itself—a little run-down, but trying to keep up appearances.

"I'm Frank Bennett from the Trout Run Police Department. I'm looking for a young woman—maybe your daughter—who drives a brown pick-up, license plate number 63-48A."

Her face lost its small glimmer of welcome. "Why? What's she done?"

"Not a thing," Frank reassured her. "I just need to talk to her. She might be able to help me with an investigation."

"It's that no-good boyfriend of hers, isn't it? I warned her he was nothing but trouble, but she wouldn't listen. Now look at her."

"Who's there, Shelly?" a deep voice bellowed from inside the house.

"Just someone who needs directions," she shouted back. "You can find Diane at the bait shop—she helps out over there," she whispered to Frank.

"Her dad don't want her driving our truck except to work—tell her to be more careful."

DIANE SARENS WAS EASY enough to spot—the only pregnant teenager in a room full of fishing rods, flies and coolers full of live bait. She sat at a table in the back, tying flies, her fingers still nimble even if her body was too unwieldy to move. Frank dropped into a chair beside her.

She glanced up. "Hi. You need something special? A cocky knight, a dry blobby?"

"No, I'm not much of a fly fisherman. I don't like getting wet."

She smiled slightly and returned to her work, looping her thin, pale hair behind her ear.

"When is your baby due?"

Instinctively, her hand dropped down and cradled her belly. "Soon."

"I saw you over in Trout Run on Saturday. At the Rock Slide."

She looked at Frank quizzically. It seemed to register now that he was a cop.

"Yeah, so? My friend works there."

"You weren't talking to a friend when I saw you. You were talking to Dr. Galloway, out on the porch. Is he treating you? Providing pre-natal care?"

Her eyes darted around the room. "Why?"

"Diane, you may have heard that a girl in Trout Run died giving birth to her baby outside the hospital. No one knew she was pregnant."

"Well, everyone sure knows that I am."

"She made a plan to give her baby up for adoption, but it wasn't a legal adoption agency. I think someone at the Cascade Clinic might have helped her, and taken the baby. Has anyone approached you about giving your baby up for adoption?"

Diane's eyes widened. She pushed back from her worktable so abruptly that it tipped right into Frank's lap, sending nippers, forceps, feathers and fur scattering into every nook and cranny of the shop.

"Hey!" someone shouted from the front of the store.

By the time Frank got him free, Diane had run out the door and was peeling out of the parking lot.

Chapter 20

Frank sat at his desk on Monday morning creating a whirlpool in his coffee with a swizzle stick. He'd screwed up the encounter with Diane Sarens—the girl would never talk to him now. Belatedly, he'd called Trudy Massinay for help. He should have thought of that before he went blasting off to Willsboro to scare the poor kid out of her wits. Trudy had promised to try to approach her, but she'd warned Frank there was not much she could do if the girl turned down her help.

He was tempted to go see Galloway again, but what would he gain? There was no crime in talking to a pregnant girl, and Galloway would claim it was an innocent encounter. And what did this latest development do to his theory that Galloway's was the mystery signature on the card in Mary Pat's car? He couldn't be both the baby's father and the link to Sheltering Arms, could he? Frank sighed and gulped down his coffee. He'd better just wait and see what Trudy turned up.

"Up to all hours hitting the books?" Frank asked as Earl slunk to his desk at nine-thirty. Here was a distraction to take his mind off his problems.

"Uh, yeah," Earl cast a nervous glance over his shoulder. "Sorry I'm late."

Frank waited until Earl started filing reports before launching his next salvo. "I guess I've been replaced."

"Huh?"

"I hear you have a new study coach."

Earl turned the shade of the sugar maple blazing outside their window. This was too much fun to stop. "All you get from me is a beer when you answer all the questions right. What does Melanie give you?"

"I happened to run into her at the Trail's End and she asked me some of my questions. What's the big deal?" Earl shut the file drawer hard enough to bring down a shower of leaves from the terminally ill philodendron on top of the cabinet.

"Happened to run into her?" Frank grinned. "I thought you hated the food there."

"I thought you hated it, too. But I hear they practically had to sweep you out the door on Saturday when you had lunch with Beth Abercrombie."

Frank's grin faded. He might have known that Nick Reilly, the bartender at the Trail's End, was a conduit through which information flowed in two directions.

"That was business," he snapped.

A little smile played on Earl's lips as he booted up his computer. "I think Beth's kind of pretty... for an older person."

Frank knew when he'd been bested. "I have someone to see. I'll be back in an hour."

<hr>

AN OLDER PERSON! WHAT the hell was that supposed to mean? Frank gunned the engine of the patrol car and rolled out of the parking lot toward Harkness Road. He'd been meaning to talk to Doug Penniman again—this might be the perfect time.

No doubt everyone in town was getting a kick out of the show—almost as funny as watching Grandpa put the moves on a blue-haired lady at the nursing home. Well, if he couldn't have one lunch with Beth without setting tongues wagging, how was it that no one noticed who was screwing around with Mary Pat?

Obviously, because she never went out anywhere with him. That made Anita's theory that Mary Pat's lover was married look more likely. And Doug Penniman's schedule meshed perfectly with Mary Pat's—they both had some afternoons free, while Judy and Billy were reliably out of the way.

As he approached the Pennimans' house, he could see Doug's truck parked out front. He rang the bell, but no one answered. Probably Doug was asleep. Too bad—he leaned on the bell again.

A bleary-eyed Doug answered the door and stood staring at Frank as if he couldn't quite place him.

"Sorry to bother you." Frank made little effort at sincerity and stepped into the house before Doug had time to react. "There's something more I have to ask you about."

"Okay." Doug rubbed his eyes. "Want some coffee?"

"I never say no to that offer." Frank followed Doug back to the cheerless kitchen, where the breakfast dishes still sat on the table. The red light glowed on the half-full coffee pot. Pushing aside a bowl with a few soggy flakes in a puddle of milk, Doug presented Frank with a cup of stale coffee.

"Excuse me for mentioning this, but things between you and Judy seem a little," Frank cleared his throat, "strained."

Doug shrugged. "All married couples have their ups and downs."

Frank stirred steadily, trying to break up the clots of sour milk that had risen to the surface of his coffee. "When things are down, it helps to have someone who's a good listener."

Doug suddenly took a great interest in cleaning up the kitchen. He rose and began pushing dishes into the sink with a clatter. "I keep my business to myself."

Frank watched Doug work. The place wasn't really dirty, just cluttered with yesterday's newspaper and piles of unopened mail. He noticed one pane of the large window that overlooked the backyard was broken, with a piece of cardboard inserted to keep out the cold air.

"Looks like you have a repair job waiting for you," Frank said, nodding toward the window.

Doug sighed. "Yeah, Billy broke it."

"Playing baseball?"

"Uh...right."

Frank noticed three brown drip marks on the woodwork next to the window. Had Doug or Judy been cut while cleaning up, or had Billy put his hand, not a baseball, through that glass? Was he subject to fits of rage? Frank didn't know much about Asperger's—he'd have to ask Trudy.

"I know you're under a lot of strain, having a handicapped son, and all," Frank said, still trying to convey that he wouldn't blame Doug for taking comfort with another woman.

Doug whirled around, his dark brows knotted together. "Don't you mention my family. Just ask me what you have to ask me and leave."

Frank felt like he had cornered a wild animal that he didn't want to shoot. "Look, Doug, I'm not one to judge. But you *are* free during the day at times, and if you and Mary Pat..."

Doug looked baffled. "That's what this is about? You think *I* knocked Mary Pat up? Jesus, even I'm not that stupid." He began to laugh, an unpleasant sound that expressed something—bitterness? relief?—at any rate, not humor.

————————◆————————

BY 6:45, THE PARISH hall already buzzed with activity. The monthly meeting of the Town Council, normally attended by no more than five or six people, had attained rock-concert popularity. Scheduled for discussion: the rights and responsibilities surrounding public demonstrations in Trout Run.

Frank stepped through door and paused. Early arrivals had reserved their places by draping their jackets over folding metal chairs, the set-up of which Augie Enright had probably stretched into an all-afternoon job. Some of the older folks were sitting down, but most people stood around chatting in groups of three of four, waiting for the meeting to be called to order.

Standing off to themselves Frank noticed the Extrom house construction supervisor Sean Vinson and a tall, tanned man with slicked-back hair. Must be Extrom himself. Was he taking an interest in local politics now that he was a property owner? Or did he consider Trout Run town council meetings part of the quaint local atmosphere he was paying so dearly for?

Frank took a deep breath and plunged into the crowd. He hadn't taken more than three steps before the assault began.

"Frank, could you please send Earl over to run the speed trap on Beaver Dam Road? The way cars go flying down there, that'll be the next place somebody nearly gets run down."

"Frank, any news on what happened to Mary Pat Sheehan's baby?"

"What a shock for poor Joe and Ann. I tell you, I took a casserole over there yesterday and Ann and I just sat down and had a good cry together."

"Hey Frank, got your gun loaded? You may need it tonight!"

"Only if these nuts are planning a protest over there, right Frank?"

Frank answered every comment and request patiently, stretching his walk from the back of the room to the front into a ten-minute excursion. He finally arrived at the stage to find Reid Burlingame fiddling with the sound system, periodically sending ear-splitting blasts of feedback through the room.

As many times as the council chairman had addressed a crowd in this hall, he remained utterly baffled by the church microphone.

"Let me help you with that, Reid." With a few deft adjustments, Frank saved half the population from permanent hearing loss as Trout Run's leader gratefully watched. Although electronically inept, Reid was quite sharp in every other way. Approaching 70, he still practiced law from an office in his rambling old house. He took these meetings very seriously, and had donned a natty, if venerable, suit for the occasion.

"Are the Fenstocks here, Frank? I like to begin promptly, but we can hardly get started without them."

Frank scanned the hall, and noticed the sea of bodies parting to allow someone to pass up to the front. In a moment, he recognized the short, portly form of Abe Fenstock muscling his way through the crowd. His two sons, Roy and Stan, trailed close behind. "Go ahead, Reid, make the opening announcements," Frank said.

Seeing Reid approach the podium, people began to scurry to their seats, and soon everyone's eyes were fixed on the stage. To the left of Reid sat the Green Tomorrow contingent: Katie Petrucci, Meredith Golding, and the bearded guy, Barry Sutter. Beth Abercrombie stood in the middle of the room behind a slide projector. To the right sat the three Fenstocks, each nervously shuffling his feet in anticipation of the public speaking ordeal to come.

Reid was not one for long-winded introductions. "We're here tonight because of an incident that happened out at Raging Rapids five days ago. Some protesters—"

Immediately, a buzz of conversation erupted in the hall. Reid rapped his gavel three times.

"Some protesters, who were exercising their constitutional right to free speech, got a little carried away and blocked the driveway to Abe's business. Then a truck, which still hasn't been found, nearly ran down some of the protesters. This whole thing has clearly gotten out of hand. Reasonable people can disagree on an issue, and we ought to be able to discuss it without resorting to violence or breaking the law. So I've agreed to give both parties some time at the podium tonight to present their cases.

"Green Tomorrow has a little slide show for us. After that we'll hear from Abe Fenstock. There will be plenty of time for questions at the end, so please don't interrupt our speakers. Go ahead Mrs. Golding."

Reid sat down and Meredith Golding took his place behind the podium. She looked straight out into the crowd and spoke without any prepared notes in a clear, steady voice. But Frank noticed her long, slender hands, resting on the side of the podium, trembled slightly. "I think most of you are aware of our organization and its mission," she said. "Some people obviously thought that Green Tomorrow would die, along with its founder. But I want to say that my husband's death has made me more committed than ever to continue our work to preserve our natural resources for coming generations."

Beth, Katie and a few other people, including Lucy Bates, applauded. Frank noticed Edwin reach out and take his wife's hand. He marveled that Meredith could talk about her husband's murder with such composure. He'd felt like crawling into a hole and shutting out the whole world after Estelle's death. But everyone dealt with grief differently. It wasn't fair to hold it against her that she wasn't a basket case.

"I know a lot of rumors have been circulating about why we want to close Raging Rapids," Meredith continued. "We're here tonight to clarify our position, and to answer any questions you may have."

Frank settled back in his hard, metal folding chair. This he wanted to hear.

"In a nutshell, we believe the Raging Rapids tourist attraction is destroying the fragile ecosystem of the rapids section of Stony Brook," Meredith began, "which is a habitat for several varieties of trout, many wildflowers, and blue heron and other rarer birds. We propose to dismantle the current system of catwalks and observation decks and replace it with a carefully constructed hiking trail which would, of course, be open to the public free of charge." This was a jab at the $7.00 fee the Fenstocks charged for admission to Raging Rapids.

A murmur ran through the crowd—nothing so blatant as a boo, but distinctly unsympathetic.

"To pay for this, and to compensate Mr. Fenstock for his business, we have written a grant proposal seeking two million dollars from the State of New York."

Now the room burst into excited chatter. "Who says the state would give them the money?" "That's a fortune! I'd take it." "Not really, he'd have to pay taxes, and then how are Abe and the boys going to earn a living?"

Meredith raised her voice over the clamor. "I'd like to show you these slides, which I think clearly illustrate why Raging Rapids should be closed." She nodded and Augie dimmed the lights, while Beth started up the projector.

"First, the concession stand at Raging Rapids promotes litter," Meredith narrated, as a picture appeared of a solitary blue heron standing regally still as an M&M wrapper swirled up against his spindly legs. Next a slide of a dark-haired teenager throwing a soda can from one of the catwalks into the brook below flashed on the screen. "That's probably your brother," someone called out, prompting laughter and scattered clapping in the darkened room. Frank smiled too. The slide proved nothing; it would be easy to set up the shot.

"More importantly," Meredith resumed, "the constant noise and traffic created by Raging Rapids is disrupting the habitat of the Bicknell's thrush, a rare native bird whose numbers are declining at an alarming rate."

"Thrushes? There's plenty of thrushes around—I got some in my backyard," someone shouted out.

"This is the Bicknell's thrush," Meredith explained. "If its habitat continues to be destroyed it will soon disappear altogether from the Adirondacks."

"So, we still got a ton a birds," a man next to Frank muttered. But he noticed that Ardyth Munger and Celia Lambert, both great bird-watchers, were sitting forward in their seats paying close attention. He looked back at Meredith Golding. He still hadn't heard her say anything that explained how Green Tomorrow got interested in Raging Rapids in the first place. He might just participate in the question and answer period himself.

"Finally," Meredith said, "we believe the system of catwalks and observation decks at Raging Rapids is quite unsafe."

In the dim light, Roy Fenstock leaped to his feet. "We've never had a serious accident in fifty years of operation," he shouted to more scattered applause.

"Sit down, Roy," Reid commanded. "You'll get your chance to respond." Roy allowed his brother to pull him back into his seat, although he continued shaking his head.

The slide on the screen now showed a very large man backing up to take a picture. His broad backside was pressed against a metal guardrail, which bulged outward under his weight. The crowd tittered, despite the man's precarious situation.

"That was repaired weeks ago!" It was Abe who burst out this time, then glanced guiltily at Reid and lowered his gaze to the floor.

"As you know," Meredith narrated calmly, "Raging Rapids is the site of many school field trips. I think you'll be interested in this series of slides." The first image on the screen showed a group of grade school children, all wearing nametags and marching along a catwalk behind their teacher. The next showed the last boy in the line lagging behind. The third showed him placing one sneakered foot on the cross support of the catwalk railing, which begged to be used as a foothold. The fourth slide showed a terrified adult pulling the child back as he straddled the railing, one foot flailing in space. The final slide showed the dizzying drop below, as water surged powerfully over huge, jagged rocks.

After a moment of stunned silence, the room burst into a cacophony of debate. "I'm never letting my daughter go there again!" "Oh, they're blowing this all out of proportion. Skiing's dangerous and you don't hear anyone saying Whiteface should be closed."

Frank glanced around the room, trying to anticipate where free speech might escalate into trouble, but after repeated, vigorous pounding of his gavel, Reid managed to bring the room to order.

"It's time to hear from Abe Fenstock. Please give him your undivided attention."

Abe came up to the podium clutching a sheet of tablet paper that had grown limp in his sweaty grasp. His short upper lip and prominent chin combined to give him a naturally pugnacious look, although anyone who knew him could tell you he was the most affable of men. Tonight he seemed neither frightened nor angry, simply determined.

"Hello everybody. I think you all know me and my sons. All I want to say is this. I don't want no two million dollars from the state. I just want to earn an honest living. People have offered to buy my land before and I always turned 'em down. Don't forget, I employ sixty people over there in the high season, and these fellas"—he gestured across the stage—"won't employ none.

Like Roy said before, we've never had a serious accident in fifty years, and we don't intend to ever have one. As far as I'm concerned, there's nothing to discuss because my family has owned that land since 1873 and we intend to keep it." Then he sat down.

Determinedly loud applause broke out in several pockets throughout the room, then Reid opened the floor for questions. Alma Kurtz immediately strode up to the stage. Short and wiry, she barely cleared the podium, but her voice rang out, doubly amplified by anger and the microphone. "I think you all know my husband and I own the Trim 'n Tidy Motel in Verona. We get a lot of business from bus tours and Raging Rapids is one of the main attractions on the bus tours. You'll lose all that business if they turn the rapids into a *hiking trail*," she spit the last words out like pieces of gristle and stomped off the stage.

Frank noticed several people in the audience nodding their heads in agreement. One head bobbed harder than the rest. It belonged to a thin, dark-skinned man sitting between two empty chairs. Frank knew he was Sanjiv Patel who had recently bought the old Mountain Vista Motel on Route 12. Deserted for more than two years, the motel had attracted kids who broke into the rooms to have sex and smoke pot. Some college boys on a ski trip had even crashed there and started a small fire. The place had become a nuisance, and Frank knew he wasn't the only person to be relieved when Mr. Patel bought it and cleaned it up.

Still, Patel wasn't exactly part of Trout Run's inner circle, and Frank had to smile as the slender man leaped out of his seat and started toward the front, then paused as if horrified by what he had done. But Reid waved him on, and then introduced him as he took the podium.

"Miss Alma is correct," Patel began, his voice quavery and high-pitched. Frank thought he probably made fewer grammatical mistakes than half the men who worked at Stevenson's, but the sing-song rhythm of his speech set him apart as foreign, exotic. "We motel owners are not the only ones who would be affected. Closing Raging Rapids would hurt Malone's and the Farmer's Market and you, Miss Beth."

Patel turned and pointed at Beth Abercrombie. "The hikers and back-packers," he said this word carefully, with the emphasis on pack, "will not be the ones to buy your vases and rugs. Not on your life!" he nodded, looking pleased that he had thought of this Americanism. "This Nathan Golding stayed at my motel, but if I had known who he was, and what he wanted to do, I tell you, I would have turned him away!"

Then he stepped back from the podium and addressed the room at large with surprising confidence. "Mark my words, closing Raging Rapids will hurt the whole local economy." With that prediction hanging in the air, he slipped back through the crowd to his seat, keeping his eyes focused straight ahead.

Now the room buzzed with debate as people twisted in their chairs to discuss this angle with their neighbors. Frank felt a pang of sympathy for Beth, being singled out for reproach in front of the whole town. But Alma and Mr. Patel had a point, and he wondered why Beth aligned herself with the Green Tomorrow group against her own best interests.

Marooned there in the center of the room with the slide projector, Beth looked like a Puritan sinner sentenced to the stocks. On all sides the people of Trout Run talked and shot her looks, but no one spoke to her directly. Frank thought she maintained her composure pretty well, keeping her eyes fixed on the stage as if simply waiting for her next projector cue, but her hands moved restlessly in her lap twisting and folding a Green Tomorrow brochure. She had nodded to him when he first took his seat, but now she refused to make eye contact.

The buzz of conversation died down as Katie Petrucci rose and approached the podium. Everyone knew full well who she was, so she just began talking. "It seems to me," she said in a preachy tone that bordered on stridency, "that we're all forgetting just what it is about the High Peaks region that attracts all the tourists in the first place. It's the natural beauty of the last remaining wilderness area in the Northeast. Without that my friends, we have nothing. We owe it to our children and our grandchildren to preserve the land, protect it, and pass it on. Forever Wild!" she shouted with a raised fist.

This battle cry produced a tumult of shouts and whistles from the audience, but how many were supportive and how many were catcalls Frank couldn't tell. "Forever Wild" was the slogan of the Adirondack Park Agency and he knew not everyone in town endorsed their efforts. Still, he could see plenty of people in the audience nodding in agreement. Rod Extrom glanced up at the podium as if he might want to say something, but Frank noticed Sean Vinson tug on his boss's arm and shake his head.

Katie had left the stage, and now the three Fenstocks had their heads together at the podium. Frank watched as Abe laid a restraining hand on Roy's arm, but the younger man shook him off and snatched up the microphone. "I just want to say that the Fenstock family loves the Adirondacks as much as anyone in this room. We've lived here for five generations and God be willing, we'll live here for five more. If any person or organization tries to take away our land, it'll be over my dead body!"

Roy's performance effectively ended the meeting. Two men tried to ask questions above the noise of the crowd, but soon gave up, and the hall began to empty out.

"What did you make of that?" Edwin asked later as Frank stood outside the church making sure all the participants went quietly to their cars.

"I don't like any meeting that ends with talk about dead bodies."

Edwin patted him on the shoulder. "Relax. It's just a figure of speech."

Chapter 21

"You're not going to believe this! No sooner did I place Mary Pat's baby with the couple in Syracuse, than I notice a bunch of posts in the adoption chat rooms from a couple looking for a baby and willing to really pay.

"Don't tell me you're going to take that child away from the new couple the way you took her from the Finns!"

"No...relax. But I hate to let this new couple get away. Maybe I'll contact them."

"I haven't even got a baby for the Braithwaites yet. Now you want two?"

"Just see what you can do."

EARL ENTERED THE OFFICE whistling. He looked different somehow—cleaner; Frank couldn't put his finger on it.

"Did you get a haircut?" Frank asked after studying him for a while.

"Uh, yeah," Earl ran his hand nervously over the neatly trimmed nape of his neck. "Why?"

"It looks good. And they trimmed your mustache, too." That was what really made him look different—trimmed and evened out, the wooly caterpillar on Earl's upper lip didn't look half bad.

"You didn't go to the Butcher of Verona, did you?"

"No, I went to the place in Lake Placid you and Edwin go to."

Frank raised his eyebrows. It wasn't like Earl to part with twenty bucks when Joe's Barbershop would mutilate your hair for half the price. Something was up.

"Do anything last night?"

"Melanie and I went to the movies."

Ah, Melanie again. Frank couldn't imagine that pairing; Earl hardly had the training wheels off his bike and now he was racing in the Tour de France.

"We saw *Berserk*, that serial killer movie. It was great!"

"Earl, that's not the kind of thing you should take a girl to on a date."

132

"She picked it," Earl protested. "She loves mysteries and cop shows and stuff."

So, maybe that was behind Melanie's sudden interest in Earl, now that she knew he planned to go to the police academy. He hoped Earl wasn't headed for a broken heart.

Earl hummed happily as he prepared to go out to run the morning speed trap. Frank opened his mouth to offer some advice, then shut it again. What the hell did he know about women? Earl was doing fine.

"Dr. Hibbert's on line one," Doris announced.

Frank stared at the blinking light for a moment. He was almost sure what the coroner was going to say. Probably poor Dean Jacobson had a couple of beers under his belt and his blood alcohol level was slightly over the legal limit. For that, he'd gotten the death sentence, and Frank couldn't help feeling like he was the executioner.

"Hi, Chuck, what do you have for me?"

"Your crash victim was pumped full of PCP. He probably would've crashed into something before long, even without you on his tail."

"PCP...angel dust? I haven't seen that around since the eighties," Frank objected.

"I know, and we never had much of it up here, even then. But I was just reading a journal article the other day—apparently it's making a comeback with the kids again. Teenagers today don't have any memory of how screwed up PCP makes you. Prolonged use leads to extremely irrational behavior: paranoia, delusions, hallucinations."

Frank felt relieved. PCP did make people crazy. There had been a case years ago in Kansas City of a college kid diving out a fifth floor dorm window because he was convinced he could fly. And Dean's grandfather had said the boy hadn't been himself lately. But relief was immediately followed by worry.

"Where the hell did he get it?" Frank asked. He'd arrested Trout Run's foremost pot dealer a few months ago for blatantly conducting a sale in the parking lot of the Mountainside. Since then, Earl had reported that the scuttlebutt around the tavern was that dope had been hard to come by without a long drive.

"Maybe over in Burlington. This article said PCP's becoming a popular party drug on campus."

"Possible, I guess. But Dean didn't strike me as a kid with a lot of U. Vermont frat-boy friends."

"You don't have to be their friend to be their customer. Anyway, finding the source is your problem—I've got patients waiting."

"Thanks for the call, Doc." Frank hung up and made a note to call Mr. Jacobson to find out who Dean's friends had been.

"Anita Veech is here to see you." Doris's voice came through the intercom dripping with disapproval.

What would Anita be doing, coming to the town office to see him? Frank crossed the room and opened the door. Sure enough, there she sat with a grimy little girl beside her.

"Hello, Anita—come on in." Frank bent down to the little girl as Anita lumbered past. Why wasn't this kid in school? "Hi there, sweetie. What's your name?"

The child squinted at him through a tangle of hair as if he were a two-tailed cat. She looked like she had never had a real haircut in all her six or seven years, but when the stringy brown strands got in her way, someone came along and whacked off the offending pieces with dull nail scissors.

"This here is my Olivia." Anita prodded her daughter. "Say hello, girl."

Olivia stared at her tattered Little Mermaid sneakers.

"She's shy." Anita lowered herself into a chair that creaked in protest. "Say, I appreciate what you done for my brother, Ralph."

Frank started to say he hadn't done a thing, but caught himself. If Ralph had wormed his way out of trouble with the Lake Placid police, there was no harm in taking the credit. "Sure. Have you come to repay me?"

"I always hold up my end of a bargain." Anita grinned, exposing her dentist's nightmare of teeth. "I know you been wondering what Mary Pat was doing out on Harkness Road so much, thinking that might have something to do with the baby and all. But she was just coming out to visit Olivia, here. Ain't that right, Olivia?"

Olivia nodded vigorously without looking up.

"But you told me she didn't visit you," Frank protested.

Anita raised a sausage-finger. "I never actually said she didn't—I just said Pap don't like visitors, and that's the truth. So we had to set up times for

Mary Pat to visit when I knew Pap wouldn't be around. See, Olivia here is real smart. Ain't that right?"

Again the nod.

"So Mary Pat would come out and help her with her schoolwork. Because I never was one much for school myself, and I'm not much help with the spelling words and the multiplying, am I, Olivia?"

A shake this time. Frank watched the performance, fascinated.

"But Mary Pat, she was real good with that stuff. She liked working with Olivia on the studying and the handwriting and the reading. That's why she was out on Harkness Road so much."

"But that last day—she was with you right before she died. Didn't you notice how sick she was?"

Anita shook her head, clucking sadly. "We never did see her that day, did we Olivia? We made a plan for her to come, but then Pap didn't go out like we expected, so I had to send Olivia down to the signpost to prop up the big stick. See, that was our signal—if the stick was leaning against the sign it meant Pap was in and she shouldn't come up to the house, right Olivia?"

Frank looked at the forlorn little bundle of rags with the bobbing head that was Olivia Veech. He could certainly see Mary Pat taking the child under her wing. He felt like doing so himself. "Why didn't you tell me this when I talked to you at the Stop 'N' Buy?"

"I didn't like to, just in case it got back to Pap. I figured it didn't really matter, since it didn't have nothing to do with why she died. But I know you been spendin' a lot of time worrying on it, so my conscience got to botherin' me."

Conscience? He didn't figure Anita had a conscience. "What about the father of the baby—have you given any more thought to that?" He didn't want to ask her directly about Dr. Galloway, and plant an idea in the mind of someone so unreliable.

Anita stretched back in her chair and folded her hands over her massive belly. Frank felt his eyes drawn perversely to the slab of flesh that hung down over her crotch. Sometime in the past seven years, Anita had had sex with a man, and he didn't care to dwell on the logistics required to pull that feat off.

"I *have* been thinking, and you know what? I think the fella was not from around here."

Typical Trout Run attitude. When in doubt, pin it on an outsider. "Why?" he asked, giving up hope that Anita really knew anything about Mary Pat's lover.

"Because it seemed like she knew he would be coming in on certain days, and she would try to get me out the door early then. It was like he passed through on a schedule, see? But I don't remember the exact days."

"Just because he came in on a schedule doesn't necessarily mean he was from out of town," Frank said.

Anita pushed off from his desk to boost herself out of the chair. "You got a point. I guess that's why you're the detective."

Was she mocking him? It was hard to know what to believe from this woman.

Anita waddled to the door, with Olivia trailing behind. As she crossed the threshold, the child turned back and met his eyes for the first time.

"I miss Mary Pat," she said. He couldn't doubt the sadness etched in her wan little face. "She was my real friend."

⸺⬦⸺

THE CALL FROM SEAN Vinson reporting vandalism at the Extrom house building site came in just as Anita left. Frank left for the scene immediately, driven by curiosity to see this house he had heard so much about.

Extrom's place was located at the summit of one of the higher peaks in the Verona range. These mountains weren't part of the forty-six named High Peaks, but the locals referred to this mountain as Beehive because of its conical shape. There were several homes nestled in the woods at the bottom third of the mountain, but the top two-thirds had generally been considered too inaccessible for anything more than a rough hunting shack. Then Extrom had come along, bought up the entire top of the mountain from several different owners, and set about building an access road, drilling a well, and installing his own power generator. What all this cost was a subject of constant speculation among the regulars at the Store and Malone's diner, with the tally rising by tens of thousands of dollars every week.

Frank turned onto the unpaved road marked with a hand-painted plywood sign that read Extrom Site. The road grew increasingly steep, winding through the dense maple and birch forest, but it had been worn smooth by the constant traffic of trucks and earthmovers. At the higher elevation the trees thinned a bit, and wind-stunted hemlocks and balsam wrapped their roots around boulders searching for some nourishing soil. Frank followed one last twist in the road, and the Extrom house appeared before him.

The house seemed to cling to the rocky peak much like the resilient trees, but there was nothing stunted about it. It cantilevered out from the mountaintop, a vast, multi-leveled structure of natural field stone, huge log beams, and cedar shakes. One wall appeared to be made of nothing but glass. The rhythmic explosion of nail guns echoed in the cool morning air as a crew of men installed shingles.

Frank parked and walked toward the house, amazed and appalled at once. Extrom's new home commanded a panoramic view of everything from Lake Champlain to the east and Lake Placid to the west. Stretched out below, like clouds beneath a high-flying plane, was a blanket of brilliant reds, yellows and oranges, broken only intermittently by a thin ribbon of road. Frank knew there were houses down there, but he couldn't see them through the dense leaf canopy. The old cliché, "master of all he surveys" popped into his head. Yes, a man would feel like a feudal lord in his castle in this place.

Frank was so intrigued by the feats of engineering that the house presented, and the stunning craftsmanship of the stonework, that he didn't even look for signs of the spray-painted vandalism that Sean Vinson had reported. Staring up at the trusses supporting one wing of the house, he jumped at the sound of a voice right behind him.

"The damage is over here."

Frank whirled around to face Sean Vinson, an exceptionally thin man wearing work boots with blue jeans and a flannel shirt that looked like they had been professionally laundered and pressed. With several silver rings on his fingers, a diamond stud in one ear, and a precision-trimmed mustache, it was no wonder Vinson came in for so much grief at the Mountainside Tavern.

"This is quite a place," Frank said. "I haven't been up here before."

"I haven't had occasion to call you until now," Vinson said as he led Frank away from the house. "But we've had a major episode of vandalism that threatens the work on this project." Vinson stopped in front of a small construction trailer at the edge of the clearing. Spray-painted in bright orange across the siding, door and window was the message: hire local or the house is next.

"Any idea what that means?" Frank asked.

"I know exactly what it means and who wrote it. Last week I had to fire three local men who were working here as carpenters, because they simply refused to follow the blueprints. I replaced them with reliable men from New York City who have worked for our firm before. Today, I came in and found this blatant threat to damage the house. I demand that you arrest these men. Their names are Richie Blevins, Pete Ringold and Dan Strohman."

Frank knew who the three men were—Richie and Pete were about Earl's age; Dan was a little older with a wife and kid. They were all struggling to stay afloat, patching together a living by working a variety of part-time jobs. He knew they were all hard workers, and probably damn good carpenters, even if they weren't used to following a fancy architect's plan. He could just imagine Dan arguing with Sean that those trusses would never hold the house up.

Getting fired from one of the best-paying gigs in the county wouldn't be easy to swallow, so Frank didn't doubt the boys had cooked up this little retaliation after a few beers at the Mountainside. But they had probably gotten the anger out of their systems now and had forgotten all about their threat. "You may be right, but I can't arrest them without more evidence than that. I'll talk to them, though."

"Talk to them?" Vinson all but stamped his foot. "The house is slated to be the subject of a major article in *Architectural Digest* in the spring. I want them locked up where they can't do any harm."

Yes, the glossy magazine spread might get cancelled if Sean Sucks were sprayed on that stonework. Frank gestured toward the trailer. "Minor property damage doesn't normally result in much of a prison term, Mr. Vinson. Trust me, I'll see that they don't give you any more trouble."

"We can't afford any set-backs."

"Seems like Mr. Extrom can afford quite a lot. What line of work is he in, anyway?"

"Communications."

"Owns some radio and TV stations?"

"*Hard*ly." Apparently, Vinson had rarely encountered such doltish naiveté. "Wireless communications. Satellites, fiber optics. This house will include a state-of-the-art communications network."

"That'll come in handy, I'm sure." Frank returned his gaze to Vinson. "I'll go speak to those fellas. They won't pull any more stunts like this."

"You'd better be right." Vinson slammed his graffitied office door in Frank's face.

On the way down the mountain, Frank caught one last glimpse of the house in his rear-view mirror. Why didn't Green Tomorrow protest this monstrosity? The massive house must've displaced more than a few bird nests. Oh, but what was he thinking? This was no monstrosity; this place had been blessed by *Architectural Digest*, whereas poor old Abe would be more likely to be written up in *Trailer Parks Today*. Maybe Green Tomorrow didn't mind assaults on the environment that were so tasteful. He'd have to ask Beth about that.

Chapter 22

On the way back to the office, Frank decided to stop in and see the Sheehans. Their front yard was covered in a thick layer of fallen leaves, another sign of Mary Pat's absence. She had probably taken care of the raking. Frank kicked through them, breathing in their warm, sweet smell. He knocked and waited. Just as he was about to knock again, the door opened. Ann Sheehan stared at him without a word, then turned around, shouted "Joe," and disappeared into the kitchen, leaving Frank on the porch.

Well, there was no doubt where he stood with Ann Sheehan; he hoped her husband might be a little warmer. Joe had apparently been down in the basement. He arrived at the door slightly out of breath, and came out to join Frank on the porch.

"Now what?" Joe asked.

No, he was persona non grata with them both now. He decided to lead off with the question about Olivia Veech, since asking about Mary Pat's lover was sure to raise Joe's hackles.

"I'm still trying to verify what Mary Pat was doing out on Harkness Road, just in case it has something to do with the baby. Anita Veech, who cleans at the Stop 'N Buy, recently told me that Mary Pat went out there regularly to visit her little daughter, Olivia. Did Mary Pat ever mention that?"

Joe let out an exasperated snort. "Oh, Olivia! Mary Pat just worried herself sick about that little gypsy. Always looking for clothes for her at the clothing bank, buying her books and crayons and such. Anita was just using that child to get money out of Mary Pat. I told her she better leave those Veeches alone, but she said Olivia couldn't help the family she was born into."

"So Mary Pat *did* go out to Harkness Road to visit Olivia?" Why hadn't Joe mentioned that possibility in the first place?

"I don't know about that. Mary Pat talked about seeing the kid when Anita brought her in to the store. I didn't even know you could get back to where the Veeches live from Harkness. I thought you had to go in by way of Route 12, then take that unmarked road."

"If Mary Pat knew you didn't approve, she wouldn't have mentioned going out there, right?" Yet another secret Mary Pat had kept from her parents, but not *the* secret.

"I suppose so." Joe no longer bothered to insist Mary Pat wouldn't have concealed the truth.

It looked like Anita's story could be true then—maybe the trips to Harkness Road had nothing to do with Mary Pat's lover. Which made Galloway all the more likely a prospect.

Frank pulled the greeting card out. "I found this in the roadside emergency kit in Mary Pat's trunk. I think it might be from Mary Pat's—" He found he couldn't use the word 'lover' to Joe. "The father of the baby. Do you recognize the signature?"

Joe accepted the card with all the eagerness of a man being handed a live tarantula. He pushed his glasses up to get the bifocals aligned for close scrutiny. "I can't make out the name, can you? But that writing looks familiar to me, like I seen it somewhere before."

"Where? Another card that was mailed to the house?"

Joe shrugged.

Frank tried to keep his tone casual. "Have you ever been to the Cascade Clinic?"

Joe wrinkled his brow at the sudden change in topic. "Yeah, once last year when I had pink-eye. That young doctor prescribed some drops and it went away. Why?"

Now there was no mistaking Frank's interest. "So, you had a prescription filled. Could that be where you saw that writing?"

"You mean you think that young doctor, the short fella, was the guy who..."

"There's some link there, but I don't have any solid evidence that Galloway is the father. It may be that he helped deliver the baby." Frank told Joe about the antibiotics he'd found with the card, and about his visit with Dr. Galloway. "Did Mary Pat ever mention him, say that he came into the store?"

Joe shook his head.

"What about Ann? Can I ask her?"

Joe, who had been cooperative if reluctant, now bristled. "You leave Ann out of this. She don't want you prying into Mary Pat's business."

Why did the Sheehans treat him like some busybody from the Store? "For God's sake, Joe, your daughter's death wasn't an accident, it was a crime. Whoever wrote that prescription knew Mary Pat was sick, knew that the birth hadn't gone well. She should've been taken to the hospital. Instead, he tried to patch her up himself, and she died. That's reckless endangerment, and it's a felony. Don't you think Mary Pat deserves some justice for what was done to her?"

If he expected Mary Pat's father to be grateful for his concern, he was wrong. Tears streamed down Joe's face. He put his hand on the doorknob and backed away from Frank. "You can't give her justice, only God can. She's in heaven now. Just leave us alone."

Frank got back in the patrol car and massaged his temples. Might as well make the afternoon complete by visiting another relative who'd be unhappy at the news he had to deliver: Fred Jacobson.

Dean Jacobson's grandfather answered the door after a protracted period of shuffling and muffled shouts of "I'm coming, I'm coming." Frank followed him into the cramped and shabby living room. Amazing how similar old people's houses all smelled—the place exuded that trademark scent of mothballs, musty magazines and burnt toast. There was no sign of a young person's presence here.

Frank broke the news of the coroner's autopsy results and the old man bore it stoically.

"Drugs. I thought that might be it, but I didn't know what to do." He raised his hands, then let them fall back in his lap. "I'm too old for this. I raised my kids the best I knew how, but I just didn't know what to do about Dean."

"How did he come to be living here?" Frank asked.

"Both his parents died within a few months of each other, his last year in high school. Dean was angry about his folks passin', but it wasn't anybody's fault—heart attack, cancer, what can you do? He wasn't prepared to live on his own, but he didn't want to take no rules from me, neither. He worked some and gave me a little money, but it was like having a boarder here—he came and went on his own schedule."

"So you don't know who his friends were?"

"He never brought anyone here, and if fellows called when Dean wasn't home, they never left a message."

"You said he'd been acting strange lately?"

Fred nodded. "He came home one night and woke me up, he was talking so loud. I thought someone was here with him, but when I came out, it was just Dean alone, pacin' around the house, talking up a storm and not making a lick of sense."

"When was this?"

"About three weeks ago. After that, it seemed like he hardly slept. He was barely ever home, but when he was he was jumpy and nervous and always muttering to himself. I guess it was the drugs makin' him like that, huh?"

"I'm afraid so. Could I look around his room, Mr. Jacobson?"

"Sure." Fred led the way to a small bedroom in the back of the house. "It's real messy. I couldn't get him to clean it up."

If the rest of the house smelled of old age, Dean's room reeked of youth: sweat, unwashed clothes, and half-eaten food, over-laid with spray deodorant. Frank lifted the gray-sheeted mattress and immediately found what remained of Dean's drug stash. But an hour of sifting through the clutter of CDs, video games, magazines and clothes didn't produce an address book, or even any scribbled phone numbers that would provide a link to his friends.

After returning from the Jacobsons' house, Frank spent the rest of the day trying to come up with more evidence to support his suspicions of Dr. Galloway, but the facts just wouldn't cooperate. Galloway had graduated near the top of his class, had volunteered at an inner city health program in Washington, and got sterling recommendations for his job at the Cascade clinic. No patients had ever complained about him to the state medical board. He had no outstanding traffic violations, a good credit report despite his high debt, and neighbors who insisted he never entertained anyone at his apartment.

Frank hung up the phone after the last unproductive call and leaned back in his chair with his eyes closed. A vision of Mary Pat's baby flickered through his mind's eye: a little bundle wrapped in a blanket with only a shock of black hair and two dark eyes peeping out. He supposed he imagined her like that because the Finns had said the baby they were offered had been dark. Galloway had dark hair and eyes, but so did Doug Penniman and a thousand other guys.

The Finns said they didn't know who the father was, but he hadn't really quizzed them on whether Mary Pat or Sheltering Arms had dropped some hint about him. Frank smiled at himself. He knew the hint he'd like to hear—something along the lines of, "The baby will be smart because the father's a doctor." Still, it couldn't hurt to call the Finns and go over that again just to see if he'd missed anything.

He found their number in his file and dialed. A few clicks on the line, then the familiar three-note tone followed by a recorded voice: The number you have dialed, 518-555-1247, has been disconnected. Click.

Frank's hand tightened on the receiver. Had they changed their number for some reason? He dialed directory assistance, and gave them the Finns' name and address. No listing. He checked his file again for the name of the school where Brian Finn worked, and called the Buchanan Open Academy.

"Mr. Finn no longer works here," the secretary informed him.

What the hell was going on? Did the Finns have the baby all along, and now had run off with her? Was the story about being scammed by Sheltering Arms a scam too? Or had Sheltering Arms come back to the Finns after his visit, because they had coughed up the extra money?

Frank asked to speak to the principal, who became extremely chatty when he learned who Frank was. "It was the weirdest thing. He came into my office on Friday afternoon while I was out watching a field hockey game and left a letter of resignation. No explanation, no two weeks notice. Nothing. I called him up and the number was disconnected. I drove by his house and there's a for sale sign up and no one answered the door.

"He's always been very reliable, because I gave him a break. With that assault conviction he had, he couldn't have taught at a public school. I don't know what came over Brian—"

Frank knew what had come over him: the lure of a healthy white infant. Never mind sex or drugs or money—a baby had driven Brian and Eileen Finn to abandon their safe suburban life and go on the lam.

The principal sighed. "And I'm going to have a hell of a time replacing him."

"Why's that?"

"He taught social studies, computer science, and coached lacrosse. That's a combination you don't find every day."

"He taught computer science?"

"Oh yes, Brian was quite a whiz with computers."

Frank increased the tempo of the pencil he was tapping on his desk. So, when Brian had told him Sheltering Arms had disappeared into cyberspace and couldn't be traced, maybe he'd been lying. Maybe Brian had the computer skills to locate the group, even though he and Earl didn't. He should've gotten the state police computer guys involved. But whom was he kidding? Meyerson would never have approved that request.

But the Finns could be tracked down. After all, what did people like that know about creating a new identity for themselves? They'd want the money from the sale of their house; they'd want to teach again. All it would take to find them was a little time and some resources.

Neither of which he had.

Chapter 23

The smell of stale beer and fresh cigarette smoke engulfed Frank as soon as he entered the Mountainside Tavern looking for the men Sean Vinson had accused of vandalizing the trailer at the Extrom place. The decor of the Mountainside was no decor at all. Bar stools covered in black Naugahyde, virtually every one marked with huge fissures oozing dingy beige stuffing, surrounded the big U-shaped bar. The linoleum floor had probably been new when Truman was in the White House. Lit solely by the glow of two color TVs suspended over the bar, and a large, red neon Budweiser sign, the bar required games of pool, pinball and darts to be played largely by feel.

Frank groped his way to a seat at the bar, waiting for his eyes to adjust to the gloom. He ordered a hamburger and a beer, and asked the bartender if he had seen Dan, Pete or Richie recently.

"They turn up most nights around seven, seven-thirty."

Frank watched ESPN until, just as predicted, Dan Strohman sauntered in at 7:10. A few minutes later Pete and Richie plopped into bar stools beside their friend. Frank wasn't sure if they hadn't noticed him on the other side of the bar, or if they were avoiding eye contact. Soon, they wandered over to the pool table. Frank followed them.

"Nice shot," Frank said as Richie sank a ball in the corner pocket.

Richie glanced up and smiled, but his next shot went wide of the mark.

"You guys working much up at the Extrom place these days?"

All three of them exchanged glances. Dan took elaborate care sizing up his shot. Richie and Pete looked down at their feet. Honestly, they were like three six-year-olds standing next to a broken vase.

"They're doing the roofing now. Isn't that a specialty of yours, Pete?"

"Uh, yeah, I like to roof. But I'm busy now with another job."

"Where's that?"

"Um...um...Schroon Lake."

"What about you two?"

146

Dan and Pete eyed each other. Dan slammed his pool cue down on the table.

"Just spit it out! That fag Sean Vinson sent you here, didn't he?"

"He reported some vandalism—graffiti spray-painted on the work trailer. A threat to do more damage. I came here to warn you that wouldn't be a good idea," Frank said.

"This ain't right! That prick accuses us and you automatically believe him because he works for that rich asshole, Extrom," Richie complained.

"The fact that Rollie Fister at the hardware store remembers selling Pete three cans of orange spray paint would tend to support Vinson's theory," Frank answered. "Let me give you a heads-up—experienced criminals tend to buy their materials where they're not well-known."

Dan gave Pete a disgusted shove. "Nice work."

"We were pissed that day when he fired us." Pete jammed his hands in his jeans pockets. "We wouldn't really do nothin' to the house."

"It was just unfair, is all," Dan chimed in.

"Why's that?" Frank kept his face stern. He was interested in their side of the story, but he didn't want them to think they were off the hook yet.

"We couldn't make heads or tails of the blue print for this section we were supposed to be framing. We went to look for Sean, but we couldn't find him," Richie explained. "Finally, we just said, screw this, and did it the way that made the most sense to us. Then Sean shows up and has a shit fit and fires us."

"But what really griped my ass," Pete picked up the story, "is that Doug Penniman was there working with us the whole time and Sean didn't fire him."

"Why not?"

Pete shrugged. "Doug seems to know The Man himself. I saw him driving Extrom's Land Cruiser one day."

"Did you ask Doug about it?"

Pete shook his head. "I saw him at the lumberyard later that week. He caught sight of me and headed in the other direction. I figure he's embarrassed he hung us out to dry. But I ain't beggin' to be taken back up there. I don't need the work that bad."

"All right." Frank looked long and hard at the three of them. "Just see that you all stay away from the Extrom place. I don't want any more trouble."

Muttering and nodding, they returned to their game. Frank watched them for a moment longer. "Say, just out of curiosity, where did you see Doug driving Extrom's SUV?"

Pete leaned on his pool cue, watching his friend shoot. "He was coming out of the road right next to the sign for Beth Abercrombie's shop."

Frank left the tavern and cruised slowly toward town. Might as well make one last patrol before heading home. He passed the Stop'n'Buy—all the lights were on, but it was empty except for the new girl hired to replace Mary Pat. The sign for Beth's shop loomed in his headlights. He looked down the dark road that led to her home and wondered if Doug Penniman might be down there. He kept driving—he wouldn't stoop to spying on the woman.

The neon sign for Mountain Vista illuminated the next rise. The no vacancy part was lit—business must be good. A raccoon scrambled across the road in front of him, still fast enough to escape the wheels of the car despite being fattened up for winter. Frank glanced into the woods where the raccoon had disappeared. Were those headlights back there?

He slowed the patrol car and turned around in the Mountain Vista parking lot for a closer look. A few years ago a developer had bought this land with the intention of building some homes back there. But he'd gotten only as far as clearing some of the trees and creating a rough track into the property before he ran out of funding. Now, couples drove back there to park and kids hung out and drank. Mr. Patel had complained more than once about noise and broken beer bottles thrown in the road. Frank positioned the patrol car so the headlights shone into the trees. He could see a car, sure enough.

He got out and prepared to walk back there with his flashlight. He couldn't see anyone in the car—either it was empty, or he was about to get an eyeful. A few steps closer and he could distinguish the color and make of the car. Beige, a small Ford. Another step. A Ford Escort. Good grief, it was Earl's car! What was he...?

Frank stopped and began to laugh. Earl was here with Melanie. Both of them lived with their parents, so there was precious little privacy at home. It was getting nippy out now, but he supposed the inside of the Escort was warm enough.

FRANK SAT ALONE AT the Formica table in front of the big plate glass window at the Store. The generically named emporium in the center of town carried just about everything but what you really needed. Dusty valentines and St. Patrick's Day cards stayed on the rack year-round; there were toothbrushes but no toothpaste; baking powder but no flour; grated cheese but no spaghetti. Frank hated to buy milk there ever since he discovered the little Styrofoam deli containers on the same shelf in the fridge held nightcrawlers, not cole slaw. But you couldn't beat the Store's coffee.

A fruitless morning spent trying to track down the Finns, interspersed with nagging doubts about Beth Abercrombie, had driven Frank out of the office in search of a fresh cup and a sticky bun to clear his jumbled thoughts. Mercifully, the place was empty except for Rita cleaning up behind the deli counter.

The sugar and caffeine weren't helping him come up with a logical reason for why Doug Penniman should be driving Extrom's car past Beth's place. He could have been going somewhere else on the road, but the only other homes back there were vacation places. Still, he might have a carpentry project lined up with one of the homeowners. But why would he be driving Extrom's expensive vehicle to a moonlighting job?

Why did he care, anyway? Was he jealous that Doug and Beth might have something going on? Doug was good-looking, in a way, but he didn't seem Beth's type. *Right. Not like me.*

Frank watched Augie Enright emerge from the side door of the church and head toward the Store. You could set your watch by that man: morning coffee break at 10:15, afternoon break at 2:45. Frank wasn't in the mood to gulp his coffee so he resigned himself to the handyman's company.

Augie's eyes lit up as he came in and saw Frank. He poured his coffee, tossed fifty cents in the cigar box on the counter and sat down next to him. "Hiya, Frank. What's new? Green Tomorrow planning any more demonstrations?"

"Nope."

"Any news on Mary Pat's baby?"

"Nope."

Augie would talk to a statue, so Frank's taciturn mood didn't discourage him. He chatted on about the weather, fishing, football, until a tall man and his little girl came in. But Augie's face fell when he called out, "Nice afternoon, eh?" and they walked right past him without answering.

The man was Rod Extrom and he'd committed the ultimate breech of Store etiquette—failure to greet all other customers, whether you knew them or not. Frank and Augie watched in silence as Extrom paid for a quart of orange juice and a candy bar. "Here, Alyssa," he said and handed the candy to the child, who had shiny black hair and almond eyes. Those were the only words he spoke, and then they left.

"Humpf," said Augie, before the door had fully swung shut. "I guess some people think they're too important to even say hello to folks."

"He's always like that," Rita said. "As many times as he's been in here, he looks right through me like he's never seen me before. And his daughter's just as bad."

"I guess she must be adopted," Augie speculated. "I seen the wife a few times and she's not oriental. You can get lots of girl babies over there in China, you know, but they won't give up any of their boys. Guess Mr. Extrom'll have to go somewhere else if he wants a son."

Frank sat up and took interest in Augie's prattle for the first time since he'd started talking, but the handyman was already on a new tack. He turned his attention to the fliers taped up in the window. "I hear that garage sale at the Feeney's this Saturday is really going to be something. But some of these signs are awful old." Augie pulled down a yellow one with musical notes floating across it. "Don't need this anymore. The summer concert series is over."

Frank picked it up. He'd enjoyed the concerts, when everyone brought their lawn chairs to the green and listened to performers in the Gazebo, ate pie and coffee at intermission, and heard the last notes die away in the dark. "Some of those concerts were really good. I liked those four girls who sang in close harmony." He was willing to chat if it wasn't about his work.

"Yeah, they've gotten a lot better since Constance Stiler came back and took over organizing them."

"What do you mean 'came back and took over'?"

"Constance Stiler's a local girl. She and her husband were both from Keene Valley. But they moved away for better jobs years ago. Then they came back after he retired, and she started organizing the concerts. She gets musicians from all over. But who knows if she'll do it for much longer."

"Why not?"

"Her husband's really failing. If he dies, maybe she'll go live near her kids. 'Course, she's friends with a lot of ladies at the church. And she does have her job."

"Job? I thought they were retired?" Frank asked.

Augie leaned forward confidingly. "No sooner did he stop working than he got that Parkinson's disease. Insurance don't pay for all the special medicine he needs, so she went back to work part time. She's a nurse over at the Cascade Clinic."

Now Augie had his full attention. "Really?"

"They say she practically runs the place. They'd take her on full time but she don't want to be away from her husband all day, every day."

"Understandable," Frank murmured. It looked like another visit to the Clinic was in order.

Augie sighed. "It's sad. You make plans, and sometimes life just don't cooperate."

Frank closed his eyes briefly and saw Estelle at the piano, Caroline tossing him a Frisbee, the command room at the precinct house. "You can say that again."

Leaving the Store, Frank nearly tripped over a bundle on the steps. The bundle raised its head.

"Why, hello, Olivia. What are you doing out here?"

"No school today. Waitin' for my uncle to pick me up."

"Where is he?"

She shrugged. "The Mountainside, probably."

This could be a long wait, and it was getting gray and cold. "You can't stay out here in that thin jacket. Why don't you go inside and wait?"

Olivia shook her head. "Ain't allowed in if I'm not buyin' anything."

Frank tugged on her hand. "Well, come on—I'll buy you a cup of hot chocolate, how would that be?"

Olivia shook her head again. "Miz Sobel don't like me. She won't let me stay in there."

Frank looked up and saw Rita glaring from behind the cash register. Probably afraid the poor kid would lift a roll of Life Savers.

"Then you better come over to my office. We'll watch for your uncle from the window."

Olivia hesitated, but a strong gust of wind convinced her. She trotted across the green at Frank's side.

"Do you want a snack?" Frank asked as he settled her in an office chair.

"OK." Her tone stayed indifferent, but her eyes darted around avidly looking for where the food might spring from.

Frank didn't know what to give Olivia from the trove of junk food in Earl's bottom desk drawer. He felt justified in plying his grandsons with Oreos and peanut butter cups because their mother had convinced them that whole wheat pretzels and yogurt were treats. But he could take no joy in offering Olivia candy and cookies, not when she probably subsisted on a diet of Hawaiian Punch and Devil Dogs and Cheetos. Her baby teeth were like two brown rows of Indian corn. No doubt her mother had put her to bed every night with a bottle of juice, or worse.

Casting about the office, his eyes fell on a sack of Winesap apples he'd bought at the farmer's market. He quartered and pared one with his pocketknife, afraid that if he let Olivia bite right into the apple, her rotten, little teeth would break off in the crispy fruit. "This is one of my all-time favorite snacks," Frank said as he set the apple on a paper towel before her.

Olivia did not seem to share his enthusiasm, but she reached out a grubby hand to take a slice. "What's that stuff?"

"Just some files I'm working on." Frank sat down at his desk and began to go through his paperwork, but he could feel Olivia's eyes boring into him.

He looked up. "So, Olivia, what grade are you in?"

"Second."

"You like school?"

"I like the library. That's where I go at recess."

"Not out to play?"

"The other kids make fun of me." Olivia's hand traveled back to the desk for two more slices of apple.

Geez, this kid could take your heart and hang it out to dry. "Do you have any brothers or sisters?" Maybe that was a safer topic.

"I had a brother, but he went away."

He hoped she meant he'd left to get a job, not to go to prison. He didn't get a chance to ask.

Olivia pushed back from the desk and headed over the shelves in the corner. "What's in here?" she asked over her shoulder, shaking a colorful bag from the bookstore in Lake Placid.

Before he could answer, Olivia had fallen to her knees in front of the shelf and slid out the contents of the bag.

"I bought some books for my grandsons. You can read them if you like," Frank offered.

Olivia picked up the top book in the stack. "*The Three Little Wolves and the Big Bad Pig*," she read the title aloud. "That ain't right."

"It's a joke—in this version, the pig's the bad guy, but it has a happy ending," Frank explained.

She shot him a dubious look. Olivia wasn't one to suffer fools gladly.

"What kind of books did Mary Pat read to you?"

Olivia's eyes lit up. "*Charlie and the Chocolate Factory*—that was a really funny book. It took us a while to finish it because...because she couldn't come to my house that often."

"What other books did you read?"

"We read *Little House on the Prairie*. She brought it with her. To my house, I mean." Olivia dropped her eyes. "I'm going to read this book now."

Frank watched her lips move slightly as her stubby finger traced down each page. She certainly seemed to have shared some favorite books with Mary Pat. And yet she seemed so jumpy when he asked her about it. Reaching the end, Olivia shut the book with a snap. "That was stupid."

Frank really liked the book. "I think they're just trying to show that it's impossible to keep your enemies locked out, so you're better off making friends with them."

"It don't work like that," Olivia stated in a tone that ended all further discussion. She crossed to the window. "There's my uncle. I better go."

Frank watched Olivia walk into the wind toward her uncle's truck. He tensed as he saw Ralph shaking his fist and stamping his foot, obviously irritated that she'd had the nerve to keep him waiting even a minute. If he hit that kid, he'd find his ass in the holding cell. But Ralph simply flung open the passenger side door, and threw the truck in gear before Olivia could even sit down.

Chapter 24

Frank didn't have long to contemplate the Veech family dynamics. A state police patrol car pulled up in front and Lew Meyerson got out. He saw Frank standing in the window and raised his hand. A moment later he was sprawled across an office chair in a most unMeyerson-like pose.

The lieutenant kneaded his eyes. "This case is driving me crazy."

It wasn't like Lew to come looking for sympathy. Frank sat down behind his desk and put his feet up. "Tell me all about it."

"The FBI has interviewed everyone who has the slightest connection with the Green Tomorrow operation out in Oregon—both opponents and supporters. Everyone can account for their time—no trips to the East Coast, no unexplained absences."

"Could they have hired someone out here to do the job?"

Meyerson shrugged. "You know the kind of low-lifes who sign on to be contract killers. How could someone like that sneak up on Golding early in the morning on a hiking trail and kill him at point-blank range? How could they even know he'd be there?"

"You're right—it seems likely it was someone he knew," Frank agreed. "Have you learned anything more about the organization?"

"A bundle. The FBI auditors have been combing through Green Tomorrow's books. Get this—the IRS no longer classifies Green Tomorrow as a tax-exempt non-profit organization. Because of all their political activism, the IRS considers them a lobbying group. It was an enormous blow to their fundraising. If you make a contribution to, say, the Sierra Club, you get a tax deduction; if you make a donation to Green Tomorrow, you get squat."

"So how do they stay afloat? Neither Golding nor his wife has any other job."

Meyerson rose and began to pace around. "The auditors are trying to follow the money trail. All they'll tell us right now is that it's *not* coming from the small donations of thousands of individual contributors."

"What does Meredith Golding have to say about it?"

"Get this—she has a master's degree in some field I can't even pronounce, but when the Feds questioned her about the books, she suddenly turned into a bimbo who wouldn't know how to write a check to pay the gas bill. 'I have no idea,' Meyerson mimicked in a high-pitched voice. 'My husband handled all that.' or 'You'd have to ask our lawyer, Barry Sutter.'"

"So where does that leave you?" Frank asked.

"Nowhere," Meyerson plopped back down in his chair. "The Feds are pressuring us to come up with more local suspects, now that none of their west coast possibilities have panned out. But we're working in the dark—they won't share a lot of what they've discovered on the financial end." Lew snorted. "It's *classified*."

Frank wasn't particularly interested in Meyerson's power-struggle problems. He honed in on the first thing he'd said. "Local suspects? Like who?"

"The Fenstocks of course. All the women who were at that protest march. All the people who spoke up at that Town Council meeting."

"Now wait a minute, no one from around here..." as the words came out of his mouth Frank knew he sounded just like a Trout Run native and he changed tacks. "Abe Fenstock didn't even know about Green Tomorrow's plans until after Golding was killed," he pointed out, in what he hoped was a reasonable tone.

"So he claims—we'll check on that a little further. And Beth Abercrombie and Katie Petrucci knew the score before Golding was killed. Maybe they're–"

"What? Double agents?"

Meyerson bristled at the sarcasm. "I thought you wanted to help. Guess I was wrong."

Now he and Lew were back to their familiar antagonism.

"I do want to help. But let's follow the most likely leads first. I just..." Was he trying to use his influence to steer Meyerson away from Beth? Ridiculous–she had nothing to hide. Did she?

"I just think," Frank continued, "that we never have gotten to the bottom of what brought Green Tomorrow to Trout Run in the first place. If we could figure that out, we might make progress on who killed Golding."

Lew relaxed a bit and nodded. "You've got a point."

"Doesn't Golding have kids from his first marriage? Are they involved in the organization?"

"Two sons," Lew stood up and bounced on the balls of his feet. "Daniel, in San Mateo, California. And Neil, an orthodontist in Nyack. Both estranged from the old man."

"Nyack's only four hours away. Did you check him out?" Frank knew that they must have, but Lew tended to reveal more information when he thought he was setting Frank straight.

"Iron-clad alibi. Was with his nurse and a steady stream of patients from eight A.M. on. Not enough time to kill Golding and get back to Nyack by eight."

"What did he say about his father's personal life? Maybe this murder has nothing to do with Golding's environmental work."

"Says he hasn't spoken to his father in over a year. I don't think he knows anything."

Maybe not, but Frank had seen Meyerson interviewing suspects and he felt the trooper had a tendency to charge ahead, trampling any subtle innuendoes. He wouldn't mind talking to Neil Golding himself, and it didn't hurt that Nyack was only twenty-five minutes away from Chappaqua. Following up a lead on a case would give him a very good reason to drop in on Caroline and figure out what the hell was going on there.

"Well, I'll keep poking around here," Frank assured Meyerson. "I'll see what I can turn up on why Green Tomorrow's so interested in Raging Rapids."

"Thanks, Frank." Meyerson nodded curtly. "I know I can count on you."

THE NEXT DAY, FRANK pulled into Caroline's driveway, right behind her minivan. Good, that meant she was home, and he was quite sure the boys would be in nursery school. He went up to the back door and raised his hand to knock, but lowered it again as he looked into the house. He could see his daughter standing in profile, holding a mug in her hands and gazing out the kitchen window. He watched her for quite a while; she never drank from the mug or turned her head toward him. Then she rubbed the back of her hand against her cheek, as if brushing away a tear.

He knocked.

Caroline jumped, then smiled as she came to answer the door. At least she looked happy to see him.

"Daddy! What are you doing here?"

He said nothing, only pulled her into a tight embrace, glad that her curly, dark-haired head still fit right under his chin. She returned the hug, but when he didn't let her go she pulled away and looked at him with her head cocked.

"What's wrong?"

"What's wrong with me? What's wrong with *you*?"

"Nothing. Nothing's wrong."

Frank banged his fist on the doorframe. "Godammit, Caroline, don't lie to me. You've been avoiding me and cutting me short on the phone. I know something's wrong. That's why I came down here. You're sick, aren't you? And you don't want to tell me."

"Daddy, don't be silly." Caroline spread her arms. "Look at me—I'm as healthy as a horse."

True, she didn't look ill, but she didn't look great either. Her face seemed strained and taut. And her pants drooped on her slender hips, like she'd lost weight.

"It's one of the boys, then, isn't it? Something is worrying you, I know it."

"The boys are fine." They faced each other stubbornly as they had so many times when she'd been a teenager. Frank remembered how she'd once stuck insistently to the story that she was sleeping at a girlfriend's house when he had incontrovertible proof that she'd been drinking and dancing at a club downtown. She didn't crack easily under pressure, so he shamelessly hauled out the parent's personal grenade launcher: guilt.

"This rift between us is killing me, Caroline. I know if your mother were here, you'd be able to tell her. Can't you just tell me? No matter how bad it is, it's better than not knowing."

Immediately, she was crying and clinging to him. "Oh, Daddy, I'm sorry," she gasped through her tears. "I just didn't want to worry you. Besides, it's nothing you can help with."

He sat her down at the kitchen table and handed her a box of tissues. "Don't be so sure."

She bristled. "You always think you can fix anything, Daddy. This is different."

He did have a tendency to think he could fix anything, from broken toasters to broken hearts. And Caroline wasn't the first person to find it annoying. He reached out and took her hand. "Tell me. Please."

She wiped her face and looked down at her trembling fingers. "It's Eric. Things aren't working out. We're separated."

He might have known it; he'd never trusted that pompous jerk. "What is it?" he demanded. "Is he running around with another woman?"

Caroline looked up in amazement. "Daddy! Of course not. Eric would never do that."

"Well then, what?"

Caroline shrugged. "We just have different values. He wants me to get rid of my minivan and replace it with some big, stupid SUV. And you know why? Because it's a status symbol. The van embarrasses him."

No one got divorced because they couldn't agree on what car to buy. She wasn't telling him the whole truth. A terrible thought popped into his mind. "He didn't he hit you, did he?"

Caroline jumped up from the table. "Don't be ridiculous. I'm telling you, we just can't agree on anything anymore. Like, for instance, he wants the boys to get special tutoring so they'll pass the test to get into this ritzy private school. Can you imagine anything so insane? They're three years old, for God's sake."

"Private school? I thought you bought this house because it's so close to that nice elementary school in town."

"Exactly. The public schools here are terrific." Caroline paced around the kitchen, waving her hands as she spoke. "But suddenly Eric says the boys won't get into Harvard if they don't go to the right prep school, and they won't get into the right prep school unless they go to the right kindergarten. It's crazy, and I want no part of it."

Frank happened to agree with his daughter about the SUV and the private school, but surely this wasn't enough to end a marriage. "All married couples have disagreements, honey. Maybe you should see a marriage counselor."

"I found a wonderful counselor. We went once, and Eric said he didn't like her and wouldn't go again."

"So you're divorcing him?" Frank couldn't keep the disapproval out of his voice.

"It's not the car and the school, per se," Caroline tossed the wild tumble of curls out of her eyes. "They're symbolic. It just shows how far apart we've grown."

Oh, symbolism. Now they were wading into deep water. All he knew was his grandsons were about to become statistics, part of the fifty percent of children brought up in a broken home. And he didn't like the symbolism of that, not one little bit.

He studied his daughter silently as she stormed around the kitchen, collecting sticky cups and spoons and slamming them into the dishwasher. All her life he'd tried to protect her from her own headstrong impulses, rarely with any success. He'd lectured and threatened and cajoled, but she'd always had to make her own mistakes before she learned anything. He supposed she'd inherited that from him. He didn't want to sit back and watch her make this mistake, but he didn't know what to do to stop her.

He wanted to deliver a sermon about the sanctity of marriage vows, the necessity of commitment, the obligation she bore to her sons. Instead, he asked her a question.

"Why didn't you tell me about this sooner?"

The anger drained out of her and she stood before him with her head hanging. "I didn't want to disappoint you. You've always been so proud of me. I've never screwed up like this before. And you and Mom had the perfect marriage—I never thought it would be so hard."

It was true; she had led a charmed life. Even when he'd thought she'd fail, she hadn't. He rose and held her in his arms, rubbing her back like he used to when she was a child. Eventually he began to tell her a story. A story about another young woman who had made a mistake and hadn't wanted her parents to know. Another girl who hadn't wanted to disappoint the parents she loved, and had paid the ultimate price.

Caroline pulled away and dried her eyes. "Oh, Daddy, that's so sad. What would you have done if I'd gotten pregnant when I was single?"

"We would have supported you in whatever decision you made: keep the baby, give it up, have an abortion. Just like I'll support you now, whatever you decide."

She smiled at him shakily. "But you do have an opinion."

"I think you should try a little harder. Find a different marriage counselor. Keep working at the problems."

Her eyes welled up again. "I don't think it will do any good. I'm not sure I love Eric anymore."

"Your mother wasn't sure she loved me, but she stuck with me."

"Oh, Daddy, Mom adored you and you know it."

"Sure, all the time you can remember. But those early days were rough. We got married too young, had you too soon, never had enough money. I was always working, or in school. I remember your mother looking me in the eye and saying those very words. 'I'm not sure I love you anymore.' "

He had her hooked now. "What did you do?"

"Luckily, we were too overwhelmed to start a divorce, and eventually things got better. I finished my degree. She started to teach. We had more money. Most of all, we each stopped trying to win every argument." Frank studied the mechanism of a pepper mill he'd picked up from the table. "I guess when all the other stuff dropped away, your mom decided she loved me after all. Thank God."

Cautiously, he looked up. Caroline's eyes blinked rapidly. "I love you, too."

Chapter 25

Frank drove the fifteen miles between Caroline's house and Neil Golding's, loudly singing his favorite old hymns.

"Sometimes I get discouraged, and think my life's in vain;
But then the Holy Spirit restores my faith ag-a-i-n."

The stone that had weighed his heart for these last few months had crumbled. Not that he didn't still worry about this crisis in Caroline's marriage. But at least now he had a focus for his worry, instead of being plagued by constant uncertainty. And now he knew the problem wasn't him.

"There is a balm in Gilead to soothe the sin sick soul," he sang as he swung around bends in the road leading through the prosperous town. "Balm in Gilead" was the song that had brought him and Estelle together. She had heard him harmonizing on the tenor line as he sat behind her in church. She'd turned around and smiled. And the rest was history.

Estelle hadn't learned until much later that he'd only gone to church that Sunday to try to finagle an introduction to her. By that time, she'd taken him on as a project, trying to train his voice and tame his ornery disposition. The poor woman hadn't had much luck with either, but she'd never stopped trying.

Frank reached a crossroads and took a left toward Nyack. Neil Golding had been quite friendly on the phone yesterday, almost as if he were hoping someone else in law enforcement would be coming to talk to him. In a few minutes Frank pulled into the circular drive in front of Golding's McMansion. He rang the bell and listened as the Westminster chimes echoed out to him. A man in his early thirties soon opened the door and ushered him into a cavernous, and completely empty, foyer. Through an archway, Frank could see a preschooler gleefully riding a plastic trike on the polished hardwood floor of what would have been the formal living room, had it contained any furniture.

Neil Golding followed Frank's glance. "We let Joshua ride in there. After all, it's his house too. Come on back here—I'll get you a soda."

Frank followed him to the rear of the huge house. Neil seemed awfully chipper for a man whose father had recently been murdered. They settled themselves on plush sofas in the family room. Toys encroached from every side—dolls and trucks galore, stacks of videos, bins of art supplies, a miniature kitchen, a tool bench, basketball hoop and even a child-sized doctor's office.

Frank pulled out a GI Joe that poked him from behind a cushion. "This is quite a set-up you've got here."

"I know it's too much," Neil said. "My wife yells at me. But I want Josh to have everything I missed out on as a kid. My brother and I never had anything to play with but wooden blocks and this awful homemade play-doh my mother used to mix up."

"Why's that?"

The floodgates opened. Probably Neil Golding's wife and friends were sick of hearing about his deprived childhood, but Frank was a fresh audience. He couldn't have shut Golding up if he'd tried. He heard about how Golding and his brother had been forced to attend a dangerous urban public school to show solidarity with the underclass, and had been denied every simple pleasure of American childhood, from *Gilligan's Island* reruns and Wonder Bread to Little League and Juicy-Fruit.

Neil Golding leaned forward, breathless with his recitation of injustice. "Once, my little brother Danny wanted this stuffed dog. He looked at it every day in the window of a store on our block. A gentle, soft, cuddly puppy—what could be wrong with that? So my mother bought it for him for his birthday. When Danny opened it he was so excited. And my Dad took it away from him and returned it to the store. You know why?"

No choice but to bite. "Why?"

"Because it was made in China. The factory probably exploited its workers. That was my father—you couldn't win with him. I've never forgiven him for that. And for what he did to my mother."

This was getting closer to the mark. "What was that?"

"For twenty years she did his bidding—living in that crummy apartment in Red Hook, working in the Green Tomorrow office without pay. And how did he repay her? He dumped her for that bitch, Meredith."

"How did he meet her?"

"She was a Green Tomorrow volunteer, just like all the others. He'd had affairs before. My mother knew about them, but they always blew over. But not Meredith—she got him by the balls. I don't know what she has, but for the first time in his life, my father was in the passenger seat and Meredith was behind the wheel."

"Well, she is attractive, and she seems like she might come from money, no?"

Neil snorted. "Pretty, rich girls from Vassar and Smith were my father's stock-in-trade. No, I think it was because she's an even bigger bullshit artist than he was.

"When he met her, he was just about burned out. He'd been doing this environmental protest gig for two decades, and what did he have to show for it? Everyone recycles their soda cans; meanwhile, the planet's burning up. Meredith came along with all these ideas for flashy, symbolic campaigns to get media attention and raise money. She breathed new life into Green To- morrow, and she convinced my father that he couldn't get along without her."

"You seem to know all about it. I thought you were estranged from your father?"

"When I was in college, I used to work in the Green Tomorrow office in the summers." Neil rolled his eyes. "It was the family business. So I was there when Meredith first came on the scene. After he left my mother, I didn't speak to him for over two years. But when I started dating Robin, my wife, she thought I should try to patch things up." Neil sighed. "She comes from a nice, normal family—she just didn't understand.

"So I started to see him again. But Meredith always found a way to horn in. I couldn't stand the way he kowtowed to her. And I couldn't listen to all her crap about email broadcasts and Web rings and media alerts. I never thought I could be nostalgic for all those candle-light vigils and rainy protest marches."

"It sounds like Meredith was taking over Green Tomorrow, pushing your father out."

Neil shook his head. "No, not that extreme. He needed her, but she need- ed him too. Meredith has no people skills. She's too abrasive. My father's charm is what rallied the troops, kept the reporters interested."

"But you stopped seeing him again?"

"We argued over that stunt Meredith organized out in Colorado."

"Bombing the earth-moving equipment? I thought it was some local supporters who got carried away?"

"That's what Meredith put out in her public statement. But behind the scenes, she was crowing about how she'd pulled it off." Neil shook his head. "She could've got someone killed!

"I never saw him after that. He came here to visit Joshua—I stayed at the office. Robin was worried I'd be devastated that we were on bad terms when he died. But you know what? I heard the news and I didn't feel a thing."

Chapter 26

Frank strode into the office the next morning with an air of determination that warned Doris to stay out of his way. He flung open the door to his inner office in time to see two heads huddled over some papers on Earl's desk snap up.

"Hello, Melanie," Frank said as he glared at Earl. "What can I do for you?"

"Uh....nothing. I was just leaving." Melanie fumbled for her purse, exchanged a long, soulful glance with Earl, and scuttled out the door.

"Do you see that girl morning, noon and night? Do you think you can find time to wedge a little work into your schedule?" Frank snapped.

"Sorry."

"What time does Katie Petrucci start up that nursery school of hers?" Frank barked in response.

"I see the moms dropping off their kids at nine."

"Good. I'll head over there now and catch her before she starts working. Then I'm going over to the Cascade Clinic."

He gulped down a cup of Doris's bitter brew, shuddered, and headed out the door to the Presbyterian Church. No one was in the church office, and Frank headed down the hall toward a door covered with construction paper leaves and letters that spelled Fall into a Good Book. Walking into the room without knocking, he found Katie and Dee-Dee Peele setting out art supplies.

"Good morning, ladies."

Deedee looked up and smiled. Katie looked up and glared.

Probably he shouldn't have referred to them as "ladies." He kept forgetting the rules. "Painting pumpkins today? That oughta be fun."

"The children will be here soon. Is there a point to your visit?" Katie demanded.

Deedee looked shocked at her friend's rudeness. "I think I'll go to the kitchen and see to the snacks," she said, and scurried away.

Frank picked up a small pumpkin and passed it from hand to hand. "I hope there's no hard feelings about the protest last week. I just want you to know we're working hard on trying to track down that truck. You haven't had any more trouble, have you?"

Katie shook her head. "A few nasty phone calls, but you have to expect that as an activist."

"You went to NYU, I believe someone told me. Is that a very politically active school?"

"It's a big school—some people are politically engaged, others just care about parties and grades," Katie answered as she struggled to pull a bag of art smocks off a high shelf.

"Nathan Golding lived in New York City." Frank handed the bag down to her. "Did you meet him when you were in college?"

"I didn't meet him there, but I heard him speak. He was very inspiring."

"So you got involved with Green Tomorrow?"

Katie shook her head and paused from filling cups with yellow paint. This little walk down memory lane seemed to be warming her up a bit. "I kept in touch with their activities. But at the time I was totally committed to helping the people of Peru, who lived in poverty under an oppressive, U.S.-backed regime. I was in Peru for almost two years."

Frank nodded sympathetically, and picked up the blue paint to help fill the cups. "You have to choose your priorities. So after that, you moved back here, started a family. Probably didn't have much time for activism when the kids were babies, huh?"

Katie sighed. "You tell yourself you're not going to let children totally change your life..."

"But they do," Frank finished her sentence with a smile. "You love 'em, but they soak up your energy like little sponges, don't they?"

"Exactly!" Katie looked pleasantly surprised at his perception. "But starting this nursery school was my way of combining my commitment to my children with my commitment to build a better world. You see, we offer a non-sexist, non-racist, non-authoritarian approach to learning..."

"And that's just what this town needed," Frank chimed in. "Get the kids away from those violent TV shows, right?"

Katie set down her paint and leaned across the table. "You wouldn't *believe* how much TV these kids watch!"

Oh, he was playing her like a fiddle now. If he could just manage not to blow his advantage. "So, I imagine your curriculum here also includes information about the environment?"

"Of course, and that's how I got interested in Green Tomorrow again. I was up late one night, searching for environmental stuff on the Internet I could use in class, when I stumbled across Green Tomorrow's web site."

Frank had already visited the site and he knew there was nothing on it about Raging Rapids, or even the Adirondacks in general. "And did it have anything useful to you?"

"Oh, nothing I could use for school, but I did sign up to be on their e-list to receive advisories about important environmental issues."

"And you received news about the protest against Raging Rapids on that list?"

Katie hesitated. "No, I got an email directly from Nathan one day at the end of August. He said he was going to be in our area and wanted to meet with local supporters."

"To talk to you about Raging Rapids?"

"He didn't mention it in the email; he told me about it when we met. Why?"

He could feel her beginning to turn on him again. "Katie, did you ever ask him how he first got interested in Raging Rapids? I mean, what even made him think to look there for environmental problems? It's a pretty obscure spot."

Katie got that "I'm ready to start spouting a lot of left wing hot air" look. "Nathan's always been concerned with threatened species. With the Bicknell's Thrush's habitat being destroyed right here in Nathan's home state, I don't think it's at all surprising that he'd get involved."

"Well, if he's so worried about that bird, how come he didn't protest the building of the Extrom house?"

Something in Frank's question made her pause; she cocked her head like a dog that hears something his owner can't. "I'm, I'm not sure. . ."

Encouraged by the hesitation, Frank pressed on. "The state police think someone local may have killed Golding. Like one of you protesters, or Abe Fenstock. But—"

A door slammed and high-pitched shrieks echoed down the hall along with the thunder of dozens of little feet. Shit! Just when he was making headway. Deedee appeared in the doorway with a crowd of kids.

But Katie seemed to stare right through them. "Deedee, please lead them in circle time. I'll be right back." She motioned for Frank to follow her across the hall to an empty Sunday school classroom.

Katie sat at a round table and ran her fingers though her wild, curly hair. She cradled her head in her hands and stared at the scarred tabletop. A minute passed in silence.

Frank cleared his throat. "As I was saying, Abe didn't even know what Green Tomorrow was up to until after Golding was killed, did he?"

Katie looked up and met his eye. "Stan knew."

"Stan Fenstock knew about Green Tomorrow's plans? Why didn't he tell his father and brother?"

"Because apparently he's wanted to cash out of the business to do something else. But his father and brother can't afford to pay him for his share. He figured the protests might push them to sell Raging Rapids, and he'd get his third."

"And Stan was perfectly open about this with you and Golding?"

Katie jumped up from her seat and began to pace around the room, gnawing on her thumb. "I've never spoken to Stan. I got all this from Nathan. He said Stan stumbled across him when he was taking those pictures we used in the slide show. When Stan realized what Nathan was doing, he offered to work behind the scenes for our side." She paused in her pacing and looked at Frank.

"But something doesn't feel right to you?"

"I don't know. I don't know if Stan really wants that money from the state. It's hard to believe he'd turn on his own family to get it. And, like you said, I'm not sure why Nathan opposed Raging Rapids, but not the Extrom house." Katie shook her head. "Nathan was very charismatic—"

"So I've heard."

"When you were talking to him, he could make anything sound reasonable. But now that he's gone...." Katie's sentence trailed off, her usual take-no-prisoners attitude evaporated.

"What about Meredith? Does she have any explanations?"

"She's nothing like Nathan. She can be very dismissive, especially if you question her judgment."

Frank was silent for a moment before he began his final approach. "Katie, I don't pretend to know all that much about South American politics, but I do remember a story that was in the papers a few years ago. An idealistic young American woman went down to Peru as a teacher or nurse or something. Somehow, she ended up providing shelter to some Shining Path revolutionaries. She got arrested and thrown in prison after a sham trial. It was pretty clear from this article that she'd been set up—the government needed to show it was cracking down, and the opposition offered her up like a sacrificial lamb. The two sides were in collusion, and the American was the dupe."

Katie's mouth had dropped open slightly. "Lori Berenson," she whispered. "She's still in prison there."

Their eyes met for a long moment, two people whose preconceived notions about each other were crumbling away.

Katie shoved her hands in her jeans' pockets and stared down at her boots. "I honestly believe the world would be a better place if Raging Rapids were turned into a hiking trail."

"And maybe it should be. But think—is that all Green Tomorrow is after?"

"I don't know. But I'll find out. I won't be played for a fool."

FRANK LEFT THE NURSERY school debating whether to go directly to Raging Rapids to confront Stan Fenstock, or hang back a while and see what Katie could turn up. He thought Katie might be more effective at ferreting out the truth, but he wasn't entirely sure that he trusted her. As he walked back into the office, Doris began flapping her left hand at him as her right hand clutched the phone.

"Wait, wait—he just came in," she yelled into the receiver. Then she turned to Frank. "It's Trudy Massinay."

Frank went into his office and shut the door on Doris. "Hi Trudy, any luck with Diane?"

"No. In fact, I'm getting sort of worried."

"Worried? Why?"

"I called her home several times and no one ever answered," Trudy explained. "I called the bait shop, and they said she hadn't come in to work since she ran out on you. Finally, I got through to the father. He was very nasty, and said something like 'the slut's taken off with her boyfriend.'

"Then I decided to go over to the Rock Slide, since you said she had a friend there. The friend claims that Diane's boyfriend has been out of the picture for months. She said she and Mrs. Sarens haven't seen or heard from Diane in days. Mrs. Sarens wanted to call the police, but the husband wouldn't let her."

"So you're telling me that–"

"Diane Sarens has disappeared."

WHEN FRANK ARRIVED at the Clinic, the parking lot was packed, so he knew what to expect inside. The receptionist responded to his request to speak to both Dr. Galloway and Constance Stiler with a grimace and a deep sigh.

Frank glared at her. "It's important."

"They're both with patients—you'll have to wait until they're through."

Five minutes passed before movement across the room made him look up from an ancient copy of *Sports Illustrated*.

"Stand there, Dora, while I make our next appointment," a familiar voice commanded. Judy Penniman stood before the receptionist's counter carefully prying an old lady's gnarled fingers from their iron grasp on her right arm. The frail woman swayed and Frank poised to jump up, but Judy had the situation under control. Gently, she placed the woman's cane in her right hand and propped her against the wall. The man closest to them offered his seat but Judy waved him off. "No, if she sits, we'll never get her up again, right Dora?"

Dora smiled faintly, sensing a joke even if she couldn't understand it. Judy turned back to the receptionist. "He wants to see her next week. Can you fit her in on Thursday morning? I already have an appointment for Nate Beegley then."

"Sure, kill two birds with one stone," the receptionist answered. "And we'll see you again Monday, right?"

Judy rolled her eyes. "Yeah, Esther and her bunions." They both laughed.

Judy never noticed Frank among the crowd in the waiting room. When she had left, Frank sauntered up to the desk. "Sounds like Judy Penniman is a regular here."

The receptionist answered without looking away from her computer. "Yeah, she brings clients in a few times a week. She works for the County Board of Social Services—bringing old folks to the doctor is a service they provide."

So, Judy Penniman also had ready access to the prescription pads at the clinic. As an LPN, she'd have some knowledge of the type of medication Mary Pat would need, but maybe not enough to realize how dangerous her condition was. Odd that two people living on Harkness Road also had connections to the Clinic. Yet, Anita claimed it was Olivia that brought Mary Pat out to Harkness Road. Could Mary Pat have made another stop on the way, or was Anita lying? But why should she?

Frank's thoughts were interrupted by a pleasant alto voice. "I'm ready for the next patient, Stacey."

Stacey pointed to Frank. "He wants to see you first."

Constance Stiler looked a little startled, then smiled. "Certainly. Come on back."

She showed him into an examining room. "We'll have a little more privacy in here."

"I don't know if Dr. Galloway mentioned my previous visit?" Frank asked.

She nodded. "Yes, he said that Mary Pat had a prescription for antibiotics that he hadn't written. I'm afraid I can't help you, either. As a nurse, I can't prescribe medications, and as Dr. Galloway told you, Mary Pat wasn't a patient here." She spoke gently and calmly, and ended her statement with a smile. Frank thought she'd be very comforting if you were sick.

"Dr. Galloway asked me to check our files again myself after your last visit," she added. "The only Sheehan we've seen here is a sixty-eight-year- old male, Joseph. The doctor treated him for conjunctivitis."

"That's her father," Frank said. "Dr. Galloway wrote Joe a prescription, which he filled months ago. That still leaves us with the question of how Mary Pat got the prescription for the antibiotic."

"May I hazard a guess?" Constance asked. "Perhaps Mr. Sheehan took a blank from the prescription pad for his own purposes. The older folks on limited incomes are always looking for a way to save money. He might have seen this as a way to extend another prescription—maybe one for his wife—without having to pay for a checkup with her physician."

Constance continued in her soft, reasonable voice. "He could have been saving it for a rainy day. Then his daughter found it and used it. He probably wouldn't want to admit that to you."

Frank supposed it was possible, but Constance seemed a little too pleased with the explanation. "What about Judy Penniman? She's in here a lot. She's an LPN."

"Judy?" Constance's brow furrowed. "What about her?"

"You both happen to live on Harkness Road. The place where Mary Pat died. The place she visited regularly during her pregnancy."

Constance smoothed her gleaming silver hair and bit her lower lip. "Ah, Judy. She has a very difficult life, you know. Her son's therapy is so expensive. I'd hate to think that she would take prescription blanks and sell them, but I suppose it's possible." She pondered this for a moment, then shook her head and met Frank's eye. "But, no. No, I doubt it. She can be a little brusque at times, but I'm sure she's quite honest."

"All right—one more question. When is the last time you saw Diane Sarens?"

Constance looked at him blankly. "Diane Sarens? That name doesn't ring a bell."

"She's a patient here. A young, pregnant, unmarried patient."

Constance tilted her head to one side and regarded him with bird-like puzzlement. "Really? The nurse on duty would check the weight and blood pressure of a pregnant patient before Dr. Galloway sees her. This girl must always have come in when Elaine was working, not me. Otherwise, I'm sure I would remember her."

Constance Stiler displayed no signs of nervousness. Either she was telling the truth, or she was the kind of liar who could trump a lie detector test. "Okay. Thank you, Mrs. Stiler. Could you send Dr. Galloway in now, please?"

Frank stood in the doorway of the examining room to make sure Constance had no opportunity in the cramped office to prep Galloway before he entered. Stacey had obviously alerted the doctor to Frank's visit, because Constance merely tapped on the door of the other examining room and nodded toward Frank.

Galloway entered with a scowl. "Now what?"

Frank saw no reason to be any more polite than the doctor. "Given any more thought to how Mary Pat Sheehan got that prescription?"

"I think it must have been the father," Galloway said. "He's been a patient here. He's a short, stocky guy with reddish-gray hair, right?"

Frank nodded.

"I remember when I was examining him, I got interrupted. Some woman came into the waiting room screaming bloody murder that her son had chopped his finger off. I had to check on him, and I left Mr. Sheehan alone. Probably, I had just pulled out my prescription pad. Yes, I'm sure that was it."

"So you're saying he stole it in advance, knowing his daughter might need it months down the line?"

"Of course not," Galloway snapped. "More likely he was planning a drive up to Canada to buy a two-year supply of blood-pressure medication. That's what all the old people do—save money or die trying."

This sounded a lot like Constance's theory. Had they planned to give him the same story, or was it really the logical explanation?

"Maybe," Frank said. "Now, there's one other little matter."

Galloway scowled. "What?"

"One of your other pregnant patients seems to have disappeared. I'm wondering if you can help me locate Diane Sarens?"

Galloway stepped backward and stumbled into a chair. He caught the chair before he fell and sank into it. Still, he didn't speak.

"Let's start from the beginning," Frank said. "Diane Sarens is a patient of yours?"

Galloway coughed. "Yes, but she's close to delivering. I turned her file over to the obstetrician in Saranac Lake two weeks ago."

"But you've seen her since then."

Galloway shook his head. "No."

"Don't lie to me!" Frank stepped directly in front of the doctor and loomed over him. "I saw you talking to the girl on the porch of the Rock Slide."

Galloway's eyes blinked rapidly and he shifted in his seat. "Oh, that...well, I just ran into her there."

"You were talking to her for some time." Frank didn't know how long they'd been there, but it was worth a shot.

"She was upset. I just..." Galloway's voice trailed off.

"Upset about what?"

"It's confidential—she's my patient."

"Let me just see if I can guess," Frank snapped. "She was upset about what to do with her baby when it's born. And you were maybe telling her how you could take it off her hands. That there might even be a little money in it for her, and the baby would go to a nice rich couple. Is that what you were talking about?"

"No!" Galloway protested. The horror on his face was unmistakable. "No, it was nothing like that. I've been trying to help her. She's got nothing to do with what happened to Mary Pat Sheehan."

"Well then, explain it. And tell me where she is."

"I can't." Galloway seemed to find some inner reserve of courage. "I won't betray her trust."

The radio on Frank's belt squawked to life, startling them both. "Frank? Frank?" Earl scrupulously adhered to proper radio procedure; something must have panicked him.

"Trout Run One here, over."

"Frank, a call just came in from the Mountain Vista Motel. Mr. Patel has been shot!"

Chapter 27

"Shot? You mean in a robbery?" Frank was already out the door as he spoke into the radio.

"I don't know. Someone who's staying at the motel called it in. I could hardly understand her, she was so worked up. I sent the Rescue Squad over there."

"Good. I'll be at the motel in ten minutes. You sit tight," he added, in case Earl got any clever ideas to head to the scene himself.

Frank flicked on the sirens and lights, urging the cars in front of him onto the shoulder as he sped past. Who would rob the Mountain Vista in broad daylight? For that matter, why would they even choose the motel as a target? Patel would be unlikely to have much cash on hand—most people paid for a motel with a credit card. Maybe the thief had been breaking into rooms looking for valuables and Mr. Patel had surprised him. He hoped the poor man hadn't been killed trying to protect some tourist's camera.

Frank soon pulled into the Mountain Vista parking lot, glad to see that the community ambulance of Trout Run and Verona had beaten him there. As he ran toward the motel, the office door opened and Roger Einhorn emerged, waving Frank in his direction. Then the volunteer paramedic disappeared back inside.

As Frank drew closer he could see something red on the sidewalk—not autumn leaves, but big splotches of bright red blood leading to the office door. He pulled it open, expecting the worst.

Mr. Patel lay on a stretcher. The little man's chestnut brown face had an ashy gray cast to it and streams of blood stained his beige pants. The right sleeve of his white shirt had been cut away and his arm was wrapped in layers of gauze. He looked bad to Frank, but thank God, he was alive.

"Roger, Mr. Patel, what happened here?"

"I have been shot!" Mr. Patel said in his high voice. "Shot as I go about my work in my own place of business!"

"Roger, can I get a statement before you take him to the hospital?" Frank asked. If there was any chance of catching the shooter, he needed information now.

Mr. Patel answered before Roger could open his mouth. "Yes, yes. I want to talk. Hospital can wait."

He turned his head toward Frank, "I am in the back taking the garbage out when I hear a loud bang. The next thing, a big force has knocked me over. Only a moment later do I feel a burning in my arm. I see the blood. I am shot!"

"Looks like the bullet passed right through the fleshy part of his arm, " Roger said. "He was incredibly lucky."

"I crawl to office, in case they shoot again. The woman in Room 10 is pulling in just then. She called for help."

Frank could see part of a grassy back yard that ran for about seventy-five feet behind the motel before turning into dense woods. "You mean the shot came from the woods?" he asked. "This wasn't a robbery?"

"No, no. No one is trying to steal from me. But I know why this has happened."

"You do?"

"Yes. It is because of that meeting on Monday. Because I spoke against closing Raging Rapids."

"But you weren't the only one to oppose it," Frank objected.

"Ah, yes. But I am the only foreigner to say this. They make of me an example, a warning, because I am Indian."

"Who?" Frank and Roger asked together.

"That group, that Green Tomorrow."

The EMTs loaded Mr. Patel into the ambulance, and it tore away, siren blaring. Frank hesitated for a moment. Everything in his experience told him it would be foolishly risky to charge into those woods by himself to look for the shooter. He had radioed the State Police for back-up, but depending on where the trooper on duty was at the moment, it could be half an hour until help arrived. The shooter was probably long gone anyway.

He started making the rounds of the guest rooms, but apart from the woman who had arrived after Mr. Patel was wounded and called in the report, all the rooms were empty at mid-day.

Roger said the bullet had passed clean through Mr. Patel's arm. Frank took gloves and plastic bags from the patrol car, then went around back to look for the bullet. Immediately he saw a small round hole in the side of the heavy yellow plastic can, but no exit hole on the other side. The bullet was somewhere in there. Frank sighed and picked up his radio. If ever there was a project that he could use Earl's help with, this was it.

Earl arrived within minutes, and Frank filled him in as they dug through bags of paper towels and soap wrappers and the remains of Mr. Patel's curry.

"So you think someone with Green Tomorrow shot Mr. Patel?" Earl asked.

Frank shrugged. "I don't want to jump to conclusions. More likely he was hit by a careless hunter. He was wearing a white shirt, you know."

"Yeah, except they're still hunting bear now, not deer. And no one could mistake little Mr. Patel for a bear."

Frank nodded as he shook the near-solid contents of an ancient quart of milk. "Still, people have been known to get a little over-eager waiting for opening day of deer season."

Earl wasn't buying it. "You don't poach in broad daylight, Frank. Why shouldn't it be Green Tomorrow? After all, they've blown things up out west."

Frank sat back on his haunches amid the sea of trash. "They could be retaliating for what happened to Nathan Golding and the attempt on Katie Petrucci. But why go after Mr. Patel? All the poor man said was that closing Raging Rapids would be bad for business."

"He explained it himself—because he's Indian."

"That doesn't fit," Frank answered. "Green Tomorrow's a bunch of ultra-left wing types. They're more likely to go after a red-neck white guy like Roy Fenstock."

"Wasn't Nathan Golding staying at the Mountain Vista the night before he was shot?" Earl asked. "Maybe they had an argument."

Frank shook his head. "Mr. Patel claims he didn't know who Golding was at the time."

Earl sank his gloved hand into a tangle of cold spaghetti in a carryout tin. "Here it is!" He held up what looked to be a 9 mm bullet.

Frank stared at it. "That's not from a hunting rifle—that's from a pistol." So it definitely wasn't a hunting accident. Had the gunman really been trying to kill Patel or just scare him off?

Earl glanced back at the woods. "You'd have to be a very good shot to even hit a man shooting from clear over there with a revolver."

The arrival of two state troopers ended their speculations. Together, they searched the woods until the fading light made it useless to continue. They found nothing.

————————— ◉ —————————

THERE WAS NO QUESTION now about waiting for Katie to uncover information about Green Tomorrow's motivations. The attack on Mr. Patel moved the talk with Stan Fenstock to the front burner. But as Frank headed out to Raging Rapids on Monday morning, Doris stopped him in his tracks.

"They're going to be too busy to talk to you," she said. "Stan took off for a long weekend and they're really short-handed. April called my house last night wondering if my Jeff could fill in."

Frank pivoted and returned to his desk. He sat staring at the phone, considering whether to call Abe now or wait for Stan to get back.

"Remember there at the end of the meeting, Abe Fenstock said something about passing up another opportunity to sell Raging Rapids?" Earl asked. "I wonder what he meant by that?"

Frank had forgotten all about it, but now he could picture Abe up at the podium, right before the whole meeting had dissolved in an uproar, making his "over my dead body" speech.

"Maybe it's nothing," Earl said. He still had trouble distinguishing between Frank thinking and Frank ignoring him.

"No, it's not nothing. It's a very good observation."

Earl beamed as Frank snatched up the phone.

"Say Abe," he began after April had put him through, "Earl just reminded me of something you said at that meeting the other day. Something about another offer to sell Raging Rapids that you didn't take. When was that?"

"Last year. Some lawyer called me from the city. Said his client was some company that wanted to buy my land. He offered me a million dollars. I said no."

"Just like that? Did your, uh, family agree that was the right thing to do?" Frank could imagine quite a family showdown over a million-dollar offer.

"I didn't even show it to them, but that wasn't the end of it. Then the guy wrote me a letter doubling the offer. Stan opened that, and he thought we ought to consider it. But Roy and I talked him out of it."

"How come? Two million's nothing to sneeze at."

"Not after you pay taxes on it and divide it three ways—it's not enough that you'd never have to work again. I'm only fifty-five, the boys are in their thirties. We're used to being our own bosses. And Raging Rapids is a great business—you get to be outside, meet folks from all over. I told my boys, you ain't going to find another deal like we got here. Best to just sit tight. So we turned him down."

Had Stan been in complete accord with the decision? "And you all agreed that was the best thing to do?"

"Yeah. Why're you asking me this?" An edge was beginning to creep into Abe's voice, so Frank let the matter drop. There was more he needed to know.

"Do you know who the client was who wanted to buy it, and what they wanted it for?"

"The lawyer wouldn't say. Why? You think this has something to do with what's going on now?"

"Could be. Someone wanted your land. You wouldn't sell. Now all of a sudden Green Tomorrow wants to close you down."

"But they want me to sell to the state. The other offer came through some fancy New York law firm."

"Do you remember the name?"

"I have the letter here somewhere." Frank could hear the sound of file drawers opening and papers shuffling. "Here it is. Arthur Noble. Levine, Noble, Howe and Findlayson, on Park Avenue. You gonna call?"

"Yeah, I think I'll see what I can turn up."

Frank took the direct approach first. He called and asked for Mr. Noble, explained that he represented Abe Fenstock, who had changed his mind and might be interested in selling his property, and was told in no uncertain terms that the buyer was no longer in the market. Who the buyer was, Mr. Noble was not at liberty to say. Good-bye.

It was what he expected. He checked his watch. Only three o'clock—people worked late in New York, so it would be at least another three hours until he could put Plan B into effect. He'd do the routine afternoon patrol and then try. It was a long shot, but it might give him something to work with.

Frank set out on his normal loop, which eventually took him past the Rock Slide. He didn't bother to stop—he already knew that Diane Sarens's friend had no further information on her whereabouts. In fact, the search for Diane had turned into a big bureaucratic tangle. Despite Trudy's report that the mother had been concerned, Mr. and Mrs. Sarens now maintained a unified front that Diane had simply taken off for a few days, as she had done before, was likely staying with friends they wouldn't approve of, and would eventually be back. They flatly refused to file a missing persons report. Consequently, the state police declined to get involved, despite Frank's urging. "You don't think the parents murdered her, do you?" Meyerson had asked, with no attempt to disguise his sarcasm.

"No, I'm afraid she might end up like Mary Pat Sheehan."

Frank remembered that conversation as he drove toward the Cascade Clinic. His conversation with Dr. Galloway about Diane had been interrupted by the call about Mr. Patel's assault. He was determined to find out what Galloway knew about Diane and her plans for her unborn baby.

He pulled into the clinic parking lot and found it empty except for one car. Odd—normally the place was packed. He walked in and found only the receptionist at work, with a large sign taped to her desk:

Dr. Galloway will be on vacation October 14-18. For emergency coverage, see Dr. Eggert in Lake Placid.

The receptionist was entering data from a large stack of charts into her computer. She did not look up until Frank spoke.

"Galloway's gone? This sign wasn't up two days ago when I was in here."

The receptionist eyed him strangely. "He got an opportunity to meet his girlfriend in Chicago. She lives in California, so it's halfway for both of them. We all told him he should go—he needed a break."

"Where in Chicago?" Frank demanded. More likely Galloway was quite nearby, delivering Diane Sarens's baby.

The urgency in his voice made the receptionist's brow furrow. "How should I know? Some hotel—his girlfriend's at a conference. I have his cell phone number, but we're only to use it in case of *extreme* emergency."

"This is an emergency—let me have it."

"I really don't think—"

"Now."

Reluctantly, she wrote it out and handed it over. "He deserves this time off. I wish you wouldn't—" were the last words Frank heard as he left the clinic.

Back in his own office, he dialed Galloway's cell phone number and immediately got a recorded voice. "The subscriber you have dialed is not available."

Wherever Galloway was, his cell phone was turned off.

At 6:15, he called the law office again.

As he hoped, this call was answered by an automated system. "Our regular hours are 8:30 AM to 5:30 PM. If you know your party's extension, you may dial it at this time. For a directory of employees, dial 4."

Frank dialed 4, then entered different combinations of letters. The first three times he tried he got various people's voicemail. On the fourth try, a woman answered.

"Yeah?" she snapped. He hoped the surly voice meant he'd reached a secretary forced to work late, not an over-achieving young lawyer.

"Hi, I work upstairs. I was just on the elevator with someone who got off on your floor. I realized after the doors closed that he'd dropped this sealed envelope. It might be important."

"Well, bring it down when you leave and slide it under the main door."

"Gee, I hate to do that—I'm not positive it's yours."

"Look, I don't have time for this. I gotta finish typing this brief." He could hear her keyboard begin to clatter as she spoke. Good. The more exasperated and stressed she was, the less likely she'd be to notice how lame his ruse really was.

"What if someone you work with really needs this? I'm just trying to be helpful." Frank tried to sound wounded.

"Well, open it and see what's in it," her voice echoed over the line. She'd put him on speakerphone so she could keep working as she talked.

"Oh, I could *never* do that. It could be very sensitive material. I'm a lawyer, you know." He'd encountered so many nit-picking lawyers in his career that it was surprisingly easy to imitate one.

"So whaddaya want from me?" Irritation rising—just what he hoped for.

"There *is* a logo on the envelope. It looks so familiar, like it's from a well-known corporation. Maybe if you named some of your big clients, I'd recognize it." He held his breath.

"Gandalf Corporation, United Messaging, Crosby and Cole," she rattled them off without hesitation. Frank scribbled frantically to keep up. Who knew if this would even lead to anything useful? He foresaw an insurmountable load of research.

"Rheim Pharmaceuticals, CynaQuest," she nattered on. "Extrom Communications..."

Pay dirt! He let her name a few more, then interrupted when she paused for a breath. "Oh, this isn't working. I guess I'll just have to come down in the morning and show it around."

"Fine," she barked, and hung up before he had to lie any more.

The next morning, Frank dialed the law firm again to perform the necessary crosscheck. "I'm trying to decipher a message left on my voicemail. I think it says to call a Mr. Knoll about the Extrom Communications deposition."

"You must mean Mr. Noble," the receptionist said helpfully. "He handles Extrom Communications." When she put the call through, Frank hung up.

Frank sat at his desk and stared at his calendar. The sound of phones ringing and Doris's relentless cackle faded away. Extrom had tried to buy Raging Rapids, but why? Could he have wanted to build his house there, beside the river? But surely he already owned the property at the top of Beehive Mountain at the time he made the offer on Raging Rapids. A quick call to the county clerk's office confirmed that.

Besides, current environmental regulations would prohibit any new building, and certainly anything as huge as Extrom's house, so close to a scenic waterway. Why did he want that land, and why had he been so secretive about acquiring it? And what was the connection to Green Tomorrow? Frank resumed staring. The calendar continued to say Monday, October 14.

Chapter 28

"*I think we may be in luck. A girl who first contacted me last spring is still interested.*"

"*Last spring? She must be pretty far along.*"

"*That's the beauty of it. She's due any day. So, no more waiting for the Braithwaites. And, she's blonde.*"

"*So was Mary Pat.*"

"*I asked about the father. He's fair and blue-eyed too.*"

"*So why did she wait so long?*"

"*She was in denial, like so many of them are.*"

"*Are you doing the delivery?*"

"*I don't want to—it's too risky.*"

"*Do what you have to do. Don't let her change her mind.*"

NEWS OF THE ATTACK on Mr. Patel quickly spread. Roger Einhorn saw it as his personal mission to tell everyone he encountered Mr. Patel's belief that he'd been shot as a warning to all who opposed the closing of Raging Rapids. And the more the story was repeated, the more people came to accept it as fact, not theory.

Irma Kurtz, owner of the Trim 'n' Tidy, regarded the assault on her fellow motel owner as a declaration of war. Within hours, she had a team of volunteers organized to keep the Mountain Vista operating while Mr. Patel was hospitalized. And she started a petition circulating that called for "the arrest and expulsion of outside agitators."

On Tuesday, Reid Burlingame dropped into the chair opposite Frank's desk and held out three sheets of tattered yellow legal paper. "Have you seen this?'

"Heard about it," Frank said as he reached for the pages.

Reid massaged his temples. "How can I respond to this? They won't be satisfied until you throw someone from that group in jail, even if you have to trump up the charges. I don't suppose you have any leads on who shot the poor man?"

"The state police are working on it. The bullet that we found is from a handgun. If the gun happens to have been manufactured and sold in New York, there will be a digital image on file of a sample fired bullet from that gun. If they find a match, we'll know whom the gun is registered to. But don't hold your breath—most crimes aren't committed with licensed guns."

Frank had been scanning the petition as he spoke. There were scores of signatures—even sensible people like Randall Bixley and Regis Malone had signed. He was about to hand it back when the last signature on the third page caught his eye, and he felt a rush like the morning's first coffee hitting his bloodstream. He recognized the writing—the first name was identical to the ornate but crabbed scrawl on Mary Pat's card. And there was a last name, also undecipherable.

"Who's this? Do you know?"

"Oh yes, Irma made sure to point it out to me. It's Sanjiv Patel himself. He found out about the petition when he got out of the hospital, and he demanded to sign. Says he refuses to be intimidated."

Frank sat in stunned silence.

"Do you really think he continues to be in danger?" Reid asked. "Are these Green Tomorrow people truly after him?"

"Huh?" Frank said, then pulled himself together. "No, no, signing this petition is meaningless. But I have been keeping an eye on his motel—the state police and I drive by several times a day. Hopefully that will discourage any more trouble. As for Irma and her crew, tell them...tell them you're pressuring me for results, how's that?"

Reid rose. "That ought to keep them happy–for a day or two."

"A day or two may be all I need."

As soon as Reid was gone, Frank took Mary Pat's card and the petition and headed out to the Mountain Vista Motel. Now things were beginning to make sense. No wonder poor Mary Pat had gone to such extremes to keep the affair and pregnancy secret from her family—worse than a criminal, worse than a married man, her lover was a Hindu. He could imagine Joe and Ann's reaction to that news.

And maybe the attack on Patel had nothing to do with Green Tomorrow and everything to do with Mary Pat's baby. Could Patel have been threatening to claim paternity? Would the people who had Mary Pat's baby kill to keep her?

Frank walked into the Mountain Vista office and found Mr. Patel behind the registration desk. Although his arm was heavily bandaged and in a sling, he looked quite chipper.

"Good morning, Mr. Patel. How are you feeling?"

"I am very well, Chief Bennett. I am so cheered by the kindness of my neighbors. They kept the motel running for me while I was in the hospital—even cleaned the rooms. It is like you say, the clouds are a different color on the inside."

Frank thought for a moment. "Every cloud has a silver lining?"

"Precisely."

He might feel the clouds were thoroughly black once he saw what Frank had to show him. "You signed this petition that's been circulating?" Frank laid the papers on the counter.

"Yes. I know you cannot arrest them without more evidence. Still, I think it is important that we show some solidarity."

"So this *is* your signature?" Frank tapped the last name on the list.

"Yes. Why?"

Frank pulled out the greeting card. "I found this card hidden in the trunk of Mary Pat Sheehan's car. It would appear to be signed by you."

Patel drew himself up to his full height, which was only five seven or eight. "A person cannot send a friend a greeting card? There is no crime in this, I think."

"No crime. But I think you were more than her friend. You know she died of complications of childbirth. I'm trying to find out what happened to her baby. Maybe you can tell me something about that?"

"How should I know?"

"Because you're the father, aren't you?"

Patel's dark eyes opened wide and his delicate fingers trembled. "This cannot be. I have no child."

Frank assumed a clinical tone. "Were you having a sexual relationship with Mary Pat Sheehan, Mr. Patel?"

Muddy blotches rose on Patel's cheeks. "Who is spreading such a rumor? I just chat with her at the store sometime."

"Look—the girl saved this card, hid it from her parents, because she cared about you. But she knew her parents would never approve. And maybe your family wouldn't be so crazy about her either. It could never work out. But then she got pregnant. And she would never have an abortion, so—"

"Stop! Stop!" Patel put his good hand over his ear. "This is a terrible thing you are saying. You have no proof of this."

Patel was right on the edge of admitting the relationship, Frank could sense it. He felt sorry for the guy, but gave it one more push. "You know, Mr. Patel, sometimes young couples use that empty lot across the road to park and make out. Before I came over here today, I called one of the fellas I've chased out of there in the past." Frank made it up as he went along. "And I asked him if he ever saw Mary Pat's car parked at your motel late at night. And he told me he had seen it—many times."

That was all it took. Patel slid down into his desk chair. Frank came around to the other side of the counter and pulled up a chair.

"Start at the beginning. Tell me everything."

"I am so lonely here. I have no friends, no family nearby. I cannot afford any help, so I rarely even leave the motel. When I go into the Stop 'n' Buy, Mary Pat is always so friendly to me, so kind. When I explain how hard it is for me to get away from the office, she says I can call in my order and she will drop off my groceries on her way home. So she starts to come here at night, and we talk. She is such a good person...I should never..." Tears slipped down his face.

"I understand. You were both lonely."

Patel nodded. "This went on for several months. Then in the spring, she came in one night and said it must stop. What we were doing was wrong. Of course, she is correct. She is a Catholic—she must marry one of the same. My mother in Bombay is working to find me a nice wife. We are both feeling very guilty. So we stop. It is hard, but I honor her wishes. I do my shopping in Verona or at the Store. I never see her anymore."

"She never told you she was pregnant?"

Patel shook his head, and spoke down at the desk. "When I heard she was dead, how she died, I was shocked. But I tell myself, this cannot be my doing.

Maybe she has another man, and that is why she stopped seeing me." Now he began to weep in earnest. "But I know this cannot be true. I was the first, the only..."

Frank got up and paced around the small reception area to give Patel time to compose himself. He had counted so much on the baby's paternity being the key to locating her. Now, it looked like he was no further along than before. He was quite sure Patel wasn't lying—Mary Pat had kept the pregnancy a secret even from her lover. His idea that the assault on Patel had something to do with the baby also seemed to be blown. Then again, just because Mary Pat hadn't told Patel he was about to be a father didn't mean that no one else knew, did it? With all those late night conversations, Patel might have some idea who Mary Pat would turn to for help, even if he hadn't known why she needed it.

When he heard Patel blowing his nose he turned around. He explained all he had discovered so far about Sheltering Arms and the Finns, the trips to Harkness Road and the prescription from the Cascade Clinic.

"What do you think, Sanjiv? Someone put her in touch with Sheltering Arms, someone helped her have the baby—do you have any idea who? Whom would she turn to for help?"

Patel did not answer.

"It's important. Other girls could be at risk. Anita Veech?" Frank prompted. "Judy Penniman? Dr. Galloway?"

"That Anita is not such a nice person. I don't like how she looks at me. I am thinking she knows about me and Mary Pat."

So maybe Anita did know all along. Why wouldn't she tell him the truth? "Were Anita and Mary Pat good friends?"

Patel shook his head. "Not friends. I think Mary Pat was a little afraid of her."

"What about Judy Penniman?"

"Mary Pat spoke sometimes about Mrs. Penniman's son, the fellow who always talks so much. She prayed for him because he is not right in the head. This was her way—always worrying about others."

"Do you know if she ever visited Dr. Galloway at the clinic?"

"I do not know this name." The tears began flowing again. "I was a coward. I should have said, 'To hell with what our families will say. We will marry because we love each other.' After all, this is America. Everyone does what they want."

Patel stood up. "I am done with being afraid. I want my daughter back. You will find her and I will raise her to be a fine, strong American girl."

Chapter 29

Frank unlocked the door to his cottage and headed for the BarcaLounger. What a day! He'd screwed Mr. Patel to the wall to get at the truth and precious little good it did him. And now, Diane Sarens, with her long, spindly legs and her beach-ball belly, had insinuated herself onto his list of women to worry about—right up there with baby Sarah, Caroline, and Beth.

He flopped down and reclined, knocking over a column of books stacked beside his chair. He'd hoped to start building the bookshelves he'd promised himself this weekend, but the latest developments in the case made that unlikely.

Frank had jettisoned most of his books in Kansas City, sending them off with new owners for twenty-five cents a pop at the giant yard sale that had marked the end of his married life. But like most of the rash decisions he'd made during those chaotic weeks, he now regretted getting rid of the books, even though he wasn't one for re-reading.

The house in Trout Run seemed cold and sterile without them, and soon he began acquiring more. Histories and biographies, mysteries, westerns, and classic novels–just about everything but poetry and science fiction. Before long the books began accumulating in dusty, teetering piles, offending his sense of order. So he'd bought some fine maple boards from Stevenson's lumberyard, but it sat in his workshop untouched.

Frank snapped his recliner forward, reached for a scrap of paper and started sketching how the shelves would fit around the fireplace. Where was that tape measure? As he rattled around in his junk drawer, he thought he heard a knock. Then again. He put on the porch light and peered out. Beth Abercrombie's face stared back at him.

"Beth! What are you doing here?" He was so surprised, he didn't even invite her in, but kept her standing on the stoop.

"Hi, uh, I hope I'm not disturbing you."

A cold blast of wind brought him to his senses. "Of course not. Come on in. How about a drink?" Then he cringed, wondering if he had anything more than that six-pack of Bud to offer.

"Thank you. That would be nice." Beth took off her coat and followed him into the kitchen.

Inspiration struck: the bottle of brandy Edwin had given him. He pulled it out, then hesitated. He didn't have those fancy glasses you were supposed to use. Oh well, tumblers would have to do.

He handed her the drink and sat across from her at the kitchen table.

"This—"

"I—" they began simultaneously.

Beth clutched her glass and started over. "I came to apologize, Frank. I was terribly unfair to you last week."

"Nah," he protested, although he'd worked himself into a lather more than once thinking about their last encounter. This reversal came as a pleasant surprise.

"No, no—I was wrong. Your concerns were legitimate."

Now what did that mean? Had she changed her tune about Green Tomorrow, or only about her reaction to his questions?

"So," he asked cautiously, "have you spoken to Katie recently?"

"Yes, she told me about your conversation. We agreed to sit down with Meredith and ask her some questions. Unfortunately, she's been traveling the last few days and we haven't been able to get in touch with her." Beth smiled. "But we will."

She seemed to think that settled it. He considered telling her about Rod Extrom's interest in Raging Rapids, but Beth kept talking.

"So, how's the investigation into Mary Pat's baby going?" she asked.

"I'm making some headway," he replied cautiously. He hadn't told anyone yet about Sanjiv Patel being the baby's father. "But I still don't know who helped Mary Pat have the baby. I think it's someone with connections to the Cascade Clinic."

"Really? I've never been there, myself. I go to a doctor in Lake Placid."

"Judy Penniman takes her patients there a lot," Frank said, watching Beth closely. "Do you know the Pennimans?"

"Just in passing." She stood up and carried her drink into the living room. "You must have a nice view of Stony Brook out this window."

He wanted to ask her about Doug being seen on her road, but now his suspicions seemed ridiculously sordid. Why risk making her angry again—Beth obviously wanted to change the subject. And looking at her face in profile, softly illuminated by his reading lamp, so did he. "I think I'll build a fire—how does that sound?"

"Terrific." She dropped down on the hearthrug beside him. He told her about his plans for the bookshelves and she told him about a new gallery in Boston that wanted to carry her work. Her long honey-colored hair, un-braided today, slipped across her cheek as she talked. Without thinking, he reached out to brush it back, and the next thing he knew, she was in his arms.

The warmth of her, her soft, clean scent unleashed an unbearable longing. Guilt, nerves, restraint: all out the window. And Beth certainly did nothing to discourage him.

He didn't recall just when or how they moved to the bedroom, but that's where he was when the sun woke him. The pillow next to him was still warm, but when he looked out the window, his driveway was empty. He wasn't sure if he was disappointed or relieved.

Chapter 30

"*Frank Bennett has been nosing around again.*"

"*Oh, relax. He doesn't know anything.*"

"*He may not understand the whole picture, but he suspects plenty.*"

"*Let him suspect all he wants. He has no proof unless you talk. All you have to do is keep your mouth shut.*"

"*This is a nightmare. I wish I had never gotten mixed up in this scheme.*"

"*But you did. And now you're going to play it out to the end.*"

"...SO BEV TRUESDALE FROM The Gables calls and says she has a party of five for the weekend that she can't accommodate and do I want them, and after I say sure she drops it on me that they expect dinner tonight!" Edwin, normally imperturbable, knelt in front of the large cooler at the Store, frantically rooting through the bin of spongy apples and brown-edged iceberg lettuce that made up the produce section.

"All I need is one lemon. Is that asking too much?"

"I see something yellow over there to the left." Frank offered what help he could as he reached for a quart of milk.

Edwin emitted a yip of glee, but then let the lemon, wizened and petrified with age, fall from his hand. He rocked back on his heels and shut his eyes. "This is just too cruel. When I lived in Manhattan I could get any-thing—kumquats, pomegranates, guavas—twenty-four hours a day at the Korean market on my block. Here, not even a lousy lemon. "

"Welcome to the North Country."

Edwin glanced at his watch. "I suppose I have time to drive to Verona for it."

"Can't you just make something else?"

"I'd make the butternut squash with coriander and pecans, but Meredith Golding is back again, and she's had that twice since she's been staying with us. I've got to make the spinach and couscous salad with lemon and dill."

Frank couldn't care less about Edwin's menu problems, but he was very interested in Meredith Golding. This was his chance to ask the questions he never got a chance to raise in that meeting. "Set a place for me at dinner, would you? You know how I love couscous."

All afternoon, Frank was restless. He dialed Galloway's cell phone number again, as he had several times over the past couple of days, and continued to get the automatic message. He agonized over whether or not to call Beth, and what he should say if he did. Several times, he steeled himself to pick up the phone and dial, but then Doris would pop in squawking a question, or the fax machine would start printing something out that he felt compelled to look at, and the moment would pass. Finally the clock showed three o'clock, and he took off with unusual enthusiasm for the afternoon patrol.

When he returned, Doris had her coat on and was ready to walk out the door. "I have to leave early today," she said, not bothering with an excuse. "While you were gone, a state trooper came by and dropped something off for you. It's on your desk."

Frank went in and found a computer printout labeled COBIS at the top. That was the handgun tracking system the state police were using to trace the gun used to shoot Mr. Patel. Could it be the complicated system actually worked for once? He scanned all the technical jargon until four words jumped out: Registered Owner—Douglas Penniman.

Frank leaned back in his chair and contemplated the stained acoustical ceiling tile above his head. Penniman's gun had been used to shoot Patel, but had Penniman pulled the trigger? Frank couldn't see what motive the man had had to shoot Sanjiv Patel.

Penniman had no relationship with Mary Pat—that much was clear now. And even if Judy was the link between Mary Pat and Sheltering Arms, why should the Pennimans want to harm Patel? Frank was sure that Patel had been entirely honest when he said he hadn't known about Mary Pat's pregnancy until after her death, and had no idea who had helped her deliver. Of course, if Mary Pat had told Doug and Judy that Sanjiv was the father, they might worry that he knew about them, even if he didn't. Frank frowned—kind of a shaky motive for attempted murder.

Maybe it had nothing to do with the baby. Patel thought the attack was linked to Green Tomorrow. But the only tenuous link between Doug and Green Tomorrow was...Beth.

Frank jumped up and began to pace the office. Those yahoo carpenters, who admittedly had a grudge against Doug, said they saw him on Beth's road driving Extrom's SUV—what did that prove? Maybe Doug had been doing some carpentry work in Beth's shop. Might as well just call and ask. He grabbed the phone and dialed before he lost his nerve, but the phone rolled over to her answering machine on the fourth ring.

He sighed and cut the connection, then dialed the Pennimans. Billy answered.

"This is Chief Bennett. Is your Dad there?"

"No. I'm getting ready to watch the baseball game. Do you—"

"How about your Mom?"

"My mom is staying with a patient. She was supposed to be home before my dad left for his trip. He's driving to Toledo. I don't like staying home by myself, but Dad said to watch the game until Mom got home. The Yankees are playing tonight, did you know that? I hate the Yankees. Who's your favorite—"

"When will your dad be back?"

"I don't know—a few days. It takes a while to get to Toledo—it's in Ohio, you know. Usually he leaves at five when he goes to Ohio, but today he left at four because he had to go Rooney's gun shop. He had to sell one of his guns, one of the little ones. Do you want to watch the game? You could watch it with me. I have some coke and chips. Okay? Okay?"

FRANK ARRIVED AT THE Iron Eagle Inn at 7:30, hoping he looked appropriately benign in his plaid shirt, khakis and loafers. He was feeling a little guilty about his conversation with Billy Penniman. The kid had unwittingly ratted out his own father, but it wasn't as if Frank had tried to trick him. He couldn't have stopped the tide of words rushing out of Billy if he wanted to.

Doug had made it ridiculously easy for him by getting rid of the gun openly at Rooney's. He wouldn't need a search warrant to get the weapon;

Rooney wouldn't want any part of a gun used in a crime. Doug didn't even know he was under suspicion. When he got back from his trip, Frank would question him. It would be nice if Meredith Golding proved as inept as Doug. Somehow, he doubted he'd be that lucky.

Frank ran into Lucy as he came through the front door. "It's just going to be the four of us, Frank. Our other guests called—they're stranded in a traffic jam on the Thruway; haven't even made it to Albany yet. So I thought we'd eat in the kitchen, if that's all right."

"Fine with me."

He trailed Lucy into the kitchen, following a wonderful scent that grew stronger with every step. Frank sighed in relief as he saw Edwin at the counter, carving a plump roast chicken. He could load up on that if the couscous was a bust.

"You need a hook," Meredith Golding was saying to Edwin as Lucy and Frank came in. She perched on a stool, sipping from a glass of white wine. "Something about the Inn that would attract media attention."

"I need a hook all right—a long one to reel customers in off the street." Edwin laughed as he greeted Frank. "You two remember each other?"

"Yes, but I'm afraid I wasn't in very good shape the last time we met." Meredith extended her hand. It felt cold and bony in Frank's grasp.

Lucy watched Frank as if he were unpredictable pet who might leap on her guest without warning. But he was Mr. Congeniality, chatting about Lucy's latest scheme to boost business and regaling them with tales of Earl's courtship of Melanie. Even Meredith laughed, as she took the seat across from him at the table, and Edwin served the food.

It was Meredith herself who brought up the subject of Nathan Golding. "This chicken is delicious, Edwin. I haven't had any in a long time." She turned to Frank with an explanation. "My husband was a strict vegetarian. I'm afraid Edwin's cooking is pushing me off the wagon."

"I lost my wife two years ago, Meredith. It's strange how your habits start to change."

Meredith's gaze met his. "Yes," she said softly, her mask of perfect composure slipping a bit.

He'd come prepared to quiz her; the tug of empathy he felt surprised him. "I'm impressed at the way you've thrown yourself back into your work. I guess it helps to stay busy."

"Yes it does." Her briskness returned. "Absolutely the best way to honor Nathan's memory."

He could feel Edwin observing him; probably expected him to make some snide comeback. Instead, Frank said, "There's something I meant to ask at the town meeting the other day, but it ended before I had a chance. I'm a bit of a birdwatcher, myself..." Edwin began coughing. "And I just wondered, how did you folks know about the Bicknell's Thrush being threatened? It's not a very well-known bird."

He thought Meredith hesitated before she answered, but maybe she just had to swallow. "We're in constant communication with other environmental organizations. A group called Species Watch publishes a quarterly report of threatened species worldwide. The Bicknell's Thrush was on it."

"But what made you connect that bird with Raging Rapids?" Frank persisted.

Edwin set his fork down and leaned forward, waiting for the answer. Lucy leaped up. "Meredith, have some more wine. Edwin, is that second bottle open?"

"I have plenty, thanks." Meredith turned to Frank. "I believe one of our supporters in the area pointed it out to Nathan. Once we visited, we could see how damaging the place was to the natural ecosystem on several fronts."

"Who..." Frank began.

But Lucy was adamant this time. "Have some more couscous, Frank." She shoved the bowl into his hands. "Edwin, tell Meredith all you had to go through to get the ingredients for this salad."

Frank backed off. Both Katie and Beth claimed that Nathan had contacted them, not the other way around. Who was this other local supporter? Surely not any of the moms from Katie's nursery school—but no one else local had participated in the protest. He waited for another opportunity to bring the conversation back to Green Tomorrow, but Lucy kept up a steady stream of chatter about the Inn, the weather, books she had read, movies she would never get to see. Frank had to admire her determination to protect Meredith.

Finally, as Lucy chirped on about remodeling plans, Frank saw his opening. "If you want to see a big building project, you should check out the new Extrom house. Have you been up there, Meredith? All those trucks rumbling up and down the mountain must be scrambling a few thrush eggs. I'm surprised you're not protesting that."

"Frank!" Lucy scolded. "Meredith is our guest. She shouldn't have to defend her position at dinner."

"That's quite all right, Lucy." Meredith turned on her "Meet the Press" smile. "A good question, Frank. Of course, we're aware of the Extrom project, and you're right, the construction does have a short-term negative impact on nesting patterns. But we feel that in the long-term, the Extrom house will actually be beneficial to the environment."

"Oh?" Frank sat back. This he wanted to hear.

"You see, the land on Beehive Mountain was owned by five different people, all with hunting cabins or plans to eventually build homes there. Extrom came along and bought them all out at a good price. Now, there will just be one home at the top of the mountain, and the rest of the land will be undisturbed. The wildlife will return once the construction is finished. It may not be the ideal situation," Meredith offered a world-weary smile, "but sometimes you have to compromise."

Damn, she was good. Enough with gentle lobs over the net; see if she could return a spike. "I understand Mr. Extrom made an offer to buy Raging Rapids a while back. Any idea why he'd want it?"

Meredith neatly used her knife to push the last of her couscous onto her fork. "I wouldn't know," she said, meeting Frank's eye without hesitation. "I've never met the man, although I believe Nathan may have spoken to him at one time. Or perhaps it was Barry Sutter, our lawyer"

She had an answer to everything, except when she didn't want to reveal something. Then she fell back on the "only Nathan handled that" routine.

As they settled back with coffee and pie, Meredith turned to him again. "So, Frank, what can you tell me about the investigation into my husband's murder? I get precious little information from the state police, and none from the FBI."

Lucy stopped with the coffeepot poised over Edwin's cup. They all stared at Frank, waiting.

He took his time pouring cream and sugar into his coffee. He wasn't sure how far he could go without bringing Meyerson's wrath down on his head. Well, he could always claim stupidity; Meyerson would have no trouble accepting that.

"They've ruled out a number of suspects," Frank said. "The major players opposing your logging action out in Oregon, Nathan's sons, his ex-wife, you. But I don't think they have a new prime suspect. They seem to be focusing now on the people involved in the Raging Rapids protest. But I don't know... that had hardly gotten underway when he was killed." Frank tapped his spoon lightly on the tablecloth. "Who do *you* think did it?"

In Frank's experience, the victim's family always had a theory. Sometimes it was right on, even if they lacked solid proof. Other times, it was completely irrational. And if the family was involved in some way, it might be intentionally deceptive. But they always had a theory.

Meredith was true to form. "I'm worried," she said. Her face had lost that PR-woman's Teflon confidence. She looked smaller than she had just a few minutes ago. "I made it my mission to raise the profile of Green Tomorrow. To make it a national player in environmental politics. I'm afraid that something I did, something I urged Nathan to say, unintentionally provoked some, some unstable person to..."

She twisted away from the table and bit down on her thumb as two tears coursed slowly down her cheeks. Lucy looked ready to spring into action, but Meredith straightened up and dabbed her face with her napkin.

"I'm sorry. Sometimes I coast along for days, feeling like Nathan's just away on a business trip. And then it hits me that I'm never going to see him again. He's really dead. And maybe I'm responsible."

Chapter 31

Frank took his morning coffee out onto the screen porch. It was nippy, but the air carried the comforting smell of hardwood fires from his neighbors' fireplaces. The meadow that ran down to Stony Brook shimmered with goldenrod and asters. Above, as far as he could see, the sky stretched deep blue and cloudless.

He felt thoroughly out of sorts.

He'd meant to have some fun this fall. For the first time in two years, he felt like having fun. Paddle through the St. Regis wilderness, climb Giant, maybe take the boys on that easy hike up Baxter Mountain and show them that blueberries don't come from little plastic baskets.

Instead, he'd let Mary Pat Sheehan and her baby, and all the craziness with Green Tomorrow consume him. With Caroline avoiding him, he'd had no chance to take the boys out. Now, the best days of autumn were already over. The blaze of autumn was so intense here, but it ended so quickly. A few freezing nights, a few big rains and the show was over. As Edwin sadly commented, the leaves were "past peak." You could still find spots of flaming color in odd, protected areas, but the grey and brown mountain tops told the story: the bleak days of winter were coming fast.

Still, today promised to be glorious. It was Sunday. Why shouldn't he take a hike? He was still waiting to hear if Diane Sarens had returned home, but sitting by the phone wouldn't make the call come any faster. The exercise might clear his mind, help him think straight.

He went inside and pulled out his knapsack and ADK trail guide. He settled on a hike up Noonmark. It wasn't as tough a climb as Giant, and the guide promised a stunning view at the peak. A big water bottle, a sandwich, some snacks, a compass, his binoculars and an extra sweater and he was ready. He glanced at the phone. Maybe he should call Beth and see if she wanted to come. They'd traded a few awkward voicemail messages since their night together, but they hadn't seen each other. He decided against it—he needed to relax, and time spent with Beth was a lot of things, but never relaxing.

Only two other cars were parked at the trailhead—that was one advantage of waiting until the tourist frenzy was over. Frank started off briskly, but it wasn't long before his heart thumped and he had to pull off one layer of clothing. He ought to do this more often. He was as thin as he ever was, but clearly his heart and lungs could use the workout.

Pacing himself, he paused more frequently to drink as the trail switched back and forth across the mountain. He reminded himself that this wasn't a race, and started to notice things like bright orange mushrooms growing on a rotten log and huge holes hammered by woodpeckers.

But when he passed a spry elderly couple he couldn't help but put on a little burst of speed. It would be embarrassing if they overtook him at the end. After two hours he was climbing, not walking.

Some young men passed him on their way down. "You're almost there—ten more minutes," they said.

Frank thanked them, although he wasn't particularly encouraged. Ten minutes for them probably meant twenty for him. But sooner than anticipated he scrambled across the smooth rock face, and pulled himself up the last ten feet to the summit.

A grin spread across his face. The trail guide hadn't lied.

Even in the unshaded midday sun the wind made the summit a good ten degrees colder than the valley. He pulled on his extra sweater and just sat, taking it in. All he could see was the hand of God at work: peak after peak rolling away into a purplish haze, the distant glimmer of Lake Champlain. This is what the Algonquin must have seen as they hunted these trails and fished these streams before white men ever suspected what lay on the other side of the Atlantic.

Frank rose and walked to another vantage point. Looking straight down from where he'd come, he could see the signs of civilization, if you wanted to call it that. Tiny, twisting black ribbons of roads. Roofs, a few open fields, a golf course, everything out in the open now that so many leaves were down. He walked to the north side of the summit and looked out. Closer than seemed possible, he saw the vivid yellow-orange of a backhoe. He pulled out the binoculars. The distinctive outline of the Extrom house loomed into view. He dropped the binoculars and got his bearings. Yes, Noonmark must have been the larger mountain he'd noticed when he'd admired the view from Extrom's place. He looked down into the valley between Extrom's mountain and this one. What he saw made him step backwards, and not just because of the dizzying drop.

Below, clearly visible through the bare tree branches, was Raging Rapids: the parking lot already filling up with belching buses, the big green building with the snack shop and the souvenir stand, the catwalks crisscrossing the brook. This would be Extrom's view seven months out of the year.

He must have bought the property impulsively, obviously in the summer or early fall when the leaves masked the imprint of Raging Rapids on the land. When he saw the problem that lay in his field of vision, he'd done what any rich man would do: he tried to buy it and fix it. But he hadn't counted on the stubbornness of Abe Fenstock, hadn't taken into consideration that some people value their way of life more highly than money.

But an entrepreneur like Extrom wouldn't be one to give up easily. He and the Goldings must have crossed paths somewhere along the line, and the scheme to shut Raging Rapids down for environmental reasons was born. After all, Extrom didn't need to own the property—just to get rid of the eyesores on it. From Extrom's aerie, a few hikers wandering beside the brook would only be tiny specks of color. A big contribution to Green Tomorrow to accomplish that would be well worth the price.

Frank didn't know if the state police auditors could actually find a paper trail between Extrom and Green Tomorrow, but it hardly mattered. Once he made Extrom's motivations clear to Katie and Beth and anyone else in town who supported closing Raging Rapids, he was quite sure the whole protest would melt away. With no local support, Green Tomorrow would be forced to pack their bags.

Still, one thing troubled him. Understanding why Green Tomorrow had come to Trout Run didn't make it any clearer who had killed Nathan Golding. But that wasn't his problem. Let Meyerson figure it out.

Chapter 32

❝ *What are you howling about? Calm down—I can't understand a thing you're saying."*

"She tricked me! The little bitch tricked me! I should have suspected when she kept stalling about meeting me. Once I talked to her, I could tell what she's trying to do—

"I don't understand."

"Don't you see? She wanted to find out who placed the ads. She wanted to find out who Mary Pat gave her baby to."

"Why?"

"She's playing detective or something. Oh, my God! We're screwed! It's all over..."

"Maybe she thinks there's money in it for her. She's still there with you?"

"Yes, but—"

"Get a grip on yourself and do as I say."

"OKAY, BUT YOU HAVE my message? You'll tell her to call me as soon as she gets in, right?" Earl hung up and looked out the window. He picked up a few files from his desk and approached the file cabinet.

The phone rang, and he lunged for it. "It's for you." He handed the phone over to Frank and resumed pacing around the office.

Frank finished his call and hung up. "What's wrong with you? You're as jumpy as a cat."

"Nothing."

"Look Earl, I can see you're waiting for a call from Melanie. If you've had some little squabble with her, you can't let it affect your work."

"I'm sorry." Earl made a great show of typing a report, but when the phone rang again, he leaped for it.

"All right. Yes, we'll look into it."

Frank looked at him inquiringly.

"A car's been sitting at the Cascade trailhead for four days. Looks like it might be abandoned," Earl explained after hanging up.

"So, what are you waiting for? Go check on it."

Earl looked longingly at the phone. "Do I have to?"

"Earl, if you think you're going to sit around here all day waiting for a girl to call you—"

"It's not what you think, Frank! We didn't have a fight. I'm worried about her. She hasn't shown up for work yet and—"

"Christ, Earl, don't be up her butt like that. You can't be checking on her constantly. Let her live her life, and you live yours. Now, go see about that abandoned vehicle."

Frank turned back to his paperwork, but he didn't hear Earl moving. He looked up. Earl stood rooted at the door, the expression on his face not heartbreak or despair, but pure fear.

"What's wrong?" Frank asked, more gently now.

"I think we did a really stupid thing. I think Melanie and Diane could both be in terrible trouble, and it's my fault."

Earl had Frank's full attention now. He came and sat across from his boss. "I did what you always tell me not to do," Earl confessed. "I talked to Mel about the case. About how we were trying to get Sheltering Arms to contact us, but it wasn't working. About how we didn't have any young policewomen we could use to pose as a pregnant girl."

Frank rubbed his temples. "And of course, she offered to help."

"I told her you'd never let her do it. But then, get this. Someone from Sheltering Arms emailed her. See, when she told us her friend had answered one of their ads last spring, it really was her. There was no friend."

"I know."

"You do?" Earl's voice rose as he got more agitated. "See, Mel got this email last week asking her if she was still interested in giving up her baby for adoption. It came from a different address than the one she had contacted, but Mel was sure it was the same person."

Frank slammed his fist on the desk. "And you didn't tell me this?"

"I wanted to, but she didn't want you to know that she was the one who'd been pregnant. She said the two of us could follow up on it, and then..." Earl looked about a hair's breadth away from crying.

"And then you'd look like a big shot, and she'd have her five minutes of fame. Jesus Christ, Earl, how could you be so reckless? How could you not share vital information like that with me?"

"Well, why didn't *you* tell *me* you knew it was Melanie who answered that ad? If I'd 'a known that, I could've convinced her to tell you everything."

"I could see she was lying, but I went along with it because I knew you liked her, and I didn't want to embarrass her."

"Never mind." Earl ran his fingers through his hair. "What are we going to do now? Mel went to meet the person at the park in Verona today."

"Went to a meeting? Don't tell me she stuffed a pillow under her shirt!"

"Actually, she had this thing they use on manikins at Sears. Her cousin borrowed it for Halloween—it's pretty realistic. Anyway she was supposed to call me and let me know who it was, and what they said. But I haven't heard from her since noon."

"What did she say then?"

"She just left a message on my answering machine. She said she met the person, but not to worry because it was—" He coughed to regain his composure. "I've played the message over and over and I can't understand the name she said, because she was calling me on that stupid cell phone, and it was breaking up. But after the name I think she said something about 'over to Harkness Road.'"

Earl's eyes widened in fear. "She must have decided to go there."

Frank and Earl tore toward Harkness Road in the patrol car. "Shouldn't we radio the state police for back up?" Earl asked.

"Not yet. We don't know for sure if she's there. And even if she is, she's probably not in actual danger." Frank tried to be reassuring, but he was worried. He'd listened to Melanie's recorded message and her voice sounded bright and chipper. That lead him to believe that Melanie knew the person who'd shown up to meet her at the park, and wasn't afraid. That meant Judy Penniman or Constance Stiler, because surely Melanie wouldn't be so complacent about an encounter with Anita Veech. She was as mistrustful of the Veeches as everyone else in town. But what about Galloway? Melanie probably knew him in passing, and she was conditioned to believe doctors were trustworthy.

Would Judy or Constance or Galloway harm Melanie? How desperate would any of them be to conceal their connection with Sheltering Arms? But why would Mel go out to Harkness Road, now that she knew the identity of the person soliciting for Sheltering Arms?

"Where are we going first?" Earl asked.

"The Pennimans." He'd already decided that the Pennimans posed the bigger risk. Doug must be in on the scheme. If he had tried to kill Mr. Patel, for whatever reason, he would be a danger to Mel. Judy had claimed her husband wasn't due back from his trip until tomorrow, but he might have arrived already. And maybe even Billy would help Judy with any dirty work.

Frank pulled into the Pennimans' driveway. No cars, neither Mel's nor Judy's and no sign of Doug's rig, but his pick-up was there. Frank leaped out and pounded on the front door.

"Police! Open up!"

No response from within. Earl shaded his eyes and peered through the front window. "I don't see anyone," he said and Frank continued to knock and ring the bell.

"Let's go around back." Still, no one answered. Frank was considering whether to throw his shoulder against the back door when Earl simply reached out and turned the knob. The joy of living in a place where people still routinely left their doors unlocked.

They stepped into the kitchen, which once again contained the remnants of the family's breakfast. A package of chicken thawed on the counter. Frank and Earl quickly searched the house: unmade beds, towels on the bathroom floor. Clearly the Pennimans had taken off this morning in a rush and hadn't been back.

"Come on. This is a waste of time." Frank returned to the car and drove straight across Harkness Road and up the Stilers' driveway. Again, no cars, but he knew Mrs. Stiler kept hers in the garage. Where was Melanie's little red Chevy?

He knocked on the back door, and when it was not immediately answered, reached to try the knob. As he did, the door opened from within. Mr. Stiler, frail and hunched in his cardigan sweater and bedroom slippers, stood before them.

"Hello, Mr. Stiler, is your wife home?"

He responded with an unintelligible sound, but stood aside for them to enter. They all three stood in the kitchen, uncertain what to do next. "Mrs. Stiler?" Frank shouted

Her husband shook his head.

Now what? He couldn't very well barge in and start looking around. "Was she here a little while ago?" Frank asked.

Mr. Stiler nodded. The Parkinson's made his face strangely expressionless, but his eyes were keen.

"Did she have a young woman with her who looked pregnant? Blonde hair, pretty?"

Again he nodded.

"Where did they go?" Earl asked. The agitation in his voice transmitted to Mr. Stiler. He edged away from them, shaking his head.

"Look, Mr. Stiler, we need to talk to your wife and Melanie Powers, the girl with her. It's very important."

He made another garbled sound, his eyes pleading.

"Did they go somewhere together in Melanie's car?" Frank asked.

A shake no, accompanied by a lot of distressed sounds. The pathetic man made a feeble effort to push Frank toward the door.

Frank caught his trembling hands by the wrists. "Listen to me, Mr. Stiler. Your wife is in trouble. If you want to keep that trouble from getting worse, you better tell me where she went. I'll ask you the questions, you answer yes or no.

"Are Melanie and your wife alone together?"

No

"Are they with Dr. Galloway?"

His eyes widened in surprise. No.

"Are they with Anita Veech?"

Mr. Stiler swayed in Frank's grasp and he lowered the man into a chair. He was truly distraught now, struggling to form a word. His lips pursed. "R-r-r, R-r-r."

"Ralph Veech?" Earl guessed. "Ralph took Melanie away?"

Mr. Stiler shook his head emphatically. He lifted his stiff right arm as best he could and pointed toward a corner of the kitchen. Frank was puzzled for a moment, then understanding dawned. "They went down the road to the Veech place?"

Mr. Stiler collapsed against the chair. They left him weeping.

Frank radioed the state police as soon as they reached the car. "We're not going to sit around and wait for them, are we?" Earl was practically hysterical.

Frank shook his head. The dispatcher had told him Trooper Pauline Phelps was in Lake Placid and was on her way. It would be a good half-hour, depending on traffic. He didn't like going in alone, but he liked waiting even less. What could Constance Stiler possibly intend by taking Melanie to the Veeches? Surely they didn't think they could kill the girl to shut her up and no one would make the connection. He thought Constance had more sense than that, but he was afraid the Veeches might take drastic action first, and think about the consequences later.

He decided to call for the ambulance too. Probably completely unnecessary, but what the hell. Roger and the boys on the squad lived for this kind of thing. He gave them strict orders to wait at the turnaround on Harkness Road. If there was any possibility of violence at the Veeches, he didn't want the volunteer paramedics mixed up in it.

Frank steered the car up the rutted dirt road to the Veech property. At least this time, he knew where he was going. Before long, he could make out glimpses of the dilapidated Veech houses through the almost bare trees. Frank pulled into the clearing and he and Earl got out of the car, the noise of their arrival echoing through the still woods.

The door to the first shack slammed open and Melanie flew out. She ran toward them across the hard-packed dirt yard, head down, dodging old tires and rusty appliances, the look of intense concentration on her face almost comical. The little ditz-brain wouldn't pull a stunt like this again any time soon. Relief unwound the coil of tension in Frank's gut.

No one saw him coming.

The dog appeared from the trees, running with startling speed. He hit Melanie at the shoulders and knocked her down so unexpectedly she had no time to put out her hands to break the fall. Her face hit the ground with the same impact as her knees and chest.

Frank was out of the car by the time the second dog appeared. Smaller than the first, he latched onto Melanie's jean-clad leg and worried it back and forth like a toy. The first dog, the same brindle-coated beast that had attacked the patrol car on their first visit, went about his work with deadly intent.

With his enormous paws planted on Melanie's back, he pinned her to the ground, her head and neck within easy reach of his slavering jaws. Frank drew his gun just as the dog lowered his head over Melanie's and bit into her scalp.

Her shrieks rent the air. Earl ran forward, but the other dog immediately came after him, baying ferociously and blocking any move to rescue the girl. Then a third dog joined the pack.

"Get back, Earl!" Frank dropped to one knee and prepared to shoot. The big dog raised his head. Saliva, mixed with Mel's blood, dripped from his mouth. Melanie writhed to get free, but as Frank took aim, the dog flattened his body, lowered his massive head over Melanie, and bit again.

"Shoot him! Shoot him!" Earl screamed. But it wasn't that easy. Frank could hit a bull's eye nine times out of ten on the firing range, a margin of error wholly unacceptable in this circumstance. He had to wait for the perfect opportunity or risk killing the girl.

Melanie's shrill screams and the dogs' deep barks blended in a horrific harmony. She struggled and thrashed under the dog, which weighed at least as much as she did. His attack grew more frenzied as she fought against him.

"Roll into a ball, Melanie! Protect your neck. Try to go limp."

Maybe if the dog thought he'd killed her he'd let up for a moment and Frank could pull off a shot. But Melanie continued to thrash, too terrified to follow instructions, if she'd even heard them.

Frank changed his position. If he could bring down the other dogs, he could move in for a clearer shot. He moved to the side so that Melanie and the big dog would not be in his line of fire, and shot the dog that was holding Earl at bay. Its body arched in the air with the force of the shot, and flopped down.

The sound of the shot caused the big dog to pause and look around. This was Frank's chance. He aimed. As his finger tightened on the trigger, the shack door opened and little Olivia ran straight toward him.

Jesus Christ, could this get any worse!

He lowered his gun—the opportunity had passed. The dog got a mouthful of Mel's yellow sweater and ripped it away, exposing the bare flesh of her back. Then he bit again.

Olivia continued running right at the dog and Melanie. That's all he needed, for the dog to turn on her. "Get back, Olivia. Go back in the house."

But Olivia paid him no mind. She slid to a stop a foot from the dog. "Cujo, release!" she shouted. The dog hesitated, but kept Melanie's shoulder locked in his jaws.

Olivia reached over and rapped him on the snout with her bare hand. "Release! Now!"

Reluctantly, the dog opened his mouth.

Olivia locked eyes with the brute and pointed her finger in the direction of one of the sheds. "Go. Go to your bed."

Frank watched in astonishment as the big dog drooped his head and tail and slunk away, followed by the second smaller dog. When cops who worked with dogs talked about how important it was for the animal to recognize which people were higher than it in the pack, Frank had dismissed it as doggy pop psychology. But obviously Cujo accepted a sixty-pound child as his social superior.

Earl reached Melanie's side first. He tore off his shirt and used it to stanch the flow of blood from the worst wounds on her back. Although her face was covered with blood, miraculously, the dog had never succeeded in biting her neck. She was still conscious, but obviously in shock. Mel needed immediate care—he'd have to deal with the Veeches and Constance later.

Frank picked her up and carried her to the patrol car. Carefully, he slid her into the back seat, where Earl cradled her head in his lap. In minutes they were transferring her into the ambulance. Earl rode along as they tore off.

Seconds later, Trooper Pauline Phelps arrived and she and Frank headed back up the rutted road to the Veeches'. With Pauline driving, Frank noticed something he hadn't seen on his first trip up the hill: a small red Chevy parked among some trees about twenty yards from the clearing where the Veeches houses were located. Melanie's car.

When they pulled up in front of the cluster of shacks, the only sign of the nightmare that had just unfolded were some dark stains on the dirt. Frank reached for the bullhorn to call the Veeches out, but it wasn't necessary. An old man appeared on the sagging porch of the second shack.

Pap Veech was as lean as his daughter was fat, but there was nothing frail about him. Big, powerful hands protruded like pruning hooks from the too-short sleeves of his faded flannel shirt. A golf-ball sized lump distended his right cheek. He moved it with his tongue and spoke.

"You killed my dog." A glob of brown spit followed the words out of his mouth.

"You people abducted Melanie Powers. I want Ralph, Anita and Constance Stiler out here right now," Frank commanded. "You're all under arrest."

"That girl trespassed on my proppa-tee. I got signs sayin' to watch out for them dogs. That's what happens when strangers get too close. She got no one to blame but herself."

The old man's brazen offensive seemed deranged in the circumstances. "Constance brought her here. You were holding her inside your house," Frank repeated.

"There ain't no Constance here."

Frank glanced around. The only vehicle in sight was a rusted pea-green Impala with three wheels. They had to have come together in Mel's car. Certainly no car had passed them on their trips up and down the dirt road that led to Harkness. He remembered something Joe Sheehan had said. "There's another way out of here. Where's Ralph?"

Pap shrugged. "Ralph left this morning and he ain't been back. That girl come sneakin' up here. She went right into Anita's place, snoopin. The dogs were protecting our proppa-tee."

"George Stiler told me that Melanie and Constance came up here."

"George Stiler? Ain't he that sick man who can't talk? Don't see how he coulda told you nothing."

The man really did plan on denying everything. Well, he'd see how long they all stuck to that strategy. Being questioned—separately—at state police headquarters might produce a variety of different tunes.

Frank walked toward Pap Veech with his handcuffs out. "You're going for a ride, Mr. Veech. And so is your daughter."

FRANK HAD PAULINE TAKE the Veeches to the state police barracks in Ray Brook while he stopped back at the Stilers' home. This time, when he knocked on the door, Constance answered.

She looked like she always did—neatly dressed, not a silver hair out of place. Her expression was serious, but not particularly nervous. She let him in without question and began talking first.

"I'm afraid I'm having a rather difficult day. I went out to run a few errands, and when I got back I found my husband having a small seizure. I finally have him medicated and in bed, resting."

"I'm sorry to hear that. I guess I should have realized he didn't look too good when I left him. But, you see, I was too worried about Melanie Powers." Frank watched her reaction intently, but all he noticed was her hands tightening their grip on the top of the kitchen chair.

"What do you mean? You were here earlier?"

"Yes," Frank checked his watch. "I guess it was about an hour and a half ago, now. I was looking for Melanie Powers. Your husband told me that you and Mel went down the road to the Veech place."

Constance took a step backward. "I have no idea what you're talking about. Who is this Melanie person? How could my husband tell you anything? He can no longer speak."

"No, but he can hear. He can answer yes or no to questions that are put to him. And he told me that Melanie Powers was here."

"You must be mistaken, Chief Bennett. My husband is very easily upset. When he's agitated, it's difficult even for me to understand what he's trying to communicate."

"Well, ma'am, I might agree with that, except, you see, he was right. He told me Mel was at the Veeches' place, and that's where I found her. When I got there, she was being attacked by the Veeches' dogs. You wouldn't happen to know anything about that, would you?"

Constance turned her back and began spraying the immaculate countertops with cleaner and scrubbing. "What could I possibly know? I don't even know the girl."

"Really? You didn't meet her in the park in Verona this morning?"

Constance pursed her lips and let loose another blast of Formula 409. "No."

"Where were you then?"

"In Lake Placid, shopping."

"In what stores?"

"I don't remember."

"Oh come on, now. There aren't that many places to go...was it Eastern Mountain Sports, the Bookstore, the outlets?"

"I was just window shopping. I needed to get out."

Frank pulled out a chair and sat, stretching his legs before him. "Poor Melanie was terribly hurt. She's in surgery now. But she's young and strong. She'll recover. And when she does, she'll tell me exactly what happened."

Frank paused. Constance lifted up canisters, wiped beneath them, and banged them down.

"You know, Constance, it might go easier with you if you just told me everything now. All about Sheltering Arms. About Mary Pat and her baby. Tell me where Diane Sarens is, and if she's had her baby yet."

Constance stopped scrubbing. "Who...?" Suds oozed between the fingers of the hand that clutched the pink sponge. "I want a lawyer."

"A lawyer? Why would you need a lawyer?"

"You obviously have it in your head that I am involved with something illegal. I won't have you twisting my words and trying to pin something on me that I didn't do. I want a lawyer."

Frank stood up. "All right, then. Call your lawyer—tell him to meet us at state police headquarters in Ray Brook."

For the first time, Constance looked afraid. "I can't leave my husband."

"Then talk to me here."

She wavered, then stepped toward the phone. "I'll get Judy Penniman to sit with him. Just give me a few minutes and I'll be ready to go."

Chapter 33

The buzzing florescent tubes in the ceiling of the police department cast the only light in the town square. There was no moon, and a dense cloud cover obscured the usual canopy of stars. Malone's and the Store were closed; all the meetings at the church were long over.

Two hundred and twenty five stitches and three units of blood later, Melanie Powers lay heavily sedated in post-op recovery. The doctors said it would be at least forty-eight hours until she could talk to Frank. The Veeches' two surviving dogs were under observation at the state police animal control unit. Pap, Ralph and Anita Veech had steadfastly stuck to their story: Ralph had been out all morning checking his beaver traps; Anita and Pap had been in Pap's house when Melanie had sneaked into Anita's place; the dogs had attacked when they discovered the trespasser on the property. All three denied any knowledge of Sheltering Arms, and the whereabouts of Diane Sarens. Pap had finally been charged with failure to control an aggressive animal, and released on his own recognizance.

Constance Stiler had followed the advice of the lawyer she had brought in from Lake Placid and had refused to answer questions. When Frank pointed out that she would be compelled to testify before a grand jury, the lawyer had merely smiled and shrugged. "When, and *if,* one is convened, Chief Bennett."

Now, all of them were back in their own homes while Frank sat in his office.

He craved solitude to plan his next move, and had commanded Earl to go home, but relented at the stricken look on the kid's face. Melanie's family held Earl responsible for what had happened, making him persona non grata at the hospital. But Earl's restless sighing and pacing were driving Frank to distraction.

"Can't you sit still?"

"I can't help it," Earl whined. "It's not fair that Melanie's hurt so bad and none of them are in jail."

"I explained it to you, Earl. We need corroborating evidence. The Veeches say Mel was trespassing. We have nothing to prove she wasn't."

"What about what Mr. Stiler said?"

"He didn't *say* anything. It's not even hearsay. It's less than nothing."

"But when Mel comes around, we'll get them, right?"

Frank sighed. By the time Mel came around, Constance Stiler and the Veeches would have had two full days to destroy evidence and cover their tracks. Even then, it would just be her word against theirs. He needed concrete proof *now* that they were running an illegal adoption business. Finding Diane Sarens would help—she might be able to identify Anita or Constance. But if she couldn't, Mel's testimony alone would not be enough to bring the whole operation down. A good lawyer could tie that girl up in knots on the witness stand.

He could see now what he was up against. They were much shrewder than he gave them credit for; they wouldn't collapse and confess.

Earl continued to yammer. "I should have known. My cousin Donald warned me about Anita Veech. He said she was really mean, and smarter than she acts."

"How does Donald know Anita so well?"

"They were in the same class at school."

"Anita went to school with your cousin Donald? I thought he was only a few years older than you?"

"That's right, he's twenty-seven."

Frank let some papers slip out of his hands onto the desk. "Are you telling me Anita Veech is only twenty-seven? She looks like she's forty."

"Nah. Maybe she's twenty-eight, or nine, if she got held back, but definitely not forty."

The fat and bad teeth had misled him. But now he remembered something Olivia had told him right here in this office. She said, 'I had a brother but he went away.' He'd assumed she had an older brother who'd left home. But if Anita had been twenty when Olivia was born, an older brother would be too young to leave home. Which meant he had to be younger than Olivia.

"What about Anita's other child, her son?" Frank asked Earl.

"Son? I never knew she had a son."

"Olivia told me she had a brother who went away."

Earl shook his head. "She was trying to put one over on you. All those Veeches lie."

"No." Frank answered out loud, but he was talking to himself more than Earl. "No, she wasn't lying. She had no reason to lie. I think Anita had another child recently, and I have a feeling I know what happened to him."

———— ◉ ————

FRANK AND THE ESSEX County prosecutor sat in the Chambers of Judge Roland Kovally. Chambers was a pretty glorified term for Kovally's very ordinary office, and "your honor" was a pretty glorified form of address for a mild-mannered, middle aged man who looked more like a social studies teacher than a judge. When he'd sized up the setting, Frank had been quite confident that Kovally would quickly grant them the court order needed to access Anita Veech's medical records at the Saranac Lake Hospital.

"Absolutely not," Kovally was saying. "You have no evidence that this woman is involved in anything illegal. Medical records are accorded the highest level of privacy. And adoption records are even more protected."

"But there's a good chance that the adoption was illegal," Frank protested. "And the father of Mary Pat Sheehan's baby was denied—"

Kovally held up his hand for silence. "You've explained all that to me Chief Bennett. Until you can bring me more evidence that Ms. Veech was involved in this illegal adoption scheme, her medical records are off limits. I think we're finished here."

"Sorry, Frank," the prosecutor apologized out in the hallway.

Frank glared at Kovally's closed door. "I thought everyone up here was a Republican law-and-order type. Where did Mr. Civil Liberties come from?"

"He falls into the 'keep government out of private citizen's lives' camp, I think."

"Fine. He wants more evidence, I'll get him more evidence."

"What makes you think Anita had her baby in the hospital?" Earl asked. They were in the patrol car on the way to Verona to see if anyone had witnessed the meeting between Melanie and Constance. "She mighta had it at home, just like Mary Pat."

Frank shook his head. "I don't know for sure, but I doubt it. You see, I don't think Anita necessarily tried to hide her pregnancy. She's just so fat, nobody noticed. And don't forget, she's only been working at the Stop 'N Buy for the past six months—before that, I never used to see her around town."

"Yeah, the Veeches really keep to themselves. You know, I heard she only took that job because they were going to cut off her welfare. This way, she gets to keep her food stamps," Earl said.

"That plays right into my idea of why she wanted to give the baby up," Frank agreed. "It used to be, you got extra welfare money every time you had another baby. It doesn't work that way anymore; you don't get anything extra if you have the baby while you're collecting—it's supposed to discourage people from having more kids they can't support. This baby was going to be a drain on the family finances, but then Anita, or maybe Pap, saw one of those ads in the paper and they realized they could actually *get* money for it if they gave it up for adoption. And when Anita noticed that Mary Pat was in trouble, she connected her with Sheltering Arms. And got a cut of the action, I'm sure."

"Couldn't you try to get Olivia to tell you more about the baby brother who went away?"

Frank sighed. "I thought of that, but a parent has the right to be present whenever a minor is interrogated. And Olivia certainly won't volunteer anything with her mother in the room."

"You could try to trip her up."

"I'm afraid, Earl. Can you imagine what Pap would do to her if she were the one to blow their cover? I can't put Olivia in danger."

"You oughta get Trudy Massinay to take Olivia away from them," Earl said righteously. "The way those people live is disgusting. They use an outhouse, for God's sake."

"It's not that easy, Earl. I know it seems to us like Olivia would be better off with just about anyone compared to Pap and Anita, but they're her family. Lack of indoor plumbing is not enough reason to take a kid away from her mother.

"No, I've decided that Constance Stiler is the weakest link. If I can scare her enough, I can get her to talk. She's not used to lying."

"Not like the Veeches. Why would a nice lady like Mrs. Stiler get mixed up with them anyway?"

"It has to be money, I think. She's running out of money for her husband's medical care. She must've been desperate for cash to get involved with this adoption scheme."

"Mrs. Stiler and the Veeches—you think that's all there is to Sheltering Arms?"

"No, there has to be someone coordinating the whole operation."

"Dr. Galloway?"

Frank shrugged. "He's got the brains for it. And I'm sure he's lying to me about Diane Sarens. But there could be someone outside the area—all that Internet stuff could be done from anywhere. I just hope I can get Mrs. Stiler to tell us the rest."

Earl looked unconvinced, but crossing the one lane bridge over Stony Brook just before the Verona town limits forced a change of topic.

"Where do you want to start?" Earl asked as Frank parked the car in the center of the two-block long main street of the village.

"You ask in all the stores if anyone noticed Melanie and Mrs. Stiler here yesterday. Don't just ask the workers, ask the shoppers. They'd be more likely to have seen them on the street, or in the park." Earl nodded, taking a picture of Melanie along to jog people's memories, although it was possible he wouldn't need it. Verona and Trout Run were part of the same regional school district, so families in both towns with kids tended to know each other. Constance would be less well known since she hadn't raised her kids in the area, but, of course, she wasn't about to give them a picture.

Frank headed directly for the town park where Mel had agreed to meet the mysterious woman who was supposed to help her give her baby up for adoption. The weather had changed dramatically since yesterday. With low gray clouds blocking the sun, the temperature barely hit fifty. The wind blew steadily from the west, carrying occasional spurts of drizzle. Frank pulled his collar up and buried his hands in his pockets as he walked the block from the main street to the grassy area on the bank of the brook.

A swinging wooden sign announced that he'd arrived at the Carl W. Fahey Memorial Park. He didn't know who Carl had been, but his tribute amounted to a picnic table, two wooden benches, a trashcan and some rickety playground equipment. Not surprisingly, the place was deserted.

He looked around. The closest building had a shop on the ground floor with two levels of apartments above. Six windows faced the park. Frank walked over and climbed the stairs in back that led to the apartment doors. No one was home at the second floor apartment, but the blare of the TV on the third floor told him he was in luck.

The door was opened by a woman in her seventies with keen brown eyes and gleaming white dentures. She looked delighted to find a policeman on her doorstep. Before long she had him settled at her kitchen table with a cup of coffee and some really excellent molasses cookies.

"You came at the right time. Oprah was just finishing up, and I can't stand that fella who comes on next. Now, you want to know who was over at the park yesterday?" She stretched forward to improve her view out the kitchen window. "No one there today, but yesterday was nice. There were quite a few folks in and out, as I recall."

Frank pulled out his photo of Melanie. "Do you recognize this girl? She was pregnant."

"Can't say as I do." She looked disappointed. "It's hard to make out faces at this distance. And everyone was wearing heavy coats."

"Did you recognize anyone who was at the park yesterday? If I could talk to someone who was there, they might remember seeing Melanie."

Her face lit up. "You know who was there for quite a while–Ruthie Phipps and her boys, Jason and Mason. I know it was her cause she's got one of those big double strollers, and she always dresses the twins just alike. This year, their jackets are bright orange. She musta picked 'em up on sale."

"That's very helpful, ma'am. You wouldn't happen to know where she lives?"

"Oh, sure. Over on Fowler Street. Pink house, second from the corner."

Frank drove there in five minutes. When the young woman answered the door, Frank had no doubt he was at the right house. Behind her on the floor rolled a writhing mass with four legs, four arms and two identical heads. The young mother quickly identified Mel's picture. "I know it was her. My little sister was a cheerleader with Melanie. But I didn't talk to her—she was so caught up in what this other woman was saying, I don't think she even noticed me."

"What did the other woman look like?"

She shrugged. "She was sitting down, and wearing a thick coat and a hat."

Great, it did no good to prove Mel was there—he had to be able to prove to Constance that someone had identified her in Verona. "Think, ma'am. Was there anything distinctive you remember about her?"

"The hat, Mommy!" One of the little boys piped up from behind her.

"Oh, that's right. Her hat blew off and rolled right across the playground. Jason chased it down for her and brought it back. And before she put it back on, I noticed she had the prettiest pure silver hair I'd ever seen."

"TRUDY MASSINAY CALLED," Doris announced as soon as Frank got back to the office. "She says to call—it's very important."

Frank rushed to his phone and dialed. Trudy answered on the first ring.

"I found Diane," she announced. "She's okay."

Now things were looking up. "Great! Where is she? I want to talk to her."

"There's no need for that. She's been staying at the battered women's shelter in Lake Placid. It never even dawned on me to check there, but when I was placing a client, there she was. Dr. Galloway helped her get in."

"A shelter? Galloway helped? What are you talking about?"

"It seems Diane's father has always been abusive, mostly to her mother, but since Diane got pregnant he's been hitting her, too. Dr. Galloway's been treating her, and he noticed signs of the abuse. He convinced her to go into the shelter so she'd be safe until the baby came."

"But why did she run out on me like that?" Frank asked.

"I guess she freaked when you started talking about adoption. Everyone's been encouraging her to give the baby up, but she wants to keep it. That still hasn't been settled."

"What do you mean 'everyone' has been encouraging her to give the baby up? Did Constance Stiler try to persuade her?"

"No, I mean her parents, her friends. I asked her about Constance—she claims she never saw her at the clinic. She only went three times, always when the other nurse was on duty."

"Why the hell didn't Galloway tell me where Diane was? What was the point of keeping the secret from me?"

"Diane said Dr. Galloway told her about a nurse he worked with during his residency. She was being stalked by an ex-boyfriend and got a restraining order against him. The police did nothing to protect her, and the guy came into the ER one night and shot her dead in front of Galloway. He's been mistrustful of the police ever since."

"I still need to talk to Diane," Frank insisted. Galloway might be honest, but Frank couldn't believe a perfect candidate for Sheltering Arms could present herself at the clinic and Constance wouldn't know about it. "Tell her I'll be there in half an hour."

———————◈———————

CONSTANCE STILER SAT in the interview room of state police headquarters looking as perfectly relaxed as a nun in a cathedral. Frank watched her through the one-way glass for a moment. He wanted badly to wipe that composure off her face. The interview with Diane Sarens had been a bust. The girl insisted that Constance had never treated her at the clinic, and that Dr. Galloway had never offered to help her give her child up for adoption. Still, she'd been jumpy as a cat, and reluctant to say much about Galloway. And Galloway was still away.

A tap at the door signaled him. Constance's lawyer had arrived—the interview could begin.

Frank took a seat opposite them. Constance's eyes met his without hesitation.

"How long has your husband been sick, Mrs. Stiler?" Frank began.

Constance looked a little startled. She glanced at her lawyer, but he nodded.

"About five years."

"And he's not going to get any better, is he?"

"Parkinson's is a progressive disease. Eventually it's fatal," she answered coldly.

"His treatment must be very expensive. Does your insurance cover all that?"

"Get to the point, Chief Bennett. This is all irrelevant," the lawyer objected.

"And taking care of an invalid must be very time-consuming," Frank went on. "I imagine your children have careers and young kids to take care of—they're probably not able to help much. In fact, if something were to happen to you, I suppose your husband would have to go into a nursing home."

Constance took a drink from the water glass on the table. "Nothing's going to happen to me. I'm quite healthy."

"I can see that," Frank replied. "I meant if you should have some legal trouble that would put you out of commission for a while..."

"That's enough! You're threatening my client. Ask her what you intended to ask about Melanie Powers, or we're leaving."

Constance looked approvingly at her lawyer, and Frank could see that he'd rattled her a little. Now he was ready to move in.

"Melanie Powers received an email offering to help her give a baby up for adoption. She arranged to meet that person in the park in Verona to discuss it. That person was you, wasn't it Mrs. Stiler?"

"No."

"I have a witness who saw you talking to Melanie in the park on Monday."

"Who?" the lawyer interjected.

"A young mother playing there with her twin boys. You probably remember seeing them, Mrs. Stiler."

"Since I wasn't there, Chief Bennett, I don't."

"This woman can identify you." Frank insisted.

"I don't know any young people in Verona. I don't see how she can say she knows me," Constance said.

"She knows Melanie, and she saw who Mel was talking to."

"Did she identify my client by name?"

"She described her in detail."

"What detail? How she was dressed?" The lawyer gestured toward the winter coat hanging on a rack by the door. "My client wears a green LL Bean jacket. I think I've seen about ten of them walking around this week—they're very popular."

Constance Stiler let go of the glass she'd been holding and sat back in her chair.

"The witness said the woman she saw had striking silver hair," Frank answered.

"Put my client in a line-up with five other mature ladies with silver hair, Chief Bennett. If your witness can pick her out, then maybe we have something to talk about. Let's go, Mrs. Stiler."

Frank waved them back into their seats. "By tomorrow I'll be able to speak to Melanie Powers in the hospital. She's going to tell me how you coerced her into going to the Veech place. She's going to explain what you did to her up there. Why don't you make it easier on yourself and tell me what part Anita and her family played in this adoption scam?"

Constance stood up. "Everyone on Harkness Road knows about the Veeches' dogs, Chief Bennett. I wouldn't dream of going up there." She fixed him with a sphinx-like smile. "When you find out what inspired that poor girl to take such a chance, do let me know."

She slid her arms into the coat that her lawyer held for her. The man opened the door and glanced back over his shoulder.

"Good afternoon. I hope this has been helpful."

Frank listened as their footsteps petered out down the hall. If Constance Stiler was the weakest link, this case was bound up in an anchor chain.

Frank stood at the nurses' station on the second floor of the Saranac Lake hospital arguing with Melanie Powers' doctor.

"She's had a terrible trauma," the doctor said. "She's loaded up on painkillers. I doubt you'll get much sense out of her."

"It's vitally important—just let me try."

The doctor scowled. "All right, but put a mask and gown on—she's at risk of infection."

Frank slipped into Melanie's room. She lay propped up in bed, her head, shoulders and right arm swathed in bandages. Her pretty face peeked out, remarkably unscathed. She glanced at him without recognition—probably thought he was another doctor come to poke and prod her.

"Hi, Melanie...it's Chief Bennett."

Her eyes, which had been at half-mast, flew open.

"How are you feeling?"

She smiled slightly. "A little better."

He could see that she was groggy. No time for pleasantries—he'd better get right to the point. "Mel, I need to ask you some questions. Who did you meet at the park in Verona?"

"Mrs. Stiler."

"Did she offer to place your baby for adoption?"

"We talked about babies. She was careful what she said, but I knew..." Melanie's eyelids fluttered.

Gingerly, Frank took her left hand in his and squeezed it slightly. Mel resumed. "I went back to her house in my car, like I was still interested in knowing more about it. Then after we talked she left me alone to make a phone call, and I slipped out the back door. But her husband saw me."

"She didn't go with you to the Veeches?" Could Constance have been telling the truth after all?

"No..." Again the eyelids dipped.

"Melanie!" he said sharply. She snapped to attention. "Why did you go to the Veeches?"

"I'm sorry," she whimpered. "I overheard something at work, and I thought I'd check on that, too."

"What?" Frank demanded.

"That Ralph is growing something up there. Plants..."

Her eyes shut, and Frank couldn't rouse her again.

FRANK ENTERED THE EMPTY office and plopped down at his desk, grateful to sit and rest.

The raid on the Veech place had gone surprisingly well. He'd been in on the discovery of the generator that ran the florescent lights and heating system that kept three hundred marijuana plants growing in a shed deep in the woods behind the Veeches' living quarters. He'd even stayed long enough to witness the uncovering of hundreds of packets of PCP. But he'd left when the state police handcuffed Ralph, Anita and Pap, because he couldn't bear the reproachful glare of little Olivia as she sat in a patrol car waiting for Trudy to come and take her away.

So he had solved the mystery of where Dean Jacobson had got his drug of choice, and figured out why Anita had been so anxious to keep him from snooping around Harkness Road, but he was no further along on proving who ran Sheltering Arms.

In the middle of his blotter lay a manila folder with a sticky note covered in Earl's childish scrawl. "Thought you might be interested in this. I got it from my Uncle Harry's brother's wife. She's a nurse. I went to see Melanie today but they still won't let her have visitors."

Frank opened the folder. Inside was a slightly crooked photocopy of a hospital form. At the top, his eyes scanned the typewritten words "Veech, Anita," before being drawn by a section outlined in yellow hi-liter. "Discharge notes: Mother relinquished baby for adoption. Baby left hospital in custody of Barry Sutter, Esq."

Chapter 34

"Are you out of your *mind*?" Frank had hauled Earl into the office where he cowered in his chair as Frank paced back and forth. "Haven't you learned one thing, *one* friggin' thing from me in a year and a half?"

Frank waved the file folder. "This is illegally obtained evidence—we can't use it. The judge specifically denied me access to Anita's records."

"Yeah, but can't we use it to pressure Mrs. Stiler? Tell her we know that the Goldings and Green Tomorrow are behind the adoption scam? Make her admit she works for them?"

"How can we do that? Think, Earl, think! Her lawyer's going to demand to know how I came upon this information. And if your cousin's father's brother's wife— whoever she is—is anything like you, she's probably blabbed her part in it to everyone who'll listen."

Earl looked particularly miffed at this assault on the honor of his extended family. "She has not. I told her how important it was to keep it a secret. Besides, she'd get in trouble at work if anyone knew it was her."

Frank still seethed. "You're a loose cannon, Earl. Why do you go off and do these things without talking it over with me first?"

"I was just over at the hospital and I ran into Gail, and well, it seemed like a good idea. I didn't think..."

"That's just it, Earl—you don't think. You. Do. Not. Think. Now get out of here."

Earl slunk toward the door.

"And I'm not writing that letter of recommendation for the police academy," Frank yelled after him.

Frank found it hard to concentrate when every drop of blood in his body felt like it was boiling through his brain. He tried taking a few deep breaths to calm down, but he'd really never bought into the whole yoga thing. He got up and kicked the wastepaper can a few times and felt a little better.

Gradually, the significance of what Earl had discovered was sinking in. Green Tomorrow was linked to Sheltering Arms. Baby-selling was just another activity the group used to raise money. He would have been content just to chase Green Tomorrow out of town when he thought all they were involved in was the attempt to shut down Raging Rapids. But he sure as hell wasn't going to let them continue to exploit young women and desperate couples—their operation might reach all over the country for all he knew.

The tricky part was he had to make the case against Sheltering Arms without using the illegal evidence Earl had produced. Without, in fact, ever revealing that he knew it. And that ruled out using the state police auditors to try to piece together the money trail between Green Tomorrow and Anita Veech, Constance Stiler and the Finns.

Constance and Anita weren't yielding to pressure. Meredith Golding would probably be just as resilient. It was time to put all his energy into finding the Finns, and Mary Pat's baby. And now he had the advantage of knowing the baby's father had never given permission for her adoption and wanted her back. He reached for the phone. Here was something he could use state police help for without compromising himself, or Earl.

<hr />

FRANK SAT IN THE COMPUTER lab of the Buchanan Open Academy looking over the shoulder of the state police computer technician. The principal of Brian Finn's school had been more than willing to give them access to the computer network. Brian's disappearance had undermined his confidence in the security of the system. "Who knows what he was up to in here," the principal complained, as he lurked around the back of the lab. "For all I know, the whole school's in here shopping on eBay and downloading porn. Can you check on that for me while you're in there?"

The technician grunted.

Frank shifted impatiently as screens full of unintelligible code flashed before his eyes. The technician tapped, squinted, tapped some more then sat back with a snort of satisfaction. He pointed to something on the screen. "Someone's been logging in remotely using Finn's password."

"Remotely from where?"

"Probably a public access computer—a cybercafé or a library. We can trace it eventually."

"What did Finn do when he got in?"

" Looks like he accessed some files, then deleted them."

"Deleted them? Can you get them back?"

"No, but it looks like Finn ran a pretty tight ship here. Everything's backed up automatically. We'll find it there. He couldn't erase the back-up remotely."

Frank settled back to watch the technician work.

"This could take a while. Why don't you go get some coffee or something?"

Frank forced himself to stay out for forty-five minutes. When he returned, the technician was pulling some documents from a printer. Frank took a copy of what looked like an email that had been saved and read:

Dear Mr. Finn:

I understand your concern for the lack of documentation. Rest assured that after we receive the final payment you will receive the certificate.

Barry

"Is that it?" Frank asked. "He must be referring to the baby's birth certificate, but he's kept everything intentionally vague."

"Look at this one."

Dear Mr. Finn:

The BM has experienced some unanticipated expenses. We will require an additional $20,000 to complete the transaction.

Barry

"BM must be Birth Mother. Can you prove what computer these messages were sent from?"

"If you know who this Barry is, we can get a warrant and seize his computer. They'll show up on there."

"Do it. And find where Finn was when he accessed this system."

Frank kept busy tracking down the Finns' friends and relatives while the technician worked his magic. By the time the computer jock called with the news that Brian Finn had used the computer at the Glens Falls public library last Tuesday, Frank had discovered that Eileen Finn's sister Brenda lived in Glens Falls.

In less than an hour, he sat in Brenda's kitchen. She bore an amazing resemblance to her sister that extended right down to her voice and gestures, even to the impeccable crispness of her clothes. "I don't know what's going on," she told Frank as she picked at the hem of the placemat before her. "Eileen came here alone on Friday the fourth. She said she came to say good-bye, that she and Brian would be away for a while, but she wouldn't say where. She wouldn't answer any of my questions. Said it was best I didn't know. Then she kissed me and left."

"Where would they go? Is there a vacation home somewhere? A town in another part of the country where they might have some connections?"

Brenda shook her head, teary-eyed now. "I can't think of anything. Why is this happening? Is Eileen in danger?"

"The adoption they were trying to arrange was illegal, ma'am. We think they took off with the baby."

"But the deal fell through. Eileen was devastated."

"That's what they claimed. But I think somehow they got her back, and now they're on the run."

Brenda shook her head. "I don't think they have the baby."

"Why not?"

"If Eileen had that baby, she'd be happy. Even if it was illegal, even if it meant giving up her home and her job." Brenda stopped her fidgeting and looked Frank in the eye. "She wasn't happy when I saw her. She was terrified. Please find her, Chief Bennett. I'm worried sick."

Frank looked around the neat, cheerful kitchen that so resembled Eileen's, heard the sound of children giggling at cartoons in the next room, smelled a pot roast cooking, and with a sickening certainty it came to him why the Finns had disappeared.

Chapter 35

Meredith Golding faced Frank and Meyerson across a table in an interview room. This was the first time they were talking to her since the attack on Melanie. By now she had to know that they had a witness to Constance and Melanie's meeting and that Barry Sutter's computer was being searched. But she also knew that all the evidence against them was circumstantial, and that no one yet had crumbled under questioning. She looked like a seasoned quarterback in a third-and-ten situation—too experienced to be cocky, but too confident to be panicked.

"Can I get you a drink before we get started?" Meyerson offered.

"No thank you, but I want to wait for my lawyer to get here."

"Sure, if that's what you want." Meyerson shrugged. "We just thought you'd be interested to hear that we're pretty certain we know who killed your husband."

Her air of studied nonchalance dropped. "That's why you called me here? That's wonderful!"

Meyerson made a waffling gesture with his hand. "We haven't actually caught him yet—we may need your help for that."

"Anything." She sat forward eagerly.

"We were just wondering," Frank took over, "if you might know where Brian and Eileen Finn might have taken off to with Mary Pat Sheehan's baby."

Instantly her face shut down. "What kind of trick are you trying to pull?"

"No trick," Frank assured her. "You see, I spent a few hours with Eileen Finn's sister yesterday and she told me quite a bit about her brother-in-law. A few things you might not know. Like how he has a hair-trigger temper when someone threatens something he cares about. Apparently he once knocked a man unconscious at a neighborhood picnic for making too many cracks about the Republican Party. So you can imagine how angry he was when you took that baby away, and broke his wife's heart."

Meredith watched him with spellbound dread. "Of course you already knew he was a teacher, but maybe you didn't realize one of the subjects he taught was computer science. Yeah, he was quite a pro. All those cryptic emails you sent him—he knew exactly where they came from.

"And one other detail about Brian Finn: he's a real newshound. Takes two newspapers everyday, addicted to CNN. He knew all about Green Tomorrow. He knew that Barry Sutter, the man arranging his adoption, worked for Green Tomorrow. But he didn't care, as long as he got that baby."

"So that was your mistake, Mrs. Golding. Not giving him that baby. Because when you told Sutter to up the ante, and the Finns couldn't pay, you underestimated your man. You thought Brian Finn would just give up and go away, but that's not the kind of man he is. He's the kind of man who takes action. He's the kind of guy who knows if you want results, you have to go straight to the top. So he didn't bother arguing with Barry Sutter or Mrs. Stiler. He took his complaint to the boss—Nathan Golding."

Meredith was leaning forward now with her elbows up on the table and her head in her hands. Frank couldn't see her eyes, but he knew she was listening.

"We went back over the phone records from your husband's room at the Mountain Vista Motel. This time, we noticed there was a call placed from your husband's room to the Buchanan Open Academy, Brian Finn's school, the day before your husband died. The state police had overlooked the significance of that. They assumed a call to a school had something to do with Green Tomorrow's environmental education program. But really, it was Brian and Nathan, arranging a meeting. At that point, I suspect Finn thought he could strike a deal to get the baby back.

"But that's where Finn miscalculated, wasn't it Mrs. Golding? Because your husband didn't know anything about Sheltering Arms, or the way you were selling babies to finance Green Tomorrow's operations. He was a very principled man—he would never have allowed that."

Frank paused, doodling in the margins of his notepad. The room was so silent, the scratch of the pen seemed to reverberate against the blank walls. "When Nathan told Finn he didn't know what he was talking about, he really meant it. But Finn had just talked to me the day before. He knew that none of the money Sheltering Arms collected ever went toward Mary Pat's medical expenses. He was sure Nathan was jerking him around, and that," Frank lowered his voice, "made him mad."

Meredith was sobbing now. "Oh, I forgot one other thing about Mr. Finn. He's a gun enthusiast. He hunts, but he also collects firearms. I've always thought that's kind of a strange hobby, collecting guns. But I guess it's no weirder than collecting stamps, or coins. Except you can't kill someone with a buffalo head nickel. But if you happen to take a small handgun from your collection to the meeting with the man you think is stealing your money and your baby and your wife's happiness, then things can get out of hand."

"Oh God! Oh, no!" was all Meredith said, then slumped back in her chair.

Silence hung in the air. Then Meredith began to speak, her eyes focused on something only she could see. "It all started as a favor. One of the volunteers, a college girl, was pregnant. She didn't want an abortion. I had friends who were eager to adopt. They met and liked each other. Barry took care of the legalities—everyone was happy. My friends made a big donation to Green Tomorrow. In gratitude, you see."

"So you just took the next logical step. Created Sheltering Arms as a money-maker to support Green Tomorrow."

Meredith didn't answer. She began to weep.

"How did Constance Stiler get involved?" Frank asked.

Meredith looked up. Her face was drained of all its usual energy and confidence. "She was the mother of that first girl whom we helped," she said woodenly. "She was grateful that we found a good home for her grandchild. We all stayed in touch. Then George Stiler got sick."

"And you realized she was a woman who could be useful to your cause. Or should I say, your business. Constance delivered Mary Pat's baby. She took her down to Albany to show her to the Finns, wearing a wig."

Meredith nodded. After interrogating Constance Stiler with such a spectacular lack of success, Frank hadn't been at all confident of breaking down Meredith Golding. But maybe the difference was that Meredith realized she'd killed the only man she ever loved, while Constance still had everything to lose.

"You're under arrest, Mrs. Golding." Calmly, Frank recited the Miranda warning. "Now, I want you to tell me who has Mary Pat Sheehan's baby."

Meredith met his eyes for the first time since he entered the room. "Their names are Sam and Theresa Buckner. They live outside Rochester."

FRANK WAS SITTING WITH Lew Meyerson when the call came in from the Rochester police. He watched Meyerson's right eyebrow go up—high emotion for Lew. This wasn't looking good.

"You searched the house?" Lew asked. Then he sighed and hung up.

"The Buckners received an email from Sheltering Arms one day after they got the baby. The email said the birth mother had changed her mind and wanted the baby back. Sheltering Arms assured them they'd have another baby ready for them in a few days, so they let her go without too much fuss."

Frank sprang to his feet. "Godammit, that bitch is still lying to us! What's she trying to pull now?"

Lew waved him back into his seat. "It's not the Golding woman. The man who came to take back the baby was a big burly fellow with blond, curly hair."

"Brian Finn."

BRIAN AND EILEEN FINN'S photos appeared on the evening news and immediately the phones started ringing. There were the usual crackpots, plus calls from well-intentioned people reporting blameless couples who bore a passing resemblance to Brian and Eileen. But one call showed promise. A woman in Malone reported renting a small furnished house six days ago to a couple with a baby who had paid the first and last month's rent and the security deposit in cash. She hadn't asked for references. Eileen's sister remembered that Brian's father had come from somewhere near there. Maybe this was an area Brian felt familiar with.

Frank and Meyerson drove toward Malone together.

"How did Finn find the baby at the Buckners'?" Meyerson asked.

"He must have just tailed Meredith and Sutter, waiting for them to move the baby. By that time, he'd already quit his job, so he just devoted himself to finding that child."

"But why not just take her away from Mrs. Golding? Why wait until the Buckners had her?"

Frank shrugged. "He would have had to take her by force from Meredith. He figured no one suspected him yet in Nathan's death, so he didn't want to do anything to give himself away. He took a gamble that he could trick the Buckners. If that didn't work, I guess he could've tried snatching the baby from them."

They crossed the city limits into Malone and Frank began to direct Lew to the house. The streets they drove down became progressively shabbier, until they pulled up in front of 162 Hauser Avenue, a Depression-era bungalow with peeling paint and a concave roof. A far cry from the trim house the Finns had abandoned on Hawthorne Lane.

Frank glanced inside the rusty Toyota Corolla parked in front of the house —a brand new infant car seat was strapped into the back. Brian Finn was a murderer and kidnapper, but a safety-conscious one.

He and Meyerson walked up the crumbling concrete path and climbed three steps onto a broad, saggy front porch. A dormer on the second floor jutted out over the porch, making its roof. Meyerson hammered on the wooden front door. "Open up, Mr. and Mrs. Finn. Police."

Immediately, they heard scurrying footsteps above them. "Sarah!" a woman's voice shrieked.

Sarah had been the name Eileen had chosen for Mary Pat's baby, Frank remembered. Absolutely no doubt now they were in the right place.

"This is Frank Bennett, Mr. Finn. Open the door, please, so we can talk."

"Talk! There's nothing to talk about." Finn sounded like he was right on the other side of the door.

"Open the door, Finn, or we'll break it down," Meyerson barked.

"You'll be sorry if you do," Brian Finn answered.

"It's over now, Mr. Finn," Frank said gently. "Get your wife and the baby and come out."

"Oh, it's over all right. Be we're not coming out. There's nothing to come out for."

"Don't talk crazy, Mr. Finn. We can work this out," Frank said.

"I'm calling for back-up," Lew mouthed. He crouched down, slipped past the front window, and jumped down off the side of the porch.

"All Eileen ever wanted was a family. We can never have that now. There's no point in going on."

No point in going on—Frank knew that feeling well enough. People had spouted all kinds of platitudes at him after Estelle's death. Time heals all wounds, a brighter day is coming, blah, blah. He'd felt like spitting in their faces. But he had gone on, even though there was no point. Just by waking up every morning and eating breakfast and putting one foot in front of the other, he'd gone on. And the point had come back, on most days, at least. He wished there was some way to tell Brian Finn that through the locked front door of 162 Hauser Avenue.

Instead he said, "We don't want anyone to get hurt, Mr. Finn. The baby's OK, so we can straighten this out." Let Finn think they didn't suspect him of Golding's murder.

He heard footsteps walking away from the door, then silence.

"Mr. Finn? Brian?"

More silence. He was just turning toward Lew when the shot rang out, so close that he reflexively dove for the ground. Lew had taken cover behind the patrol car and had his weapon drawn.

"Are you alright?" Lew shouted.

"Yeah. The shot was inside, right in the hall, or this front room," Frank answered. "Mr. Finn?" he called, but didn't expect an answer.

Lew was on the bullhorn. "Mrs. Finn, please come to a window with the baby and let us see that you're all right." They waited, but there was no sound or movement from inside the house. Three more local police cars pulled up.

"I'm going in around the back." Frank said.

"No! You don't know that Finn is down. It could be a trap," Lew shouted. "I'm calling in the SWAT team."

Great. When he had wanted Lew's help with this case, he'd shown no interest. Now he had to horn in and complicate things. Once those SWAT yahoos arrived with all their gadgetry and armor poor Eileen Finn would be so terrified she'd never come out. The whole thing would spiral out of control. He'd met the woman. He knew if he went in now he could talk her out.

"Just watch my back, Lew." Frank walked through the narrow path between the house and its neighbor and came out in an overgrown backyard. Cautiously, he looked through an uncurtained window. The kitchen appeared to be empty. He tried the back door, but it was locked. He used his penknife to slice through the window screen, pulled an old wheelbarrow under the window to raise himself and silently slid up the old double-hung window. He climbed through onto the kitchen table, then stood and looked around.

The place had fifties-style metal cabinets, and faded Formica counters. Clean baby bottles were lined up next to the stained porcelain sink. Two doors led out of the kitchen. He looked through the nearest one into the dining room, empty except for a card table with a laptop computer set up on it. Through an archway he could see part of the living room: a grungy plaid sofa and a scarred coffee table.

He turned toward the other door out of the kitchen. A narrow hallway led to the front door and the staircase upstairs. Just past the newel post, a large man's foot and part of a blue-jeaned leg were visible. Flattening himself against the wall, Frank edged closer. A trickle of blood made its way down the hall to meet him.

Frank made it to where the stairs were low enough to look through the bannisters. Brian Finn sprawled across the lower part of the staircase, the shaft of a powerful Glock semiautomatic in his mouth. The top of his head was now an integral part of the dingy wallpaper pattern in the hall.

It was what he had expected, but still shocking. He closed his eyes for a moment, then went to look into the living room from the hall doorway. The room was empty: Eileen and the baby must be upstairs.

Gingerly he stepped around the body on the steps. The creaking stair treads announced his approach. "Mrs. Finn, it's Frank Bennett, from Trout Run. I'm coming upstairs now." He kept talking slowly and calmly. "We're going to get an ambulance for your husband. Everything will be all right now." He hoped she hadn't come out in the hall.

He reached the upstairs landing. There were just two bedrooms and a bath. He pushed the closest door open—a lumpy double bed, neatly made, consumed the whole room. The bathroom was unoccupied. In the other bedroom, Frank saw a corner of bright yellow and pink fabric moving.

He peeked through the door. Eileen Finn sat in a rocking chair holding a sleeping baby. She kept her eyes focused resolutely on a picture of Pooh and Tigger on the opposite wall, as her feet pumped the chair back and forth. The baby was nestled in the crook of Eileen's left arm, her little mouth slightly agape.

"Mrs. Finn?" He extended his hand. "Come on now, it's time to go."

Eileen Finn raised her head and looked at him for a long moment. Then she lifted her right hand from where it rested on the chair cushion. In it she held a tiny silver handgun, the kind of small-caliber revolver that had ended Nathan Golding's life. She leveled it at Frank's heart.

Chapter 36

It took Frank's brain a full second to process what his eyes saw.

A woman with a baby in her lap was holding a gun on him. He knew she wasn't thinking clearly—he could practically see the disjointed thoughts ricocheting around behind her glittering eyes. But the hand that held the gun was steady, disturbingly steady.

What had he been thinking charging in here by himself, all because he wanted this thing resolved and didn't have the patience for a drawn-out standoff with the SWAT team? He criticized Earl for going off half-cocked, but who was the cowboy now?

Frank shifted his stance slightly; Eileen tracked him with the gun.

There had been a time when he wanted to die, when he would have welcomed this predicament. But he realized that time was past. He didn't want his life to end in this crummy house, shot by this pathetic woman.

"Mrs. Finn, put that gun down. If you put it down now, no one will ever know you drew a gun on a police officer. We'll pretend it never happened."

"I'll kill you if you try to take my baby away. I'll kill anyone who tries to take her."

"No one's going to take her," Frank said, in what he hoped was a reassuring voice. What the hell was the woman doing with a gun in the baby's room, anyway? Did she walk around armed while she took care of the kid? Then it dawned on him. Brian had intended for them both to die. But he couldn't bring himself to shoot his wife, so he left her with a gun to do it herself. But she hadn't. Yet.

"You're lying to me. They'll never let me keep her now. Brian was right."

"No! Brian was not right." What could he say to this woman? She had lost everything—what could he hold out to her?

"Don't do anything foolish, Mrs. Finn. Think of Sarah. When she gets older, she'll want to know about her birth, her background. If you kill me, or kill yourself with that baby in your lap, can you imagine what the newspapers and TV will do when they get a hold of the story? This will follow Sarah around for the rest of her life. Don't do that to her."

He saw her hesitate. He bit back the impulse to say any more. Just let that sink in. Finally, the hand with the gun dropped to her side.

"Let me be alone with her for a few minutes, to say good-bye."

"Slide the gun over to me first, Mrs. Finn."

The little silver gun came skittering across the floor and stopped at his feet. Frank picked it up, and with a wary glance over his shoulder, stepped out in the hall. He heard Eileen murmuring and singing to the baby. He radioed to Meyerson and told him everything was clear, and to take Brian's body out of the hall.

After about five minutes, the chair stopped rocking and Eileen appeared in the doorway, and held out the baby to him. "You take her," she said, and went back to the rocker to wait.

Frank let the state police have the arrest. What joy was there in taking that poor broken woman into custody? Outside, amid all the commotion of squad cars and ambulances and the medical examiner, the baby still slept in his arms. The thatch of jet-black hair, the tawny skin, the delicately formed features were all from Sanjiv.

Then the sun moved out from behind a cloud. The brightness and the heat on her face awakened her, when all the noise had not. She looked up at him—another stranger in her short life—and he expected her to cry. Instead, a gummy smile spread across her face, and the sweetness, the innocence, the joy in that smile was pure Mary Pat.

Chapter 37

The days following the resolution of a big case were usually ones of quiet satisfaction, but ever since finding Mary Pat Sheehan's baby Frank had felt like Typhoid Mary, spreading misery wherever he went.

The Sheehans had greeted the news that their granddaughter had been found with icy silence. Over seventy-five couples around the country had been informed that the adoptions they'd arranged through Sheltering Arms were illegal. Constance Stiler had agreed to a plea bargain with the DA that would have her serving two years at the Albion Women's Correctional Facility for her role in the adoption ring and her reckless medical treatment of Mary Pat Sheehan, which meant her husband would have to go into a nursing home. Doug Penniman was also in custody, since the forensics tests had proved his gun had been used to shoot Sanjiv Patel. Patel was still awaiting the outcome of the tests that would prove he was baby Sarah's father; in the meantime she was in a foster home. And so was Olivia Veech.

Anita, Ralph and Pap Veech couldn't make bail so they were in the county jail awaiting their trial on drug possession with intent to distribute. The DA would happily have charged them with participation in the adoption ring, but Constance insisted that although Anita had sold her own baby to Sheltering Arms, and recommended the same solution to Mary Pat, she wasn't actually on the payroll.

After her brief lapse in judgment, Meredith Golding had come to her senses and hired a high-priced lawyer. Her upcoming trial would probably make Court TV ratings soar.

Trudy Massinay had taken one look at the homes of the rest of the extended Veech family and decided Olivia would be better off in foster care. But Olivia hadn't adapted well, and the first family who'd taken her in soon gave up on her, as had the second. The list of eligible foster families in Essex County wasn't very long, and word had soon gone out that Olivia was trouble.

Frank's day had gone straight to hell when Trudy called to say she couldn't find another family to take Olivia and might have to ship her out of county to a group home for troubled children.

Frank felt the greasy burger he'd eaten for lunch rise up in his throat. "I'll take her," he volunteered.

"We don't normally place little girls with single men who work full time, Frank."

Couldn't just one thing in this damn case work out well? Was that so much to ask? "If I find someone appropriate, can you push the official paperwork through so they can take her?" Frank asked.

"Yes, but who—"

"Just give me a few hours and I'll get back to you."

LUCY SAID YES BEFORE he even had the request out of his mouth, but Edwin was adamantly opposed.

"We don't know anything about taking care of traumatized children," he objected. "She needs experienced parents."

"She just needs someone who understands her," Frank said. "Someone who doesn't assume that she's no good because of who her family is. Besides, if it doesn't work out, you can always give her back to Trudy, like the others did."

"Please, Edwin, let's try," Lucy begged. "She needs us."

Edwin's face had a look of stony anger that Frank had never seen before. He hadn't really thought about the trouble he might be stirring up between Edwin and Lucy when he'd raced over to the Inn with this plan to save Olivia. Still, he couldn't help feeling that he was right, that of all the children in the world, Olivia was perfect for Edwin and Lucy.

"The kid's as sharp as a tack, Edwin. She loves books, spends her recess in the library. She's a little diamond in the rough who just needs some polishing."

"We have to take her," Lucy cried. "You're being selfish to say no."

"Selfish! What's going to happen when Anita gets out of jail and wants Olivia back? You'll be heartbroken, Lucy, and I'll be left to pick up the pieces. Have you thought about that, Frank?"

"Actually, I have. With the quantities of marijuana and PCP we found, Anita will probably be in jail for a good ten years."

Edwin sighed. "All right, we'll take her."

Amidst the screaming and squealing from Lucy that followed, Edwin locked eyes with Frank. "You'd better be right."

Frank left the Iron Eagle confident that he had done Edwin a favor, even if his friend couldn't see it yet. The radio produced more static than music in the low-lying areas between the Inn and his house, so he switched to loudly singing, "Lord I Want to be a Christian." He broke off in the middle of the third "in-a my hear-art" when a hand-lettered sign on bright yellow paper caught his eye. "Moving Sale—Everything Must Go." Traveling too fast to make the turn down the narrow road to Beth Abercrombie's shop, he turned around and backtracked.

As he got out of his car, he passed two ladies leaving the shop with shopping bags, clucking about bargains. He entered to find the shelves half empty, and Beth sweeping up mounds of Styrofoam packing peanuts.

"Hi. What's going on?" He knew it was lame to come in here acting like nothing extraordinary had happened in the past two weeks, but starting in with explanations and apologies and reassurances seemed just as awkward, so he took the easier approach.

Beth stopped sweeping and studied him with unblinking green eyes. "I'm moving to Oregon," she said finally. "My older son is there, and the younger wants to move west when he graduates, so there's no reason for me to stay here."

"I see. This is kind of sudden, isn't it?"

"Not really. There's a vibrant arts community in Portland—I've considered moving before. The time seems right...now."

"Look, Beth, the way everything turned out. I'm sorry, but—"

She interrupted him with a sharp bang of her dustpan against the side of the trashcan. "There's no need to apologize, Frank. You were right about Meredith. I was right about Nathan. I guess it never occurred to either of us that we could both be right about Green Tomorrow."

So, she still had her back up. He didn't see how any of this was his fault, but there was no point in arguing. "You heard about Mary Pat's baby?"

"Yes, I hope it all works out for Mr. Patel. He's a nice man and he's been through a lot."

"We've arrested Doug Penniman for shooting him. I can't quite figure what his motive was, though. Meredith and Extrom both swear they knew nothing about it—not that either one of them can be trusted. Still, I don't see what purpose it served Extrom to have Sanjiv shot."

Beth began crumbling a packing peanut, making a mess where she'd just swept. "Is there any doubt that Doug was the shooter?"

"The bullet came from his gun; his prints are the only ones on it. He had kept it in a locked gun case, then he tried to sell it. He was in town that day."

"I think..." Beth's voice came out raspy and hoarse. She cleared her throat and tried again. "I think I might know why he did it."

"You do?" He thought about the night he and Beth had been together when she'd brushed off his questions about Penniman driving by her house. What was she going to tell him now?

"Do you know who lives down the road here?" Beth gestured behind her.

"It's all vacation homes, no?"

Beth nodded. "And one of them has been rented by Sean Vinson while he's supervising the work on Extrom's house."

Frank's blank expression was enough to keep her talking. "Sean let Doug drive Extrom's SUV, since they couldn't take the chance of being seen together in Doug's truck."

"What do you mean, 'take the chance'?"

Beth took a deep breath. "They were involved. With each other. You know, romantically."

Finally the light bulb went on. "Doug Penniman is *gay*?"

Beth shrugged. "Well, bisexual, I guess. I often walk down the road to the pond in the evening. I saw them one day, embracing, but they didn't see me. I kept my mouth shut—I know how difficult these things can be. A friend of mine left her husband for another woman. It was devastating for everyone."

"But wait a minute, what's this got to do with Mr. Patel?"

"You know that empty lot across from the Mountain Vista? People use it as—"

"I know—a lover's lane."

"Well, I've heard Mr. Patel gets upset because kids leave beer cans, and make noise late at night. So when he sees cars in there, sometimes he goes over and chases them away."

"So you think Patel must have caught Doug and Sean in the act? And Doug tried to *kill* him?"

"Face it, Frank. His life in Trout Run would effectively be over if *that* got out."

"Why didn't you tell me this sooner?" Now it was his turn to get testy.

"I didn't figure it all out until after you arrested Doug. I didn't think at first you needed to know about the affair with Sean—it was Doug's private business."

They glared at each other. "You know, you're as stubborn as I am," Frank said.

A glimmer of a smile tugged at her mouth. He stepped forward and took her in his arms. For a moment she stood stiffly, then relaxed into his embrace.

"Good-bye, Beth. Good luck in Oregon." He kissed the top of her head.

She tilted her head back and kissed him full on the lips. "Good-bye, Frank."

Chapter 38

"What are you doing tonight?"

"Nothing much."

"You wanta come to the Mountainside? I'm going to shoot some pool with my cousin Donald and his friends."

The no formed reflexively. The smoke at the Mountainside made him cough. The music was so loud he had to just smile and nod when people spoke to him. His eyes couldn't adjust to the dim light. Then he thought of the TV dinners stacked in his freezer, the books beside his recliner, his bed neatly made.

"Sure, I'll come. Thanks for asking."

"You wanna drive? My car's at Al's for a tune-up. Donald was going to pick me up, but it's out of his way."

They drove in silence, passing through the green and coasting down the long hill that preceded the steady climb to the Mountainside. Things had been a little strained between them since the incident with Anita Veech's medical records.

"So, how's Melanie?" Frank finally asked.

"I don't know. We broke up—she'd dating a physical therapist from the hospital now."

"Oh—I'm sorry."

Earl shrugged. "It's no big deal. She was a little crazy anyway. A girl who works with Donald is going to be at the Mountainside tonight with some of her friends. I'll check that out."

Frank smiled. So much for the heartbreak of young love.

"I hear Beth's moving away."

"Yeah, all the way to Oregon."

"That's too bad."

Frank could feel Earl's eyes studying him for a reaction. "I think she feels like starting over in a new place. I can understand that."

"Hey, guess who else is moving away? Stan Fenstock—he's going to Nashville." Earl elaborated before Frank could ask why. "He wants to be a country singer. He's sung at bars and fairs around here, but I guess he decided he's going to try to make it in the big leagues."

"Good riddance," Frank said.

"Why do you say that?"

"I think Stan is the person who tried to run you and Katie down, but I can't prove it. This plan to move to Nashville makes sense. He must've wanted his share of the money from Raging Rapids to finance his singing career."

"Yeah, I heard Roy and Abe were pretty pissed when they found out Stan was helping Green Tomorrow. But why would he want to hurt Katie—they were on the same side?"

"I think he just wanted to stir up as much controversy as possible to scare his father into selling. He knew the stunt with the truck would get Katie and everyone else more riled up."

A huge full moon was creeping up through the trees. The bare branches of the birches swayed before it. The wind blew hard enough to push the car toward the center line. It wouldn't be long before the first snow.

"When do I have to have that letter of recommendation written?" Frank asked.

Earl's head snapped to the left. "It's due in November. I thought you weren't writing it?"

"I'm sorry I threatened you like that." Frank kept his eyes glued to the road. "It's just... I want you to understand that when you do the wrong thing for what you think is the right reason, it always comes back and bites you in the ass."

Out of the corner of his eye he could see Earl studying his seat belt with great interest.

"But I'm still going to write the recommendation."

"Thanks, Frank." The last vestige of tension between them dissolved. "Say, I wonder who'll buy Beth's house? It's a real pretty spot. Maybe someone from somewhere far away will want to start over in Trout Run."

"Maybe. Anything's possible."

FRANK AND TRUDY MASSINAY sat in Malone's eating apple-cranberry pie and drinking coffee. They were the only mid-afternoon customers, and Marge had scowled at them for taking a table instead of seats at the counter, but they wanted the privacy.

"So how did it go when you brought Olivia to Edwin and Lucy's place?" Frank asked.

"Lucy fussed all over Olivia and Edwin was stand-offish. I predict Edwin will be the first to break through to her. This placement will work, I can tell."

"That's a relief—maybe I'll go and check on them tonight."

Trudy shook her head. "Keep your distance for a while, Frank. Olivia feels a lot of guilt over her mother's arrest. You're all tied up in that. Give her a chance to get her bearings before you visit."

"She shouldn't feel guilty—it's not her fault her mother is a drug dealer."

"She's seven, Frank. A very bright seven, but she still thinks like a child. In her mind, she's responsible for everything that happens in her world."

Frank gave a half-laugh. "When do you outgrow that? I'm forty-seven and I think that way. Now that I've got Olivia settled, I'm dwelling on the Sheehans. Seems like there ought to be a way to get them to help Sanjiv with little Sarah."

Trudy paused with her fork poised over her pie. "Don't worry about Sanjiv. He's doing fine. They threw a baby shower for him over at the church–twenty-five Presbyterian ladies, one Hindu man, and enough pink onesies to clothe every baby between here and Albany. And his cousin in New Jersey has introduced him to a nice Indian widow with two little boys."

"I'm not worried about Sanjiv; I'm worried about the Sheehans and Sarah. If Sarah's going to be raised in Trout Run, how can they go around pretending she's not their grand-daughter?"

Trudy's eternally affable expression slipped, and Frank saw a darkness he didn't think she was capable of. "The same way they pretended not to know their daughter was pregnant."

"But they didn't know," Frank protested. "I saw how shocked they were when I told them."

"I don't buy it, Frank. Maybe Joe didn't know, but Ann sure as hell did."

"How can you be so positive?"

"Ann's an obsessively clean housekeeper. You mean to tell me she never noticed that there were no wrappers from tampons or pads in the trash any-more, never a drop of blood on Mary Pat's panties when she did the wash?"

"Mary Pat was an adult—she must've done her own laundry."

Trudy rolled her eyes. "I've worked with Ann at church functions, Frank. She was always boasting that she did all the wash herself. She has some arcane methodology that has to be followed. The woman irons her dish towels, for God's sake."

Frank smiled. From the condition of Trudy's blouse, it was pretty clear the iron was used as a bookend at the Massinay house. Trudy's argument made sense, but he still wasn't entirely convinced. "But if Ann knew Mary Pat was pregnant, that would mean she knew Mary Pat was planning on having the baby with no one but Constance to help."

Trudy's shaggy eyebrows went up in an inverted V. "Exactly. I think Ann Sheehan knows she's ultimately responsible for her daughter's death, Frank. That's why she can't bear to see her grand-daughter."

Frank sat in a rocking chair at the Mountain Vista Motel, right behind the curtain that divided Sanjiv's living quarters from the main office. He'd taken to dropping by the motel several times a week after work, to see if Sanjiv and Sarah needed anything. He'd even eaten dinner there once or twice, after Sanjiv convinced him that not all curries were spicy hot.

Tonight, after much persuasion, Sanjiv had agreed to leave Sarah with Frank while he shopped in Verona. The baby had sucked down her bottle, let out a tremendously unladylike burp, and now lay sleeping in Frank's arms. He knew he could put her in the crib without waking her, but he enjoyed watching the rapid rise and fall of her chest, the occasional flutter of her long lashes against her cheek, the way her clenched fists gradually unfurled as she sank into a deep sleep.

The bell over the motel door sounded and Frank sighed. Now he would have to put her down, while he checked in the guest. He rose and peeked through the curtain. Joe Sheehan stood on the other side of the counter.

Frank opened the curtain and stepped into the office with Sarah still in his arms. Joe's mouth dropped open. "What are you doing here?" he asked Frank, but his eyes were already focused on the baby.

"Baby-sitting." Frank moved out from behind the counter. "Is this who you came to see?" He shifted the baby so she faced outward in his arms.

Joe came closer to study the sleeping baby, but didn't touch her.

"You can hold her," Frank said, offering Sarah up.

Gingerly, Joe took the baby into his arms. But his hands and jacket were cold from the outside air, and Sarah's eyes opened. She studied her grandfather solemnly with big, dark eyes.

Frank watched them. "She hardly ever cries."

"Just like Mary Pat," Joe whispered. He cradled the baby's dark head in his pale, freckled hand.

"What made you come over tonight?"

"Ann's at bingo," Joe said.

Did the man think he could just sneak over here and see his granddaughter on the sly whenever his wife's back was turned? Frank was about to lash out when he caught himself. It wasn't for him to decide—Sanjiv would have to determine what was best for Sarah. He tried to be more conciliatory. "You know, Sanjiv has wanted to get in touch with you, but he was afraid you were angry with him."

Joe merely shook his head, his gaze never leaving Sarah's face. "Not angry."

"So then why don't you—"

Joe raised his eyes to meet Frank's. "I can't," he said softly. "It's time to go get Ann now." He handed the baby back. "Don't tell her father I came."

Frank stood at the door staring until Joe's taillights disappeared into the night. Sarah had dozed off again in his arms, oblivious to the way her life—all eight weeks of it—had changed so many others.

He thought about Alma organizing everyone to keep the Mountain Vista open when Sanjiv had been in the hospital, and the ladies at the church throwing that shower. He thought about Dr. Galloway and Trudy looking out for Diane Sarens, and Lucy and Edwin taking Olivia. There was a lot of goodness in this town. Too bad Mary Pat and Sanjiv hadn't trusted in that—things could have turned out so much differently.

As he watched out the door, a car on the road slowed to turn—probably Sanjiv returning. But instead of making a right into the parking lot, the car turned left into the empty lot across the street. Another pair of lovers.

Maybe he should put Sarah in her crib and go roust them out of there. He'd be doing them a favor, even if they didn't recognize it. Then he smiled at his own foolishness. Whatever drama was underway across the road would play out without his direction.

He sat back down with Sarah in his arms and rocked.

THE END

Turn the page to read Chapter One of the next Frank Bennett Adirondack mystery, *Blood Knot*.

Blood Knot

Frank Bennett Adirondack Mystery #2

Chapter 1

Irene Delafield was dead and Frank Bennett was glad.

It wasn't the first time he'd been happy to hear of someone's passing. When Ronald Beemis, serial child molester, had been shanked in the exercise yard of the Missouri state prison, Frank couldn't help but feel that the world was a better place. And when Osvaldo Merguez and Tyrone "Teeko" Mills had taken each other down in a blaze of semiautomatic gunfire over contested drug turf in Kansas City, Frank had joined his fellow cops in a genial celebration at their local bar.

Irene Delafield didn't have a rap sheet; she was the organist at the Presbyterian Church in Trout Run, New York—but what she did to the fine old melodies in the Presbyterian Hymnbook was positively criminal. Under Irene's inept fingers, "Jesus Christ Is Risen Today" became a dirge. She was so flummoxed by the syncopations of "A Mighty Fortress Is Our God" that she lost the entire congregation before the first verse ended and left each person valiantly singing whatever he thought best.

As the widower of a very fine church musician, Frank couldn't bear to listen to Irene play. When he occasionally got in a churchgoing mood, he headed down to the Congregational Church in Keene Valley, where the organist put on a creditable show. Frank's flagrant disloyalty did not go unremarked in his adopted hometown. He was, after all, the police chief of Trout Run and should set an example.

So he had chosen the first Sunday in November, All Saints' Day, to rejoin the fold now that a heart attack had taken Irene off the organ bench for good. And it hadn't been bad. The service had ended with a rousing rendition of "When the Saints Go Marching In" that made sitting through Pastor Bob Rush's meandering sermon worthwhile.

He was still humming under his breath when Reid Burlingame and Ardyth Munger cornered him during fellowship hour.

"Good to see you here, Frank," Reid said. As chairman of the town council, Reid was his boss, so Frank was glad his attendance had been duly noted. "What did you think of today's music?"

Frank swallowed the last morsel of his crumb cake. "Terrific. Stepping outside the hymnal with that last number, no?"

"Matthew wanted to play it, and Bob said it was okay," Ardyth explained.

"Matthew?"

"Matthew Portman. That was him playing the piano during the service."

"Ah, *that* Matthew." Matthew Portman was only fourteen years old when he had filled in on piano last year while Irene visited her sister in Toledo, and church attendance had risen dramatically. After that, Pastor Bob had thoughtfully encouraged Irene to take more vacations, but she had clung to her organ bench with barnacle-like tenacity, and Matthew hadn't gotten another shot.

"Did you see this?" Ardyth tapped the back page of her bulletin, which proclaimed in boldface print: Hymn Sing and Pie Social, Saturday, November 14. "It's a fund-raiser so we can send Matthew for organ lessons."

Reid beamed. "We've had a real stroke of luck. Oliver Greffe, the music teacher at the North Country Academy, is quite an accomplished organist. He's agreed to instruct Matthew. It's another example of the good things that school is doing for our town now that it's under new management."

Frank braced himself for another one of Reid's rah-rah speeches. He'd hardly had a conversation with the man lately that didn't revolve around what a boon to the local economy the new North Country Academy was proving to be. The academy used to be a third-rate boarding school catering to kids who couldn't get into—or had been kicked out of—better institutions. But its remote location and indifferent academic reputation had finally driven it out of existence at the end of the last school year. Trout Run greeted the news with a big yawn—although technically within the town limits, the school had never seemed like part of the community. Only one person from Trout Run taught there, and all the local kids went to Trout Run Elementary, then on to High Peaks High School.

Then, at the end of the summer, a man named MacArthur Payne had bought the North Country Academy and the place had been reborn as what

Reid liked to call a "therapeutic school." Frank, who hadn't mastered political correctness, referred to it as "that high-priced private reform school."

"So Matthew's going to the North Country Academy for organ lessons, huh," he said. "What'll they do if he doesn't practice—lock him up?"

Reid glared at him. "Frank, that's a very unfair remark. You—"

"Joking, I was joking!" Geez, Reid had really lost his sense of humor over this place.

"The lessons will be here in the church, where the organ is," Reid explained. "Plus, Matthew will be able to walk here."

"His father won't help out at all," Ardyth interjected. "He wasn't going to let Matthew take the lessons until Pastor Bob went and spoke to him. Those poor kids are really struggling without their mom."

Ardyth had a tendency to dwell on misfortune, while Reid was a determined optimist. "That's why the organ lessons are such a godsend. And, have you heard about the latest two people to get good jobs at the academy? Lorrie Betz and Ray Stulke."

Frank's hand hung suspended over the Danish tray. Lorrie had crammed more heartache into thirty years of living than most people manage in a lifetime. And Ray was Trout Run's foremost blockhead. "What in the world are those two qualified to do at a school? Cleaning?"

"Oh, no. They're going to be Pathfinders."

"The only path Ray can find is from his barstool to the john. What kind of position is a *Pathfinder?*"

"Fine for you to be so cavalier, Frank," Reid said. "You have a good, secure job. Most people in this town aren't so lucky. We're losing our young people because there are no opportunities for them here. And with Clyde being so sick, we can't count on Stevenson's Lumberyard to continue as our prime employer."

Reid straightened the lapels of his tweed sports coat. "This town needs to diversify. If MacArthur Payne makes a success of this school, it will be a source of good steady work with benefits for years to come. Steady work keeps people out of trouble. *You* should appreciate that."

Ardyth studied her shoes as if she'd never seen patent leather before. The thump of the big coffee urn being hauled away broke the uncomfortable silence, and Frank grabbed the opportunity to leave as Ardyth began helping with the cleanup.

He trudged across the green toward his truck, trying to shake off the sting of Reid's words. Last night's jack-o'-lanterns mocked him, their cheerful gap-toothed grins now transformed into grotesque snarls by the gnawing of hungry squirrels.

Unspoken in Reid's tirade was the fact that Frank was an outsider who'd taken the position of police chief away from a local. True, the job didn't pay well enough for a man to support a family. For twenty years his predecessor had combined the police chief's job with furniture refinishing to make ends meet.

Herv's retirement had touched off a great debate: increase the pay of the chief's position and induce a local man to train for the job at the police academy, or abolish it altogether and turn Trout Run's law enforcement over to the state police. In the middle of the fray, Frank had washed up on the town's doorstep: a man with twenty years' experience marred by one big mistake that had forced his resignation, willing to work cheap because he had a decent pension from the Kansas City force. His hiring had been an uneasy compromise, and Frank knew, even though Reid would never be so crass as to remind him, that he had cast the deciding vote in Frank's favor.

Now with a few unguarded wisecracks about the North Country Academy, he'd given Reid the impression that he didn't care about the fortunes of other people in town as long as his own bread was buttered.

Frank looked up at the towering peak of Mount Marcy in the distance, and the smaller mountains that tumbled toward the town, shutting out the problems of the wider world. If he knew what was good for him, he'd start showing some enthusiasm for the North Country Academy. But really, how excited could he get about a school that imported scores of juvenile delinquents into his jurisdiction?

Continue reading by downloading Blood Knot[1].

---

1.   https://www.amazon.com/Blood-Knot-mystery-Adirondack-Mysteries-ebook/dp/
B00Y3DE6NM/ref=tmm_kin_swatch_0?_encoding=UTF8&qid=1486735339&sr=8-3

THANK YOU FOR READING *The Lure*. To help other readers discover this book, please post a brief review on Amazon[2] or Goodreads[3]. I appreciate your support!

Receive a FREE short story when you join my mailing list[4]. You'll get an email whenever I release a new book. No spam, I promise!

Like my Facebook[5] page for funny updates on my writing, my travels, and my dog. Follow me on BookBub[6] for news of sales. Meet me on Twitter[7] and Goodreads[8], too.

---

2. https://www.amazon.com/Lure-mystery-Bennett-Adirondack-Mountain-ebook/dp/B00WTGB7V4/ ref=sr_1_1?s=digital-text&ie=UTF8&qid=1486736494&sr=1-1&keywords=the+lure

3. https://www.goodreads.com/book/show/25499619-the-lure?ac=1&from_search=true

4.   http://swhubbard.net/contact/

5.   https://www.facebook.com/swhubbardauthor/

6.   https://www.bookbub.com/authors/s-w-hubbard

7.   https://twitter.com/SWHubbardauthor

8.   https://www.goodreads.com/author/show/746045.S_W_Hubbard

Read these other mysteries by S.W. Hubbard:

Frank Bennett Adirondack Mountain Mystery Series

Blood Knot[1]
Dead Drift[2]
False Cast[3]

1. https://www.amazon.com/Blood-Knot-mystery-Adirondack-Mysteries-ebook/dp/B00Y3DE6NM/ref=tmm_kin_swatch_0?_encoding=UTF8&qid=1486735339&sr=8-3

2. https://www.amazon.com/Dead-Drift-mysteries-Adirondack-Mountain-ebook/dp/B00HE34YX0/ref=tmm_kin_swatch_0?_encoding=UTF8&qid=1486735475&sr=8-4

3. https://www.amazon.com/False-Cast-mystery-Adirondack-Mountain-ebook/dp/B01N2U1IBW/ref=sr_1_1?ie=UTF8&qid=1486735547&sr=8-1&keywords=false+cast

Palmyrton Estate Sale Mystery Series

1. https://www.amazon.com/Another-Treasure-romantic-thriller-Palmyrton-ebook/dp/B009ZFP3DA/
ref=sr_1_1?s=digital-text&ie=UTF8&qid=1486735685&sr=1-1&keywords=another+mans+treasure

2. https://www.amazon.com/Treasure-Darkness-romantic-thriller-Palmyrton-ebook/dp/B00QXWYUF0/
ref=sr_1_1?s=digital-text&ie=UTF8&qid=1486735788&sr=1-1&keywords=treasure+of+darkness

3. https://www.amazon.com/This-Bitter-Treasure-romantic-Palmyrton-ebook/dp/B01CKEZ4BS/
ref=sr_1_1?s=digital-text&ie=UTF8&qid=1486735834&sr=1-1&keywords=this+bitter+treasure

4. https://www.amazon.com/Treasure-Exile-read-all-night-mystery-Palmyrton-ebook/dp/
B079CQYVQY/ref=cm_cr_arp_d_product_top?ie=UTF8

About the Author

S.W. Hubbard is the author of the Palmyrton Estate Sale Mysteries, *Another Man's Treasure*, *Treasure of Darkness* and *This Bitter Treasure*, and *Treasure in Exile*. She is also is the author of the Frank Bennett Adirondack Mountain Mystery mystery novels set in the Adirondack Mountains:, *The Lure* (originally published as *Swallow the Hook*), *Blood Knot*, and *False Cast*, as well as a short story collection featuring Frank Bennett, *Dead Drift*. Her short stories have appeared in *Alfred Hitchcock's Mystery Magazine* and the anthologies *Crimes by Moonlight*, *The Mystery Box*, and *Adirondack Mysteries*. She lives in Morristown, NJ, where she teaches creative writing to enthusiastic teens and adults, and expository writing to reluctant college freshmen. To contact her, invite her to your book club, or read the first chapter of any of her books, visit: http://www.swhubbard.net.

Thank you.

Made in the USA
Las Vegas, NV
22 February 2023

67953919R00144